TWICE THE HARD CASES!
TWICE THE HONEYS!
TWO PISTOL-HOT ADULT
WESTERNS IN ONE BIG VOLUME!

BODIE BEAUTIES

"Bastard! You shot me!" the gunman said.

"My calling card," McCoy said from where he hid behind a boulder. "Who hired you? Was it the men who held up the stage and killed the guards?"

"Don't know what you're talking about. Jesus, I'm bleeding to death."

"Tell me who hired you and I'll take you down to Doc Rogers."

"Not if I kill you first."

"You tried and missed. Now it's my turn!"

FRISCO FOXES

Fresh blood soaked into the gunman's shirt as he pressed his left hand to his chest. "Damn! My firin' hand! You busted it all up!"

"I could've done worse. Was it worth it?" Spur asked.

The wounded man's body trembled as pain boiled through him. "Anything's worth them dies!"

The word thundered through Spur's brain but he showed no surprise at the mention of his secret cargo—the dies for the twenty-dollar gold piece. "You may be crazy, but you're not dying. They'll get you patched up in jail."

Clutching his broken hand, the downed man reached into his shirt with his good one. "You're dyin', mister. You are!"

The *Spur Double* Series from *Leisure Books:*
DODGE CITY DOLL/LARAMIE LOVERS
DAKOTA DOXY/SAN DIEGO SIRENS
COLORADO CUTIE/TEXAS TEASE
MISSOURI MADAM/HELENA HELLION
RAWHIDER'S WOMAN/SALOON GIRL
INDIAN MAID/MONTANA MINX
ROCKY MOUNTAIN VAMP/CATHOUSE KITTEN
SAVAGE SISTERS/HANG SPUR McCOY!

SPUR

BODIE BEAUTIES
FRISCO FOXES
DIRK FLETCHER

LEISURE BOOKS NEW YORK CITY

A LEISURE BOOK®

August 1993

Published by

Dorchester Publishing Co., Inc.
276 Fifth Avenue
New York, NY 10001

SPUR

BODIE BEAUTIES

1

Wesley Urick saw the shadowy figures in the trees and knew instinctively that they had trouble. He drew his six-gun and blasted a shot into the cool California night air rousing the six armed men inside the Concord stagecoach that jolted along a high mountain trail from the booming mining town of Bodie toward Bridgeport.

"Trouble!" Wesley shouted, bringing up the double barreled Greener.

A rifle snarled in the woods, a heavy sound like a big Sharps-Borchardt, Wesley thought. A fraction of a second later the .45-70 round from the rifle slammed into his chest, tore through his heart and out his back, taking a two-inch chunk of his spinal column with it.

The dead body that seconds before had been Wesley jolted off the high seat of the Concord, pitched to the side and smashed into the ground as the stagecoach rumbled on past.

By then a dozen guns had barked from the woods on both sides of the coach. The attackers had picked the perfect spot, the man with the reins directing the four horses knew. At this point they were at the steepest up slope on the route and he had been forced to slow to a walk to negotiate the hill and the rutted stage road.

From inside the coach, six well armed men began returning fire. All had rifles and pistols, but there were few chances to see the attackers.

A high pitched scream stabbed through the darkness and the coach stopped abruptly.

"Bastards shot a lead horse!" one of the six guards inside the coach shouted over the gunfire. "Make your shots count. Whoever is out there knows what they're doing."

"Goddamn, I'm hit!" one of the guards inside the crowded coach shouted. Then he pitched forward against another guard who had his Spencer repeating rifle aimed out the window, the other guard dead before he fell. He saw a rider in the darkness of the woods and fired. There was a moment of satisfaction as he saw him blasted off the horse.

But ten seconds later six rounds came through the open curtain where the guard with the Spencer sat. Two of the hot chunks of lead bored into his skull stripping all life from his suddenly limp body.

Another Wells Fargo Stage Lines guard, Frank Gaston, crowded lower in the Concord. He sat on the floor, his Remington repeater angled over the low door. Both the shotgun guard and the driver had to be dead. They would go in the first volley. Now two more inside had died.

"Ain't worth it!" Frank shouted. "Let's give the bastards the gold." He went on in a much calmer tone as the three other men inside stopped firing.

"Hell, I ain't gonna die for somebody else's gold. Not for three dollars a day, I ain't."

The other three guards agreed.

"Stop shooting!" Frank called out. "Enough! Dammit, we give up! You done killed half of us now. Ease off and you can have the fucking gold!"

The men firing weapons on both sides of the coach slowed their shooting and then stopped. A voice came out of the blackness. "How many alive inside?" a heavy voice asked.

"Four. Only four."

"Throw out your weapons, rifles and six-guns," the voice snarled.

The guards threw out eight rifles and six pistols.

"That everything?"

"Damn right!" Frank bellowed.

Somebody in the darkness laughed.

"Get out one at a time and lace your fingers in back of your necks. Now!"

The four guards did as they were told.

The clouds slid away from the moon and brightened the scene. The driver lay sprawled just behind the coach. Frank couldn't see the shotgun guard.

Men on horses still shrouded in the darkness, moved up slowly.

"Well now. Look a' here. You gents ain't Pinkertons, know for damn sure. Just local hires pretending to be guards."

A robber rode in on the other side of the stagecoach and stepped up to the driver's seat where he opened the front boot.

"Got it!" the man shouted. "Strong box is up here and it's heavy as hell!"

"Get it out of there," the leader in the darkness ordered.

The coach rattled as two men tugged the strong

box out of the boot and tossed it to the ground.

Saddle leather creaked as men dismounted. One moved into the soft moonlight in front of the four prisoners. He turned quickly as someone shouted. The kerchief that had been hiding his face came loose and fell around his neck.

He looked up at the four men, pawing at the cloth to cover his face.

"Lenny! You bastard!" Frank shouted. "What the hell you doing here? You're Lenny and I use to play poker with you at the Richstrike Saloon!" Too late, Frank realized what he'd done.

"Oh, damn, Lenny, I promise I won't ever breathe a word. Give me a horse and I'll be in Oregon in a week and claim I never been in California. Won't tell a soul, Lenny, I promise!"

Lenny drew his six-gun and leveled it at Frank. "Shit, Frank, didn't know you was gonna be on this run. How'n hell was I to know? Not a damn thing I can do now, Frank. If'n it was just me, you could ride. But, hell, you know these other gents won't hear of that."

A shot blasted into the stillness on the other side of the coach.

"Get that strong box open?" Lenny asked.

"Damn right, come look!" a voice beyond the rig shouted.

"Bring the whole box around here and don't open it," Lenny snapped.

"Lenny, you can't do this," Frank pleaded. "Look, there's four human beings here. You can't just execute us, shoot us down in cold blood. You just can't do that. They can't be paying you enough. . . ."

Lenny shot Frank Gaston in the chest, then once

more in the side of the head as he fell. The sound of the first shot sent the other three guards on the Wells Fargo stage into action. They charged away into the darkness in three different directions.

Lenny shot the closest one through the back of the head, sent two bullets at the next one but missed. Three more pistols and a rifle roared in the mountain air, and the other two guards fell in the moonlight along the deserted mountain stagecoach trail.

"Make sure of them," Lenny said.

A few minutes later, he heard a pistol blast once, then twice.

"Damn sure of all four of them now," a voice said in the blackness.

When the two men lugged the heavy strong box around the stage, Lenny found some dry grass and twisted up a torch, then lit it with a stinker match and lifted the lid.

Inside lay fifteen gold bars, each weighing five pounds.

"Don't any of you get any wild ideas or even think about taking off on your own," Lenny said. "California ain't big enough for you to hide. Your skin would be worth five-thousand dollars to me if you try it."

He picked up the bars, hefted them. "Yeah, worth more money than we ever saw before, but it ain't ours. I saw Les get knocked off his mount. He hit hard?"

"He's dead," a voice answered.

"Damn, he was good. Two of you drag him back off the trail and pile some brush over him. Somebody else bring his horse around."

When the holdup men got back from hiding the body, Lenny had the gold bars split between his own saddle bags and those of the horse Les had ridden. He tried a lead line on the nag and then Lenny studied the immediate site.

A few minutes later he began giving orders. One man cut the dead horse out of the leather harness, and using his horse, dragged the carcass to the edge of a small canyon, twenty feet from the trail, and rolled the stiffening animal down the fifty foot dropoff.

They drove the stage to the same place, shot the three horses, and toppled the stage over the bank, dragging the horses with it.

It took them longer to find the dead guards but when they did, their bodies also were dumped into the open grave of the canyon. When they were done, no trace remained of the stage.

"Let's ride," Lenny said. "When we get back to town you'll all get paid. Anybody who wants to ride out, should head for Nevada. For the money you made tonight, you can afford a small vacation."

Lenny kept the other five men ahead of him as they rode along the trail toward Bodie. They had hit the gold stage about fifteen miles from the mining town, and now went back over the easy trail at a canter, eating up almost six miles an hour. It was still dark when they came to the outskirts of a sleeping town that showed lights around the gold and silver mines and stamping mills and in some of the saloons along Main Street.

Lenny pulled his men to a stop just outside of town and dug into his pocket.

"Like I told you before, you each get a hundred dollars. That's more real money than you've seen in a long time. Don't spent it all in one day in Bodie or Captain Trevarow will have you in jail before you can spit. He's old, but he's smart. Better if you ride out to Auroa or Hawthorne where it won't matter if you whoop it up a little."

"Figured since we done such a good job, we'd get a few dollars more," a whining voice said from one of the men in the darkness.

Lenny eased his six-gun from leather. "You get $100 or you get three cents worth of lead. Which you want?"

Lenny paid the last man. He sat his horse and rolled a smoke while he watched them ride away. Two of them said they would stay in town. The other three chose to keep riding right on through toward Nevada. Lenny was pleased, there would be three fewer witnesses to worry about.

He caught the lead line to the second horse and angled around the main part of town to the west. He climbed the hill behind the town where the mines dotted the landscape. A quarter of a mile beyond the Standard Stamp Mill, he came to a mine works and tied the horses to an office hitching rail.

A cigar glowed in the darkness of the porch.

"Figured that was you, Lenny," the voice said.

Lenny jumped, then grinned. "Yeah, and right on time. Got something for you."

"All of it?"

"Seventy-five pounds worth."

"Let's take it around back," the same even voice said.

"Ran into some trouble. Lost one man. Somebody recognized me so we had to make sure nobody talked."

"All eight of them?"

"Yes."

"Christ, gonna be hell to pay."

"Just couldn't be helped."

They stopped at the back door of a long low shed, lifted the saddle bags off and carried them inside.

Two coal oil lamps burned brightly. The room was next door to the area where raw gold was melted down and poured into molds with the mine's name stamped proudly into the top of each bar for all to see.

The tall man with handlebar moustache and long sideburns took the gold bars from the saddle bags and stacked them on the table.

"Fifteen, right. You say you lost a man?"

"Yeah, Les. Shot through the heart."

"Tough. You can have his pay."

"Thanks, I earned it. You offered me a thousand besides if I brought back the gold."

"That, plus a bonus."

The tall man's voice had a faint note of sarcasm and Lenny looked up. The grin on his face changed to a scowl and then the start of a scream as the .45 the tall man held fired and the heavy round smashed into Lenny's open mouth, traveled upward through the roof of his mouth and into his brain where it tore up a dozen vital nerve centers before it shattered into ten fragments which lodged against his thick skull bone.

The tall man called softly. "Newman. You have a job to do."

The man who came through a side door was about forty, stooped, with a reddish complexion from too much sun, too much foundry heat, or too much whiskey. He had a crooked face, damaged by a mule that had kicked him when he was a boy. His cheek had been caved in and never repaired. The flesh under one eye was torn and still sagged to the side, and his mouth was ripped and healed with a large scar and pulled down to one side and usually dripped with a disgusting drool.

Newman nodded, didn't seem surprised to see the dead man. He simply picked up Lenny's body and dragged it out the door. He slung it over the saddle of one of the horses and tied it on securely. He would dump it well out of town where it might not be found for months.

Before he moved the horse, he went back into the workroom and mopped up the blood, then waved to his benefactor and hurried out to dispose of the body.

The tall man wearing a black suit preened his moustache and hefted the bars. He frowned at the name on the top of each one: STD-BODIE. They were from the Standard Mining Company there in Bodie. That would be changed soon enough. He moved quickly through the mostly dark head-quarters building of the mine until he came to a door where he knocked. He could see light under the panel.

A voice answered and he opened the door a foot and talked around it.

"Everything is going according to plan. We have the seventy-five pounds of bars and will get to work on them shortly. By morning they will be completely safe."

"Good. Give me a report in the morning."

The tall man said he would, closed the door and hurried back to the foundry room. He had come up through mining, knew every phase of the operation. That's why he made such a good manager of this mine.

Now he took off his suit coat and vest and built up

the fire. Then one by one he put the gold bars in the heavy iron cauldron where they would melt.

As they did he added a like number of gold bars already cast with their own imprint on them. When the gold was melted and mingled, no chemist on earth could tie it down as coming from any particular seam or vein of raw gold ore—so not from any one mine.

Also with their own imprint on the bars, they could send them to the mint in San Francisco and not an eyelash would be raised.

The man worked quickly, efficiently, and when Newman returned, the disfigured little man helped do the pouring for the new bullion bars. Newman was an expert at his trade and the tall man welcomed his help even though it was hard to look at the ugly face.

When they completed the pouring and the molds were cooling, Newman gave his superior the money he found on Lenny's body, more than three hundred dollars.

"Thank you, Newman, that will be all. And remember, not a word of this to anyone, or I'll cut your balls off so you'll never again be able to go see Miss Lily's girls up in Virgin Alley, you understand?"

"Yes . . . yes sir. I don't talk. Never have."

Newman stood watching the tall man for a moment, then hurried out the door to his small shack on the mine grounds where the mine owner said that he could live.

After preening his handlebar moustache again, the tall man smiled. They had just cleared $74,700 for the company, and he was determined to have his ten percent of that. The mine owner had promised him that—and he would collect.

2

The Wells Fargo stage came toward Bodie from the south along the regular stage road from Bridgeport. Spur McCoy stretched in the close confines of the coach and then stared out the window at the booming mining town on the far fringes of California next to Nevada.

It had been a tiring stage ride from the end of the railroad at Sacramento, and Spur was happy to see the town. It was laid out north and south along Main Street on a flat that was nearly two miles long and about half a mile wide. The back side of the town, now home to from ten thousand to thirteen thousand souls, sloped up into the low ridges that had provided the reason all these people were here—gold and silver ore.

More than a dozen smoke stacks belched smoke where wood furnaces provided steam for the mine works and the stamping mills. Even from a mile away he could hear the clanging of metal on metal as the stamping mills turned rocky gold ore into a finer consistency that could be worked.

Spur McCoy leaned on the window watching the town come into closer view. He was a tall man, two-inches over six-feet, and a rugged two-hundred pounds. He wore his reddish brown hair a little long around the ears, but that was because he seldom found time to sit for a barber. His full moustache met sandy muttonchop sideburns but his chin and neck were shaven clean.

Curious green eyes stared out at the world and his tanned and windburned face showed that he spent as many hours in the weather and under the stars at night as he did indoors.

A drummer sitting beside Spur looked at the town and chuckled. "Don't look so rough to me," the drummer said. "Heard about a little girl who was moving here with her parents and she said, 'Good-bye God, we're moving to Bodie!' "

Spur laughed and began checking the buildings on the outskirts of town. The cemetery showed to the left on the first slope up from the flatland. Down lower he saw a sign on a wood frame building that proclaimed it was Moyle Storage.

To the right of Main Street he saw three or four houses and a larger building that looked like a church. Close by Main stood the Moyle Bottling Works. This place had grown ten times the size it was the last time Spur had hurried through five years ago. Gold did strange things to a town.

Spur McCoy came to Bodie to look up an old friend. Spur was a Secret Service Agent of the United States government. The service had been established by Congress in 1865 specifically to protect the currency from counterfeiting. Since then it had taken on the police duties of any matter that crossed from one state line or territory into another.

Spur had joined the agency shortly after it began and was a crack shot with pistol, rifle, shotgun, derringer, and an excellent horseman. He was in great physical condition and an expert at hand-to-hand fighting with fists, knife or staff. He was unabashedly a ladies' man and they couldn't keep their hands off him. They found his rugged good looks, his Harvard education, soft spoken manner and his gentleness so unlike most of the Western men they knew.

Spur's father was a well known New York merchant. After graduating from Harvard University in Boston, Spur had worked in his father's firms for a while. Then he went into the army as a Lieutenant and served the Union army for two years before going to Washington, D.C. to be an aide to an old family friend who was a U.S. Senator from New York.

After he joined the Secret Service, he was soon appointed to head up the Western region of the agency with headquarters in St. Louis. He had as his area all those states and territories west of the Mississippi River.

The big Concord stage jolted over some ruts, then rolled into the canyon of Bodie's main street with stores and offices and shops along both sides for a good half mile.

Bodie was wood. Spur could see no stone or brick buildings as he rode down Main to the Wells Fargo stage office across from the Occidental Hotel. Spur had heard tall tales about the bad men of Bodie, now he probably would see a few of them in action. He had come to town from Sacramento to visit an old friend, Sheriff's Captain John Trevarow.

The county seat had been in Bridgeport since

1864, Spur knew, so that's where the County Sheriff was. John said he had been appointed Chief Deputy for Bodie, had been given twenty deputies, and the rank of Captain. His letter had been concise.

"McCoy, I'm getting slow and won't admit it except to you. It's the damn rheumatiz in my right hand. I can still shoot good as ever, but it's the draw. I look like my Aunt Matilda drawing out of leather.

"Not too sure that I can hold my temper if one of the young punks around here wants to make a name for himself and call me out. Had one or two want to try, but I joshed them out of it.

"It would be dandy if you could pay me a visit next time you're out this way and maybe discourage some of the local riff-raff who think they're fast but ain't never seen a real fast draw."

The letter was dated two months ago and caught up with Spur in Denver. He hoped the old lawman was still alive.

Spur swung down from the stage at the depot, caught his carpet bag from the top and stashed it at the U.S. Hotel, the best in town and across Wood Street from the Occidental. His room cost a dollar a night. He paid for three days in advance, then went to talk to Sheriff's Captain Trevarow.

The Bodie jail sat on the corner of Bonanza and King Streets, north of the hotel and a block west of Main. Captain Trevarow's office was there as well. A deputy at a small desk just inside the door pointed west.

"Captain and two men just went up to Virgin Alley," the young deputy said. "Peers a customer of one of the ladies of the evening had some trouble."

Spur thanked the deputy and walked along King Street to where it began climbing the upgrade to the

Bodie houses of ill repute which perched there on the side of the hill. They had been neatly segregated from the "proper" citizens so none of the "nice" ladies would be contaminated.

He found Virgin Alley next to Maiden Lane and Virtue Street, with thirty or forty men and demi-mondes gathered around some kind of a confrontation outside the fancy Highgrade brothel.

Spur worked his way through the shirtsleeve crowd. Even though it was August, at 8,500 feet there's always a little bite in the air and the ever present Bodie wind blowing that varied from light to sturdy.

When Spur got to the center of things he saw a barefoot man in his undershirt and pants waving a six-inch hunting knife at two sheriff's deputies. Both had on badges but that didn't deter the knife man.

"I wanta fight the sheriff!" the man yelled. Spur could see blood on the edge of the blade the man held. A second man lay near his feet with a six-inch gash on his upper arm that he tried to hold together with one hand to slow the bleeding.

"Where's the goddamned Sheriff?" the knifer bellowed.

"I'm the best we've got for a sheriff," a tall, slender man who looked to be about sixty said and stepped forward. "County Sheriff is over at Bridgeport. You new in town?"

"Want to kill me a sheriff," the man said. Now it was obvious to Spur that the knife wielder was drunk, almost too plastered to stand up. He transferred the bloody knife to his left hand and let his right hang beside a six-gun holstered on his hip.

"You're packing a piece, Sheriff, you draw first," the drunk thundered.

"No cause for this, mister. You just put down the knife and come down to the jail and sleep it off. Then you'll be back to work tomorrow."

"Want to shoot me a fucking Sheriff!" the drunk screamed.

The people watching all edged back. Those behind Captain Trevarow and the drunk hurried to one side to get out of the line of any possible shooting.

"The Sheriff is over in Bridgeport. I'm Captain Trevarow, head of the sheriff's office here. Why don't we talk this over. You got drunk and you cut up that man. He needs to get over to Doc Rogers before he loses that arm. You come along now peaceful like and we'll only charge you for stitching up the arm. Fair enough?"

The drunk drew his six-gun. He was better than most, but still not very fast, Spur decided. The drunk put the weapon back in his holster and looked up, blinking away some film over his eyes.

"Damnit, want to kill me a Sheriff!"

Spur eased up beside Trevarow and glared at the drunk. His .45 Colt was tied low on his right leg in its usual place. The well oiled weapon was loaded and ready. The leather was polished with neatsfoot oil and supple.

"Mister, you just pretend I'm the Sheriff, all right?" Spur said evenly. "Now look over there at that weathervane on top of the house. You see it?"

The drunk scowled for a minute, turned and nearly fell, stared at the house, then nodded. "Yeah, see it. So what?"

"Watch," Spur said.

Some people said they never saw his hand move. In the blink of an eyelash Spur drew the Colt, thumbed back the hammer and fired from the hip. The roar of the six-gun going off startled the crowd.

The "W" on the weathervane caught the .45 slug, gave off a clang and the weathervane spun around a dozen times from the impact.

The men in the group stared in surprise. It was a four-inch square target at more than eighty feet.

"Christ' a'mighty! You see that shot?" one of the men shouted.

"Talk about fast! That was so damn fast I barely saw his hand move!" someone else added.

Spur holstered the weapon, moved his feet to a slightly wider stance and looked back at the drunk.

"Now, let's just pretend that I'm that Sheriff you want to kill. You go ahead and draw against me, just anytime you're ready."

The drunk's eyes were still wide in wonder.

"You . . . you really did that? He hit the weathervane?" The drunk looked around at the others.

They nodded.

"Damn right he did," a fancy lady wearing a petticoat and little else said.

"Yeah, he did. You wanta be dead, crazy man, you just go ahead and try to outdraw him," another voice said.

The drunk turned back to Spur. He pushed the bloody knife into a sheath and stared again at the tall man a dozen feet from him.

"Are . . . are you somebody? A fast gun or something?"

"What do you care? You want to draw against a Sheriff. Go ahead." The deadly, cold tone of Spur's voice shocked the drunk back another step. He hit a rock in the street, stumbled and fell.

The two deputies helped him stand up. He shook off their hands.

"What's your name?" Spur demanded in a tone that brought a sure response.

"Wanamaker, W. W. Wanamaker. Why?" the drunk asked.

"Sometimes they don't know what name to put on a grave marker," Spur said softly. His hand moved slightly next to his holster, fingers relaxed, ready.

Slowly the drunk held up his hands. He shook his head. "No offense, mister. I think I'll go with the Captain there, have a nice sleep in his jail."

The deputies lifted the pistol and knife from Wanamaker's belt, caught both his arms and walked him down the slope toward King Street and the Bodie jail.

The crowd slowly dispersed, the excitement over. Some of the soiled doves tarried, watching the tall stranger who had backed down the drunk.

Spur turned to the man beside him. "Morning, John. Thought I'd stop by for a visit."

Captain John Trevarow let out a long held breath, grabbed Spur's hand and shook it, his face breaking into a delighted smile. "McCoy, you have no idea how glad I am to see you."

"I have some idea. Buy you a beer?"

An hour later at the Philadelphia Beer Depot, Spur and Captain Trevarow had corned beef sandwiches and caught up on each other's news.

Spur was surprised how John had aged. He was maybe sixty-two, six-feet tall and now not only thin, but on the gaunt side. His skin color wasn't the best either and Spur watched him carefully as he listened.

"Got into Bridgeport about three years ago when I was moving around. They needed somebody over here who could whip this town into shape. Lord knows I tried. This town has too much money, too many wild women and too much booze. You know there are three breweries in town? *Three of them,*

24

and all turning out more beer than we can drink."

"Place looks prosperous," Spur said.

"Yeah, it is. Looks civilized, too, but it ain't. Some days we average a killing a day. Been a week now without a shooting death. That worries me." Captain Trevarow sipped his beer. "Hell, ten years ago I'd have eaten this town alive. Now, I ain't so fast. I can shoot straight as anybody, but getting the damn thing out of the leather takes me just too damn much time.

"Now, take that slasher drunk up at the cat houses. Probably a right nice gent when he's sober. Trouble is the only time I see these guys is when they're drunk or mad or when they go crazy." Trevarow sighed. "Don't know how much more of it I can take, McCoy. I might be dead right now if you hadn't walked up when you did. It was getting about as nasty as it can before the lead starts to fly."

Spur finished his beer and had another bite of the sandwich. Best corned beef he'd had since he left Chicago.

"John, I understand what you're telling me. If it's any help, you're not the first man to go through this. I've known two of the old gunmen, big names you'd recognize in a second. They both came to a point where they knew if they wanted to go on living much longer, they had to hang up the gun belt.

"One did, he's a popular man now back in Massachusetts. Says he's going to run for the state legislature. The second one couldn't break the chain. He got gunned down in a call out in Virginia City. Some kid who hadn't even started to shave yet beat him and killed him in a half-a-second on one cold winter day."

John Trevarow looked out the window at the dirt

street with piles of horse droppings, each with a thousand flies around it. When his eyes turned back to Spur he seemed to relax a moment. "You're telling me to quit my job, hang up my gun?"

"Not quit your job. This should be a desk job here anyway. Hire whoever you want to for street patrol and door knob checks. Send out three deputies to stop gun fights and to bring in prisoners. That shouldn't be your work. Hell, John, you're a Captain, you're in law management now."

They went on talking and eating their sandwiches. Spur remembered how Trevarow had pulled him out of a tight spot in Kansas six years ago. It had been a small job, pick up a counterfeiter and his plates from the sheriff in a little Kansas town and bring the prisoner and the evidence back to St. Louis.

When Spur went to get the man out of jail, it turned out the gent had six brothers and three brothers-in-law who all owned shotguns and pistols and loved to use them.

For two days they had a standoff with the brothers outside the jail, while Spur, Trevarow and the prisoner remained inside. Nobody could move, nobody would back down. Spur didn't want to get anybody killed over some bad five dollar bills.

At last Spur slipped the gagged prisoner out the back way after midnight and rode half the night to get away from the brothers, while John Trevarow put up a big fuss in the front office of the jail haranguing the men about how they were violating Kansas law and how he'd have them all brought up on charges of obstructing justice and inter-fering with a peace officer. The charges would get them each five years in the Kansas penitentiary.

By the time John Trevarow had talked himself hoarse, two of the men had slipped around and broke in the back door and found their brother gone. They almost strung up John before he shot one in the shoulder and two more in the legs and backed them down with his own pair of Greeners, one in each hand, with two barrels each and four loads of double ought buck.

As a demonstration he blasted a wooden box in the corner of the jail and shattered it. The in-laws backed down and Spur was well on his way to St. Louis.

Spur finished his sandwich and pushed back from the table as he watched a man come in the front door, look around and go up to the barkeep. His clothes were dusty and there was a line of perspiration on his forehead, as if he'd just come off a long ride.

"Hell, Spur, maybe you're right about hanging up the iron," Trevarow admitted cautiously. "Lord knows I hate to go out where I know I might have to draw fast. But maybe I've done enough law work with a gun. Maybe it's time I concentrate on the other aspects of law and order."

"Then do it. It's what I'd do if I was in the same situation. Damned right I would."

"Captain Trevarow?"

Spur looked up and saw the man he had just watched come in. Spur's hand swung down near his holster automatically.

Trevarow glanced up and nodded. "Yeah, that's me, son. What can I do for you?"

"Deputy at the jail said you was here. My name is Orval Kemp. I'm from Salt Lake City in Utah. I got something to tell you." He looked at Spur.

"It's all right. He can hear whatever it is. Sit down. You had a beer yet since your long ride?"

"No, sir, but I don't drink. I'm sorry to be the

bearer of bad news. I just rode in from Bridgeport along the stage road. Twelve, fifteen miles out on that part where the trail winds up along a gully, my horse acted up. Seemed like he was spooked. I got him calmed down and tied him to a tree and looked around.

"There was stage tracks and all on the road such as it is. Then I saw one set of tracks that cut away from the trail toward the edge of the drop off. Never seen nothing like it before, Sheriff. A stage went over the side!"

"How far down was it?" Spur asked.

"Not more than fifty, sixty feet. That's why I was surprised at first that I didn't see survivors."

"Everyone was killed?" Trevarow asked.

"All shot to death, Sheriff. All men. I counted seven but there might be another one underneath a horse or the coach. All the horses had been shot, too."

Captain Trevarow grabbed his hat and reached for his purse to pay the tab. "Which way was the coach going?"

"Can't be sure, but seemed to be heading for Bridgeport."

"Can you take us back to the spot, Mr. Kemp?"

"Figure I should, Sheriff."

"All men, you say, seven of them, and going toward Bridgeport? Damn! There's only one good explanation and I don't like it." The Captain looked at Spur. "You feel up to a ride in the noonday sun?"

John went to the Wells Fargo office while Spur walked to the Kirkwood Livery Stable to rent a horse and saddle. They all met in front of the U.S. Hotel and John Travarow looked grim. He made the introductions. The new man with him was Ingemar Johnson, manager of the Wells Fargo stage and freight office there in Bodie. His face was set in a deep scowl and he barely acknowledged the introductions.

The four riders turned south on Main and rode out of town up the first slope and along the stage road south and west toward Bridgeport.

Johnson rode ahead with the man who found the wreckage. He asked him a stream of questions, but Kemp knew few of the answers.

Captain Trevarow rode beside Spur. "Johnson is the manager of the Wells Fargo stage. If he's right, those seven men Kemp found could have been Wells Fargo guards."

"Why seven?" Spur stopped. "A gold shipment was on that stage?"

"That's the way we've been sending out gold now for three or four years. Up to a hundred pounds of bullion goes in a strong box, and Wells Fargo guarantees it delivered to the mint in San Francisco in thirty-six hours.

"No passengers are permitted, and they send along seven heavily armed guards and the best driver they have. Never lost a shipment before. But Johnson says it sounds like it could be the stage he sent out last night about four A.M. Nobody ever knows when the gold is being sent, and by midnight hardly anybody is up to see the rig leave from the back of one or another of the mines where it picks up the gold."

"But somebody knew about this one," Spur said.

"You figure it's the gold stage?"

"A driver in Bridgeport said the stages going into Bodie are always full these days, almost nobody coming out. Why else would seven men be leaving Bodie except as Wells Fargo guards?"

It took them just over two and a half hours to ride

to the spot on the trail where Kemp stopped. He showed them the drop off and tied up his mount.

Johnson swung off his horse, dropped the reins and slid down the slope to the wreck below.

Almost at once a wail of despair echoed up the canyon.

By the time Spur and Captain Trevarow skidded and slipped down the side of the gully, they found Johnson sitting on a rock with tears streaming down his face.

He nodded when Captain Trevarow asked him if this was the gold shipment stage.

"I knew every one of these men. They were like brothers to me. We'd never lost a guard before on any of our runs out here! Not in six years. Now eight men all at once!"

Spur checked the men he could locate. All had been shot. None of them had weapons. He found the battered strong box and carried it over to Johnson. They could see how the lock had been shot off.

"That's our strong box," Johnson said. "We've got to take the bodies back to Bodie for a Christian burial."

"We can't today, Mr. Johnson," Spur said. "We'll send out a wagon tomorrow to bring them back."

Johnson stared at the face of one of the dead men a dozen feet away. "Eight of them! God, what am I going to tell their wives? What can I tell my superiors? Do I just write them a dispatch saying I lost a $25,000 shipment of gold? My God, that's as much money as I make in fifty years!"

"We better be heading back for Bodie," Captain Trevarow said.

They had to help Johnson climb back up to the horses. All the way on the three hour ride home he kept repeating over and over that all eight of them had been murdered. All eight!

Spur and Captain Trevarow had checked the killing site carefully. There was not a clue as to who had robbed the stage. There were horseshoe tracks, but nothing distinctive. Most had long since been trampled by a stage going each way pulled by four horses and numerous horseback riders. Nothing at the site would help them find the killers.

It was dark by the time the four men rode back into Bodie. Johnson had pulled himself together, and went directly to the Standard Mining Company office to give them the news about their shipment. He never hesitated, it was his job and he would do it without fail.

Spur turned in his mount at the Kirkwood livery and went with Captain Trevarow for a dinner at the U.S. Hotel. Both men were tired. Spur destroyed a one-pound steak with all the side dishes as he listened to John tell him about the town.

"We mushroomed from fifteen-hundred to ten or twelve thousand in about two years. Never seen anything like it. But when you get right down to it, we're only an overgrown gold mining camp. People around here brag that Bodie has absolutely the worst climate in the country. In the summer it's hot and desert dry, and the wind always blows. In the winter it's freezing your balls off cold and usually about six to eight feet of snow. This will never be a resort where city people come to take the mountain air."

"The mines are the only basic industry here then," Spur said. "If the mines all went dry tomorrow, how long would Bodie last?"

Captain Trevarow snorted. "Last? Maybe a year as people used up their savings. Without the mines there's no income. Nothing could survive here. This would be only another mining ghost town."

They didn't talk long. When the food was gone they went their separate ways. Trevarow had a room at one of the smaller hotels and ate out. He had never married.

Spur said goodnight and walked upstairs to his second floor front room and started to unlock his door. He missed the keyhole with the skeleton key and the door swung inward slowly.

Before the door had opened an inch, Spur had his Colt .45 out of leather and the deadly muzzle led the way as Spur McCoy stepped into his room.

3

Spur pushed the unlocked door to his room inward an inch. At once he saw that a lamp was burning inside. He rammed the door open and stepped to the side of the door jamb where the wall protected him. No shots blasted through the opening. He peered around the door frame and laughed.

"Pretty little Jessica!" Spur drawled as he stepped into his room and closed the door.

A girl sat on the bed reading a magazine. Her shoes were off, her legs crossed and she wore only a thin cotton petticoat. She hugged her knees a minute, big brown eyes staring at him, long blonde hair tousled around her shoulders.

"Hi there, cowboy. It's been a long time." She jumped off the bed and bounced into his arms, her hands tight around his neck. "It's so *good* to see you! It was Salt Lake City, if you've forgotten. I got in a little trouble and you managed to set everything straight and get me a ticket on the stage."

"Three years ago, Jessica."

"I saw your fancy shooting demonstration in Virgin Alley. You always been so good with a six-gun?"

"Helps a guy like me stay alive." He carried her to the bed, kissed her cheek and sat her down. He dropped beside her. "Now, tell me all about what you've been doing, where you've been, and how many marriage proposals you've turned down."

Jessica smiled, then lifted her brows with a little shrug. "Spur McCoy, you know what I've been doing. I've been to Sacramento, San Francisco, Portland and down to San Diego. I love that little town. Now I'm starting to work east again."

"You are a traveling girl. How long have you been in Bodie?"

"Six months. It's a good town to winter over in. They work two or three shifts underground rain, snow, sleet or shine so there's always plenty of money, and customers."

"For as long as the boom lasts. Somebody said there were thirteen-thousand people here now."

"They'll stay as long as the gold holds out," Jessica said. "But not me. Another six months or so and I'll be buying a ticket down to the railroad at Sacramento. I'll hate to leave. I'm working for the best lady I've ever met. Her name is Miss Hetti and she runs the Highgrader House of True Pleasure."

Jessica reached up and kissed his cheek. "Now, you handsome, wonderful man, tell me what you've been doing these past three years."

"You know what I've been doing, working for the government, getting shot at, winning more than losing, not dead yet, and not getting overpaid."

"Short and sweet." Jessica went to her knees on the bed and gracefully lifted the thin petticoat over her head, revealing her sleek figure. She was barely five feet tall, slender, with small hand sized breasts with bright pink areolas and darker nipples that now hardened and rose.

"Business first, Spur McCoy. Remember in Salt Lake I told you I owed you so much I could never repay all of it. Least I can do right now is make you a payment. Then I want to talk, and have a beer, and talk some more."

She pulled his face down to her breasts and maneuvered one to his mouth.

"You have any arguments with that, cowboy?"

Spur bit her nipple gently, felt her respond. "I'm taking you away from your gainful employment."

"Tough titty. I told Miss Hetti about you and she said I had the night off. You've got to meet her, she's a marvel. Almost sixty now and straight and slender and in charge. She won't allow a gun or a knife in the rooms. The gents got to check them in the lobby or they never get upstairs. If I was smart I'd stick with Hetti. She's got six or seven girls who have been with her in two different towns now."

Jessica moved his head to her other breast and sighed. "Hey, I promise not to cry, but you mind me talking a little?"

"Talk away, pretty girl."

"Good. I would have anyway, I always was a big talker. But I've been thinking a lot lately about whoring. As long as I don't get a disease, it ain't hurtin' me none. Oh, I get slapped around sometimes, but Hetti makes whoever does it pay twenty dollars and gives it to the girl.

"Usually it's like I'm just a thing some man uses to get his prick hard so he can pump it off. By that time most of them are snorting and bucking like a range bull anyway and they don't care where they stick it.

"But once in a while a real gent will come in. His wife is having a baby, or she's gone back east, and for a half hour I get treated like a lady. Those are the men who really make love, not just have sex. That's the way I felt with you in Salt Lake. It was a real treat. I mean, you even thought about how I was feeling and what I wanted to do. That . . . that's so damn unusual."

She pulled his face up to hers. "Nice man, Spur Charles McCoy." Jessica grinned as he looked up sharply. "Yep, I know your real given name. Wager there ain't six people in the whole wild west who knows your Christian name." Jessica smiled at him and kissed his cheek.

"Just wondering, nice man, Spur Charles McCoy, if you'd consider giving a whore like me a real kiss right on the lips?"

Spur kissed her. He knew more about Jessica than anyone but her family. She would never be a whore to him. He kissed her gently, then wet her lips with his tongue and felt them open. He caught her shoulders and gently pushed her down on the bed, suspended himself over her fragile body, and kissed her again.

She purred softly deep in her throat. When he eased away from her she opened her eyes, and blinked away tears. "McCoy, you kiss me about three more times that way, and I'm going to start following you around like a puppy dog. I'll hound you to take me with your wherever you go, and I'll even learn to shoot a derringer and a little .25 pistol to help you in your business.

"You just turn me into buttermilk and chocolate candy and fancy lacework that is so fine!" She knuckled away moisture from her eyes and traced the lines of his jaw with one delicate finger. "Damn, McCoy, you turn me into a little girl again. I get to thinking about a cottage of my own with flowers around it and maybe even a white picket fence and a husband and at least two little babies and a buggy out front. Isn't that ridiculous?"

"Not ridiculous at all, Jessica. It's past time you retired and moved to a warm climate and opened a boarding house. San Diego would be a good place. It's growing, and it has a future. You think about it."

She nodded, then pushed Spur away from her, rolled him on his back and sat on the bed as she undressed him. "You remember I liked to peel the clothes off you? I still do.

"You kidding about a boarding house in San Diego? That would take five hundred dollars, maybe even a thousand. I don't have that kind of money. Sure I have some, but not that much."

She stared at him a minute from her deep brown eyes, then she shook her head of blonde hair.

"Now don't try to confuse me when I'm paying off an old debt. I'm going to enjoy making this payment."

When she stripped down his pants and his short underwear, she cooed and bent and kissed his erection.

"Glory! I was afraid maybe you had fucked him down to a nub! Glad to see him so bright and huge!"

Jessica sat on Spur's stomach, straddling him, then bent forward until one breast hung over his mouth. "You see anything you'd like to take a bite of, please go easy. I don't have enough tit to let you chew off much." As she said it she ground her hips against his stiffness and Spur groaned in delight.

She let him chew a moment, then lifted her hips

and moved lower so she could angle his shaft into her.

"As I remember, you like the first one fast and furious," Jessica said.

She settled down on his lance, yelping in satisfaction as it penetrated deeper and deeper inside her. At last she bent and kissed his lips.

"The party is yours, Spur Charles, whenever you want to start."

Spur roared his pleasure and thrust up at her. Then she began bobbing and moving forward as if she were riding a race horse, and at once Spur felt the double action on his shaft.

Jessica supported herself on her knees and elbows as she rode him. Spur felt things moving too quickly. She always had excited him in a few furious moments.

Now he surged upward again and again. Then with one final thrust, he launched his seed into her and again pounded a dozen times before he was empty and panting like one of the steam rigs that lifted the cables that came up from the mile deep gold mines.

Her inner muscles gripped him, massaging the last bits of juice from McCoy. Then she lowered herself to cover him and they both panted and rested.

Five minutes later she lifted off him and sat looking down as his eyes came open.

"You're as fast as a sixteen-year-old boy, you know that?"

"When I grow up I'll do better."

Jessica laughed and it made her eyes light up and one dimple punched in on her cheek. "Spur Charles, you could not possibly get any better. Even if you aren't grown up, I like you this way. Never change."

"Everything changes." He told her about John Trevarow.

"Really? He's got half the men in town still scared of him. They know his reputation. I never even figured that he was slowing down." Jessica frowned. "But his color isn't good. Have you noticed? His skin is kind of pale, unhealthy looking."

"Might be some sickness. Don't let on I talked to you about it. Half this lawman job is having a good reputation with a fast gun. I think he's going to stay in the office most of the time, now."

She jumped off the bed, her breasts bouncing and her bare little bottom jiggling as she hurried to the side of the room and brought out four bottles of beer from a paper bag. They had been cold once from ice from the Bodie ice house. Now they showed sweat stains but were still chilled.

She opened two bottles, gave him one and sat cross legged on the bed beside him tipping the second.

"A boarding house in San Diego? Were you kidding?"

"No. Buy an older house with eight or ten rooms, rent out four or five bedrooms, throw in two meals a day, and you can make a good living. Then if one of your renters takes your fancy, you might even wind up getting married."

"With my luck the second boarder would be an ex-customer from the Highgrader here in Bodie. What would I do then?"

"You'd have a heart to heart talk with the gent, and tell him you'll blow his brains out if his breathes a word of your former life. Most men will be glad to see you making it on the other side."

A far off look came into her brown orbs and she

smiled. "I remember our house back in Cleveland. We had a yard with grass in it and everything. I even had a puppy that grew up into a strange looking mutt that we called Rover. I think he sired about a hundred litters in that neighborhood."

"Think about San Diego."

"A real daydream. Impossible."

"Not really. The stage was robbed of the gold shipment. If you don't know, you would have heard tomorrow. There could be a reward for capturing the robbers. They killed eight men in the process."

"How awful!" She frowned. "A reward?"

"Men who rob and kill often spend lots of money soon afterwards. Watch for anyone in that mood, or talking about lots of money. Sometimes men talk more in a crib than they do in a barroom. Remember, whoever robbed that stage, also killed eight men."

They finished the beers and Spur patted the bed beside him. Jessica curled up beside him.

"Now it's your turn," McCoy said. "Tell me what pleasures you the most, anything you want, any way. It's time for Jessica to have exactly what she wants for a change."

"Glory be, no man ever talked to me that way before."

Spur's hands crept over her body, pausing at the pleasure zones and soon he had her panting.

It was halfway to daylight before they got to sleep that night, and both of them were smiling.

Captain Trevarow had sent a wagon out to the stage robbery site as soon as it was daylight. The wagon rolled into town slightly after noon, and Spur had only just got up and shaved. He let Jessica sleep while he dressed and slipped out the door and arrived at Bodie jail the same time the death wagon did.

"Roll on down to the undertaker," Captain Trevarow said when he looked at the wagon filled with the corpses. "Hooperman will have a field day because most of those men have family in town."

Spur followed the rig to the undertaker and saw the name I.C. Hooperman on the sign outside the door. The place was on an alley down from the jail half a block on Bonanza Street.

Spur watched a short, fat man inspect the cargo.

"Eight!" he said at first, alarmed. Then nodding. "Yes, yes, of course we can take care of them. Have the families been notified? Be sure the Captain tells each family so proper arrangements can be made. They'll want correct clothing and perhaps some extra nice coffins."

He stopped and looked up at Spur. "You must be McCoy. Heard about you costing me gainful employment yesterday. I can't win them all. Name's Hooperman, I. C. Hooperman. Everyone calls me Hoop."

Colt took the surprisingly strong handshake and returned the man's big grin. "Deadly business you're in, Hoop."

"Not as deadly as yours. You drop them, I pick them up and plant them. But you know, none of them have grown yet!" Hooperman slapped his thigh and roared with laughter at his own small joke.

"Let's hope they don't sprout all over the cemetery. That would be a mess."

Hooperman laughed again, this time until tears came to his eyes. "By damn! Glad we got somebody in town with a sense of humor. I get tired of trying to make jokes to folks who don't appreciate them. Fact is, I always wanted to be an entertainer. Get up and tell jokes and funny stories and regale the crowd. Fancied myself with some show troop going from town to town.

"Then I had to help in the family business." He pointed around him at the undertaking parlor's back room. "My dad died two years later and I had a ready made business. I've been laying out folks and getting them dressed in their Sunday best ever since."

He helped the men carry in one of the dead guards and came back panting.

"Hey, McCoy, did I tell you the one about Doc Rogers? He told his patient, Herman, that he had only six months to live and then gave him a bill for ten dollars. Herman was shocked by the news but told Doc Rogers he could only pay him a dollar a month. 'In that case, you have ten months to live,' Doc Rogers said."

Hooperman doubled over howling with laughter. Spur joined in and when they both recovered, Spur motioned to the bodies.

"I'm working with Captain Trevarow. If you see anything unusual with the bodies, or find any papers on them we should know about, be sure to send us a message."

"Deed I will, McCoy. Good to know there's a man in town who can still laugh."

Spur went back to the jail and talked with John Trevarow.

"Not much farther along then we were last night, 'cept for one thing." He pointed to his gunbelt and the well worn .44 that now hung on a coat hook on the wall. "Decided to leave the blamed thing over there as long as I can. Maybe forever," Trevarow said.

"Good, we're making real progress in keeping you alive. Also, I met the local humorist, Hoop. He's going to be busy today."

"He'll have to use blocks of ice from the ice house. That'll be four funerals today and three tomorrow. Right, he's gonna be damn busy."

"Talked to the Wells Fargo people this morning, yet?"

"Nope. Hoped you'd want to go along. I got this government agent in town, I might as well make good use of him."

"Fact is, this is close enough to government business that I can be official, since the gold was heading for the United States mint in San Francisco. Let's go."

Ingemar Johnson was in no better a frame of mind that morning than he had been when they rode back from the death scene the evening before. He had shadows under his eyes, and jumped at every little noise. His hands wrapped around a large coffee cup and he sipped at the brew frequently.

"I sent a long letter to the company on the morning stage. As soon as the stage hits Sacramento, they'll send a wire to San Francisco. Then we wait for word. I'm not sure what else I have to do—besides find the murdering bastards, get the gold back, and then hang all of them!"

"Wondering if there was anything you know that we could start working with, Mr. Johnson," Spur said. "I know your security is tight. But you've been shipping gold out of Bodie now for two or three years at least. A lot of people must know how you do it. Have you had any unhappy employees lately who have been discharged, caught stealing, got mad at the company and quit? Anything like that?"

"No!"

"Take your time, Mr. Johnson, and think it through. Every company I've ever seen has had a few unhappy workers. It's normal. A driver, a freight man, maybe a guard who would know the set up."

Johnson sipped the coffee. Spur saw a half empty pint whiskey bottle in a partly opened desk drawer. No wonder Johnson loved his coffee this morning.

"All right, I'll think about it. Go back over the records. I'm . . . I'm still so damn angry . . . ."

He walked to the window taking the coffee cup with him. After two sips he came back.

"You're right. Somebody knew the gold was going out. They had to. Here at our firm the people who knew were me and one clerk. We have to give the guards four hours notice of a run, so that means seven more knew about it, and the driver. But it seems highly unlikely that one of them would tip off a robber who would then kill the inside man."

"Means the share of gold is that much bigger for the survivors," Captain Trevarow said.

"My God! I'm not used to dealing with that kind of humanity. I just can't imagine it. Whoever it was knew exactly where to stop the stage. The climb up that hill means the rig has to come almost to a dead stop to make the corner and then head up the slope."

"Who at the mine knew about the shipment?" Spur asked.

"Oh, the superintendent, of course. The head bookkeeper, a trusted man, and I'd say at least one man in the bullion storage area. At least three of them."

"So ten of your people, and three at the mine,"

Spur said. "I'd tend to go along with you on the guards and the driver. Any holdup means a risk for those on board. That leaves your clerk and the three at the mine."

"Could we talk with your clerk, please," Trevarow asked.

"Of course. He's been with us since the start. Six years we've been struggling here. I'd trust him with my virgin daughters and my wife's jewelry. I'll have him come in."

Ten minutes later they finished talking to the clerk. He had the imagination and ambition of a dried prune. Spur saw no way possible that the man could have planned the robbery or been any part of it. He was about fifty years old, a bookkeeper and clerk, and that was his whole life. Matching sets of figures in books were the most exciting elements in the universe to him.

"Where do your guards assemble?" Spur asked.

"They don't. We pick them up one at a time along the route. By the time we get to the mine we have our six men inside."

"That's smart. Do you always leave at four A.M.?"

"No, we go as early as first darkness, and as late as five A.M. It's different each run."

"How many trips a month with gold?"

"Depends on production. Last month we made four trips. This month it will probably be six."

"Is it always $25,000 in gold?"

"No, but never less than that. Never more than $50,000 which is about 150 pounds of bullion. More than that won't fit into our standard strong box."

Captain Trevarow stood. "Ingemar, is there anything else you need to tell us?"

Johnson shook his head, drained the coffee and

sighed. "Wish to hell I could point a finger at the traitor, but I can't."

Outside the stage office, Spur looked up the slope. "Is it about time for us to go talk to the men at the Standard Mining Company?"

"I'd say so. Right now the head man we should see is one of the Cook brothers, Dan by first name. He handles most of the above ground end of the Standard. I'm sure he'll want to meet with us."

As they walked up the hill toward the Standard stamp mill, the clang, clang, clang of the metal rods pounding down on the gold and silver ore to crush it became louder and louder. Spur realized he had heard the sound before and quickly that morning had relegated it to a normal background sound and dismissed it.

It was what every resident of Bodie had done. It was only when the stamping mills stopped pounding, that the Bodie people looked around and asked each other what had happened.

The Standard Mining Company's office was situated east of the stamp mill and slightly up hill. Inside, the sound of the mill was muffled, and when they walked into Dan Cook's office, heavy draperies on the windows reduced the sound even more.

Dan Cook smiled at them and held out his hand for the introduction. When he heard the name he nodded.

"Yes, Mr. McCoy. I've been reading about you in some of my reports. You work with the government in some sort of law agency, and you are greatly active in the West. I assure you what I have heard is all good.

"I'd assume you gentlemen are here about the robbery. Tragic, just tragic. Eight souls blasted into oblivion that way. Do you have any leads about who did it?"

"We were hoping you could help us there, Mr. Cook," Spur said. "Who here at the Standard knew the shipment was going out, and who loaded the gold?"

"Surely, you don't think . . ." Cook stopped. "Yes, of course, if we don't know who was involved, then everyone must be suspect. I understand. I ordered the shipment. My head clerk, Mr. Vance, did the paperwork, and a trusted employee in the retort room and vault, Niles Ogden, removed the actual bullion from the vault and put it in the strongbox and signed it on the stage. The driver signed a receipt, which I have here for the seventy-five pounds of gold bullion."

"Just you three?" Captain Trevarow asked.

"Yes. Never more. If the hour is too late, I usually load the gold myself. I try never to ask an employee to do something I won't do myself."

"Did anyone outside see the gold being loaded?" Trevarow asked.

"Wouldn't be normal that they would, that time of night. It isn't a shift change. Doubt if anyone noticed. Rigs go charging around here all the time with goods, and wood."

"Seems reasonable," Spur said. "It looks like the way the robbery was planned, the men must have known in advance when the gold would go out, rode into position, and waited for the rig. Just witnessing the gold being loaded wouldn't allow the robbers time to beat the stage to the robbery site."

"Is there anything else you can tell us, Mr. Cook?" Trevarow asked.

"Not that I can think of. The gold was insured,

guaranteed delivery by Wells Fargo, so it isn't a loss. But we're shocked by the deaths of the eight men on the stage. We'll do everything we can to bring the murderers to justice."

"Mr. Cook, could we look at your retort room and the vault, and would you show us, physically, how the gold is moved from there to where the stage sat that night?"

Cook did. It proved nothing for Spur, and gave him no new ideas as to how the information could have come into the wrong hands. The more he thought of it, the more he realized that there had to be a traitor here, a betrayer of the confidentiality of the shipment of gold. But who?

The two law men walked back toward town, moving to the side of the street to avoid a convoy of huge freight wagons loaded down with firewood.

"That's the lifeblood of our town," Captain Trevarow said. "As you can see, we grow no firewood anywhere around here. It all must be freighted in from the Bridgeport area and north of there. The more people who move here, the richer the wood haulers get. If this keeps up much longer, wood will be worth more per pound than silver or gold!"

"They use it to produce the steam for the mills and lift works on the mines, and to heat the houses in winter?" Spur asked.

"We don't have any coal here, so we use wood. Last winter one of my neighbors kept telling me that the man next door to him kept stealing wood off his wood pile. Hard to prove something like that. The man said just wait, he'd get proof.

"That night my neighbor split up a new pile of wood and hollowed out one piece, filled it with black powder, then glued it together. Along about midnight the house next door blew up when the stolen wood in the heating stove burned down to the black powder. That was the last time that gent ever stole a stick of wood.''

They passed more wood rigs heading for the stamping mill, got back to Wood Street and headed for Main. Just after they turned past the U. S. Hotel a young man ran into the street and waved at Spur.

"Hey there, fast gun. Hear you think you're pretty good with that tied down iron.''

The speaker was not much over twenty, wore a fancy shirt with button down pockets and a big silver belt buckle, jeans and cowboy boots. A black, flat topped hat perched on his head.

Spur and Captain Trevarow angled away from the man but he ran in front of them and fired a shot in the air.

"Hey you, the tall, ugly one with the mutton chop sideburns and moustache. The one who says his name's McCoy. Can you talk, or are you too much of a coward to look a real man in the eye?''

Spur turned and eyed the young man. He was thirty feet away.

"I'm McCoy, and I'm not half as drunk as you are, little boy. Why don't you go home and tell your mama to wash out your mouth with soap.''

The young man colored, saw some people watching, and let his right hand hover over his tied down six-gun.

"You just bought yourself a gunfight, McCoy. I can take you, I'm twice as fast as you are. Only one way to prove it.''

Spur laughed. "Boy, you been reading too many of them dime novels about the West? You really think you're good with that iron?''

"Better'n you, old man.''

"You got twenty dollars in your pocket?'' Spur

asked.

"You damn well know it."

"Good. I've got no reason to kill you. So we'll set up a little contest." Spur flipped a double gold eagle in the air and caught it. "Here's my twenty, where's yours? We'll let Sheriff Trevarow here hold the money."

"What the hell you talking about?"

"What's your name, son?"

"Quade, Gerry Quade. A name everybody's gonna know cause I gunned down fast gun Spur McCoy."

"Not quite. We do it this way. We set up two bottles on a fence, pace off thirty feet, and on a signal we both draw and shoot at our bottles. The one who breaks his bottle first, wins the twenty dollars. The best thing about this is you'll still be alive."

"You don't have a chance of beating me, McCoy."

Spur snorted. "Kid, I've seen twenty just like you. Half of them are dead by my gun or somebody else's they challenged. Why don't you want to live long enough to grow up? Make you a deal. You break your bottle first, and I'll let you have a go at me, no rules, a call out shoot down. Agreed?"

"Damn right!"

Captain Trevarow took the young man's twenty dollars, then found two quart sized whiskey bottles and sat them on a fence in back of the U.S. Hotel down by Bodie Creek. Then he paced off thirty feet from the bottles and drew a scar on the ground with his boot.

Quade snorted as he looked at the distance.

"Thirty feet," Spur said. "If that's too far we can move closer."

"Shoot, old man, don't talk."

Spur nodded at Trevarow.

"All right, both of you take your places and get your stance. Don't touch your gun butt. When I call out FIRE, both of you draw and fire. The one who breaks his bottle first, wins."

He let the men settle down on their marks.

"Ready. Both ready? Set. Both set? FIRE!"

Spur's draw was clean, smooth, a blur as his .45 fired, blasting his bottle into a hundred pieces before the other man's weapon cleared leather. Spur fired again shattering the second bottle. He holstered his weapon and turned toward the young man.

"Welcome to the land of the living, Gerry Quade. Next time you challenge a man, make sure you're not half drunk, and make sure you see him shoot before you bet your life. Today you would have lost."

Spur and Captain Trevarow walked away watching the young man as he slowly pushed his unfired .44 into leather. Trevarow handed Spur the two twenty dollar gold pieces.

Two men hurried up, grabbed Quade by the arm and walked him away down the street in the other direction.

"Damn, Quade, you idiot, you almost got yourself killed right there," one of the young men said to his friend.

That was when Spur noticed that Captain Trevarow was not wearing his six-gun. Good, Spur thought, then returned to the problem at hand. Who knew about the gold shipment, and where were the killers right now?

4

Spur walked the streets of Bodie that afternoon trying to figure out who set up the robbery. The best suspects were the two bookkeepers and the bullion man at the Standard. But he'd met all three and not one seemed like the type.

Of course, when fifty years of wages are involved, a lot of normal men can go off the deep end.

Bodie was turning into a real little frontier town. The more people who crowded into a place, the more people it took to handle the needs of all those bodies. They needed wood, they had to have food from the outside, thousands of horses and mules were involved to haul in the goods and provide all those necessary services.

There were freight wagons by the hundreds to haul supplies and gold ore to the stamping mills. Three blacksmiths in town did little except make horseshoes and nail them onto unshod hooves. Bodie had a little of everything now, even jewelry stores, fancy ladies' wear shops and one hat store.

The whole town was built of Jeffrey pine, which was loaded with pitch. Much of the lumber that built Bodie came from the Mono Lake mills to the south. The stores were shoulder to shoulder down Main Street and close together over most of the rest of the town. Spur shuddered at what would happen if one of them caught fire.

The residents had thought the same thing and had erected a fire house just down from the Occidental Hotel on Main. Bodie had plenty of water in case of a bad fire.

Spur leaned against a building on Main and let the warm August sun soak into his bones. Before long the snow would be flying in Bodie, there would be ten or twelve feet of snow and the temperature could drop to 30 even 40 degrees below zero. To add further injury, the wind gusts in a storm could whip up to a hundred miles an hour. In spite of the warm sun, McCoy shivered. He had no intentions of staying in Bodie for the winter snow sliding sports.

The idea that had sparked in his mind an hour ago grew and blossomed and Spur kicked away from the wall and walked down to the Wells Fargo office. Ingemar Johnson, the depot manager, ushered him into his private office and closed the door.

"Any ideas who could have let out the information about the shipment?" Spur asked.

Johnson shook his head.

"Then I have an idea. I want to sign on as a guard on the next gold shipment. When is another one scheduled?"

Johnson scowled. "Is this a good idea?"

"Best way to find out who hit the stage is to stop the next attack, beat them back with firepower and follow the attackers back to their lair. If we capture them, one of them eventually will talk, even if it's to save his own neck from stretching a half-inch of hemp.''

Johnson stared at the letter he was writing to one of the dead men's widows. He took a deep breath, scrubbed a hand over his face and nodded.

"I guess we have to try it. You'll be notified four hours ahead like the other guards. Fact is, I'm having trouble hiring guards now. I've jumped the pay to five dollars a day, but still there are few takers.''

Johnson dropped the pen on his desk and drank from his coffee cup. "Damn! but I hate writing letters to these new widows. It's almost like I was in the war again.''

Spur said he understood the feeling, bowed out of the office and remembered that he hadn't had any food since he got up about noon. He picked one of the smaller restaurants and ordered the special of the day, beef stew, Bodie style. It was the best stew he'd ever eaten with whole potatoes, long carrots, lots of parsnips and tomatoes, chunks of cabbage and half a dozen other vegetables.

At four-thirty that afternoon a messenger found Spur and gave him a sealed envelop. Inside he found this message:

"Meet the Wells Fargo stage tonight at Wood and Union Streets near the Standard at 8 P.M. You'll be paid $5 a day as a guard. Yes, a shipment goes out just after darkness tonight.''

Spur rode shotgun on the gold stage since nobody else would. Johnson had met them at the Bodie mine and explained that they would be taking the regular route for the gold stage: out the road northwest to

Aurora, Nevada, then to Wellington, Gardnerville and on to Carson City. From there it went across to San Francisco's U.S. Mint.

Johnson told Spur that he varied the route from time to time hoping to change the pattern enough to keep the shipments safe.

When they picked up the gold at the Bodie mine, Spur and the other six guards watched the surrounding area, but nothing moved, and no mine employees were near. They hoisted the strong box into the front boot, the men climbed inside and Spur went on the high front seat beside the driver. Then they charged quietly into the night.

The first hour went by swiftly. Inside the coach it was quiet, but the men had been instructed not to sleep, and to watch out the windows at all times.

Spur soon caught the trick of staying on the swaying, jolting high seat by bracing his feet and knees as he kept looking around on the moonless night. He could see less than fifty feet in any direction.

Canute Edwards handled the reins for the team of six like the veteran he was. There were hills steep enough on this run for six horses. Canute had been driving stages for nearly twenty years, he proudly told Spur.

"Started out back in fifty-nine in Missouri. Not much to worry about back there, mostly getting talked to death by some up top passenger. Carried sixteen on one trip. One gent kept getting drunker and drunker until he finally fell off the top. He rolled down a hill, but he was so drunk, he never even knew he fell."

The stage didn't go through the middle of Aurora, didn't stop at the Wells Fargo depot there. It would be a tipoff to any robber to see seven armed men on a stage and moving at night. They skirted the little Nevada town and rushed back on the road north to Wellington.

Spur cradled the Remington double barreled shotgun in his arms as he scanned the way ahead.

Canute kept up a steady stream of chatter. "Not much chance of anybody jumping us along here. We got fifteen miles of open country. Then we could have a spot or two where some ratfaces could make a try at us. My guess is we go through without even a mean look from anybody tonight. Hear you're some special government man out here to hang these killers?"

Spur put the Remington in a bracket inside the seat and picked up the Spencer seven shot rifle the company provided. He felt more at home with the Spencer. He'd save the scattergun for close range work.

If he lived that long. Spur knew the shotgun guard on a stage was the first target of holdup killers. The second victim was the driver or the lead horse, depending on the angle and the situation. But the shotgun guard went first. He lifted his brows as he listened to Canute explain how the stage coach driver used to be the toast of the town.

"Hell, when I was younger I could have me any of the pretty women in town when I'd whip in on a stage and end my run. They just seemed to think it was glamorous and dangerous and somehow very thrilling. For ten years I thought they were thrilling too, then I got married for a spell and she stopped all the catting around. Mostly."

When they came to the first heavily wooded section, Spur tensed, but there was no attack. They wound up the steepest grade on the run and again came through without any trouble.

Three days later Spur rode back to Bodie with the other guards in a regular Wells Fargo stage free of charge. There had been no trouble; the new driver and guards took over in Carson City for the run to San Francisco.

Spur slumped in Captain Trevarow's office.

"Everything quiet here?"

"About as usual. Two knifings, twenty-two drunks slept overnight, six shootings but they were such bad shots that only one man was wounded." Trevarow shifted uneasily in his chair, toyed with a five dollar gold piece and shrugged.

"Hell, you'll find out soon enough. Logan Wilde is in town."

"Wilde, *the* Logan Wilde? The same man you had a small situation with in Cheyenne about ten years ago?"

"Same backshooting bastard. He must have got out of prison. I'm surprised some jealous husband or some honest gambler hasn't pumped six slugs into his worthless carcass by now."

"He's in Bodie. Does he know you're here?"

"Yes. He came here to find me."

"Wilde must be in his fifties now."

"He's fifty-one and bragging about it. Claims he's as fast now as he ever was. He's been throwing up a pint whiskey bottle with his right hand, drawing with his right and shooting the bottle before it hits the ground."

"That's not much."

"We know that, but it's showy, and he's got damned near the whole town in his pocket. When he thinks he's scared me enough, he'll come around. I still haven't put on my gunbelt. Just what the hell am I supposed to do, McCoy?"

"The first thing is to keep your six-gun on the shelf. Don't wear it and don't let him goad you into a fight. Any way you can have your deputies arrest him?"

"He's carefully staying clean. Not even cheating at cards, just brags a lot, tells great stories about his exploits. No way we can touch him."

"Maybe I could rile him a little, get him . . ."

Trevarow held up his hand. "No sir! Not a chance. I don't want you anywhere near this man. I know how fast he was. No telling how fast he still is. I've seen you shoot, but I'm no judge of a thousandth of a second anymore. That could be the difference between living and dying. I'll figure out something."

"He won't wait around long."

"I know that, damnit!" John Trevarow shook his head. "Sorry, Spur . . . sorry."

"You have time to go over for a beer?"

"No. I've been staying out of the saloons last couple of days."

"John, there's sixty-five drinking spots in town. What's the chances of you and Wilde being in the same one at the same time?"

"Depends how hard Wilde looks for me, and how many men he hired to tip him off when I walk in."

"Yeah. Guess you figured out the ride to Carson City was a complete bust. We didn't even see a jack-rabbit, let alone get held up."

"Way it goes in law work. You been at it long enough to know you got to be patient."

"True. I'm gonna go have a couple of beers, get the stage dust out of my throat."

John Trevarow didn't look up as Spur left. It took McCoy twelve stops before he found Logan Wilde. He was shorter than Spur had remembered. He'd seen the lawman/outlaw/showman twice before, once when he was town marshal of a small place in Kansas, and again with a small wild west show out of Cheyenne.

Wilde was not more than five-feet seven. He looked his fifty years, with a pot belly and a sag to his features, especially around his eyes. He wore his hat in the saloon, cowboy style, as contrasted to most of the miners who watched him. When he came out of his chair there was a momentary hitch as he favored one leg, then he shifted his weight and grinned at the crowd.

Now he had fifteen drinkers around him lapping up his tall tales of being a fast gun desperado. He even told them about the one bank robbery he and two other guys pulled back in Nebraska ten years ago and nobody ever figured out who did it.

Spur bought a beer and drank it from the bottle, watching the show from a distance. Then Wilde had the apron bring out an empty beer keg and set it on a chair next to the alley wall.

"Now, gents, my bet is that I can hear a call to fire, draw and shoot and hit the keg before you can count off three seconds. Any takers."

Wilde looked around the saloon in astonishment. "You mean there's isn't a single man here who'll risk a thin one dollar gold piece to see me shoot the cork out of that empty beer keg?"

At last one man held up his hand waving a dollar bill.

"Well, now, that's a start. Who wants to be the counter? You have to say: One thousand and one,

one thousand and two, one thousand and three. Say it out loud at just about that pace."

The barkeep walked over and said he would give the word to fire, if somebody would count. He took the better's dollar bill and one from Wilde and belched.

"Hell, I'll do the counting," a man at the end of the bar said. "I can still get to three."

"I'll tell you when to fire," the barkeep said, evidently bored, maybe because he did this same routine a dozen times a day. "You ready, Wilde?"

Wilde stretched his right arm, took an eighteen inch stance facing the keg from twenty feet and nodded.

"Fire!"

The counter started: "One thousand and one . . ."

Wilde's hand darted to his holster, his finger lanced into the trigger housing, he pivoted the weapon up still in the holster and fired before the man could say one thousand and three. He used a trick swivel holster with a hole in the end to fire through. Spur had seen them before, but never used quite so efficiently.

Wilde took the dollar and grinned. "Now, gents, just to make it more interesting, I'll give you five to one odds that I can't hit the barrel before our counter gets to one thousand and two! Do I have a few takers? I can't try this without considerable money being on the table."

This time a dozen men crowded up to the poker table and began putting down money. One man bet twenty dollars. Each man talked with the barkeep and when the amount was settled, the apron put the money on the table and covered each stack with poker chips from his pocket.

"Any more sports want to see me go home without my shooting irons as I try to pay off these ridiculously high odds?"

One more man came down and bet five dollars.

The barkeep checked his pad of paper. "That's eighty seven dollars bet, Mr. Wilde. If you lose, you'll owe me four hundred and thirty-five dollars."

Wilde pretended to sweat. He wiped his brow, looked at the men.

"Can we cut those odds to three to one?" he asked.

They shouted him down.

"Come on, shoot!" somebody said.

"Yeah, I'm buying a new rifle with my winnings!" another called.

Wilde looked at them. "Damn you! You didn't have to bet so much. Hell, I'll remember Bodie as the town where I lost my shirt, my purse, and my favorite gun. Where can I get four hundred and thirty-five dollars?"

"Shut up and shoot!" A heavy voice called from the crowd.

Wilde shrugged, wiped sweat off his brow again, then settled his Stetson in place and flexed his hand.

"Come on, fast draw, don't let us down now!" Wilde shouted.

The barkeep seemed bored, not caught up in the drama of the moment.

"You ready, Mr. Wilde?" the apron asked.

"Yeah, in a minute. Let me concentrate. I'll nod when I'm set, then you call out, and the counter starts counting." He took a deep breath, shook both hands, then flexed his right over his gun butt. Now Spur saw that the holster was cut a little lower than most to allow his finger to slide into the trigger housing as his thumb cocked the hammer.

Wilde nodded.

"Fire!"

"One thousand and one, one thousan . . ."

The six-gun fired, the bullet thunked into the beer keg and the audience applauded, then booed.

Wilde turned, concern on his face. "Mr. Counter, how did you count me?"

"Count? I got to a thousand on the two but never said two. I'm afraid that you've won."

The men jeered the decision. Wilde picked up the eighty seven dollars, gave the chips back to the barkeep and ordered a beer for every bettor. As the barkeep passed the man who counted, Spur saw him slip the man a five dollar bill. There was no way that Wilde could have lost the contest with the fix in for the counter.

Spur finished his beer and drifted outside. It was mid afternoon. The town bustled with heavy hauling rigs, bringing in supplies for the winter. It was an eighteen mile haul to Aurora, and about the same to Bridgeport. Teamsters shouted and swore at their mules and horses.

One rig with sixteen mules hauling it rolled down Main Street heading for the Boone General Store and warehouse at Green and Main. The teamster yelling at the mules said he had 40,000 pounds of goods in his two wagons and hadn't even made a dent in the boxes waiting to come in.

People expected a long, hard winter. One old timer said he got his signals from the jackrabbits. He hadn't seen one now for two months. He claimed they all had headed for the Owens Valley fifty miles to the south.

Spur stepped off the boardwalk and out from

under the overhanging second story porches that covered the boardwalk in front of most stores the length of Main Street. He saw Captain John Trevarow heading across the street a half block down. Almost at the same time he heard a man laugh and looked to the boardwalk on the other side.

Logan Wilde stepped into the dust of the street and pushed his black coat back so it exposed his .45 in the trick holster.

"Damn my hide if it ain't that low down skunk I've been looking for, John Trevarow. You wouldn't be hiding behind a badge, would you, yellow John?"

The two men stopped twenty feet apart.

"I'm gonna kill you, Trevarow, in a clean, honest draw and shootout."

"I'm not armed," Trevarow said. "I don't intend to be armed. You shoot me now and my friends here will see you hang for murder."

"Get a gun, you asshole!" Wilde snapped. He walked closer. "You want everyone to know what a coward you are?" He shouted the words so all could hear.

"I'll get a gun for you, you son of a whore!" He looked behind him. "Bring me a six-gun somebody," he bellowed.

Nobody moved.

"Bring me a gun, now, dammit!" Wilde screamed. At last a man came forward and handed a weapon to Wilde. The gunman walked up to Trevarow and pushed the barrel inside the lawman's belt on his right side.

Wilde turned his back to Trevarow and walked away twenty feet and spun around.

"Now, you gut shooting bastard, you have no excuse. You can draw or not, up to you. I'm calling you out for killing my brother by shooting him in the back in Kansas. I'm counting to three, then I'm going to kill you. Draw if you want to, or don't draw. No jury would convict me long as you have a weapon in your belt."

Wilde turned to the crowd that had assembled as if by magic. More than a hundred people watched in silence from a safe distance to each side of the gunmen.

"You all see that he has a weapon. If he doesn't want to defend himself, that's his funeral, right?"

A few in the crowd shouted agreement. Most stood, wondering what would happen. Spur began to move toward the pair.

"Wait a minute," Spur called.

Wilde ignored him. "One!" Wilde shouted. He adjusted his rig, moved his feet a little farther apart.

"Two," the gunman called.

Spur started to run but he knew he'd be too late. Then as he watched in astonishment, a woman surged from the boardwalk less than two feet behind Wilde and charged at him from the side. At the last moment she brought out a six-inch hunting knife and swiped it at Wilde's throat.

As if the whole thing had happened in frozen bits of time, Spur saw the blade slash across Wilde's throat. Immediately a spurt of red blood shot ten feet into the air and fell to the dusty street.

The woman raised the knife to cut him again, but Wilde turned and looked at her in shock and surprise. He tried to bring his gun hand up to his pistol, but spurt after spurt of rich red blood gushed from his right carotid artery. Four seconds after the slashing, Wilde dropped to his knees. His right hand came up to try to stop the flow of blood which now sprayed out in a steady stream.

Spur ran forward but it felt as if he were struggling through waist deep water.

Wilde looked up at the woman once more, then his eyes rolled back in their sockets and he fell face down into the pulverized dust of Main Street.

Spur charged up to the spot, took one look at Wilde and knew he had bled to death. He held out his hand and the woman gave him the knife, then she collapsed in Spur's arms.

John Trevarow hurried up, touched the man's throat on the uncut side and shook his head. He looked at Spur's unconscious burden.

"Take her over to the jail. We'll have to find out why she did that." Spur looked down at one of the old time fast guns and headed for the jail. Sometimes the Bad Men of Bodie turned out to be human after all.

It was two long blocks up to the jail and before they reached there, the woman he carried revived.

"I can walk," she said, surprising Spur. "We going to jail?"

"Yes, ma'am."

"I figured we would. Been planning to kill Logan ever since I seen him in town. He's so careful. Knew once he started counting he would be concentrating on his draw, that's when I could get close enough to him. He's dead, isn't he?"

"Yes, but you better not say anything else until Captain Trevarow talks to you."

The sheriff borrowed a horse and rode beside them the last block to the jail.

They gave the woman a wet cloth for her forehead, and sat her in the best chair in Trevarow's office. Then the Captain decided it was time to begin. "Your name?"

"Captain, you know me. I'm Sweetheart."

"I mean your real name, the one your mother gave you."

"Oh. Glynnis Funkhouser."

"How old are you?"

"Twenty-eight."

"You work in Virgin Alley?"

"Yeah, I'm a whore. That's why I killed Logan. We was married once. I still got the certificate in my gear. Still married, far as I could tell. The bastard sold me into a whore house in New Orleans. They needed northern girls down there. Locked us up every night. We was all prisoners. He got a thousand dollars for me but he promised that he'd be back in a month and pay off the thousand and we could move on. Fucker never came back. Never had no idea of coming back."

"He was a white slaver?"

"Don't know, but he sold me to a whore house. I finally got away . . . had to stab a man to get out and then I run and run, but the only thing I could do to make a living by then was to lay on my back. That was six years ago. So here I am. I swore that if I ever saw Logan Wilde again, I'd kill the bastard. So I saw him and I waited, and I killed him!"

Spur looked at Captain Trevarow.

"Let's go find that marriage license, Mrs. Wilde. That will help us believe the rest of your story."

They found it in her current house of employment on Maiden Lane. Spur checked the date. It had been issued in the state of Mississippi on November 9, 1873. It was signed and witnessed and looked as legal as possible.

John thought on the matter for a few seconds, then waved Sweetheart away. "The whole story will be in the next issue of the Bodie Standard newspaper. As far as I'm concerned, it's a matter of self defense . . . with some time between the death dealing deed by the deceased before the attacker had a chance to return in kind."

Spur grinned. Western mining camp justice might be a bit strange at times but it was wonderful.

"If the general population does not complain about my decision, we'll consider the matter closed. But, if enough of the folks in town put up a protest, we'll have to have the judge go over the matter next time he's in town."

Sweetheart kissed Captain Trevarow tenderly on this cheek and smiled.

"I guess I'm sad I killed him, but what he done to me is a bit worse than what he got. I'd say he's the one who come out ahead. Leastwise nobody is gonna shoot him down as he gets older and slower on the draw."

Captain Trevarow stared at Sweetheart a minute.

"First thing you know we'll be giving you a medal for saving the poor slob a fate worse than death." He turned and walked out of the sporting house without another word.

Sweetheart shrugged, Spur waved at her not to worry about it and caught up with the local law.

"Don't say a word!" Trevarow snapped when Spur fell in stride beside him. "On this one I'm damned either way. I let her off scot free, and the blabbermouths will say I did it cause she just saved my life. I bring her up on charges, and the other side will say she rid Bodie of a card cheat and cad and ne'er-do-well and our fair city is much better off without the likes of him smelling up the place."

"Yeah, you got the tough part, John. All I have to do is solve eight murders and try to find out who stole cash money that is equal to fifty years of my pay.''

Captain John Trevarow of the Sheriff's office snorted and turned in at his office as Spur McCoy continued toward his hotel and what he hoped would be a nice bath in a real bathtub with soap and big fluffy white towels.

5

Colt had his bath. Two men brought a large copper tub to his room and four buckets of hot water and three of cold. When the water cooled off he got out.

That evening he had a lonesome dinner at the U.S. Hotel dining room and then walked the town, investigating some of the 65 saloons he hadn't been in. Half of them had dance hall girls and rooms upstairs.

From all the wild stories he'd heard the last couple of years, Spur figured there'd be a gunfight in every saloon every night. Wasn't true. Most of the patrons were worried only about having a drink or two, or winning at faro or poker or one of the other games of chance.

It was nearing midnight when Spur tried one more saloon, the Gymnasium, ordered a beer and stood at the bar to watch the rituals. Spur was about to leave when he saw a man walk in the door and look around. His six gun was tied low on his left hip and his left hand never strayed far from the polished butt.

Spur knew the signs, a gunman pure and deadly. The man looked around and walked past the game tables until he grunted with satisfaction and stopped in front of one. He reached down, caught the poker table by one hand and tipped it over through a vacant chair. The two men at the table came to their feet sputtering and screaming.

One of the players looked at the gunman and then slowly backed away. The second poker player quieted and watched the small drama.

"Been looking for you now for two years, Yates," the gunman said in a quiet voice. "Usually back-shooters like you don't live this long."

"I don't know who you are, Mister," the player said. He still backed up, his glance darting toward the door, but he must have decided it was too far away to try for. He came against the bar and could move no farther.

"Never seen you before, Mister, now back off," the card player yelled in protest.

"Not a chance, Yates. Vern Yates is the name you used to use over at Denver. You figured you was a big man back there, remember?"

The gunman stood lean and ready, nearly six feet tall with a slender frame, a thin face and deep set, sharp black eyes. He wore a fancy gambler's shirt and vest under a black jacket, dressed up for Bodie.

"Never been to Denver," Yates said, his voice unsteady.

"Your wife Belle remembered me. I just stopped by at your house. That woman of yours is good fucking, better than most of the whores I've used."

Yates growled, his hand moved toward the gun on

his belt, but he didn't draw, never even touched the weapon.

"I got no fight with you, Deadman. Sure, I was in the posse, but I never fired a shot at you."

"Two other gents I conferred with say you lie. They say all three of you fired up a storm, but you was the only one to hit me. Know they didn't lie. Men on their deathbeds always tell the truth.

"Right now, Yates, we settle accounts. All you have to do to clear your name is go for your gun, draw and shoot me dead. That is, if you can."

Yates began edging for the door.

"One more step and I gun you down right here whether you draw or not, asshole Yates! You want a chance to live, you do it like a man and draw!"

By that time the men in the saloon had all moved to each side of the pair who stood about fifteen feet apart. Wild shots killed more innocent bystanders than participants in these affairs and the onlookers knew it.

Some of the men knew Yates, who ran the hardware store. They knew he came from back east somewhere, but so did everyone else. There wasn't a native born in Bodie old enough to lift a mug of beer.

The man Yates had called Deadman snorted. "You trying to decide how to die, Yates? Maybe you'd feel more at home if I turned my back so you could have a good clean shot. You're a coward, Yates, and your fat wife is a whore!"

Yates screamed. His hand darted for his gun in a move that would beat almost anyone in the room. He was fast, he had probably been a gunhand in his day, but the man he called Deadman was faster.

Deadman's left hand whipped downward and the blued six-gun slid out of the holster faster than Spur thought possible. Deadman's right hand brushed back over the metal as his palm cocked the hammer.

Deadman already had the trigger pulled and the hammer fell forward firing the first shot. It caught Yates in the right shoulder and spun him around. Deadman's weapon fired three more times, so quickly it sounded like one long explosion. The last three rounds also hit Yates, one in the chest, one in the throat and the third in the forehead.

His body slammed against the wall, dislodging a southern style whiskey jug where it had hung on a nail. It shattered on the floor. Yates died when the second round hit his heart. He leaned against the wall a moment, a corpse already, then fell to the side and pitched to the Gymnasium floor.

Spur had watched the deadly drama from the end of the bar. He stared at the gunslick and worked the name over in his mind. Deadman . . . Deadman . . . then he had it. Billy Deadman, wanted in most Western states, but few lawmen tried to take him. He often traveled with three partners and was one of the fastest quick draw men in the West.

Spur had never seen him before, but he would remember him now. Blazing fast on the draw and deadly accurate.

Yates had his six gun clear of leather but never got off a shot.

Deadman held his iron on Yates until he was sure he wasn't moving. Then slowly he holstered the .45 Colt and looked around.

"Anybody have any problem with how Yates died? He drew, I drew, it was a fair fight. Now if somebody wants to go get the sheriff or whatever law you have in this town, I'll be right over here at the bar having six straight shots of whiskey."

By the time Billy Deadman walked to the polished counter top at the stand up bar, the apron had poured six shot glasses full of whiskey and lined them up.

Deadman flipped the barkeep a silver dollar and started working on the line of glasses. He stood six feet down the bar from Spur. The two men looked at each other a moment, then Deadman glanced away.

That was when Spur knew the man was a true professional gunman. He used his guns to kill people, not play games.

That was when Spur also knew that before either of them left town, there would be a deadly contest between the two. Spur had no argument with the man, not yet. But he was somehow sure that before he was through in Bodie, this Bodie Badman would be standing across a room or a street from him as both waited to draw.

About five minutes later one of the deputies came in, talked to the barkeep and wrote down his statement, then moved up to Deadman and spoke in hushed tones with him. The chatter in the saloon died out, but still no one could hear what the lawman and the gunman were saying. A moment later the deputy nodded, folded up a small notebook he had been writing in, and walked out the door.

Spur followed him, found the U.S. Hotel and dropped on his bed. It was a lot softer than sleeping under the stars.

Spur got up early the next morning, had breakfast, then walked up to the jail. Captain Trevarow sipped at a cup of coffee in his office. Spur joined him.

"Boys brought in a dead man yesterday. Body dead five or six days. Shot once in the heart, and so close his shirt still showed the powder burns. He's a local named Lenny Abbott. He drifted around. Mine worker for a while, then worked topside, and even did some wood hauling. Nobody seems to know who he worked for last."

"Five days? About the same time as the gold robbery?"

"About. You think there's a connection?"

"Never know. See what else you can find out about him."

"Yeah, we'll do that. I figured just some grudge fight. But there might be a connection."

"What about this Wells Fargo guy, Johnson? Is he honest? He's in a position to know everything. He could grab a shipment, the mine gets paid back by the company, and he winds up with a profit of $25,000."

"Could happen. Has before. But I don't think this time. One of the dead guards on that robbed stage was Johnson's brother-in-law. He wouldn't set up his own kin to be gunned down."

"The killing part could have been by chance. Why would robbers kill everyone on board a stage they cleaned out?"

"Could be any number of reasons."

"But the biggest one is if one of the guards recognized one or more of the robbers. Say I yell out: 'I know you, you're Ingemar Johnson from Bodie' and everyone hears it. Hell, the masked robbers can't just walk away. One or more have been identified, everyone heard the name. The one robber would soon lead to the others. So the robbers must become killers to protect themselves."

"Damn, it probably happened that way. Most robbers out in this neck of the woods don't gun down a whole coach full of folks."

"So this Lenny was a local?"

"Sure, been around two, at least two, three years."

"So lots of people could know him. Even some of the guards might know him—that is, if he was involved in the robbery."

"Possible." Trevarow continued the story. "Say he gets back with the gold, tells his boss how the killings happened, and the top man guns Lenny down to reduce the witnesses and maybe the only contact between the robber/killer and the man who hired them."

"Could happen. Oh, you know that Billy Deadman is in town?"

Trevarow let his chair's front legs drop to the floor. "God, no! Deadeye Deadman? Thought he was still in Kansas."

"Probably got too much warm lead flying around him there. He killed a local last night, an old grudge."

"I heard there was a gun fight, but I haven't read the reports yet. I've never tangled with him, anywhere, never even met the man." Trevarow scowled. "You just be sure you don't kick his spurs. He's a real good man with a six gun."

"I saw him in action last night."

"So?"

"So he's the fastest and the best shot I've ever seen, bar none. Not even you were that fast. So I don't go looking for a stupid gunfight. Never when it's for bragging rights as fastest gun in the state."

"Good. I like having you around town—above ground!"

Spur stood. "Heading down to the Wells Fargo

office. Want them to check on gold shipments.''

Ten minutes later, Spur asked Ingemar Johnson his question of the day.

"Has any one mining company been shipping out more gold than it normally does? You can figure the averages for each of the firms and what they're doing now.''

"Yes, yes, I see. If one small firm suddenly shipped out an extra $25,000 in gold bullion, it could mean something."

"How better to market stolen gold bullion than to melt it down, recast it in your retort room in your own bullion molds, and then ship it to San Francisco?'' Spur asked.

"I get the idea. I'll check the records for the past year, showing the total shipments for each mine for each three month period.''

Spur thanked the manager and stepped out of the Wells Fargo office onto Main and turned north. An errant plank in the boardwalk had lost a nail and sprang up two inches. Spur stumbled on it just as a rider on a passing horse fired a six-gun at him from fifteen feet away. Only the stumble saved Spur from serious gunshot damage.

Spur jumped to his feet and glared at the horse and rider who now pounded north on Main. Spur looked along the street, saw a man just stepping down from a horse.

Spur rushed up to him. "I just got shot at, can I borrow your horse?''

Before the man could protest or answer, Spur grabbed the reins, stepped into the saddle and jolted the horse up the street.

"Bring her back!'' the owner shouted after him.

Spur waved and kicked the mount in the flanks to

urge her on. The bushwhacker turned off on the next street to the right, which was Union Street. When he saw Spur close behind, he turned left again and rode down a lane in back of the U.S. Hotel to the north, and soon came to Main and pounded past the Bodie Bank and the Moyle warehouse.

Spur's horse was not the fastest, but she seemed to have good staying power. The gunman turned off the street and angled around the old tailing ponds on Bodie creek, then rode into the hills to the north and east of Bodie which was dotted by trailings and overburdens from hundreds of mine tunnels.

The bushwhacker kept moving north, riding along the side of the ridges so his mount didn't have to climb upward. Spur kept chasing him. Now and then the man ahead looked back. He shot twice, but the range was too great.

Once he dodged behind a small mine shack but Spur made a wide turn around it and didn't afford the man an easy shot. He tried, missed, then raced away to the north again.

An hour later they left the last of the mine diggings. They were in open country with only an occasional sagebrush bush showing in the rocky, sandy soil.

Spur guessed they had climbed a thousand feet so were near the 9,500 foot level. There were no trees and no grass up here. The man's horse slowed. For a few paces it limped, then found the gait again.

They came to a flat area and Spur kicked his tired mount into a gallop, closed the distance between them quickly and he fired three fast shots from his six-gun. One of the rounds narrowly missed the bushwhacker, the second sliced through a quarter of an inch of his right shoulder, and the third caught the horse in the head as it turned to look behind.

The horse went down, screaming and kicking in a death struggle.

The gunman rolled behind the horse for some protection and leveled in his six-gun. Spur dropped off his mount and began to stalk his enemy slowly. He moved from one small depression forward, and saw that his target was still behind the horse.

Now he was close enough to call to him.

"Throw out your gun and live," Colt bellowed.

"Go to hell!" the answer came back.

Spur put a round into the horse's dead body.

"Who hired you to try to kill me?" Spur yelled.

"Your wife, you bastard!"

Spur saw a large rock he could use for cover. He fired twice at the bushwhacker, then surged up and ran ten yards to the rock. He felt a hot round of lead slash past him as he dove to safety behind the boulder. Now he had an angle on the gunman. He could see his legs. Spur reloaded his Colt so it held six rounds, then leveled in the weapon across his arm and fired.

A scream of pain billowed from behind the horse.

"Bastard? You shot me!"

"My calling card. Who hired you? Was it the man who held up the stage and killed the guards?"

"Don't know what you're talking about. Jesus, I'm bleeding to death."

"Tell me who hired you and I'll take you down to Doc Rogers."

"Not if I kill you first!"

"You tried and missed. Now it's my turn."

"No!" the man screamed, trailing off the word as he burst from behind the horse, a six-gun in each hand as he charged the rock where Spur lay.

Spur shot him again in the leg and knocked him down. But the gunman staggered up, screamed and charged again, firing with both hands, pinning Spur down. At last Spur pushed around the side of the boulder and fired twice. The bushwhacker was only three feet in front of the rock. The two rounds hit him in the chest and stopped him in his tracks. Slowly his arms dropped to his sides and he turned and fell on the rock.

He was dead.

"Damn!" Spur said. Now he'd never find out who sent the man to gun him down on the street in bright daylight. He went through the man's pockets. He found two new double eagles, probably his blood money. There was a letter from Ohio written to Bobby Hennessy. He had been working at the Standard Mine at one time.

Probably half the men in town had worked the Standard at one time or another. The only other paper was a slip from a laundry with Chinese markings and a bill of sale for a .44 caliber revolver at the price of two dollars and ninety five cents. The gun had been bought that morning.

Spur sat there in the rarified air of the mountain and looked at the dead man. Who was so worried about what Spur McCoy was doing that they hired this man to gun him down? Somebody in town would know the man, know where he worked, who he knew. Spur's one fear was that the man might be a drunk or a down and outer who someone had rescued, sobered him up, bought a gun, given him a horse and pointed out the target.

Two hours later, Spur had walked back to town with Bobby Hennessy draped over the borrowed horse's back. He dropped the body off at Hooperman's undertaking parlor.

Hoop smiled and carried the dead man on his shoulder back to a marble slab in his "work" room.

"More business! I knew you'd be good for business soon as you hit town. You and that Deadman guy could increase my income. Hey, Mr. McCoy, I tell you about the loafer who came by here yesterday? I asked him if he was looking for work. He said not necessarily, but he did want a job."

"Hoop, your jokes are getting worse and worse."

He grinned. "Sorry, McCoy, I guess I'm at a dead end!" He roared with laughter at his own pun and Spur rode back to Main Street and found the man whose horse he had borrowed.

"Any damages to my Princess?" the man asked.

"None at all. She's a fine beast." Spur gave him a silver dollar and walked up to the jail.

Sheriff's Captain Trevarow had some news for him. "We've found out that Lenny Abbott has been in town for four years. He's worked for five different mining companies, including two now out of business and the Standard, the Bodie and Bechtel. That's as far as we are on Lenny."

He eyed Spur. "Heard somebody got shot at on Main Street a couple of hours ago. Was it you?"

"True. I left the bushwhacker's body with Hooperman. Here are his personal effects and papers. His name was Bob Hennessy."

"Hennessy? That one I know. Yeah, had kin in Ohio. A lot like Lenny, he couldn't seem to hold a job for long. I've seen him in saloons lately mooching drinks and finishing off anybody's mug of beer who forgets it for a moment."

"So anybody could have hired him to take a shot at me."

"After they sobered him up, got him a clean shirt, rented him a horse and bought him a gun. According to this receipt, he got the gun today. I'll have a man check to see if the mercantile clerk remembers if anybody was with Bobby when he bought the piece. Then we'll check the livery, too. But chances of finding out who rented the nag for him are slim."

"No way I could keep from killing him. He was on top of me with two guns blasting out hot lead."

"Happens."

"I'm going over to Wells Fargo and see if I can talk Johnson into setting up a fake gold shipment. Nobody will know it's fake except about four of us. We might get lucky."

"Hopefully if you do they won't kill the whole guard force. You gonna sign on Billy Deadman as a guard?"

"Not likely. I'm hoping he rides out of town to a warmer climate since his work is done here."

"Don't count on it. He's still here. Living it up and causing a stir in Virgin Alley. Last night he ordered three girls for all night."

"Damn, nobody's got any secrets in this town—except when they hire a no-good to bushwhack a citizen."

It took Spur a half hour to talk Ingemar Johnson into the fake gold shipment.

"Look, we can put seventy-five pounds of lead in the strong box. Lead is only a little heavier than gold. Nobody needs to know except the bullion man at the mine and the superintendent. All of our people and the guards will think it's a real run. Let's head for Bridgeport this time and see what happens."

Spur set up the coach differently for this trip. He

placed quarter-inch iron plates on the inside of the
coach to deflect rifle rounds. He removed the panel
behind the high driver's seat and took out one of the
inside seats so the driver could stand on the floorboards of the coach inside and his head would be
high enough so he could look out over the driver's
seat and drive. It would give him protection from
any first shot, yet still allow him a view of the
horses.

To help his view, the cushion that usually is on the
high bench was taken off as well. It made a strange
looking stage coach, but Spur figured it was worth a
try. He tried two drivers before he found one who
would drive the coach that way. The man hitched it
up and took it on a trial run over some back roads
until he was sure he could maneuver the team from
such a low position.

Spur made sure all six of the guards inside the
coach had Spencer repeating rifles and the sheet
iron protected firing positions. There would only be
seven men in the coach including the driver and no
shotgun guard on the high seat.

The rig rolled out at midnight, stopped at the
Bodie mine where Johnson had arranged to pick up
seventy-five pounds of pure lead. They charged out
the Bridgeport road south and west, and Spur
McCoy hoped this would be the night the gold
robbers would make another try.

Spur and the guards waited. They rode and
watched. The driver cursed. He was getting tired of
standing up. The coach rolled past the three best
spots for an attack and nothing happened. At four
A.M. Spur called the rig to a stop. He explained to
the men it had been a dummy run, designed to lure
the robbers into another attack, one they wouldn't
win.

Spur ordered the stage to turn around and head back for Bodie. One of the men grumbled and was teased because he had what they called 'a bit of poon on the side' in Bridgeport.

The driver asked if he could get back on top where he belonged and Spur said he could.

The men slept the four hour ride back to Bodie. The driver had no one to talk to except the horses and even they got tired of his stories so he began singing to them. At least it kept him awake.

The rig pulled up at the front door of the Wells Fargo office in Bodie about 8 o'clock as any other rig would, only it had dropped off the guards at three places just inside town.

Spur supervised the unloading of the strong box and then went to his hotel to try to finish his half a night's sleep. A letter in his key box caught his attention. By the time he got up to his second story room he had read the note inside.

"Dear Mr. McCoy. I understand you spent some time in New York City. My people are from there. I thought we might have a pleasant chat while dining this day. Could I expect you about one-thirty?" It was signed Mrs. Milly Bechtel. "Oh, my home is at 67 Second Street. Please advise."

Spur went back to the desk, wrote a note, and gave the clerk a quarter to find a boy to deliver it to the widow. Then he went upstairs and fell into his bed and slept four hours. It was half past noon when he woke up. He had an hour.

He shaved, washed up, put on a clean shirt and a pair of trousers, a tie and a jacket. He needed a haircut but that would have to wait. From the room clerk he discovered that Mrs. Bechtel was the widow of the developer of the Bechtel Mine #3. Now she was sole owner and operator. She had a mine superintendent who did most of the day-to-day operation, but she kept her hand on the controls.

"She's what, fat and fifty?" Spur asked.

The clerk laughed. "No indeed. Widow Bechtel is about thirty-five, tall and slender, dresses well and has a fine figure."

Spur thanked him and walked toward the house. At least the time might not be totally wasted. He would get a meal and see a pretty face.

But that wasn't his major problem. He'd tried two dry runs. What did he have to do next to smoke out the robbers? General Halleck back in Washington was probably wondering what he was doing, taking so long to get to a telegraph after his last assignment. Another couple of days here, then he'd have to head for Sacramento with or without the solution of the robbery/massacre.

Ahead he saw an unusual sight in Bodie, a small white house with a picket fence and in the front yard, three blooming rose bushes. Old timers said nothing but hops and sagebrush would grow in Bodie because of the severe winters.

Spur paused to admire the roses. All three bushes were in five gallon buckets. He guessed the owner of them took them inside the house during the winter season.

A woman in her thirties came around the corner, saw him and smiled. "I hope you're enjoying my rose garden," she said. "These are the only roses in all of Bodie."

"Beautiful, ma'am, simply beautiful. Oh, could I buy one of the red blooms?"

"I usually don't pick them. They last so much longer on the bush."

"I'm going to see a lady for dinner, and I thought a rose might be a welcome gift."

"A lady, well. Certainly. How can I stand in the way of a gentleman and a lady." She snipped a red bloom with a foot long stem, trimmed off the thorns and all but two leaves and handed it to him.

"My compliments to you and to the lady. I'm sure she'll know where it came from."

"I thank you, you're most kind. What was your name?"

"Mrs. Wilson. Mrs. Emma Wilson. Enjoy."

Spur found the Bechtel house, a grand three story affair with a bay window, and a porch along the length of the house in the grand style. It was by far the most lavish house he had seen in Bodie. Most houses here were square boxes with low ceilings so they would be easier to heat, more utilitarian than fancy.

At the front door, he lifted a brass knocker and let it fall against a heavy brass plate.

A small, delicate, beautiful Chinese girl opened the door, smiled shyly and motioned for him to follow. They went through a small hallway, then into a parlor that was grand. It reminded him of one of his father's houses in New York. Warm toned wood dominated the room in the furniture, in a wall panel, and around a massive stone fireplace.

On the walls hung three oil paintings that were bold and colorful and of excellent quality.

At a small table ready for two near a bay window, sat a red headed woman who watched him with interest.

"Good afternoon, Mr. McCoy. I'm Milly Bechtel. It's good to meet you after hearing so many good things about you. I feel I must be the social leader in town, so welcome to Bodie."

Up close her skin was flawless, a soft not quite pinkish white to go with her hair color. Her wide set eyes were of the palest green and the red/green combination made him think of a Christmas tree. A delicate nose commanded a well formed mouth that showed just a touch of self applied color.

"I hope I pass approval," she said with a smile.

"I'm sorry, how rude of me. But it isn't often I find amazingly beautiful women in Bodie. Thank you for inviting me. The hotel food is becoming quite the same."

"My pleasure to have you come, especially since you have said nice things and brought me a rose. It must have come from Emma Wilson's garden. She's a marvel with flowers."

Spur handed the rose to her. She sniffed it delicately, then gave it to the small Chinese girl who placed it in a bone china vase and set it on the table.

"Now, our table is complete! I miss the vases and vases filled with flowers that I always used to have on occasions like this."

They began the meal with a robust white wine, then had diamond shaped sandwiches made of some sturdy brown bread, buttered with mayonnaise and stuffed with the best marinated roast quail meat he had ever tasted.

"Would I be impolite if I asked for another of those delicious sandwiches?" Spur asked.

At once the Chinese girl brought him two.

"I love watching a man enjoy a meal," Mrs. Bechtel said. "Now tell me about yourself. Somebody said you were a college man."

Spur laughed. "I haven't heard that term since I left New York. In most of the country it has little meaning. Yes, I grew up in New York City, then went to Harvard for my degree in business."

"How marvelous! I attended a small woman's

college for one year, then I married Harry . . . eventually I wound up here in the gold mining business."

"That's very brave of you. This is such a male dominated business."

"I am good at knowing who to hire. I find the best men to do the job, pay them more than anyone else, and make money. That seems to be what everyone is trying to do. Even when the wood supply gets short toward the end of winter, the wood sellers raise the price as high as thirty dollars a cord. Usually, it costs eight to ten dollars in the summer and fall. Now that is what I call good business!"

She watched him a moment.

"Tell me more about what you do. I'm always on the watch for good people. Maybe I could hire you, with your business degree and all."

Spur laughed. "No, I'm afraid not. I know nothing about the mining business. I'm in town to visit an old friend, Captain Trevarow. Haven't seen him in four or five years, so we have a lot of catching up to do."

"So we should have a social occasion in your honor, a party or a dance, something."

"I'm not good at parties, Mrs. Bechtel, but thank you for the thought. I was here five years ago, and the growth of the town has been tremendous. Just how big do you think Bodie can get?"

"Gracious, I have no idea. I'd say it may be somewhere near the peak. We haven't had a really good new strike in any of the mines now for six months. The top of the boom may be coming soon. Once that happens it's all down hill with the scrappy ones hanging on until the last seam of gold has been dug out."

"All good things come to an end," Spur said.

"I've lived in three mining towns. One of them little more than a tent city that never reached the wooden building stage. I know about empty dreams."

The Chinese girl came in and cleared away the things. She watched Spur every moment she was there, he noticed.

"Me Ling is such a good helper. She's fascinated by you. She speaks only Chinese."

"She's beautiful."

The girl sensed their talking about her and took the last of the lunch things and left.

"May I play the piano for you? It's one of my treasures. I had it shipped out here by boat and wagon. A piano tuner worked on it for two weeks to get it back in condition to play."

"I'd enjoy hearing you play, Mrs. Bechtel, but I do have an appointment I must keep in about fifteen minutes. I've enjoyed the meal, and the fine company. This room is outstanding. It looks something like one that was my mother's favorite in our Park Avenue house. Truly amazing."

He stood. "Thank you again for a wonderful time. Perhaps I can hear you play another time soon. I'm sorry, but I really do need to go now."

"I understand. Business, even though you're here on a friendly visit. Perhaps sometime in the evening would be better for you. I'll be in touch with you, Mr. McCoy."

She walked him to the door. He kissed her hand as he left, and she seemed about to say something, then stopped.

Spur hurried down the walk to the street. There had to be a way to rout out the killers. It was his job to figure it out. He headed back to the jail, hoping that by now the sheriff's deputies had found something about the dead bushwhacker that would tie him in with the killers.

6

Sheriff's Captain Trevarow shook his head. "Sorry, McCoy. That's all we can find out. A tall man with a fake red beard and heavy glasses bought the gun with Hennessy early this morning. The same man rented a horse at Kirkwood Stables an hour later. Then the red bearded man vanished.

"Oh, Kirkwood wants you to pay him twenty dollars for the horse you shot. I took it out of the forty dollars you found on Hennessy's body, so you're off the cowcatcher on that one."

"This outfit sure covered its tracks. They knew if something went wrong we'd check back on Hennessy. Dammit, John. We're right back where we started."

"Maybe not, Spur. A man who claimed Lenny's body said far as he knew, Lenny still worked at the Bechtel Mining Company as of last Friday when he disappeared."

"Bechtel. Doesn't mean a thing. I just had dinner

with the owner of that mine. Seemed like a right respectable lady."

John grinned. "Figured Milly might be making time with you. She's been something of a spicy item since her husband died. All very proper, of course. A lot of woman, that Milly."

"So what the hell are we supposed to do now?" Spur asked, his impatience beginning to show.

John chuckled. "How long you been at this law work, McCoy? You know what to do, we sit and wait, keep our eyes open, and hope that the killers make a mistake."

"This isn't a bank robbery, John. The killers can't spend gold bullion."

"But the actual holdup men must have been paid in cold cash. Where are the big spenders? I haven't heard of any lately around this town."

"Maybe they rode on to Bridgeport. Why come back here?"

"Unless this was where the boss was, and where they had to deliver the gold."

"If Lenny was one of the gang, he sure isn't going to spend much. You've talked to the girls up in the fancy lady houses?" Spur asked.

"Yep. First thing. Things seem to be more quiet than usual up there. Don't ask me why."

"I'm no good at waiting, John. Never have been. Think I'll go get a beer." He stopped. "What about Chinatown? Anybody up there be of any help? Sometimes they see things we don't."

"I don't talk Chink too good. Most of them don't speak any English at all. My best contact is Chou. He's a kind of head boss up there. I've got everyone listening."

"Good, time I did some serious drinking."

"Got a later engagement with the widow Milly?"

Trevarow asked.

"No. If I did, I wouldn't share all that woman with you anyway. Go find your own girl." Spur grinned as he stalked out of the office and back up King Street to Main.

Six, two-mule wagons went by loaded down with tightly packed four foot cordwood. From the looks of it the wood was all split pine. A sign on the side of the last load offered the wood for sale to the first customer for $12 a cord.

As Spur looked around the community he now noticed that cord wood in four feet lengths was stacked everywhere. In back of the Standard Stamp Mill he had seen a huge pile of neatly stacked and split cord wood that was a hundred feet long, twenty feet wide and eight feet high.

August was the time to be laying in the winter's wood supply for certain. An item in the Bodie Weekly Standard newspaper said there were now over 19,000 cord of wood in the Bodie community and half again that much would be needed before the snow closed the roads to all except freight sleighs.

Spur followed the last wagon and saw it pull in at a vacant lot across from the U.S. Hotel. The lot was jammed on the far end with stacked cord wood. A short man with a derby hat sat in a chair next to a small shack as he talked to a man and his wife. They argued for a moment, then the man produced eleven dollars and gave it to the salesman.

Spur walked up on the end of the sale.

"Right, Mr. Vernon. Have it at your place within the hour. Yep, I know the house. You be there to tell the driver where to put it. We don't stack, just throw it off. Right." The couple went down the street and Spur moved up to the small man.

"Business looks good," Spur said.

The man stood but was still only five feet tall. He held out a soft, pink hand.

"Indeed it is, stranger. My name is Zentner, Stump Zentner, in case you need to know. Need some good pine cordwood? I can cut that twelve dollar price a bit."

"Sorry, can't use any. I don't own a stove."

Stump scowled. "You're gonna freeze your balls off before Spring." He frowned. "You funnin' me, right? We got Hoop to make all the bad jokes we need in town. You really don't have a stove?"

"Be moving on long before snow time, Mr. Zentner. I've never seen so much firewood in my life."

"Fiddlefoot, huh? Okay, by me. Mills and steam lifts are what use most of the wood. I used to have a contract with the Bodie, but some jackass cut the rate to seven dollars a cord and I wouldn't meet his price. Course they buy two, three hundred cord at a time. Makes a man plumb tired just thinking about all that axe, saw and sledge work."

Spur waved and moved on up the street. He hadn't been to the Chinese district yet. Spur retraced his steps past the jail on King Street and into the Chinese houses and a few shops. They seemed self sufficient. He knew there were a few Chinese laundries in town but he wasn't sure what the rest of the people did.

These must be the workers and their descendents who came to the country to help build the transcontinental railroad that was completed back in 1869. Over ten years ago. Spur received some angry glances and after a block or two he turned and walked out of the district.

It seemed like a whole new world in there, and not one that he really needed to enter at the moment.

As he left he saw a miner moving in that direction. He seemed to be drunk, but hardly staggered. Spur thought of warning him, but the man had been there longer than Spur. The Secret Service agent watched him for a while. He wore a full set of whiskers that were now half white and half black and four inches long. He probably could take care of himself. Spur went back to Main Street to see what he could dig up about the killers. Somebody had to know something.

The miner Spur saw continued up King Street, turned off in a narrow lane between closely bunched shacks and houses until he saw what he wanted, a young Chinese girl who rushed from one building to another.

She wasn't fast enough. The miner moved quickly, cut off the girl's escape and grabbed her by one arm. He spun her around and pushed her against an unpainted building.

"Yeah, Chink poon on the hoof! Damn, I'm gonna find out for sure if this Chink stuff is cut sideways. Everybody says so." He laughed, pulled the girl close to him and whispered something in her ear.

She chattered at him in Chinese, then she screamed. The miner slapped her hard, bouncing her head to one side.

"Shut up, Chink-O. Quiet time. My name is Big Al and I don't take no shit off nobody, specially some stick thin Chink poontah like you."

In one swift move he grabbed the light fabric of her blouse front and jerked downward. Seams parted and fabric ripped and her blouse and thin chemise ripped to her waist exposing her small breasts.

"Yeah, least ways these Chink poon got tits," the miner yelped. He pushed up against her now, his hips grinding hard at hers. She screamed again, and three Chinese men appeared in a doorway behind them. The miner spun around, drew a knife from his boot and waved it at them.

"Just back off, Chink-heads. None of your god-damned business. Back off!" He waved the knife again and they moved into the doorway.

Big Al turned, pushed the knife back in his boot and rubbed her breasts. Then he tried to open the buttons on his fly. With just one hand he had trouble. The girl screamed again and clawed finger-nails down his cheek leaving red scratches that started to bleed through his beard.

"Fucking Chink whore!" the miner screeched. He slapped her. She jerked away from him and ran but he caught her quickly. Two Chinese men jumped from another doorway in front of the girl. Both had foot long knives and they advanced on the miner. Big Al held the girl in front of him now, his arm tightly around her stomach holding her as a shield.

"Get out of here, dirty Chinks! You got no cause to get messed in this."

The two men advanced, their deadly knives ready.

"You come a step more and I'm gonna slit this pretty poon's throat. Now you don't want me to have to do something like that, do you boys."

They made no indication that they understood. Now they moved apart and came at him from angles, cutting off any escape.

"Goddamn, you boys don't believe me."

Big Al swept the sharp blade across the girl's throat, then pushed her at one of the men making him stumble. The miner charged the second one, took a cut on his arm, but drove his blade into the man's upper chest.

By then two more Chinese men jumped out from

doorways behind him. One darted in and before the miner knew they were behind him, the man struck him on the back of the head with a four foot long staff. Big Al went down and unconscious on the ground.

When the miner woke up he stood in a building with three lamps lighting it. It was dark outside and around him he heard nothing but Chinese talking with each other. A glass of water had been sloshed in his face and he came fully awake and realized he was naked and standing with his hands above his head where they were tied to a cross rafter on the open ceiling.

"What the hell?" he shouted. An inch-thick staff thudded into his left kidney and Big Al bawled in agony. He vomited and just as he recovered, someone hit him in the other kidney.

When he could look up, Big Al saw the Chinese man he had stabbed in the shoulder come up and hold a long thin knife for Big Al to see.

Chou said something to the man, showed him the knife again, then pointed at his bandaged shoulder.

"Yeah, so I stuck you. Little bastard, you asked for it."

Chou shook his head, put the knife carefully on Big Al's arm and drew a six inch line as blood flowed. The cut wasn't deep, perhaps a quarter of an inch, but blood filled the wound and spilled down his arm.

Big Al screamed and tried to kick the Chinaman, but his ankles had been tied together.

"Bastard!" the miner roared.

Chou made a slight bow to Big Al and handed the blade to another Chinese who stood behind him. The man spat in Big Al's face, then made a cut, this time on his cheek. Blood flowed and dripped off his beard.

Big Al screamed again.

The Chinese man bowed and handed the blade to the next man in line. For a moment Big Al looked at the line of Chinese that stretched to the back of the room. He screamed.

Someone slapped his face. He looked at the man who stood there.

"My name is Chou. I am protector of my people in this small city. We retain our customs. Today you killed a niece of mine, a fine young girl. Now you will suffer your punishment. May your god forgive you and your soul rest in peace."

"What the hell? I don't go by no damned Chink law."

The knife made its ritual slice on his body and more blood appeared.

"Get me out of here, Chou! Go get the Captain, Trevarow. Damnit, Chou, I ain't no damn Chink!"

A small woman next in line reached up and slapped him in the face. She screamed at him a dozen words, them made a foot long slice across his stomach and watched in satisfaction as the blood puddled along the slash and ran down into his pubic hair.

When she left, Chou spoke again. "That was the dead girl's mother. She wanted to slice off your penis. I told her no. She asked our god to burn your feet in hell for a thousand years and to move the fire up your body an inch every thousand years after that."

Big Al Grogotsky looked at the line of Chinese and felt the knife slice into his flesh again, and he was morning-after sober. He realized for the first time that he was in deep trouble and this was one jam he might not live through.

* * *

The next morning Spur stopped at the Sheriff's office. He was on his way to see Jessica who had sent him a note that said she had someone who wanted to meet him at ten that morning at the house just off Bonanza.

Captain Trevarow motioned Spur to follow him and they went down Bonanza a ways to the undertaker. A man had been laid out on the marble slab in the back room. He was naked, but it was hard to tell. His entire body was marked with hundreds of individual knife cuts. There were angry slashes through his four-inch beard, but none across his throat.

"That's the hard way to die," McCoy said, looking at the body. "The man suffered more than any human being should have to."

"Never seen that before," Trevarow said. "Heard about it, being around the Chinese."

"The death of a thousand slashes," Spur said. "The Chinese reserve it as a method of execution for the most terrible of crimes against their people. This guy with the beard could be the one I saw walking into that area yesterday. Any idea what happened?"

"Not a clue, and I never will know. I let the Chinese take care of things in their little village. Chou is the head man up there now and he does a good job."

"Something like this means the man killed somebody, more likely somebody young who would have had a long life to look forward to."

Hooperman came up wiping his hands on a towel. "Maybe the slob died before they were through carving him," the undertaker said.

"Not a chance. The idea is not to kill him, just make him suffer. All of those wounds have bled. That means his heart was still pumping. The worst cut won't bleed once the pump stops. No reason blood should run out when there's no pressure in the pipe."

Hoop made a deep bow to Spur. "The man is a poet, a scholar. I'd give a cheer if this wasn't such a *grave* moment." Hooperman held his sides as he roared laughing.

"Eventually, the victim dies of loss of blood," Spur said. "Of course, that could take half the night."

"He's been dead about four hours," Hoop said, lifting one hand and letting it drop. It went back to the slab slowly as rigormortis worked its way into the flesh.

Spur and Trevarow walked back to the jail.

"Nothing to get the morning started off right like a nice fresh body," Spur said. "You want a blood red steak for breakfast?"

Trevarow took a swing at him but missed.

"Anything more on your two dead suspects?"

"Not a word."

"I got a note from one of the fancy house girls this morning. Might prove to be a lead."

"Can't tell till you ask," Trevarow said.

Spur found the right house, went up to the door and started to knock, but a sign said: "Come on in!"

He knocked and then went inside. A floozy in a robe hurried out of sight. Spur rang a small dinner bell on a stand up desk at the side of the room.

Jessica hurried in through a draped door.

"You're early as usual, Spur McCoy. Around here nobody gets up until noon. Hetti wants to meet you. She said ten, but ten-thirty will be better. I heard about the slice job last night. That gives me the shivers."

"You don't have to worry about the Chinese.

None of them will bother you, if you don't hurt them. My guess is that some drunken miner killed somebody in Chinatown last night, and they served justice in their own way, a life for a life."

"I still shiver." She stopped, reached up and kissed him gently on the lips. "Now, let me tell you why I asked you to come. First, I want you to meet Hetti. She's a dear, the best lady I've ever worked for.

"Hetti is a prim and proper lady from Boston. The gossip is that she's still a virgin at sixty-two, but I couldn't say. She demands absolute ladylike behavior of her girls until they get behind closed doors. In the parlor we are fully clothed, we all carry fans, our hair is fixed nicely, and we wear just a little makeup, not all painted like the dance hall girls. She calls us a quality product. We can't use bad language either. We have to take a bath twice a day and we can't use too much perfume."

"Even now you smell good," Spur said.

"Good. Hetti also demands absolute gentlemanly conduct from our customers. No weapons are permitted in the rooms. They have to check six-guns, knives and hideouts in the lobby. If a girl finds a weapon on a man she throws it out the window.

"Any man gets out of line we have two huge black men who come in and pitch them out into the street. Once last month a guy got belligerent, a mean drunk, I guess. He slapped Wanda and she screamed for the boys. These two blacks, who stand about six-feet-six each and weigh about 285 pounds, rushed into her room, carried the drunk out, and sat him down on the porch. He swore at them and slugged one. Then they took his pistol and knife, picked him up, carried him to the street and threw him into the dust. They dumped the rounds out of his six-gun and threw it down the street. About a dozen people were on hand to laugh at him.

"Well, like I said, Hetti is about sixty, rich some say, and she charges twice as much as any other house on the street. That makes us feel kind of special."

She squeezed Spur's hand. "I'm just so glad to see you. I'll never forget what you did for me in Salt Lake."

Jessica fluffed out her long blonde hair and smiled. "McCoy, I head something the other night and Miss Hetti said I have to tell somebody. Usually we don't, but this is too important, she said."

Jessica looked at a Seth Thomas on the wall, and stood. "Let's go see her."

They went down a hall and to a fancy door. Jessica knocked and a few moments later it opened. A tiny woman of about sixty stood there in a dignified, expensive dress. Her hair was pure white and carefully set on top of her head. A diamond necklace showed around her throat and she smiled and waved them inside with a hand that had three rings.

"Yes, the government man, please come in."

Spur looked at her trying to remember. At last he smiled and nodded. They sat down on expensive upholstered furniture in a bit of an old fashioned parlor, and Spur-smiled. "It's good to see you, Lotti," he said.

Jessica looked at him in surprise.

"Yes, McCoy. I wondered when you were going to remember. You couldn't have been much over twenty at the time."

"Twenty-one, and my first trip to New Orleans."

"Jessica, dear, you are not hearing any of this."

"No, ma'am."

"Neither am I, Hetti. Jessica said she heard something important. I'm really stumped on this one. I've got no leads, nowhere to go, and ten dead men glaring at me in my sleep."

"Charles, we might be able to help. The important parts, Jessica."

"This guy was celebrating, an all nighter. He was more than a little drunk on champagne. He gave me a twenty dollar tip at the start of the night. Then he got to talking. He was a big talker. Bragged about all the rotten, illegal things he'd done. Most of them were out of the state. He said that wasn't nothing. Just his practice, his training ground.

"Then later he asked me if I'd ever seen anything worth twenty-five thousand dollars. I said all the time, my diamonds and jewels. I just put it down to drunk talk.

"He mentioned the same figure two or three times, and then I remembered the Bodie Standard talked about that was how much the stolen gold shipment was worth."

"Tell Spur what you did then, Jess."

Jessica walked to the window and looked out through the heavy drapes, then came back. "I know we're not supposed to, Hetti, but I deliberately got him talking about the money again. Pretty soon he admitted he didn't have the money, but he did own that much gold, for a few hours. That much gold in his possession, he said, gave him a feeling he'd never had before."

"Did he say what he did with it, where it went, what happened, anything else about the gold?"

"No, he got so drunk he passed out and I couldn't wake him until morning. He just slept off all the champagne."

"We know who the man is, Spur," Hetti said. "I felt that with those eight murders, we didn't have to worry about our rule of client confidentiality."

"I'm glad. Who's the man?"

Jessica looked over at Hetti who nodded.

"His name is Eli Johl," Jessica said. "He's the mine superintendent and manager at the Bechtel Mine #3."

Spur whistled. "Yeah, yeah! We may be getting somewhere."

"This helped?"

"It's a start. Before, we had nothing."

"The Bechtel is owned by the widow of the founder," Hetti said. "I've heard that it isn't doing all that well."

Jessica nodded.

"Yes, Jess, you run along. Send in some of that good wine and those little crackers we like."

When Jessica left Spur took her hand. "I knew Jessica in Salt Lake a few years ago."

"She told me about it. You can do no wrong in her eyes. Mine either. Where have the years gone?"

"You used them well. Jessica says the girls would die for you, that you run the best house in town and that you protect them like jewels."

"They are jewels, my jewels."

A small Chinese woman brought in a bottle of wine and two glasses and a moonstone dish filled with small cheese flavored crackers.

"You may do the wine," Hetti said.

Spur uncorked the bottle and poured. The crackers were good.

Hetti smiled as she watched Spur. "You're just as intense now as you were then," she said. "A government man. I know you're itching to get back on the case. I know, I know."

"First, a toast to the good old days."

"I can drink to that."

The wine was tangy, robust. Spur drained his glass and reached for Hetti's hand. "Thanks for the help. It may get us moving down the right road. Take care of Jessica."

Jessica was waiting outside the door to lead him out of the house. All was still quiet as the working girls slept in. At the door Jessica kissed his cheek. "I want to see you again before you leave. I'll get another night off."

"Soon," Spur said. "You've really helped a lot." He tipped up her chin and kissed her lips, then turned and hurried down the steps. He had an entirely new slant on the case.

The manager of the Bechtel would certainly have the whole facility of the mine and the retort room available for his uses. Say he did arrange the robbery, one of the guards identified one of the robbers and they had to be killed.

It was possible that Lenny drew the wrath of Elí and he was wiped out. Maybe that left no connection between the robbery and Bechtel? That was what he had to work on.

7

Spur stepped into the Wells Fargo office, waved at the people there who knew him by now and walked back to the manager's office. Johnson was in.

Spur sat in a chair beside the desk, took a cup of coffee from Ingemar and sipped at it.

"So? Have you caught my robbers yet?"

"Working on it, Mr. Johnson. Just wondered if the Bechtel Mine has a gold shipment scheduled for sometime soon."

Johnson looked up quickly, a questioning frown on his face.

"Matter of fact . . ." he stopped. "The Bechtel hasn't been doing all that well. They ship out maybe a hundred and fifty thousand a year. That's not a whole lot of trips. Why would you wonder if they might have a shipment about now?"

"Just a guess. Did you average out those gold shipments like we talked about?"

"Did. So far it looks like everybody is on

schedule." He looked down a list. "Except . . . except the Bechtel. If they are working the same vein at the same level, they should have another shipment of twenty to twenty-five thousand ready the end of next month."

"But they've set one for tomorrow night?"

"Yes. Another guess?"

"No, you looked so upset I figured it had to be. Bechtel isn't due yet. Where do you suppose they got the new gold bullion?"

"Not for me to say," Johnson stammered. "Look, I've shown you more of our company records now than . . ."

"Relax, Johnson. What we're doing here is trying to run down some killers and some gold robbers, and save your firm twenty-five thousand dollars. You've got to help. I need a copy of those figures for Bechtel's shipments for the past two years."

Johnson looked out his window, then nodded. "Damn, I guess it won't hurt. If it will help . . ."

"It will. I want that same rig we used before and the same driver if he's available. We'll keep him inside the rig. Be my guess that tomorrow night won't be a dry run for us. Say Bechtel is somehow behind the gold heist, why not steal their own shipment and multiply their profits?"

"Yes, it makes sense when we talk about it. But Milly Bechtel?"

"Nobody says the widow has to be involved. One of Hetti's girls had a big-spending, big-drinking, big-talking customer the other night. He kept chatting about how beautiful twenty-five thousand dollars in gold was. We know who he is, and think we have a real good lead. It all might pay off tomorrow night."

Johnson nodded. "The same driver is in town. I'll

schedule him and six guards and you, like that fake run. We'll leave at ten P.M. heading for Carson City through Aurora."

"Good enough, Ingemar. This time I want the gold to be stolen. We'll instruct the guards not to resist too strenuously. We make them think we're defending it all out, but let them win without getting anybody killed."

"I don't understand. Why let them steal more gold?"

"I won't be on the stage. I'll have a team of six deputy sheriffs riding behind the gold wagon, back far enough to be out of sight. As soon as the gold wagon is hit, we'll ride up to make sure that the robbers aren't killing anyone. Then when the heist is over, we'll follow the gold robbers and see where they go, find out the boss, nab him and the stolen gold, and solve the whole thing."

"Is that possible?" Ingemar asked. "A lot of things could go wrong and we'd lose more gold."

"Might happen, but not with good planning, and good men. You put in seven guards and the driver, and keep him inside the rig. Then the only thing that can get killed is a lead horse."

Ingemar hit his coffee which probably was whiskey laced again. Spur watched him. His nerves were shredding.

"You really . . . you really think it'll work?"

"I do, and I think the robbers will know when we're leaving and which route we take, before we go. I'm not sure how they do that."

"Let's try it. If I don't get that twenty-five thousand back, I'm going to be fired anyway. They can only fire me once for losing two gold shipments."

"Sounds good to me, Mr. Johnson. I'll meet you at

the Bechtel Mine #3 with the deputies.''

Spur walked back to Main Street feeling better than he had in a week. He went to see John Trevarow and explained to him about the talk with Hetti and then with Johnson.

"Looks like you've got a good loop on these varmints, McCoy," the Sheriff's Captain said.

"Not yet. We've got some tracks. You assign me six deputies who can ride well for tomorrow night and we'll have a better handle. Then I want to put three or four men in a line outside of town about a mile in case they get away from us."

"No problem there, Spur."

"Good. This time we have a real shot at them, because I think they'll hit the stage. But we haven't got the gold or the culprits yet. Even if they do come from Bechtel it could be any one of fifty people."

"Could, but probably ain't."

"Gold bullion. As I understand it, each mine pours the molten gold into forms and each mine has its name in the form, right?"

"True. On top of the bullion bar it will read STD Bodie, for the Standard; BODIE Bodie for the Bodie; BECHT Bodie for Bechtel; and so on."

"So one mine can't sell another mine's bullion."

"Not unless they remelt it and recast it in the retort room using their own molds."

"I heard once that a chemical analysis of gold could pinpoint where it came from, which mine, which vein. Is that true?"

"Might be. Virginia City gold would be different than ours. But I'm not so sure that gold mined from one end of this vein would be different than gold mined from the other end of it."

"So I'll make a big bluff when I have to," Spur said. "If it gets down to that fine a line."

Spur left the jail and headed toward his hotel. He saw Captain Trevarow come out behind him and stand in the sun a moment. That was when a gunshot sounded and the Captain's hat spun off his head. Two men came across the street and stopped thirty feet away from the lawman.

"Hear you're an old time gunsharp, Captain," one of the men called. "Hear you're about the fastest thing in town. We've come to find out just how fast you really are."

Spur had turned as soon as he heard the shot and now walked back to the jail and stepped up beside the lawman.

"Afternoon, gents. Thought this party needed a little bit of evening up."

"We didn't invite nobody else," the taller one said.

"Invited myself, and I got forty-five good reasons why I should stay, right here on my hip. You objecting?"

"The big gunman don't have his pistola with him," the other gunman said. He stood loose, hand near his weapon, knees slightly bent. Spur knew he would be the fastest.

"Duffy!" Trevarow called. "Bring me out my gunbelt!"

A deputy ran out of the jail a moment later with the leather and Trevarow strapped it on.

"Boys, you don't have to do this," Sheriff Deputy Travarow said. "It's an even match now. You want to, you just keep your hands away from iron and walk up to Main Street and have a drink. No reason anybody needs to die here today."

"Hey, I'm not worried about it. You, old man, you're the one who should be worried. Figure I take you out, and then your friend here who butts into other folks' business. Then I find that other guy in town, what's his name? Deadman, Billy Deadman. I hear he can shoot a bit."

Spur relaxed, moved a foot or so more away from Trevarow, then watched the two gunmen thirty feet away. He had no idea how good either one was. The short one first.

"Any time you're ready . . . " Before Spur could finish, the visitors went for their weapons.

Spur's draw was smooth, liquid fast. He caught the butt, lifted the weapon, dragged back the hammer and when the muzzle slanted up he put his first round through the shorter man's chest, blasting him backward. The tall one was slower, his gun still coming out when Spur saw Trevarow fighting to get his weapon out of leather.

Spur timed it and just as Trevarow's gun muzzle was coming up, Spur fired again, the bullet blasting into the tall man's belly, punching him sideways into the dust, his gun jolting three feet from his hand.

Spur and John Trevarow moved forward checking the gunmen. The short one was dead. The tall one swore softly.

"Sombitch! Nobody is that fast. I had the old man dead to rights! Nobody is that fast." He screamed, doubled over and blood came pouring out of his mouth. Then he bellowed in pain and the sound died as a final gush of air whispered out of his dead lungs.

Three men ran up. They looked at the dead men, then at the lawman.

"You gave them every chance, Captain," one of the men said. "You told them to walk away."

"But I didn't . . ."

"You did what you had to do, Sheriff. That should discourage some of the other young savages in town who think they can draw a .45 on you!"

Captain Trevarow looked hard at Spur. At last he nodded. "Yep. Deed it should discourage them."

There were thanks in his eyes. He pointed to two men. "Get these bodies down to Hooperman. Ain't a far walk from here. Can't have this sort of thing littering our streets."

More men arrived, and a sprinkling of women. The bodies were carried away and Spur and Trevarow went back into the jail.

"John, I didn't even notice that you didn't have on your guns."

"No matter." He waved toward his office and the men went in and closed the door.

"That's absolutely the last time I try to fast draw," Trevarow said. "You saw what happened. If you hadn't picked the fastest gun to take out first, I'd be on that marble slab right now. The tall one was slow as sin and still he beat me. Leastwise I got my muzzle up before you killed the second one. Thanks for waiting so it looked like I shot him."

"When are these young gunsharps going to give up and let a man stay retired?"

"Hell, McCoy, you know the answer to that. Probably never, at least as long as the six-gun is important in the West. Maybe about the turn of the century things will ease off a little. I won't be around to see that day."

"Might surprise yourself. That's only twenty-one more years. You'll hit eighty at least before we stuff your boots upside down on somebody's fence posts."

"Damn well hope so." Trevarow sat down, took off his hat and wiped sweat off his forehead. "Christ, I thought I was dead out there. Would have been if it hadn't . . ."

Spur held up his hand. "You're still wearing your iron."

Trevarow stood and took off the belt, checked the five loads still in the cylinder and hung it on a nail in the wall.

"Hope to hell I can leave that thing over there."

"I'm betting that you can," Spur said.

Captain Trevarow began writing out the paper work on the two dead men and Spur headed down to his hotel where he had been going before.

At the desk the clerk gave him an envelope along with his key. Upstairs in his room he read the note. It was from Mrs. Bechtel:

"Mr. McCoy. We never did get around to talking about New York when you were here. Could I possibly persuade you to have supper with me tonight, about seven? I hope so. We have so much to talk about and people from New York so seldom come into a small town like this. I look forward to seeing you tonight for supper. If for any reason you can't come, send me a note."

It was signed Milly Bechtel. He noticed the absence of the Mrs. on the name. It probably meant nothing. On the other hand, a nice quiet supper with their prime suspect mine owner couldn't hurt a thing. He might do a little questioning, on a relaxed basis, of course.

Spur changed jackets to one of well worn jeans material, had a sandwich and a cup of coffee at the Laurel Palace Chop Stand, and meandered along the boardwalk down Main trying to reason out any new angle on the gold robbery. The Bechtel seemed to be the prime suspect. Every clue so far pointed that way, but how could he be sure?

Ride the gold wagon and hope it was hit was the best plan. They could surrender, make sure the guards weren't killed and then follow the culprits. That would take two forces, one on the coach, one following at a safe distance. Just the way he had set it up. He hoped it would work.

Spur ambled down one side of Main and up the other. Scattered among the sixty-five saloons were three times that many other businesses. There was about anything now in Bodie that a man could want, from garters to goiter medicine.

Doc Rogers had help now with three more doctors in town and even a dentist or two. Mr. Nobel at the Standard Market was showing an interesting variety of fresh fruits from Sonora and Sacramento. There were apples, pears, bananas, apricots and strawberries in season.

Spur stopped at the San Francisco Market on Main. Peaches were twenty cents a pound. He bought two and ate them as he walked. The market also had fresh vegetables of most kinds, even tomatoes at fifteen cents a pound. He paid a dollar for a nice watermelon and figured he'd take it with him as an offering to the widow Bechtel.

At the newspaper office he saw an advertisement from Aurora in the Bodie Standard that the Exchange Market had beef at six cents a pound when bought by the quarter.

On the other hand, milk was scarcer in Bodie because there was little graze for the cattle. Mr. Huntoon advertised that he'd deliver milk for fifty cents a quart.

Spur leaned against the newspaper office front wall for a minute to soak up some sun. Even in August Bodie had its chilly moments during the day. At last he figured out it was the wind which seemed in a rush to get across the 8,500 foot level of the mountains and on to the east. He had no idea where it was going.

He could come up with no other prospect than the Bechtel people. Who would have the retort room available to melt down and recast the gold? The manager, maybe a foreman. Now it was wait and see.

That evening at just before seven, he arrived at the widow Bechtel's mansion in a sparkling clean shirt and jacket, tie and clean trousers. Even his boots were shined.

The small Chinese girl opened the door, smiled, and led him into the parlor. Mrs. Bechtel sat playing the piano. She knew several of the old Civil War songs.

"Mr. McCoy. Right on time. So nice that you could come. I try to play a little every day so I don't lose my skills, such as they are."

She moved from the piano bench to the upholstered couch and waved him into a matching chair.

A moment later the Chinese girl, Me Ling, came in with drinks on a silver serving tray.

"A little branch water and whiskey will set up our dinner nicely, Mr. McCoy."

They lifted off the glasses and she raised hers in a toast. "To your good health, Mr. McCoy, and may all of your enterprises be profitable."

"I'll drink to that. You sound like you're becoming a real businesswoman, Mrs. Bechtel."

"I'm trying. How is your business in town progressing?"

"Slowly, I'm afraid. I had thought of buying into one of the mines while I was here, but nothing seems available right now—at least nothing that seems worthwhile."

"Empty holes are cheap in Bodie," she said.

Spur sipped his whiskey. It was from a fine stock.

"I would guess that you're not married, Mr. McCoy. You wear no ring."

Spur laughed and nodded. "Right you are, so far no woman would have me. I'm a fiddlefoot at heart, a bumblebee buzzing around the pretty flowers."

"Interesting way to put it. Me Ling has our supper ready, let's go into the dining room."

The dining room was elegant, carefully furnished and decorated to rival the best rooms in New York or Washington. Thick carpet covered the floor over a pad of some kind. The dining room table was set for two but could easily seat twenty. Its polished mahogany and cherry wood gleamed through twenty coats of rubbed varnish.

An old fashioned cut glass chandelier made to hold fifty candles glowed with a dozen that had been lighted around the edges. It was a room perfectly set up by a person with an artistic eye and plenty of money to work out those ideas.

Two places were set side by side at the near end of the long table. He held her chair and then sat beside her.

"Mr. McCoy, I hope you're hungry because we're on the wild side tonight. We have bear roast, venison steaks, wild turkey and oysters for our meat course."

"I'm getting hungry already," Spur said.

The salad came first, a mixture of several vegetables with a dressing on it that was as good as the carrots and lettuce and celery and tomatoes.

"You said before that Mr. Trevarow was a friend of yours. I've heard you spend a lot of time over in his office."

"True. He's a policeman and trying to rid himself of his old fast draw reputation. It's hard for a man with a name like he had to hang up his guns."

"You are something of a fast gun yourself, aren't you, Mr. McCoy?"

"A minor talent, Mrs. Bechtel. I'd much rather be a partner in a profitable gold mine. But those making money don't want any investors, and those who want investors aren't anywhere near making any money."

Milly Bechtel laughed. For the first time Spur noticed what she wore. It was a one piece dress that was cut low for the backwoods of California, exposing the surging tops of her breasts. The dress was a pale green, reflecting the color of her eyes and contrasting with her red hair.

"You're staring at me again," she said with a laugh.

"I know, I enjoy watching a beautiful woman who knows how to dress well. An old failing of mine. New York, we were going to talk about New York. Where did you live?"

"Fifty-ninth Street and Third Avenue. There wasn't much there at the time. That was almost fifteen years ago."

"You wouldn't recognize it now, much has changed."

"My father worked on the street cars, so you see I come from humble beginnings."

"Right now you're not living humbly. This is a beautiful house, an exquisite room, better than most of the best in New York City."

"Thank you. I do what I can to be civilized, even in Bodie. I freeze every winter here. You probably won't be staying over the winter."

Spur laughed. "Does anyone stay the winter in Bodie who can get away?"

They both laughed.

A half hour later the meal was finished.

"Come, it's time you had my fifty-cent tour of the house. This isn't the only interesting room."

She showed him a huge kitchen.

"We made this by taking out two walls, adding the fireplace and the two cookstoves along that wall. We dug a well just hoping we'd have a pump right in the sink, and we do!"

The kitchen was a delight for a cook, and it smelled of fresh bread and spices and herbs.

Milly caught his hand as she led him up the open staircase to the second floor. They went past the first door then into the next one.

She swung her arm to present the view: "My bedroom," she said, looking almost shy for a moment.

Then she leaned forward and kissed his lips and pushed against him until her breasts flattened against his chest. Slowly her lips came from his but only an inch, and she held him tightly. "Spur McCoy, this is where I've been wanting to get you since the first day I saw you on the street. It took me almost an hour to find out what your name was."

She clung to him but one hand worked between them and rubbed at his crotch.

"Spur McCoy, you have a choice. You can submit to my lovemaking like a gentleman, or you can wait and let me seduce you. Either way, I hope you'll enjoy it."

This time it was Spur who bent and kissed her. He forced her head back and his tongue battered at her lips a moment until they parted and he tasted the wine from dinner.

Slowly they sank to the bed and lay side by side. Milly's eyes were closed, her hand still massaging his crotch and quickly found the start of his hardness.

"Yes, yes, yes! I can't wait to see him."

Spur's hand worked down under the bodice of her dress, lifted fabric and then circled one of her generous and now warm breasts.

"Spur, I hope I've got enough tits to satisfy you. Men always like them big."

"The ones I like best are the ones hot and pulsating in my hand," Spur said. He kissed her, guiding her onto her back, where he lay heavily on her for a moment, then sat her up.

"The dress," he said.

She stood and did a little dance for him, working it up over her hips, then to her shoulders and at last pulling it over her head, sending her hair flying. She threw the dress across the room and stripped a thin chemise over her head as well.

Her breasts were firm, with small pink areolas around ruby tipped nipples that were nearly flat. She walked up to where Spur sat and stood there, waiting.

Spur chuckled, then sucked one orb into his mouth and chewed on it like a new born babe.

"Those have to last all night, don't chew them off yet," she said, moving his head to the other morsel. She pulled away and started to undress him.

"You like me to do this?" she asked.

Spur nodded, catching a breast in each hand. "The anticipation is half the fun," McCoy said, surprised at how large and firm her breasts were. This girl was big all over.

She got his jacket and tie and shirt off, then let him remove his cowboy boots and socks.

For a moment she looked at his trousers, then she pushed him over on the bed on his back and began to kiss his erection through the cloth.

"First impressions are important," she said

smiling. "I want to see Mr. Dick here at his biggest, throbbing best."

She kissed each button off, pushed her mouth inside the open fly and blew hot air through his underwear onto his cock. Spur growled. Milly pulled down his pants, then in one quick motion jerked down his shorts.

"My god!" she crooned. "My aching pussy! Now that is what I call a worthwhile prick!"

She sent a dozen kisses up his shaft, then licked off his purple head before she sucked him into her mouth. A moment later she came off him, stood and wiggled out of the tight drawers that buttoned at the side and extended halfway down each leg.

Spur grinned when he saw the red bush at her crotch. "I'll be damned, you're a real redhead!"

"Right, more red pussy hairs than you can count."

She crawled up his body where it lay on the bed, moved higher and let her breasts swing down tantalizingly to his mouth, then moved higher until his face was directly under her red bush. Spur pulled down on her hips until his mouth found her nether lips and he licked them off until she shrilled in pleasure and climaxed, jolting sideways on the bed, her hips pounding into the covers as her whole body rattled and shook in a series of three spasms that left her panting and wailing.

She looked up in amazement. "God, McCoy! You're only the second man who ever did that for me. Most of them cut and run about then. Christ, you even look like you enjoyed sucking me off that way."

"If both of us don't enjoy it, then it's no good. Come here."

She rolled to him lifting her breasts toward his

mouth but he shook his head. He put her on her back, spread her legs and lifted her knees. Then his hand worked down through her red muff until he found the small node that he rubbed gently.

"My god, Spur! again?" Almost at once she thundered into another climax, jolting from side to side, pulling his face down on her breasts and not able to let him go.

At last Spur pushed away so he could breathe as the climax eased off. She gave a big sigh and leaned up and kissed him hard on the mouth.

"It's your turn," she said. She pulled him over her and lifted her legs to his shoulders.

"Find me," she cooed.

He did, daggering in at that unusual angle and bringing gasps of surprise and wonder from her.

"Heard it could be done but damn, what a wild feeling! Don't you ever come out of there, that's strange, wild, wonderful!"

Spur began to move, he had to move or die. Slowly he worked his shaft around and in and out and she purred, then moaned in ecstatic pleasure as the beat moved faster. Soon her hips tried to play a counterpoint as the passion grew.

"Oh, my god! Oh, my god! Oh, my god!" she squealed. Spur hurried then, blasting into her hard and fast as he felt his own peak nearing. She shouted and he bellowed in release as they both climaxed at the same time, a shuddering pounding, thrashing melee of arms and legs on the bed.

When they both came down from the peaks, they lay half off the bed and edged back on it, then collapsed in wonder and joy and peace.

"Darling Spur McCoy, there is nothing in the whole world that is as good as what just happened. Nothing in life. This is the ultimate experience of the humanoid. There's nowhere else to go, no worlds to conquer, no rivers to cross. Damn, but I tend to get philosophical when making love has been extremely wonderful. But it doesn't happen often, not this good. We'd make one hell of a team, in and out of bed."

"I don't know anything about gold mines."

"Neither do I. I hire men who know, who can do the job and make money. I manage money."

"I don't have any of that at all."

"No, no, silly man. The trick is to use other people's money. I didn't have a dime when Warren married me. Now I'm worth several hundred thousand. Making more all the time. How's that for a dowry?"

"I could always rob a gold shipment. That would give me a nice little nest egg."

"Too risky. They always get caught."

"This bunch this week hasn't. I hear they got away free and clear. Nobody even has a clue who they might be."

"We'll wait and see. It's still too risky. I married my money."

"You looking for a new husband?"

"No, only a stud who can fuck me as good as you did tonight. Want the job?"

"Got a job, back east—but it's an interesting proposition. Are you always this good in bed?"

"Always, sometimes better, but not often. You?"

"It's always good for me."

Milly rang a small bell on a bedside table. The bedroom door opened and Spur looked for something to cover himself with but Milly laughed.

"Spur, you're dressed properly for the occasion. Look."

Me Ling opened the door fully and smiled. She

was as naked as they were. She brought in a whiskey bottle and a pitcher of water and carefully poured two fingers of whiskey in each of three glasses, then filled them halfway with water.

She was so slender and curveless she could be mistaken for a boy. Mature but tiny, almost flat breasts gave the only hint of her womanhood. A soft dark triangle of hair nestled in her crotch.

"Me Ling has come to play," Milly said. "Often the two of us play together, but it's more fun to share a man between us. Would you like to be between us, McCoy?"

Already Me Ling was at his crotch urging him back to the proper condition. It took her only a minute. Me Ling squealed in delight as he came up strong and stiff. She caught his hand and put it over her small breast.

"Me Ling speaks almost no English, and never when we play. Now the only way you can communicate is by touch."

Spur stroked her legs, then pushed his hand between them and one lifted into the air opening her heartland to him.

Before Spur realized what she was doing, she had bent and caught his erection and sucked all of it into her mouth. She began bobbing her head up and down. Quickly he pulled her away before he lost his control.

Spur turned and watched Milly who sat beside him. "Just what kind of games do you want to play now?"

Milly smiled. "Any kind of games that three can play. But first it's Me Ling's turn with you, then we do something different and creative. You be thinking up the ways."

It was nearly four A.M. when Spur came away

from the finely built house and walked toward his hotel. There was no one on the street. He was exhausted, but remembering the remarkable things the small Chinese girl could do.

Behind him in her bedroom, Milly Bechtel watched Spur until she was sure he was going to the hotel. She frowned into the mirror at her naked form, then thought about Spur McCoy.

She took three deep breaths reasoning it through. It was nothing he had said, it was a feeling she had. And in the past her feelings had almost always been right. She went to a door that led into an adjoining room and roused a man who slept in a large bed.

"Wake up, Deadman," she said. "Come on sleepy-head, time to get up. You have a job to do."

"Huh? What time is it?"

"Morning, as far as you're concerned," Milly said. She sat on the edge of the bed.

"Still dark out."

"Good, then it should be easier for you. I have another job for you. You better be good, Billy Deadman, because I know this other guy is damn fast. Before tomorrow night I want you to kill Spur McCoy. He didn't accuse me of anything, but something doesn't feel right. He knows too much. I think he's more than he admits, maybe even some kind of a lawman. That should give you extra incentive, Deadman.

"Now get that pretty naked body of yours out of bed, get your pants on and kill Spur McCoy before the sun comes up—if you can."

8

Billy Deadman reached for the naked woman, but she slipped away.

"Not now," Milly Bechtel said with a hint of regret. "Just as soon as you kill Spur McCoy we'll do anything you want, any way you want!"

Billy nodded and dressed slowly and with care as he always did. He made sure of everything as he went, nothing was ever left to chance. That was how he had stayed alive for so long.

Deadman asked Milly where the hardware store was, left by her back door and five minutes later pried off the simple lock on the back of the store and stepped inside. He used matches to find what he wanted in the back: a steel box that contained a carton of dynamite sticks.

He'd used them before, lots of times. He took three sticks, tied them together with wire, then found the detonator caps outside the steel container and took one from the sack. He pushed it into one stick of the powder and inserted a foot long fuse in the outer hollow half of the detonator. Then he left the hardware, not bothering to cover up anything and leaving the back door unlocked.

That afternoon he had made certain what room in the U.S. Hotel Spur McCoy had rented. It always paid to think ahead. He had the second one over from the center on the second floor. He figured Milly might want Spur taken out, and Billy was always ready to do a job when the money was right. Some in town said McCoy was fast with a six-gun. No sense taking a deadly chance when it wasn't required.

Deadman watched Main Street for five minutes. He saw no deputies walking and checking doors. Nothing moved. He was in a doorway a building down from the U.S. Hotel.

Now he walked naturally from the store and in front of the hotel. When he was directly below the window he wanted, he paused at the side of the building and lit a cigar. At the same time he lit the dynamite fuse and let it burn while he counted to twenty. He had cut a foot long length of fuse, so it should burn for a minute. Deadman knew he dared not let the fuse burn too long.

Now!

He took three steps into the street until he could see the window, threw the bomb with enough force to break the glass. The dynamite smashed the window and landed inside. Deadman walked down to the corner and then ran along the side of the hotel in the darkness. He was half a block away when the blast went off.

Deadman walked through the darkness of the alley until he came to the Bechtel house and went in the back door. Milly sat at the big kitchen table. She wore a warm robe. She had started a fire and boiled two cups of coffee. She poured him one.

He gulped down some of the hot brew, then threw the cup across the room and grabbed her, ripping open the robe to be sure she was naked underneath. He pushed her shoulders down forcing her to the kitchen floor.

"Right here?" she asked.

"Damn right, right here!" he barked. "Killing people makes me feel just sexy as all damnation!"

When Spur McCoy stumbled into his room shortly after four A.M. he thought something seemed different. He wasn't sure enough to do anything about it. The truth was he had consumed far too much of Milly Bechtel's sweet mash whiskey and the added drain of having sex several times with two not only willing but insatiable ladies, left him not quite sober and extremely tired.

He fell into bed, reached for his .45 where it usually hung when he dressed up for a night with a lady, but didn't find it. Before he could get up to look, he slept.

An explosion a few minutes later roused him but he didn't fully awaken. He heard a lot of yelling and shouts, but no one banged on his door so he went back to sleep.

With morning came his pounding head and he pulled the cover over his head and slept until noon. Then he got up and looked around.

He was in the wrong room. He must have been drunker than he figured. Spur gathered up his clothes, opened the door and looked down the hall. No one was there. He went back to the stairway, found room 204 and started to go in.

There was no door. It lay shattered against the opposite hall wall. The inside of the room was blackened and in tatters and showered with plaster from the ceiling. The window had been broken out. He smelled the familiar odor of cordite and blasting powder. Someone had bombed his room last night after he got to sleep in the wrong spot.

Spur found his gun hanging undamaged on the bedpost. From what he could tell the bomb had come in the window and rolled toward the bed. The mattress had absorbed some of the blast, but still the room was a disaster.

He put on a pair of more serviceable pants, stuffed a shirt inside, then buckled on his gun and gathered up what was left of his carpetbag and his clothes. He took all his belongings back to room 6 where he had spent the night. Then he marched downstairs and complained about the blast in his room.

The man behind the counter had gone white for a moment when he saw Spur, then caught his breath. "Mr. McCoy, you're alive!"

"No thanks to that bomb last night. You know who threw it in the window?"

"No sir. But how . . . how did you stay alive in there?"

"That's my little secret. I'm now in room 6, but don't record it and don't tell a soul, not even the manager, or I'll strip your tongue out and beat you to death with it. Not a word!"

Spur had two cups of coffee and a bowl of oatmeal for his breakfast and lunch, then about one o'clock headed for the jail.

Just outside the hotel he almost bumped into Billy Deadman who stared at him in surprise, then anger.

Deadman walked past him, then spun around.

"Yeah, you're Spur McCoy!" Deadman barked.

Spur stopped and turned slowly. "I don't think we've met," Spur said carefully, knowing the man and his reputation.

"No, we've never met, but only because you were to yellow to call me out. I've seen you draw. You're about fast enough to outdraw my old maid aunt. She's eighty-four and in a wheel chair."

"My friends were right about you, Deadman. You're not only vulgar and stupid, you're ugly, too."

Deadman grinned. "Now that's not a nice thing to say, little man. Would you care to back up those words with that hogleg of yours?"

"Why should you die so early in the day, Deadman? Are you the jackass who threw that bomb in my window last night? You're the only one in Bodie shit-dumb enough to do it."

"I'm calling you out, McCoy!" Deadman screamed. "Nobody talks to me that way and lives! You're a dead man, you don't know it yet! Right now, right here!"

Spur let his right hand fall to his side. He shifted his feet apart a little more and stared at Deadman.

"It was you with the bomb, wasn't it? Who paid you to try to kill me, you yellow bellied river rat?"

"I did it as a public service!" Deadman bellowed.

They stood thirty feet apart now, facing each other. Deadman had moved to the middle of the street and Spur angled the same way. People behind each man scattered. Doors down Main Street slammed shut. One man dropped shutters over his big plate glass window.

"Anytime you're ready to die, asshole!" Deadman thundered.

A moment later a shotgun roared, then a voice

jolted into the silence that followed it.

"Hold it! Both of you. This is Captain Trevarow. I've just banned gunplay in the city limits. No stand downs, no gunfights, no fast draws. Both of you look at the sidewalk. There's a shotgun on each one of you. Either man goes for his gun, one of my deputies will blow your legs right out from under you with a load of birdshot. Won't kill you, but you'll walk with lead in your ass for the rest of your life.

"Now, easy like, both of you take your weapons out with a thumb and finger and drop them on the ground. Do it now, dammit!"

Spur looked at Trevarow and saw that he held a shotgun, too.

Deadman stared at Spur. "This your set up, McCoy?"

"Don't know anything about it, Deadman."

Slowly the two gunmen reached for their weapons, unseated them with finger and thumb and as if on signal, dropped them in the dust.

There was no question what would happen next. Both roared like bull bears and charged forward. Spur sidestepped the slightly bigger man's charge and slammed a fist into the back of his neck.

Deadman roared in pain and anger and spun, only to find Spur on top of him with two short hard jabs with his right fist and a roundhouse left that caught Deadman on the point of his chin. The big man staggered back a moment, shook his head and charged forward.

Spur landed two hard jabs on Deadman's nose, breaking it and bringing a gush of blood, but the heavier man's progress seemed slowed not at all as he thundered into Spur, grabbed him around the back with his hands and then tripped. They fell and rolled in the dust and directly over some horse droppings.

The fall broke Deadman's grip and Spur jumped up. There was no reason for the men to inform each other that there were no holds barred, anything went: eye gouging, ball busting, ear tearing.

Spur changed his tactics. As soon as Deadman levered to his feet, Spur charged and jumped, slamming both feet into Deadman's unprotected chest. Deadman spilled backwards, caught off balance and sprawled in the dirt. Spur dropped to his hands and knees and was up in an instant.

Deadman shook his head to clear it. The kick to his chest had rattled him more than hurt him. He had never seen anyone fight that way before. Spur had boxed on the team at Harvard, and two years ago had an old Chinese in San Francisco teach him the basic arts of self defense using feet and hands as weapons. He had learned only two or three kicks and a few hand movements, but they had proved effective.

Deadman got up on his hands and knees, then pushed to his feet and circled Spur. He rushed forward and threw a handful of dust into Spur's eyes. He had picked it up when he was down. Spur saw it coming, closed his eyes, but still some of it got into his eyes. Deadman charged, caught Spur in a bear hug again. Spur butted him in the face with his head, then when Deadman increased the pressure of the squeeze, Spur lifted both his hands and clapped his palms together on both of Deadman's ears at the same time.

The tremendous increase in pressure slamming into the delicate bones in Deadman's head broke his hold and he screamed in agony of the pain.

Spur moved in at once, kicked him in the stomach,

then slammed rights and lefts into Deadman's jaw until he wavered. Spur doubled up both hands into one fist and used it like a hammer to pound a mighty blow down on the back of Deadman's exposed neck.

He went down and out.

A cheer went up from the two hundred people who had crowded around to watch a real grudge fight. There hadn't been one in the street in daylight for nearly a month.

Spur found his brown, low crowned hat, the one with the Mexican silver pesos around the headband, and walked carefully over to the store fronts and sat in a chair. A deputy brought him his six-gun.

"Captain Trevarow says you better come down to the jail until Deadman cools off," the deputy said. "Deadman won't take this without trying to kill you for sure."

"It would have been over by now if he hadn't butted in. You tell him . . ." Spur stopped. "Yeah, he might be right. I want some clean clothes, and to wash my face. Tell Trevarow I'll be down there directly."

Spur went back to the hotel, feeling every blow and bruise he had just received. He went up to his new room, washed up and changed his shirt, then made sure his gunbelt was full of rounds and pushed a box of fifty more in his pocket.

The deputy was right about one thing, Deadman wouldn't take a beating and walk away from it. He'd want satisfaction on the end of a blazing six-gun. It was time Spur gave him the chance.

Spur checked his weapon. He cleaned it, making sure the cylinder was well oiled and functioning perfectly. The action was smooth and fast. Then he holstered the weapon, checked the curl of his brown hat and went out the door.

His next stop was at the Kirkwood Stable where he rented a good horse and saddle. He would use it this afternoon and tonight as well on the gold run. First he had to deal with Deadman.

He rode back down Main and found Deadman walking along, watching every face he met.

"Over here, Deadman," Spur called.

Deadman looked up.

"Get yourself a horse. I'll meet you just outside of town to the south whenever you get up nerve enough to ride out."

Deadman swore and started to draw, but Spur was out of any kind of range. He glowered, then pushed his weapon back in leather.

"Yeah, half an hour, McCoy. You figure out what you want on your grave marker!"

Deadman asked a man on the street something, then rushed down the street toward the livery.

Spur rode out of town slowly. It would take Deadman a half hour to get a horse and ride out. He stopped at a well at the bottle works for a drink of cold water, then continued out to the rise that overlooked the town. Spur got off his mount, a sturdy bay, and quieted her, then walked around kicking rocks.

Yes, he was stupid to give Deadman a chance at him, but he'd learned that with a man like Deadman it was better to get it over with. If he didn't make it a fair fight, Deadman would bushwhack him the first chance when he stepped out of the hotel, or out of a saloon, and nobody would know who killed him.

This way it could be over quickly, one way or another. He knew Deadman was fast. Maybe it wouldn't come to that. Once he got out here away from the crowd, Deadman might act differently. But would it be more rational, or wild and crazy?

Spur saw Deadman coming, cantering along at a good pace as if he were eager to get started on the killing.

Spur mounted up, checked his six-gun in his holster and waited.

Deadman stopped fifty yards away and stared at McCoy. "You really ready to die, Spur McCoy?"

"About as ready as you are. You still want to go through with this? You can ride for Bridgeport and nothing will be said."

Deadman laughed. "Not a chance."

He swung up a rifle from his boot and pulled it to his shoulder. Spur dove off his horse to the right, keeping the animal between him and the rifle. That son-of-a-bitch!

The rifle snarled once, then quickly again, and Spur realized that Deadman had a repeating rifle. Spur hit the rocks and dirt on both hands and knees, then his shoulder as he rolled. He clawed at his six-gun to make sure it stayed in place.

Damn! He had trusted this bastard and he probably would die for that trust!

He heard the first round thud into the bay. She let out a bellow, then the second round hit her as she was falling and she screamed as she hit the ground and kicked the air in a death struggle.

Spur rolled away from the horse and searched for some cover. There was almost none. A rain run off gully barely two feet deep cut through the side of the hill. Spur rolled into that and lifted his six-gun over the lip of dirt. He could see Deadman walking his horse slowly forward.

He would come as close as he could and stay out of range of the six-gun. Spur had made shots with a pistol at fifty yards, but the elevation needed made it a guessing game. Still, if that was all Deadman left him.

Spur knew he would not lay there and let Deadman come up and drill him with rifle rounds. As soon as Spur had an open shot at Deadman past the dead horse, he tried. He lifted the muzzle of the Colt and sighted in. There was almost no wind today.

Spur fired. He saw Deadman jolt and swing the horse back a few yards. The singing .45 slug had come close enough to worry Deadman. That was something.

"I got all afternoon, McCoy. I can come in and finish you off anytime I want to."

Spur decided on the silent approach. He crawled down hill where the little ditch became deeper. Fifty yards down it grew into a ravine six feet deep. Spur kept low so Deadman could not see him and crawled along the ditch.

"Where the hell are you, McCoy, you coward. You afraid to face me?"

Spur kept moving. Every foot of distance he got down the little gully gave him more cover, more options, more operating room. He kept his six-gun in his hand for instant action if Deadman rode up fast.

Every minute, every second now gave him better odds at living.

Spur heard Deadman's horse galloping along the small ravine but not quite close enough to spot him.

McCoy came to a place where a small sage bush grew above the side of the gully. Spur pushed up two feet and peered over the dirt at where he thought the rider might be.

The gunman sat on his horse, staring in the other direction. He still held the rifle with the butt on his thigh and the barrel in the air. It was also ready for instant action—instant death.

Spur crawled again.

His strategic position was bad. Sooner or later Deadman would figure out that he was in the gully and he would simply ride down it until he saw Spur and gun him down with the rifle staying well out of pistol range. Spur had to get him close enough so he could kill Deadman's horse if not him. The horse would be an easier target at thirty to forty yards.

As he worked down the grade, Spur could now lift up to his hands and knees. He looked ahead toward the bottling works and the first few houses on this side of town. They were still a quarter of a mile away. He would never make it before he was ridden down.

His mind reeled back to years before and he thought of the time he was in Arizona tangling with the Chiricahua Apache. Yes, the in-plain-sight trick!

Now he looked at the bottom of the small ravine. It was over three feet from the top. At this point it flattened out a little and there was a deposit of silt and sand and probably some gold dust in the sand. How deep was it?

Quickly he began digging with his hands. He lay the pistol to one side within easy reach and dug. Five minutes later he had a section eight inches deep, a foot wide and six feet long. He needed another ten minutes. Furiously he dug with his hands in the soft sand. Then he sat down in the hole he had dug and stretched out his legs in the ditch in the sand. Quickly he covered his feet and legs with the sand he had dug out until it was nearly flat.

Now he covered his hips and as he stretched out on his back in the ditch like crater, he kept covering himself with sand until only one arm was free. He used a thin handkerchief over his face and sprinkled it with the sand lightly to cover it, yet allow him to see through.

His left arm was under the sand and his shoulders and head. His right arm was hardest. He had to keep it ready for a quick shot, yet still out of sight. At last he burrowed it into the warm sand with another handkerchief over the weapon itself filtered by a skiff of sand.

He relaxed. The trap was in place. Either Deadman would find him, not be fooled and kill him quickly, or he had a chance to surprise the gunman.

Spur held his breath as he heard a galloping horse. The beast went by fast on the left side of the gully. Spur saw Deadman looking at the ravine, but staring mostly downstream. Twenty feet down the bend in the small runoff the arroyo straightened and Deadman could see it for the quarter of a mile where it emptied into what sometimes was Bodie Creek. He saw that Spur had not moved down that way.

The rider stopped and stared back along the ditch. Slowly Deadman turned and walked his mount back toward where McCoy lay. He was not even looking at the bottom of the ditch. Evidently Deadman had decided that McCoy was not there. He probably was trying to figure out where the man had disappeared to.

Spur held his body rigid for a moment, then relaxed.

The horseman came closer. Fifty feet. Too far.

Spur watched through the haze of the sand on the handkerchief. Thirty feet. Not yet.

McCoy breathed softly, then held his breath and tightened his grip on the .44. He prayed that the sand had not got into the cylinder works on the Colt. Twenty feet.

When the big horse and rider were directly beside Spur, not six feet away, Spur lifted up from the sand in one heave, screamed an Apache war cry and fired four times at the man and the horse towering ten feet over him.

Spur saved two rounds. He saw the first hit the man in the thigh. It was a terrible angle for a killing shot. From his low position he couldn't even see Deadman's head or torso. The second round missed high, the third hit the horse in the side of the head, and the forth hit the animal's head as well.

As soon as he fired the shots, Spur surged up from the ground in one fluid motion, charged down the ravine twenty feet and slid to a stop as he dropped down under cover again.

He lifted up and peered over the edge of the rocky soil toward the rider. He saw the horse down and kicking in a death struggle. Spur never liked killing a horse, but better the horse than Spur McCoy. It simply had to be done. He watched for any human movement.

A body rolled away from the downed horse. Spur snapped a shot but missed. He reloaded his Colt, putting six rounds into the chambers, and letting the hammer down gently.

Where was Deadman?

Did Deadman still have the repeating rifle?

Deadman stood and looked at Spur. He was out of pistol range. He shook his fist.

"You bastard! You killed my horse, you jammed my rifle. But I'll hunt you down and kill you with my bare hands if I have to."

He turned and jogged to the west, away from town toward some higher hills and rugged canyon.

Spur followed him at a safe range. What was Deadman trying to do? Twice Spur sprinted over a flat place, trying to get within pistol range, but each time Deadman saw him coming and ran faster to keep out of range.

At last Spur saw the plan. Deadman headed for a rocky, boulder strewn gully a half mile ahead. There were a few spindly shrubs but no real trees. What did he hope to gain there?

As they came closer, Spur understood.

Cover.

Deadman would be first into the boulder strewn gully. He would have the advantage of selection and he also could find cover and command the entrance to the canyon. He could get in a position where Spur would have to expose himself to a killing shot to advance any farther.

Twenty minutes later, Deadman vanished into the boulders. Spur sprinted at right angles to the route Deadman had taken so he could enter the boulders fifty yards away from where Deadman wanted him to. If he moved quickly enough Deadman would not have time to duplicate his lateral movement.

As he ran he pumped his arms and sucked in every bit of the rarified atmosphere that he could. He was never a gifted runner at sea level. At 8,500 or 9,000 feet, the air is much thinner and has much less oxygen than the usual 21 percent. Spur soon felt the lack of oxygen to his muscles.

He panted and gasped as he raced behind the first large boulder forty yards from where Deadman had entered. For the moment he was safe and he now had equal tactical advantage.

In the game of hide and seek where the loser dies, a man is extremely careful in his movements. Spur knew the odds. He had never been in quite this situation before. He climbed to the top of the boulder and looked over. Thirty yards ahead he spotted Deadman beginning to climb up the big rock he hid behind.

Spur dropped down before Deadman saw him and moved to the side of his protection, then darted forward almost ten yards to another boulder before Deadman got into position to see him.

The advantage! He had it now. He knew where Deadman was, and the gunman had no idea where Spur was. He peered around the side of the boulder without his hat on and saw Deadman flat on top of his rock. The range was still too great.

He watched again and as soon as Deadman slid back out of sight, Spur dashed ahead to the next cover he had selected which was no more than ten yards from Deadman. When he got there he would wait and let Deadman walk into his gunsights.

Spur settled down in his new position, his weapon up and ready. Five minutes went by and Spur began to wonder if he had figured Deadman right. Then he heard a rock kicked ahead. There were two smaller boulders between the large ones. Both were the kind a man would have to sprawl out behind to get good cover.

Another minute passed, then Deadman stepped out from behind the big rock, his six-gun ahead of him, eyes alert. At first he missed seeing Spur where he lay at the base of the big rock behind a blush of green grass. When he found him his .44 came down and then he laughed.

Spur had heard the slight rattling at the same time. Without moving his head he looked in front of him and a foot to the right and saw a coiled rattlesnake, its tail rattling gently. It was merely curious. Twin black eyes stared at him and the forked tongue darted out to sense if this creature was dangerous.

Spur couldn't move. If he did the reptile would strike him. It was barely eighteen inches away from his face, half that from his gunhand.

"Well now, looks like Mother Nature did me a little favor," Deadman brayed. "You would have gunned me down without warning, if our little friend there hadn't got the drop on you. McCoy, sometimes luck runs all bad. That Indian trick was great, but you should have killed me instead of just hitting my leg."

He laughed again. "Yeah, no sense wasting a three cent round on you McCoy. We'll see how long you can wait out that rattler without moving. I'll give you about three minutes, then you'll try something. Course the second you try to move, snake eyes there will nail you. I'll just sit down here and wait and watch."

Deadman sat down without taking his gaze off Spur and the snake. The man was right. Spur knew he could stay still for ten minutes if he had to. But it wouldn't matter. Even if he outbluffed the snake, Deadman would gun him the second the snake left.

Alternate attack plan. New strategy. What had he done in the Civil War? Nothing came to mind.

"Ease off there, McCoy. You're a dead man either way, just watch and wait and enjoy your last few minutes on this blessed green earth."

Spur watched him. He hated the smug, all knowing look that the gunman wore. A movement to the right of Deadman caught Spur's attention. He checked it and looked away. The triangular head of a large rattler had edged within an inch of Deadman's hip. When Spur checked back the large rattler had coiled so close he was almost touching the man's left hip. The beady eyes studied this new element in its living space.

"I'd say another two minutes, maybe, McCoy. Want to confess anything, or have me send your belongings to a next of kin?" Deadman laughed. "Hell, I wouldn't do that anyway. Certainly not any cash you might have hidden on you."

"You're the one who should worry, Deadman. There's the biggest rattler I've ever seen coiled an inch away from your hip. I don't think the big guy trusts you."

"Good try, Spur. I figured you could do better than that. You mind if I light up a good cigar and don't give you one? I enjoy a good cigar after I do a killing." His left hand slid down toward his pocket.

In a movement so fast Spur could barely follow it, the rattler's head struck the hated human arm three times. The last time it couldn't get its fangs out. As soon as he realized he had been bitten, Deadman tried to leap to his feet. He stumbled, his .45 discharged into the rock and then he lost the weapon.

The moment the gunshot sounded, Spur's rattler turned to check the danger from behind. Spur saw the change in angle of the deadly head near him and he moved his six-gun and fired, blowing the rattler's head off its body.

Deadman screamed the second the first strike poured the rattlesnake venom into his wrist. He struggled to his feet and shook his arm to dislodge the snake, then kicked at it as it slithered off into a rocky hole between two boulders. The creature was more than six feet long and as big around as a grown man's arm.

Spur came to his feet, checked for more rattlers then looked at Deadman.

Deadman leaned against the rock.

"I'd say you were in deep-shit trouble, Mister Deadman. How many strikes, three or four?"

Deadman didn't hear the words. He dug for his knife, but instead of attacking Spur, he made a slit on his wrist over one of the bites.

"Suck the poison out!" Deadman shouted. "Yeah, I heard that you cut the fang mark and suck out the blood and spit it out." He stared at the slice he had made on his wrist. "Damn that hurts!" He bent and sucked at the cut, then spit and sucked again.

Spur found Deadman's gun and pushed it under his gun belt.

"I heard that sucking idea works once or twice out of about fifty bites," Spur said. "Not that I want to discourage you."

"Shut up!" Deadman screamed. He looked at his wrist, then back toward Bodie. "I'll hurry and get to Doc Rogers. Let him do the cutting. He's got that little suction cup thing."

"Walking back to Bodie would be the worst thing you could do," Spur said. "That will speed up your heart, and your circulation, and move the poison deeper through your system where it will kill you."

"Then I'll run, get there faster!"

Deadman came past Spur, headed for the open land and soon was jogging along toward Bodie. In their pistolero standoff they had worked almost two miles from the town. Spur figured Deadman would get about halfway. Spur trailed along behind him, watching and waiting.

Deadman only made it a half mile, then got so dizzy he had to sit on the ground for a while. When his vision cleared he ran again, but a hundred yards later he screamed and fell into the dirt.

"I can't see!" Deadman bellowed.

"It'll clear up in a minute. How's your arm?"

"Hurts like hell." He looked at it. Already it had swollen up over the bites. It had turned red. "Hot, it's also hot and hurts like it's on fire!"

"I told you not to run, Deadman. But you know everything."

"Yeah, everything. How come you didn't die in that bomb blast?"

"I was in another room last night."

"Just my luck."

"Like you told me, Deadman, sometimes you get a run of luck but it's all bad. Seems to be your problem."

"Yeah. Hey, will you carry me into town?"

"Never make it, you ran too far. Lift your left arm."

Deadman tried and couldn't. Tears streamed down his face. He screamed out all of his frustrations and anger.

"I've gunned down some of the best in my time, and now I get beat by a damn rattlesnake?"

"Looks like it."

Deadman tried to stand. He at last got to his feet and stumbled toward town a half dozen steps, then plunged into the dirt face first.

He rolled over sobbing. "Christ, oh Christ! The pain is like nothing I've ever felt. I can't take it. Shoot me, McCoy. End it for me!"

"I'm not an executioner, Deadman. Although I'm sure you deserve to be killed."

"McCoy, how long will it take. I can't even move my legs now."

"Two hours, maybe three."

"You stay here?"

"Nothing else to do until midnight. You know anything about the stage gold robbery?"

"Hell, no. Not my style."

They sat there in the dirt for a few minutes.

Deadman screamed. "McCoy, you've got to kill me. At least give me my gun and one round."

Spur stood, let out a deep breath. It was what he would want in the same situation. The poison was too far into the man's system. Not one bite, but three, maybe four. Nothing could save him now, not even Doc Rogers.

Spur took Deadman's pistol from his belt, opened the cylinder and emptied out all but one round. He moved the cylinder so the loaded round would be the next to fire.

"Put your hand over your shoulder and I'll give you the weapon. Best way to make sure is to eat the muzzle. Push it to the top of your mouth. Can't miss that way."

Spur watched him a minute. "You sure you want it this way?"

"Yes, dammit!" Deadman said. His speech was slurred now.

"You try to gun me with that one round and I'll shoot you where it hurts, but I won't kill you. Understand?"

"Yes."

Spur extended the muzzle of the weapon over Deadman's shoulder from behind him. It took Deadman three tries to grab the barrel. When he had it, Spur walked away from the dying man.

Deadman made no attempt to shoot Spur. With great difficulty he turned the weapon around, holding it in his right hand. He made two tries before he got the muzzle in his mouth.

Then almost at once a muffled shot slammed through the rocks and hills above Bodie, California.

Deadman's head jolted back and upward as the

large lead slug smashed through the roof of his mouth and into his brain. It shattered ten vital brain complex centers, then bored out through his skull taking a four-square inch chunk with it.

9

It took the rest of the afternoon for Captain Trevarow and Spur to get the body to Hooperman and return the saddles and tack to the livery. Spur paid $25 for his dead horse and told Kirkwood at the livery to bill the county for the other horse.

Back in the office, Spur and Trevarow worked out which men would be assigned to ride with Spur on the gold run.

"You want five deputies so you can trail along in back of the stage?"

"Right, John. If we knew where the killers would hit the stage we could go there and wait, but we don't. They could take it any of a dozen places, the driver told me."

"You want the men saddled and ready at 9:30 in back of the Kirkwood livery, right?"

"Yes, and each man should carry a Spencer repeating rifle and fifty rounds."

"That we can do. Just don't get none of my boys

shot up."

"Do my best. Right now I'm going to catch some sleep. We'll be up all night, I'd guess."

That night a little before ten P.M. Spur met the gold stage after it had moved well away from the gold pickup point at Bechtel Mine #3. The stage driver sat on the top seat and waved at Spur in the darkness.

"Got to talk to all of you a few minutes," Spur said. The driver stopped the rig and the guards looked out.

"Tonight we're going to be robbed, I'd bet my horse on it. I've talked to Mr. Johnson at Wells Fargo. They're paying you to defend this shipment. But tonight, we want to get held up and cleaned out."

He heard the guards whispering.

"We think we know who robbed the last stage and killed those eight men. But to prove it we have to let them rob you again. The secret this time is don't put up too hard a fight. Try to miss the attackers if you shoot. Make certain you don't kill anybody. Everyone have that straight?"

"Tonight we get robbed."

"How we know they won't take the stage over, then shoot all of us like last time?" a guard asked from inside.

"Good question. That's why I and five deputy sheriffs will be trailing along behind you. We'll be out of sight but we'll be there. As soon as we hear shooting we'll close in fast. If they start to shoot anybody, we'll blast them and take our chances on proving who they are. I don't think they'll hurt any of you. They want the gold, not more trouble about dead guards."

Spur waited and watched them. When nobody complained he moved on.

"Any man who wants to quit this trip can do so right now, no questions asked, no problems with hiring on again. Anybody want out?"

He waited and no one spoke.

"All right, let's get moving. Keep everything as usual, natural. The driver can stay inside or outside, your option. I'd suggest you stay inside, then to stop the rig all they have to do is shoot one of the lead horses. Let's roll!"

Spur met the sheriff's deputies in back of the livery and told them exactly what they were going to do. All seemed a bit grim faced as they rode out. They trailed the stage keeping it in sight for the first five miles as they headed out of town north toward Aurora on the way to Carson City, Nevada.

Another mile and Spur slowed his men until they couldn't see the stage in the darkness. The stage rolled at its usual pace along the rough road, wound around the ridge and down the other side.

There weren't any trees here to cover the robbers. Spur had been over the route, and he breathed a little faster when the stage passed the first danger point, a steep upgrade.

Nothing happened. He moved his troops up a little closer now as the stage rolled down hill, made a sharp turn at the bottom to go across a dry stream bed and then a run through a hill speckled with eight and ten foot high boulders. This was danger point number two.

Spur heard the first shot, a rifle, that rang loudly in the quiet night air. The sound of the screaming animal came almost on top of it, and the familiar sound of the rattling stage ahead of him slowed and then stopped suddenly.

A dozen more shots blasted into the scene and Spur and his men walked their mounts forward so the robbers couldn't hear them coming.

They were at the very edge of visibility when Spur stopped them. He edged his mount ahead along the side of the road. Now he could see the robbers. Six mounted men had the stage surrounded. He wasn't sure if anyone inside had fired a shot.

Some of the robbers laughed. Few words were spoken. Voices could be remembered. He saw the strong box tossed off the stage. It smashed on the road but didn't open. Three pistol shots later the robbers cheered and Spur saw them distributing the gold bars into the saddlebags.

He tensed. Now would be the time to murder the guards if they wanted to. Instead the riders all mounted up, fired pistols in the air and turned back toward Bodie.

Spur dug his heels into his horse and rushed back toward his deputies. He motioned for them to move into the boulder area well off both sides of the trail.

"Hide! They're coming this way." Spur said quietly.

The last man had just ridden behind a big boulder when the robbers came galloping down the trail. They were singing and shouting, hoorahing as they swept past, evidently delighted by the easy robbery and hoping they would get paid extra.

When the riders went past, Spur and a deputy called Jones moved after them. McCoy had instructed the other lawmen to come along slowly behind. Six sets of hoofbeats behind the robbers could be heard.

Spur and Jones rode hard for a moment to catch

up, then when they could hear the riders ahead, they slowed. After a quarter of a mile gallop, the raiders eased off and let their mounts walk. Spur and Jones followed their example, staying far enough back in the darkness in the open land so they couldn't be seen, but close enough so they wouldn't lose touch with the six outlaws.

At four miles per hour, the two groups worked back toward Bodie. Spur watched the stars and figured by the position of the Big Dipper on its way around the North Star, that it must be nearly twelve midnight. They should be back in Bodie before one if they kept going at this rate.

Suddenly Spur held up his hand and he and Jones stopped. The men ahead were making no noise. He listened. A saddle creaked. Then the sounds came again. Men laughing, saddles groaning as men moved in or out of them.

"Pass that damn bottle over here!" a voice shouted. Then everyone laughed.

"Best two hundred dollars I ever made," another voice said. The voices kept sounding ahead, evidently as a bottle passed from one hand to another.

About five minutes later a stronger voice sounded.

"All right, that's enough. Let's ride back to town so I can pay you off. Mount up."

They all moved again. Spur walked his mount forward slowly, then faster until he had them in the fuzzy, hazy half light from the quarter sliver of a moon.

He and Jones followed them for another hour, then they stopped.

The leader's voice came clearly. "Listen to me!

155

Bodie's about half a mile ahead. I'd just as soon none of you stayed in Bodie tonight. Head for Bridgeport. They've got some new girls there, I hear."

Some shouts went up.

"Come by me one at a time and I'll pay you, but first I have to get all of the gold bars in my saddle bags. Come up now and deliver."

All was quiet for a while. Then the stronger voice came again.

"Now, I've got it all. Come by for your pay."

As each man got his money he whooped a yell and rode off.

Spur counted five men leave, then he and Jones moved forward slowly. Ahead in the dimness, Spur saw a lone man and a horse. The horse had its saddlebags stuffed full and a gunny sack evidently holding gold bars tied to the saddle. The man walked beside the horse down the hill toward Bodie.

McCoy wasn't surprised to see the robber leading his horse toward the area well up on the slope where the Bechtel mine showed in the moonlight.

Captain Trevarow had promised to have three or four men watching the back approaches to the Bechtel Mine #3, just in case. The plan was to let the robber go inside the mine buildings, then they would have the evidence they needed. Spur and Jones moved cautiously following the robber with all the gold.

When they came to the first buildings, Spur and Jones left their mounts and moved in shadows and along the sides of buildings as the man walking the horse headed for the retort room.

He paused outside, looked around, then put the bars of gold in the gunny sack from the saddle bags, and lifted the 75 pounds, carrying it to the door. He pushed it open and slipped inside.

Spur and Jones ran up to the door. Out of the darkness came Trevarow. They nodded.

"You ready, Captain?" Spur whispered.

"I think we got the bastards!"

A muffled shot sounded from inside the building and Spur kicked the door open and charged inside, his six-gun in his hand.

The scene froze in time for a moment. Eli Johl, a tall man with handlebar moustache had just lowered his pistol. The man who brought the gold slumped against the wall with a bullet hole in his forehead.

Spur's Colt fired at the same moment Johl looked his way. The round tore into Johl's right shoulder, slamming him backward a step, knocking the weapon from his hand.

The only other person in the retort room was Mrs. Milly Bechtel.

Spur nudged the sack of gold bars on the floor. "Those are the gold bars, Sheriff," Spur said. "I saw this man steal them from the Wells Fargo stage, pay off his men and bring the gold here."

Sheriff's Captain John Trevarow's face hardened. "Mrs. Bechtel, Eli Johl, I'm charging you both with stage robbery, with the murder of the eight Wells Fargo guards and with the death of this man on the floor."

"He tried to rob us!" Johl said through the pain from his shoulder. He held a handkerchief against the wound to slow the bleeding. "That man broke in here, put our gold in the sack and was trying to get away . . ."

"Shut up!" Spur shouted. "We know what happened. You're lucky I shot at your shoulder.

This way you can testify against Mrs. Bechtel and how you were following her orders." Spur held his gun but bent to examine the man he figured was already dead against the wall.

"Gentlemen, I don't have the slightest idea what you're talking about," Milly Bechtel said. "Mr. Johl asked me to come see some new pourings he'd made, and then that dead man broke in and tried to steal the bullion . . ."

"Won't work," Captain Trevarow said.

Deputy Jones shifted as he watched the scene. He had out his six-gun but felt a little strange still holding it now that one man was dead, another wounded and weaponless, and just a woman watching.

Captain Trevarow holstered his weapon and turned to Deputy Jones.

"Better get over to his office and bring Doc Rogers," Trevarow said.

When he turned back toward Mrs. Bechtel, she already had pulled a derringer from her purse and shot deputy Jones in the chest. He went down in a flailing of arms and legs.

Mrs. Bechtel turned the weapon toward Spur McCoy who was just standing up from examining the dead man.

"McCoy, don't move any farther or you're dead. You heard the shot. Drop your weapon. Now, McCoy! You too, Sheriff! Take it out slow and throw it over here by me. Carefully."

Trevarow did as she said. "Where do you think you're going, Mrs. Bechtel? You can't get away."

"Don't bet your wages on it, Sheriff. Eli, tie both of them up, quickly. Somebody might have heard the shots."

Eli found some heavy twine and tied all three men's wrists and ankles. He had put a bandage of sorts around his shoulder to stop the bleeding.

Mrs. Bechtel picked up Spur's weapon and the Captain's as well. She pointed to a small wheelbarrow. "Eli, put the gold in there and let's go for a walk."

Spur watched them go outside. There was still a lantern burning in the retort room. He tested the knots. They were tight.

"Jones, how you doing?" Spur asked.

"Hurts like hell. Missed my heart at least."

"Hang on. John, can you roll over here so I can untie your hands?"

"Worth a try."

It took them nearly ten minutes to maneuver around and for Spur to untie the Sheriff's Captain's hands. Then he freed the other two. Spur edged open the outside door and watched, but saw no movement. "Jones, you better go get that shot looked at. Can you walk?"

Jones nodded.

Spur slid outside with Trevarow.

"Where would she go?" Trevarow asked.

"Head for Bridgeport, is my guess," Spur said. "She might stop and bury the gold somewhere first, then try to get lost in Bridgeport or on toward Sacramento."

"Be damn handy to have a telegraph about now," Trevarow said.

"She won't ride a horse, a buggy maybe. Does the mine have a stable, any rigs? Wagons?"

John led Spur on a short run across the mine area to a small stable built in back of a storage shed. A bearded man was just about to blow out a lantern.

"Damn, Sheriff. More people out and about tonight."

"Mrs. Bechtel. Did she just have you hitch up a buggy for her?"

"Yeah, how'd you know?"

"Was Eli Johl with her?'

"True. Said they had to drive to Aurora fast to be there for an important meeting tomorrow. Something about buying another mine."

"Anybody else going with her? Any riders for protection?"

The bearded man scratched his head under a bill cap. "Dad blamed but you sure know a lot. Yeah. She asked me to try to get two men from the mill to ride along with them. But I couldn't find anybody who would do it, not even for ten dollars. They left about five minutes ago."

"Thanks," Spur said.

Both men ran for the horses that Spur said were close by. They had seen Deputy Jones head over to the doctor's office.

"We can stop by at the jail for hand guns," Trevarow said. "You still have that Spencer?"

"In the boot," Spur said. "Then we head out south."

"What if they go north?"

"Not a chance."

A half hour later Spur knelt in the trail that led out of Bodie to the south and west and found recent buggy tracks.

"We're on the right track!" Spur shouted and they stepped into their stirrups and rode.

"They in a one-horse buggy?" Trevarow asked.

"Looks like it. One horse for damn sure, making good time along here, but that can't last long."

Spur and Trevarow galloped for a quarter of a mile, then let the horses slow down to a walk for a mile before Spur lifted his mount into a canter.

"Eat up five to six miles an hour this way with most horses," Spur said. "That buggy be good if it can average three miles an hour."

"Eli Johl is wounded, that might hold them up a bit. He could bleed to death if he doesn't wrap up that shoulder."

They rode hard for a half hour, then stopped and listened. They couldn't hear anything ahead. Spur took some dry grass, lit it with a stinker match and checked the trail ahead of their horses' prints.

"We still have a hot trail here. Can't be too much farther ahead of us."

Again they rode. They topped a small rise and Spur motioned for them to stop. This time they could hear the jangle of harness and the creaking of a going-dry wheel hub.

Both riders kicked their mounts into a gallop and shortly they saw the buggy in the misty darkness ahead of them. Spur put a pistol shot over the top of the rig, but the driver urged the horse to pull the buggy faster.

"Remember, they've both got guns!" Trevarow shouted.

Spur nodded, pulled the Spencer from his scabbard and sent a .52 caliber round through the top of the buggy. It didn't slow the rig a bit.

A pistol cracked from the back of the buggy, then again. Spur and Trevarow slowed and hung back out of range.

"I'll get in front of them," Spur said. "The trail takes a long circle route here. I can cut across and beat them, then stop them from in front."

"I want them both alive," Trevarow said.

"So do I. I'll think of something. You keep firing now and then to let them know we're still here."

Spur cut into the open country next to the trail. All he had to worry about were gophers or squirrel holes. He charged the horse across the dry, barren hill away from the stage road, then turned when he was lost in the darkness and cut back toward the trail ahead.

It wasn't much of a long arc, but Spur figured it would be enough with his better speed. When he came back to the stage road he saw the first few spindly trees along the route. He rode ahead into a small grove and jumped down, searching the ground. He found what he was hunting, a four-inch thick tree that had died and fallen over years ago. It had branches and was about twenty feet long.

Quickly Spur grabbed it and tugged it free of the ground and grasses, then ran with it into the trail so it lay across the stage coach road.

When the horse saw it, the animal might stop, try to go around it or plow into it and stumble. It was the best chance Spur had to stop the buggy without shooting the horse.

He tied his mount to a bush and lifted out the Spencer, levering a new round into the breech.

The harness jangled in front of him and in only a few seconds the buggy came charging down the trail toward the small roadblock. With good luck the horse might not shy and charge straight across. The buggy would bounce mightily, but could get over the roadblock. It was possible.

Almost too late the horse saw the obstruction. She shied to one side. The driver tried to pull her back, then the animal was into the small branches.

The mare felt the limbs on her legs and stopped suddenly. The traces creaked and the single-tree rattled. The light buggy bumped her forward two feet, but the horse refused to draw the buggy a bit farther.

"Ease out of there with your hands up!" Spur barked. He shot over the buggy with his pistol for emphasis, then jumped two feet to the side in case there was return fire.

Only silence came from the buggy.

"I said, get down from there, or I'm going to start shooting inside the rig!"

This time a figure stepped out. A man. His hands were in the air.

"Don't shoot, I don't have the gun."

"Lay down on the trail, now!" Spur bellowed.

The man lay down.

"Mrs. Bechtel, you might as well come out. The chase is over. You've lost."

Three shots thundered from the blackness of the buggy. One slapped through an inch of Spur's left arm. He spun around and fired twice into the buggy. Then he ran forward, made it to the back of the buggy and moved quickly around it.

Trevarow rode up.

"She's gone," Spur said. "She just took three shots at me and must have ran into the brush over there." Spur sent two rounds from his pistol into the small brush and smattering of trees to the right of the buggy.

Spur glared into the darkness. "John, you take care of things here. Check to see if the gold is still there, and then tie up Johl. I'm going to get this hellcat and bring her back for trial. Oh, first, could you tie my bandana around my arm. She nicked me with a shot.''

Trevarow put a pressure pad under the bandage to help stop the blood, then tied it tightly.

"You're going to try to find her in the dark?''

"If she moves I'll know it. If not I'll find her when it gets light. Can't be more than three hours now until daylight.''

Spur looked at the darkness of the woods, and without another word charged twenty feet into the thin trees and brush. Once inside the light growth, he stopped and listened. He heard nothing.

There was no rush, he had the rest of the night and then all morning. If she ran, she wouldn't get far. He still carried the rifle and his Colt.

Ahead maybe twenty yards he heard a branch snap, then another. Spur fired toward the spot but high so he would not wound Milly Bechtel.

A scream of fury answered his shots. Spur moved ahead gently, not breaking a twig, stepping down only when he was sure that it would not make any noise. He moved ten yards before he heard more noise.

It came from straight ahead. The leaves on the light brush killed any attempt the moon made to break through with some faint light. It was as dark as a coal mine.

Spur moved ahead again, and this time the sounds came from his right. The growth followed a small water course, which probably was wet only after a good soaking rain. He stepped that way cautiously.

Two shots blasted from the direction ahead, but the rounds went well behind him. Spur did not return the fire. He walked faster now. They were working uphill. The gentle little valley and the growth would peter out soon.

Spur heard sounds again, up hill. He ran ten yards toward the spot, making no attempt to be quiet, then dove to the ground. A pair of shots blazed in the darkness. They came from directly ahead not fifteen feet.

"If you're the one back there, McCoy, you're a dead son of a bitch. I know how to use these .45's I have. I used to practice twenty rounds a day with one I own. Come on and get me, McCoy."

As she spoke he used the sound of her voice to cover his movements as he worked another five feet forward.

Then she ran to the side. He heard the sounds. She was moving out of the brush! It didn't make sense. Why? He moved silently to the edge of the growth in time to see Milly Bechtel fade into the darkness of the barren, rocky soil covered slope that extended upward.

A few clouds that had been flirting with the moon swept away and he saw her standing in a formal dueling pose, sideways, pistol up and ready. He stepped into the moonlight then dodged to one side and back into the darkness of the brush as she fired.

Spur dropped to the ground and rolled to the side. Milly laughed. "I told you I could use this weapon."

"Sure, but how many rounds do you have left? Did you bring a spare box of .44 rounds with you, or are they still in your reticule back in the buggy?"

"Oh, damn!"

"It's a long walk to Bridgeport, Milly. Why not give it up? You'll get a fair trial."

Spur rolled deeper into the darkness and Milly fired twice again. The rounds came seriously close to where he had been speaking.

Spur thought it through. He could stumble around out there on the side of the hill looking for her. The chances of finding her waiting for him with two cocked .44's was too great.

He could sit here and wait, watching until dawn, then take the rifle and go out and track her down. She wouldn't go far in the darkness. Even if she did she would be worn out by dawn and he could find her quickly.

He chose the wait method and settled down. Twice he heard shots in the distance. They came from up the slope somewhere, so she was moving. She must have thought she heard him coming up below her.

Spur dozed once. A squirrel ran through the brush and he came awake with his six-gun. He heard the animal again and tried to stay awake.

Just at dawn he moved to the very edge of the growth and looked out. The ridge sloped up a quarter of a mile. It was as barren as most of the rest of the timberless slopes around Bodie. A splotch of sage here and there, a few weeds, a wild flower or two and that was it. Nothing a person could hide behind.

He rubbed his eyes, reloaded his six-gun and moved out at a brisk walk up the slope. He found her tracks almost at once. There seemed to be no try at hiding the direction of travel. She had continued up the slope about halfway, then doubled back toward the stage road again.

She would wait for the first stage or wagon to come along heading for Bridgeport and ask for a lift. Spur moved faster then, found where her prints entered the brushy section again and now walked with more care. He checked the landscape ahead, watched for places she might be hiding.

Twenty minutes later he came back to the stage road. In a powdery dusty part of the trail he checked it carefully. There were insect trails and mice tracks over the stage coach and wagon tracks. The bugs came out at night, so the tracks had not been made early this morning. No wagon or stage had been past here going either direction.

So where was Milly Bechtel?

Her tracks stuck to the road a ways, then vanished into some small brush along the side. It led nowhere. Spur jogged to the end of the small trees and found her tracks on the stage trail again.

He jogged forward, the rifle in one hand, his six-gun in the other. He topped a small rise and started down a mile long hill. Milly sat at the edge of the road two hundred yards ahead. She seemed to be rocking back and forth.

Spur sent a shot over her head with the rifle. She didn't seem to notice. He put another shot that dug up dirt in the road five feet in front of her, but the woman didn't move.

McCoy walked toward her slowly, his six-gun ready. At a hundred yards he could see little, but at fifty, he could tell she sat in the dust of the trail, her arms were folded and she rocked forward and back, forward and back. Milly faced him and she appeared to have neither of the weapons she had the night before.

Spur moved up cautiously. Unless the guns were under her skirts somewhere, she didn't have them.

"Milly, are you all right?"

She didn't reply.

"Milly, I've come to take you home with me, are you ready to go?"

Again, no response. Spur heard something behind him and looked over his shoulder to see a buggy

167

coming. Two horses trailed it on leads and he saw John Trevarow driving.

Spur put the rifle down and touched her shoulder with his hand. "Milly?"

There was no response. She looked straight ahead and now he could hear a little tune she was singing. Something about "Now I lay me down to sleep . . . ." It was a child's prayer at bedtime.

The buggy stopped a few yards away. Spur motioned Trevarow to come and see her.

"Mrs. Bechtel, it's time to go back to Bodie now," John said.

There was no response.

Spur holstered his pistol, saw John draw his. Spur knelt in the dust beside her, took her hand and lifted her. She stood with no more urging. Spur felt a little self conscious doing it, but he patted down her skirt to be sure there was no pistol hidden in it. Then he led her to the buggy and she sat in the seat but continued to stare straight ahead.

Eli Johl looked at her and snorted. "Crazy as a loon. I had a cousin that did that. Never said a word again as long as she lived. Her mind just snapped." Johl looked away, then turned to McCoy. "This robbery was all her idea, the gold robbery. She said we could get rich and sell the mine and go live in St. Louis or maybe Chicago."

Captain Trevarow brought up Spur's horse.

"Mr. Johl here has agreed to turn state's evidence against Mrs. Bechtel if we let him testify for the prosecution," Trevarow said. "He explained to me in detail how they robbed the first Wells Fargo stage. One of the men's mask slipped and a guard recognized him the way we figured. After the robbery they melted down the Standard bullion and recast it in Bechtel bullion molds."

"Did you agree to get him a light sentence?" Spur asked.

"No. We talked about it. But now with Mrs. Bechtel beyond prosecution, I don't see why we should let Eli off for the ten men he killed or caused to have killed."

Spur smiled. "Good, I might even stay around to watch the hanging. Now, let's get this thing turned around and head back to Bodie. We've got gold here to return to Standard, and a bunch of law man kind of things to get done."

10

The first project Spur and Captain Trevarow did
involved convincing Doc Rogers that he should hold
Milly Bechtel in the one small patient room he had
at his medical office.

"Doc, you can watch her and deal with any
medical problems that we never could in jail. I'll put
through the formal charges but she needs to be
taken to the state Insane Asylum. She's crazier than
a hooty owl."

As they talked Milly sat on a chair in the office
looking straight ahead. She responded only to touch
and motions. Spur was not sure if she could hear or
if she understood the words.

Doc washed out the bullet hole on Spur's left arm.

"Lucky, son, the slug missed the bone. Gets nasty
when a round smashes an arm bone. Put you out of
business for six months at least. Now this kind of
thing I can deal with. With them mental problems,
the crazies, I just don't know what in hell to do for

them.''

"Doc, all you have to do is keep her in that room with a bolt on the outside. County'll even buy the damned bolt and put it on. Come on, Doc, I got no facilities to take care of a woman over at the jail.''

"So you think I do? Somebody's got to feed her, change her clothes, clean up after her. Maybe even watch she don't kill herself. How long would it be?''

"A week, Doc, maybe two. You figure out the cost and the county will pay for her keep.''

"Not a boarding house I got here, John.'' He finished bandaging Spur's arm and relented. "All right, she can stay. Maybe she'll snap out of it.''

Captain Trevarow took the 75 pounds of gold bars back to the Standard Mining Company. They told Dan Cook that the Bechtel had melted the bullion and recast them into Bechtel imprints. He should do the same thing turning them into Standard again. He was surprised and pleased. He gave Captain Trevarow a receipt for the 75 pounds of gold which he would turn over to the Wells Fargo company.

They stowed the buggy back at the Bechtel mine. Production had stopped. There didn't seem to be anyone to take over. Sheriff's Captain Trevarow appointed two men from the Standard as temporary administrators of the company until the legal entanglements could be worked out. They had operational powers only.

Dan Cook and a man from the Bodie mine met with the men and arranged an overview committee to keep tabs on the functioning of the mine until some legal arrangements could be made. Whoever now owned the mine, the Bechtel heirs or estate, would be well protected.

Spur filled out the final report at the sheriff's

office and then headed for his hotel and a good long sleep.

Captain Trevarow was pleased with the way the whole operation had turned out. They had nailed down the gold robbers and killers. He was still questioning Eli Johl in his cell to get the names of the first band of robbers who had shot down the guards. He had two of them, including Lenny whom they had found dead. That left four more. He would get the names and put out wanted notices on them all.

Trevarow left the jail for a walk over to the Chop House for his usual midday bowl of soup and cup of coffee.

Ahead on the boardwalk two miners were snarling at each other. The insults turned into name calling as Trevarow approached.

"You're nothing but a thieving mine rat!" one man shouted.

"Mine rat, am I?" the other screamed. "How would you know when you live at the bottom of the outhouse pit!"

People began moving away from the pair. Both had six-guns on their hips.

Trevarow walked up as the man's hands hovered over their weapons. They stood ten feet apart. Somebody was going to be killed.

Trevarow jumped between the men, holding his hands out palms out, fingers up in a stop motion.

"Hold it, you two jackasses!" Trevarow bellowed. "If there's any killing gonna be done in my town, then I'm gonna do it. Gunplay in Bodie is illegal. You fire that weapon and you spend thirty days in jail whether you hit anybody or not. You wound somebody you get six months at hard labor, most likely wood splitting. You want that?

"Let's say you get lucky and actually kill somebody. Why then you're gonna hang. No questions. No self defense garbage. You kill somebody in Bodie, I'm gonna get you hung. Had enough of this damn foolishness."

The men's hands eased away from iron.

"Haven't I seen you two drinking together? I thought you were friends."

"Friends? With that bastard?"

The other man snorted. "Aw, hell, I won't spark her no more. You can have her. I'll find me another girl. Just . . . just don't say I never done nothing for you."

"Hell, Will, guess I got a little het up at you. But I saw her first. Ain't that many pretty gals left in Bodie."

The two men stared at each other a minute.

"Hell, Will, let me buy you a beer. Maybe she's got a sister."

The two men walked away talking about the nice girls in town, and wondering who to take to the dance coming up at the Union Hall on Saturday night.

Will motioned to the crowd.

"All right, the excitement's all over. Move along here. Don't clog up the boardwalk. People have business to do along here without wanting to walk in the street."

Spur had walked back to his room at the U.S. Hotel. As soon as he stepped inside, he glanced around quickly. Nothing had been changed or moved. He locked the door, pushed a straight back chair under it and fell on the bed. As he did he felt something. When he picked it up it was a piece of paper.

"McCoy. I figured you'd be home sometime last night. You never did come. I got free and come down for a nice quiet evening with you. Maybe later." It was signed Jessica.

Spur grinned, pulled off his boots and his shirt, then dropped on the hard bed and was sleeping almost at once. He didn't even have time to think about food.

After the sheriff had his soup and coffee, he lit up a short black cigar. It had been a good day so far: the murders and gold robbery solved and a put down of a shootout on the street.

For the first time he realized that he had talked the gunnies out of shooting and he wasn't even wearing his own .45. Yes, he had done it. He didn't *need* his six-gun. He could take care of a lot of the small problems around town just by talking it out with the people involved.

Back on the street, he walked the town. He hadn't done that for a month or two. The jeweler came running out of his store when he saw Trevarow.

"Captain! Look at this. Somebody gave me a counterfeit twenty dollar gold piece. I always check the gold, but somehow this one slipped through."

"Could I see it?" Trevarow asked.

The merchant held it out and the lawman took it. He could see it was a poor imitation. "I have an expert on counterfeiting from Washington who's in town. I'm sure he'll want to see this poor imitation."

"But . . . but what about my twenty dollars?"

"The coin is worthless. Maybe fifteen or twenty cents worth of gold over the lead."

"But I can give it to someone else."

"Then I'd have to arrest you for passing a counterfeit coin. I'll take care of it. Sorry, it's your loss. Be more careful of the coins you accept."

"Yes sir," the jeweler said and went back in his shop.

Trevarow shook his head. Anyone stupid enough to take that spurious a gold coin as genuine, deserved to lose the twenty dollars. He almost relented. The twenty dollars was probably all the profit the man made all week.

Down the street a shot blasted into the usual noises and the clanking of the stamp mills. Trevarow hurried in that direction. He found a man standing over another, a six-gun in his hand. The man on the ground had a wound to his chest.

"Somebody go get Doc Rogers!" Trevarow shouted. "You!" he said, pointing to a man standing nearby. The man turned and ran to the doctor's office.

Trevarow ignored the gun in the man's hand, pushed him aside and checked the victim. He was still breathing. The bullet had missed his heart but probably hit a lung.

Trevarow stood slowly. The shooter still held the gun. "This man was unarmed," the law man said.

"He called me a liar!" the gunman shouted. "Nobody calls Marvin Anderson a .liar and gets away with it."

"Are you a liar?" Trevarow asked.

The gunman looked up quickly just in time to see Trevarow's right fist crash into his jaw and the lawman's left hand grab his right wrist in a vice and shake the gun to the dust. Trevarow spun the man around, forcing his right hand upward behind his back.

A Deputy Sheriff ran up then, and the Captain pushed the gumman toward him.

"Lock him up," Trevarow said. "We'll see if we charge him with murder or attempted murder."

Doc Rogers came a few minutes later, panting and out of breath. He knelt on the boardwalk beside the wounded man and scowled.

"Still alive, but he's unconscious. Get a door so we can take him over to my office. That bullet has to come out or he won't have a chance to live."

Trevarow ran into the hardware store and came back with an unpainted door. They put the victim on it and four men carried it toward Doc's office.

"Let me know what happens, Rogers," Captain Trevarow said. He waved the people away and they went about their business.

He turned in at a saloon, the Gold Digger, and asked for a beer. The barkeep drew him a mug full from a keg and grinned. "On the house, Sheriff. I like to have you drop in now and then. It tends to quiet down any unruly customers I have. And the poker games suddenly become as honest as rummy games in a preacher's parlor."

The captain nodded his thanks, but tossed a dime on the counter anyway. "I'll be around, time to time, but I pay my way and I expect my deputies to pay also. I don't want to hear about you trying to bribe my men with free drinks."

"No sir, Captain Trevarow, I wouldn't do that. I like it better that way."

"Good. Things are going to start shaping up around this town or I'm gonna be knocking heads. You can help spread the word that gun play and wild sprees are over in Bodie."

Trevarow finished his beer, waved at the men in the saloon and walked out the door.

The barkeep wiped sweat off his forehead when the lawmen had left. "Damn but that man is tough! I saw how he stopped that gunfight up the street. You can tell everyone that John Trevarow might

have hung up his six-gun but he's still as tough as
hell. Just don't mess with Sheriff Captain Trevarow
or you're looking for more trouble than you can
handle.''

Some of the men at the bar lifted their mugs of
beer in agreement.

Spur McCoy had slept until late afternoon, then
went into the dining room for the biggest dinner on
the menu. It had just come and he was starting to
eat, when a young man no more than twenty-five
walked in and stared at him.

A moment later the man came over to Spur's table
and stood three feet back. Spur saw him and knew in
a second what he was. Gunman. There was no
mistaking the pose, the tied down leather holster,
the hogleg hanging loose, ready and the gunhand
that hovered over the butt of the weapon.

"I'm looking for Spur McCoy," the young man
said.

"You found him," Spur answered but went on
eating as if the man wasn't there.

"I hear Billy Deadman died yesterday."

"True."

"How did he die?"

"He ate his own .45 muzzle and put a slug through
the top of his head."

"Liar! Billy would never do that,''

"If you knew him so well, where were you when he
needed you?"

"I . . . I was busy."

"Did you go examine his body closely and see the
three sets of rattlesnake fang marks on his left
arm?"

"Liar!"

"Sonny, that's the second time you've said that.

If I was the type to get upset easily, I'd have to teach you not to throw around dangerous accusations that way. You have a chance to withdraw the words."

"Not a chance. I know Billy. He was fast. You could never beat him. He'd never kill himself."

"You ever been bitten by a rattlesnake, boy?"

"No. And I ain't no boy. My name is Dorsey."

"Well, Mr. Dorsey, if you've never been bit once, let alone three times on the same arm, how do you know what you would do and wouldn't do when the burning, searing, unbearable pain started to gush through your bloodstream like liquid fire?"

"Didn't come here to jawbone you, McCoy. Last thing Billy said to me was he had a skunk to kill and he'd be right back, half hour at the most."

"Said that, did he? I called him out for a showdown outside of town and he brought a rifle and started shooting from fifty yards. Killed my horse first thing. A real sportsman, your friend Billy. Is that how he built his reputation?"

Dorsey's face got red, he couldn't speak for a minute, then he sputtered. "Damn you! He never did no such thing. He could beat you fair and square!"

"Like the night he threw a bomb in my hotel room. That was fair and square? Your hero was a sidewinder who killed however he could, maybe even face to face. But I couldn't swear he did it honest, cause I've never seen him try that."

"Outside, McCoy! Right now! I'd gun you down in here but it might upset the people's dinner. Out!" He drew his six-gun and Spur knew he was fast. He held the gun leveled at Spur as they stared at each other.

Spur stood slowly, kept his hand away from his

pistol and went into the lobby.

"How about the alley, then your wild shots won't kill anybody."

"My only shot will be in your heart, McCoy."

They walked to the alley, Spur ahead. He had no fears that this kid would shoot him in the back. The young man wanted to prove that he was faster, better.

In the alley, Spur stopped and turned around. Dorsey stood thirty-five feet away.

"You ready, big gunman with a bigger mouth?" Dorsey asked.

"Whenever you are."

They stood facing each other. A woman came out of a store down from the hotel, then hurried back inside. Two men stood at the end of the alley, then scurried back to the street and safety.

Spur watched Dorsey, his eyes would give away his move.

There had been no conscious thought in Spur McCoy's head that Dorsey was drawing his six-gun. Suddenly Spur's hand flew up his side, the gun butt slammed in his hand and his left palm stroked back the hammer to full cock. Then the weapon continued to rise and fired in a blinding fast move that was mirrored on the other end. Both rounds went off at almost the same time making one booming roar in the alley.

Spur felt the bullet hit his side. It slammed him halfway around. He kept his weapon trained on Dorsey who looked at McCoy with wide eyes, then he staggered backwards with the force of Spur's .45 slug and fell to one side, his weapon skidding away from his hand.

Spur walked forward slowly. His left hand covered a red spot on his left side where blood oozed through his shirt. Dorsey lay crumpled on his back and his side. Somebody ran out of the hotel and rolled Dorsey over on his back.

"Damn, right through the heart!" the man said. "He was dead before he hit the dirt! What a shot, and from thirty-five maybe forty feet!"

Spur looked at the man. "Call the Sheriff's Captain. Tell him I'll be over to Doc Roger's place when he wants to talk."

Trevarow found Spur there twenty minutes later. He had taken statements from three witnesses in the dining room, and the one man at the scene.

"Another inch to the right and you would have been in deep trouble, young man," Doc Rogers said. "Just missed your kidney and your bowel. Went clean through. That's two more bullet holes in your hide. How many does that make now?"

"A few, Doc. Now hush up, the law is here to arrest me for holding a gunfight in the city limits."

Trevarow snorted. "You were damn lucky, McCoy. That boy was fast. Probably a good thing you didn't know the rest of his name."

"More than Dorsey?"

"Yeah, Little Boy Dorsey."

McCoy whistled. "The kid who gunned down three Texas Rangers and took out that bank? The one who is getting called an executioner because he plain likes to kill people?"

"The same one. He was the only one recognized on that bank job. Chances are that Billy Deadman was one of the other three men. Deadman always did travel with a pack."

"Dorsey was fast. If he'd been a little more accurate, we both would be dead right now."

"Seen it happen, but only once." Trevarow snorted. "Damn sure it wasn't around Bodie. Most of these miners and wood men in town couldn't hit the floor they were standing on with three shots."

"I guess I'll live, Sheriff. How much is my fine?"

"No fine, I'm running you out of town—in a week or so when you start to heal up. Oh, Johnson, the Wells Fargo guy wants to see us, something important. You feel like taking a walk or you want a horse, maybe a buggy?"

"I'm ready. Doc, how is Milly?"

"About the same. She won't eat, but she'll take food when we feed her. Strange damn thing. Like she just turned off a switch and won't live normal but don't want to die."

The two men said goodbye to Doc Rogers and walked up to the Wells Fargo office. It was almost six o'clock by then. Johnson waved them into his office.

A tall slender man wearing all black sat in Johnson's usual chair behind his desk. There were some reports spread out in front of him. He looked up and then stood.

Johnson made the introductions. The new man's name was Jacob Linden, vice president in charge of security of Wells Fargo.

"I'm from the San Francisco office. Wanted to come out and see if we could get to the bottom of this robbery. The company doesn't like to lose twenty-five thousand dollars on a secured shipment. Gives other robbers ideas."

"Mr. Linden, I'd say the man most responsible for the recovery of the gold was Mr. McCoy, here," Johnson said.

"What's this all about?" Spur asked.

"Why, the reward, of course," Linden said. "Now that the gold has been recovered and we've had a release from our guarantee by Standard Mining

Company, we are more than pleased to present the reward to the one most responsible for the recovery of the gold."

"That's good of you, Mr. Linden, but I'm not the right person. I'm a federal law officer and not allowed to accept rewards. The person who gave us the key to the whole case was Jessica Wright."

Captain Trevarow looked up at Spur with surprise.

Then the Captain nodded. "Yes, she was the one who angled us onto Eli Johl, and the Bechtel. Without her lead we wouldn't have the slightest idea who did it."

"Well, then, I'll make out a bank draft in her name for the amount of five percent of the recovery, that's one thousand, two hundred and fifty dollars. What was that name again?"

Spur told him.

"Why don't I go bring Miss Wright down here to the office so Mr. Linden can present the bank draft to her?" Spur asked. "I'm sure that he'll want to thank her in person as well."

"Yes, yes, that's a good idea, McCoy. Now that this is all cleared up, I'll want to do an inspection of all our facilities here tomorrow, then take the stage out."

"I won't be more than an hour. Why don't we meet right here," Spur said.

They nodded and Spur walked out of the Wells Fargo office and headed for Virgin Alley. When he told Jessica about her sudden wealth, she thought he was joking.

"Big companies like Wells Fargo don't give whores like me no reward," Jessica said.

He caught her by her shoulders. "Jessica Wright, that's what I told him your name was because I didn't know your other one. I didn't see any reason to tell him about your current occupation. That is, your ex-profession. As of now you're the widow Wright heading for San Diego to open that boarding house!"

She threw her arms around his neck and kissed him. Then her eyes widened. "Oh, glory! I got to get fancied up in some proper clothes. Do I have any? That one dress might do. And I got to do my hair and take off most of my face paint . . ."

"You have an hour," Spur told her.

"I'll need two days!"

They made it is just under an hour. Mr. Linden was properly impressed by the demure widow, Jessica Wright. Captain Trevarow hardly recognized her, and Johnson had never seen her before. The little ceremony went off nicely.

"I'd think it would be best not to let this get in the newspapers," Spur said. "The whole story of the recovery is fine, but the news about the reward might just make somebody want to steal gold and then be the one to 'find' and return it."

Linden agreed with Spur and no word was to leak out to anyone outside of the room.

Twenty minutes later, Spur and Jessica slipped up the back stairs at the U.S. Hotel and walked into Spur's room.

"I never did get to finish my supper. You stay right here and I'll go down to the dining room and have them send up a great dinner for two. Don't tell me what you want. You rich women will have to get used to being waited on."

He came back a few minutes later and their dinner followed in another twenty minutes. They had roast beef, oysters and trout to start, together with four kinds of vegetables in cheese sauce and three deserts. There were two kinds of wine.

"Mercy, I'll be fat as a poland china hog," Jessica said.

"Not a chance. First we eat, and then we get some exercise and work off all of the fat."

"What kind of exercise?"

"We'll think of something."

She grinned, then sobered. "You really think I could make a go of it in San Diego?"

"Damn right! The town is growing, going to be a real city one of these years. Nice little seaport there, and plenty of sun and open spaces. Not much rain, but eventually they'll figure out how to bring in water. Why not give it a try?"

It took them nearly an hour to do justice to all the food. Spur couldn't remember when he'd eaten so much. Everything was well cooked and the foods were all his favorites.

When they were through with the big tray, he sat all the leavings in the hall, and locked the door.

Jessica patted the bed beside her and he sat down. She reached over and kissed his lips gently.

"How . . ." tears filled her eyes. "How can I ever thank you, Spur McCoy, for . . . for the other time, and now this. I've never even heard of that much money!" She took the bank draft out of her reticule and stared at it.

"Sometimes I can make twenty dollars a week, but I never get to keep it all, and even so . . . I bet I couldn't save a thousand dollars in five years!"

"So, by telling the sheriff about what you heard, you just saved five years out of your young life."

She blinked, and then blew her nose. "I still . . . I still can't believe it. I told Hetti. She said Godspeed.

She's been more a mother to me than my real mother.''

Spur kissed the tears off her cheeks.

"Couldn't have happened to a nicer lady.''

"This widow Wright. What if somebody asks me to see my marriage license and my husband's death certificate?''

"Nobody will. Most folks can't prove that they're married. Out here in the west it isn't where you come from or who you are, it's how you act and what you do. You act respectable, and everyone will believe you're who you say you are.''

"Come with me, McCoy! Help me get established in San Diego and stay a month or so.''

"Hey, I've got a job to do. A boss to report to. Which I better think about doing. I'm glad there's no telegraph here. Where is the closest one . . . Sacramento, probably. Maybe Carson City.''

"You're wounded! You can't go back to work for days yet!''

"Maybe I could squeeze out two or three days to recuperate. That is if I had good nursing.''

"You've got the best nurse in all of Bodie!''

"Good, Doc Rogers will be pleased.''

She fiddled with the little jacket that went over the top of her dress.

"Spur, do I still have to act respectable? I mean, in here with you?''

"What did you have in mind?''

"Well, since I'm a widow and all, I was thinking I might test you out for husband material. Test you in the only way that most women think is practical.''

"In bed?''

"Exactly.''

"Mrs. Wright, I don't think it would be unseemly of you to do that. What married folks, and unmarried folks do behind the closed door of their bedroom is nobody's business."

"Mr. McCoy, I like the way you put things."

She slid out of the jacket and stood and quickly whipped the dress over her head. Then she sat on the bed in her tight white drawers and the chemise that couldn't quite conceal her pink tipped breasts.

"Mr. McCoy, I'd like to give you a test. First you have to kiss me about twenty times—just anywhere that you want to. Then if you pass that test, we'll move on to some others that I have in mind."

She grinned at him.

"Mr. McCoy, I'm starting the test right now."

Three days later they left Bodie on the stage and headed out to Bridgeport, then retraced part of their route to get to Sacramento.

Jessica still had the Wells Fargo bank draft safely hidden in her reticule. She had saved almost two hundred dollars and that would be plenty to get her all the way to San Diego.

They registered in the California Hotel as Mr. and Mrs. Charles Wright, and Spur left her there and found the telegraph office. The wire he sent was clear and concise.

CAPITOL INVESTIGATIONS
WASHINGTON, D.C.
GENERAL WILTON D. HALLECK

IN SACRAMENTO. MUST GO TO SAN FRANCISCO ON URGENT PERSONAL BUSINESS. CONTACT ME THERE AT PACIFIC HOTEL WITH ANY NEW ASSIGNMENT. LEFT BODIE, CAL. TWO DAYS AGO AFTER SOLVING EIGHT

MURDERS IN A GOLD ROBBERY. U.S.
MINT GOLD INVOLVED, SO I BECAME
INVOLVED. READY FOR DUTY TWO
DAYS HENCE.

When he got back to the hotel, he found that
"Mrs. Wright" had visited three shops in Sacramento to fill out her wardrobe. The clothes were respectable, well made, and well within her budget.

"I must have something to wear on the boat to
San Diego. You did say the boat would be the best
way to go."

Spur laughed and agreed with her, then took her
out to dinner.

That night as they lay in the bed, Spur McCoy
thought ahead to San Francisco. It had been a year
or more since he'd been there. He wondered how it
had changed. It was a dynamic city. He tried to remember the last problem he had heard about there.
He'd been in New Mexico at the time.

Perhaps Fleurette Leon in his St. Louis office
would have something ready for him to tackle once
he got to San Francisco. He hoped she would.

"Hey, you were a thousand miles away," Jessica
said.

She rolled over on top of him and he realized she
had taken off the nightgown. She rubbed against
him, bent to kiss his lips and grinned. "Hey, I have
you for only another two days. I'm going to do my
best to wear you right down to a nub before I'm
through with you."

Spur laughed. "That's a challenge that I don't
want to pass up," he said and reached up and kissed
her lips.

FRISCO FOXES

1

"You're dead, mister!"

Spur McCoy spun around, his firing hand sliding down to the holster strapped to his right thigh. He gripped his .45, swung it up and searched for the man who'd yelled at him.

The deserted Hastings, Arizona Territory street was shot through with inky shadows. Spur studied the darkened buildings and black alleys, looking for some sign of movement.

He let the saddle fall to the ground behind him and stood upright, knees slightly bent, gripping his Colt with a firm, steady hand.

Nothing. No sound, no voices. Spur sighed. He was just keyed up. The job had been easy, too easy. Maybe he was just expecting trouble.

Boots pounded in the dirt somewhere to the right, across the street near a false-front. The echoes seemed to emanate from the alley between Feingold's Dry Goods and the Thompson Hotel. He studied the wide passage but saw no movement, no greyish figure, no glint of moonlit steel in its blackness.

Raucous music mixed with liquor-charged voices blasted out from the saloon half a block down as the doors burst open. A drunken cowboy stumbled out, reeled and lurched back inside.

Silence settled around him again.

"Show yourself!" Spur barked.

The man snorted. "Hell, I ain't that stupid! Got you right where I want you. Now give 'em here!"

"Give you what? Make sense, asshole!"

Feet rustled in the alley again. Spur still couldn't see the man. He cursed. If he hadn't spent so much time playing poker in that smoky saloon he'd be snoring away in his cold hotel bed by now.

Guess I'll have to flush him out, Spur thought. He'd circle around the dry goods store and surprise the gunman from behind.

Soft kerosene light blossomed from the hotel's alley-facing windows as he began to move. Some-one—perhaps that pretty blonde-haired serving girl—had lit the lamps. The glow illuminated a tall, wiry man leaning against the wall of the dry goods store.

The gunman peered at Spur, clumsily gripping a six-gun in his left hand. Surprised by the light and suffering from alcoholic confusion, the man stared wildly as he realized he'd lost the advantage.

"Damnation!" he drunkenly thundered.

"What in hell do you want?" Spur asked, sweetening his aim on the suddenly nervous man.

"You know what I want," he blurted. "It's what you've been carrying around for two weeks. And it's what you're gonna give me right now!"

"What, my poker winnings? You could've won 'em from me at the table. You're stinking drunk. Go crawl in a corner and sleep it off." McCoy approached him cautiously.

Did he know? And if so, *how*?

"The hell I will!" he said, smirking. "You just hold it right there, mister! Come any closer and I'll . . . I'll plug your heart full of lead!"

Spur laughed as he approached the man with

short, deliberate steps. "You got me shaking in my boots," he said sarcastically. "You're so drunk you couldn't hit your right ball, if you had one."

The left-handed man's face reddened at the insult. "No one talks to me like that, asshole!" he said. "No one! Now give 'em to me!"

"You really wanna die that bad? I'm tired of playing games. Back off and throw down your weapon." Spur's voice was harsh.

"Like hell!" The man's arm shook so violently he nearly dropped his revolver.

The man's features came into sharper view as Spur approached him. He was sweating, the veins on his head popping out. His closely-spaced eyes darted from side to side. The gunman's chest heaved with labored breath.

Gunman? Hell, Spur thought. This guy was scared to death. He'd probably never aimed at a man before.

"That's close enough. No more time," the wiry man said. He twisted up his face in anguish. "It's now or never! You've got my ticket to more money than I could ever make in this hell-hole and I'm gonna take it from you!"

His aim shifted up and down as if he couldn't see Spur clearly. His emaciated body shook with fear.

"Do it," Spur yelled. "Go ahead. Try to blast me into hell. Give me a good reason for splattering your worthless guts all over the goddamned street!" He stopped ten feet from the shivering man.

Rage surged through the left-hander. His finger squeezed. The revolver spat.

The shot slammed harmlessly into the dust five yards from McCoy's boots. Before the explosion finished echoing between the false-fronted buildings, Spur blasted a slug into the drunkard's left hand.

The hot metal ripped into the man's extremity, splintering bones, severing nerves and arteries on its path of destruction. Blood, looking dark brown in the thin light, spurted out of the wound as the gunman's weapon rattled to the dust-filled street.

The thin man went down, clutching his shattered hand. His face went white and a howl of rage-infused pain strangled out of his throat.

"Jesus H. Christ!" he screamed.

Spur moved closer, his long-barrelled Colt .45 trained on the laboring chest. "What the hell do you want? An executioner? Sorry, that costs extra."

He glanced at the saddle before swinging his head back to the man. Good; it was still there.

The left-hander's face distorted with pain. "You know damn well what I want," he spluttered. Fresh blood soaked into his shirt as he pressed his left paw to his chest. "Damn! My firin' hand! You busted it all up!"

"I could've done worse. Was it worth it, lefty?"

Spit drooled from his lips. The wounded man's body trembled as pain boiled through him. "Hell, yeah, it's worth it! Anything's worth them dies!"

The word thundered through Spur's brain but he showed no surprise, no emotion at the mention of his secret cargo. "What the hell're you talking about?"

Doors banged open. Yells rang through the sleepy town as residents hurried outside to watch the excitement.

The thin man howled. "Goddamn it hurts!"

"It's just your hand. You may be crazy, lefty, but you're not dying. They'll get you all patched up in jail."

Clutching his broken hand to his narrow chest,

the downed man reached into his shirt with his good one. "I ain't dying, mister, you are!"

Spur drove a bullet into the man's chest long before he had the opportunity to use the suddenly revealed derringer. The man's eyes grew wide with shock as the slug blasted an inch-wide hole through his heart.

The left-hander's body shook as his big pump exploded. His arms and legs jerked spastically for several seconds before going limp. A long, hissing breath passed out between the dead man's lips as his blank eyes centered on the thin moon hanging above his motionless form.

Seven men and a brave dance-hall girl crowded around Spur, craning their necks, whooping and talking.

"He dead, Smitty?" the young woman asked the man next to her.

"Course he's dead!"

The whore whistled. "Hell, I ain't never seen a dead man afore, only men dead between their legs."

"Shut your pretty little mouth, Angelique, and get back to work!" the burly man thundered.

Spur stepped back, away from the crowd, still looking at the recently departed.

"Now you just hold it right there, mister."

The voice, cracking with youth, seemed to be directed to him.

McCoy sighed. What now? He slowly turned around as the curious residents of Hastings, Arizona Territory continued to comment on the deceased.

A stocky young man, carrying a rifle, warily approached McCoy. He looked barely old enough to shave. "Mister, you're under arrest for killing Frank Johnson."

"Ah hell, Enos, leave him alone! It was self-defense, plain and simple," a grizzled man said. "Saw the whole thing. Wow, what a show!"

"Yeah, Enos, just like Dodge City!" another called.

The star pinned on the youth's chest told Spur all he needed to know.

"Is that true?" Enos asked him.

"Yeah."

The boy glanced at the dead man, then back up at Spur. His fresh face wrinkled with thought. "I'm the law around these parts," he said hesitantly. "At least, since this afternoon when the sheriff rode out with a posse to find the man who robbed Mrs. Ortega."

"Look, deputy, I'm gonna get my saddle. We'll talk about this in your office."

"I—I—"

Spur shot him a steel-eyed glance. The kid clamped shut his thin lips, smiled nervously, then nodded.

McCoy retrieved his saddle, flung it over his back and followed the greenhorn to the sheriff's office.

Once there, Spur explained as much as the kid needed to know. He didn't tell the sweating youth everything, just enough to put off any more questions.

"But—but why was Johnson tryin' to kill you?" Enos asked, scratching his sandy-haired scalp. "He wasn't good for nothing, but he never hurt nobody. Not as long as I've seen him around town."

"How in hell should I know?" Spur growled, glancing at his saddle. No sense in spreading the word around; too many people seemed to know.

"I don't understand—"

"Look, maybe he lost two dollars at the poker table. Maybe his missus wouldn't give it to him—"

"He don't—*didn't*—have a missus," Enos said, blushing.

"Maybe he just threw too much whiskey down his throat and had to prove he was a man."

"Maybe," the boy said thoughtfully. He rubbed his double-chin.

"I'm only passing through here, deputy. I don't have time for your local trouble. And I need my sleep if I'm gonna catch the ten o'clock stage in the morning." He hefted his saddle and started for the door. "You have any problem with that, boy?" McCoy curled his upper lip, arched his left eyebrow and dared him with his eyes.

Enos looked away and fumbled with a bag of fixings. "No. Heck, they all said it was self-defense." He shrugged and smiled blankly. "I guess it was."

Grunting, Spur hefted his saddle and slammed outside. He walked to his hotel with measured steps, went up the stairs, unlocked the door, shut it and pushed the key into the lock. Inside he threw the saddle onto the bed, kicked off his boots and flopped down on the hard mattress.

He rested his head on the saddle, smelling its rich, new-leather scent, and thought of the treasures it contained. They were so valuable that gunmen were willing to risk death to obtain them.

At six-foot, two-inches, two hundred pounds and thirty-two years of age, Spur McCoy was the top agent in the newly-formed Secret Service. After a distinguished career in the infantry during the Civil War, McCoy had joined the service as soon as it was created by Congress in 1858.

The reddish-brown hair that touched his shirt collar and rode along his upper lip was usually covered with a low-crowned, gray Stetson. Mutton-chop sideburns ran down his cheeks almost to his jaw.

Countless women had long ago decided that Spur McCoy was ruggedly handsome, just as men beyond number had been brought to justice through the actions of his mind, body and a variety of weapons. He was the best shot in the service.

After serving in Washington for six months, Spur had won the job of agent in charge of the entire west, from St. Louis all the way to the golden beaches of California.

He rarely heard from the top man in the Secret Service, William Wood, who'd held down a desk job in Washington ever since being appointed by Abraham Lincoln. Every president since Lincoln had re-appointed him.

His direct superior in Washington, General Wilton D. Halleck, sent Spur on various assignments through that modern miracle—the telegraph.

McCoy's latest job was transporting and guarding two brand new dies—one for each face—of the $20 double eagle gold coin. He'd picked them up at the Denver Mint and was on his way to deliver them to its sister plant in San Francisco.

Security on the movement of the dies had been tight. To confuse anyone who might try to steal them, General Halleck had sent out two other couriers at the same time from the Denver mint in different directions. Only a few top men knew that Spur McCoy had the real dies.

No one, however, knew where he'd hidden them. Just hours before he was to leave Denver Spur had called at the home of a saddlemaker on the out-skirts of town. He'd woken up the balding Prussian and told him he wanted a small, cloth-wrapped metal box hidden inside the saddle Spur had bought from him that very afternoon.

McCoy halted the man's protests and natural curiosity by pressing a crisp $50 bill into his hand. He told him that the box contained something very precious to him and he wasn't about to lose it.

After stuffing the money into his pocket the man had studied the saddle, searching for the best place to secrete the goods. Done with this he ripped seams, tearing into the saddle just deep enough to allow the box's placement within it.

Finished, he restitched, pushing the heavy steel needle through the thick leather with gloved hands. His bald pate glistened in the warm light as he worked to piece it back together.

After the minor saddle surgery Spur had surveyed the Prussian's handiwork. The dies were completely invisible. They should be safe until his arrival in San Francisco—if he could hang on to the saddle.

Spur had been given a circuitous route to the city by the bay, hopping from one small town to another, riding stage coaches for most of the way. He was nearly halfway to his destination and had had no problems—until that night.

McCoy snarled as he thought of the skinny, left-handed man, of how he'd been forced to gun him down. Spur had felt no satisfaction while killing the drunken, knee-shaking coward. No sense of power or glory had flooded through him as he'd looked down at the dead man, only hollow relief that he'd managed to guard the dies for one more day.

Word of them had leaked out. No doubt about it. The man certainly knew of them, and others probably did as well. He could expect more trouble along the way. Hell, he was willing to bet on it.

But how had he found out? Frowning, Spur mentally checked the door—yes, he'd locked it—rested his rifle over his chest, threw his hat onto the floor and closed his eyes. He'd wonder about that in the morning.

This wasn't going to be an easy assignment.

2

A bump stirred Spur to consciousness. He opened his eyes, coughed up a load of trail dust and looked out the tiny, square window. Endless miles of harsh, dry desert stretched out in a never-changing panorama of desolation.

He shifted his gaze to the women who sat across from him in the bouncing stagecoach. The two old biddies, their fat bodies wrapped in endless layers of stiff, black taffeta, stared balefully at him, eyes full of accusations. Beads of sweat squeezed out on their pale foreheads below wide-brimmed black sun bonnets.

Spur cursed to himself and turned back toward the window.

They'd been glaring at him like that ever since the stage had left Hastings, Arizona Territory at ten that morning. In an attempt to quell their loathing he'd tried to engage them in friendly conversation but the old hags had kept their lips and knees pressed tightly together, gripping their beaded purses before their huge bosoms as if to safeguard their womanhood.

Spur sighed. Easy conversation always made long trips more pleasant but he knew he wouldn't get that from these two biddies. They seemed convinced that he was eagerly waiting for the right

moment to jump them, rip their dresses and
shawls and corsets from their gross bodies and
plunge deep where (he was sure) no man had gone
before.

They glanced at each other, nodded and returned
their stares at him.

He smiled as the clattering, jolting stage passed
a stand of sagauro cactus. Hell, he had better
things to think about than two stopped-up old
women whose beauty, if indeed they'd ever
enjoyed it, had long ago died on the vine.

He thought of the morning. McCoy had slept
through the night without problems and had gone
into the dining room for breakfast. As the blonde-
haired, beautiful, hotel owner's daughter had
served him Spur fought off the urge to feast on the
firm nipples that poked through her high-necked
gingham dress. Instead of satisfying his bulging
crotch he'd filled his rumbling stomach with stacks
of flapjacks drowned in Vermont maple syrup,
sizzling bacon and freshly-laid eggs. He'd washed
down the hearty meal with two cups of strong,
bitter coffee that she poured from a stained metal
pot.

Afterward, though, when he was splashing cold
water on his stubbly chin to wash away spots of
dried egg yolk, a soft hand knocked on his door.
He'd wiped his face with a coarse towel and,
stripped to the waist, opened it.

The blonde-haired beauty's gaze lingered on his
chest before lifting to his face.

"I'm—I'm sorry, sir, but I was wondering if you
needed a—a—" A blush flooded through her
cheeks.

"A what?" Spur asked, surprised but delighted
at her boldness. She didn't seem the kind of girl
who'd come calling at a strange man's hotel room,

even if she worked there.

"A special sendoff?" she asked.

Then Spur saw the fire in her light green eyes, in her parted, dry lips. It must have been burning all morning. No wonder she'd given him seconds of anything he'd asked for. She nearly swooned.

He gripped the nameless girl's slender waist, feeling the tight corset beneath it, as she swayed beneath him on unsteady feet.

"Little lady, are you sure you—" Spur began.

"Take me!" she whispered, with surprising passion. "I've waited for this!"

Spur shut the door behind her. He wasn't about to ask any questions as she straightened up and rubbed her sleek flanks against his groin. Spur slammed his mouth down on hers as he ripped the pearl buttons from their cloth holes on the back of her dress. She moaned as he pushed his tongue between her soft lips and nuzzled it against her.

The blonde—McCoy never did learn her name— arched her back as he freed the last button and tore the high-waisted, gingham dress from the body.

Blood pounded into Spur's groin. The girl felt his erection as he pushed it against her soft crotch and ravished her mouth.

The dress slipped from her shoulders and arms and hit the floor. Spur pulled his lips from hers, stepped back and drank in her beauty.

Naked save for the tight white corset fastened around her waist the blonde girl's body was luscious—wide hips with a dark, mysterious patch between them; a narrow waist and creamy white breasts that jutted above her corset. The perfectly round, voluptuous hemispheres were so large that Spur knew he'd never fit them into his mouth. At least, not all of them.

His erection pressed painfully against his pants

as she looked up at him with wide green eyes, unashamed at her nakedness.

"Do I please you?" she asked timidly.

"Please me! Yes, hell yes!"

"Then what are you waiting for?"

"Hell!" What *was* he waiting for? McCoy bent and captured a hard, red nipple between his slick lips. He chewed on it softly, sending groans of desire shooting from the girl. Spur sucked half the breast into his mouth. He was aroused, hard, and ready for the girl's unexpected sexual offer.

"I can't wait any longer!" the blonde said, panting. "I've been watching you all morning, wondering how it looks, how it feels. Get that thing out!" Her eyes were wild with passion. "Take me now, mister! Ride me!"

Spur ripped open his fly, releasing his monster. The girl flushed as his huge erection swung up between his legs. It jutted out majestically from his hairy crotch.

"Land sakes!" the blonde said. "That's what I've been waiting for. Hell, it's *more* than I've been waiting for, more than I could imagine!" She dropped to the floor, laid on her back and lifted her hips, exposing her blonde vee.

McCoy walked to her, pushed his pants to his ankles and, in one swift, well-aimed motion, stretched out over her and slid his hard penis full-length into her slot.

She arched her back and squealed in delight as he filled her. Their pubic hairs intertwined as Spur moved gently back and forth inside her, opening her, stretching her as she'd never been stretched before, savoring the wet, tight sensations that flooded through him.

Lust shot through his body. Spur gripped her firm buttocks and pumped hard, fast, each plunge nearly taking her breath away as their hips bounced together.

Straining his neck Spur suckled her right breast, pushed it into his salivating mouth, lightly chewing on its hard tip as he worked over her moist, willing opening.

Long before he wanted to, long before he'd begun to satiate his sudden passion, McCoy felt excitement boil within him. He plunged harder, deeper into the young woman's yielding opening, until his frantic thrusts sent the blonde girl into a clenching orgasm.

"Yes! Yes!" she said. Her face and breasts flushed a bright red and her hips rose to meet his driving thighs.

Spur ejaculated deep within her, spurt after spurt, thrust after thrust.

Their slick bodies molded together as they shuddered through their climaxes. Spur, edging off from the brain-shattering experience, flopped down onto her slender form. He felt her heart pounding through her chest as his own matched it in speed and tempo.

Her mouth found his wet lips. They kissed, long, slow, lovingly, as waves of warm passion washed through them.

Hours later, Spur still relished the experience and enjoyed recalling it, but wondered about the left-handed drunkard who'd tried to steal the dies from him. How the hell had the man known about them, and that he had them? McCoy would never know.

He sighed and opened his eyes. The old woman to the left, the slightly less ancient of the pair, dabbed a lace handkerchief to her forehead, looked quizzically at his face, then glanced down.

Her thin, pale lips parted in surprise and shock.

"You . . . you *animal!*" she screamed, flinging the handkerchief at him. "Agnes, look! I knew it!" she shrieked.

As the second woman dropped her gaze Spur wondered what had caused the outburst, until he felt the familiar, erotic tightness between his legs. Memories of that extraordinary woman and her eagerness to please him and herself that morning had, understandably, aroused him.

He laughed at the two terrified women, crossed his legs and settled his hat over his face.

They wish, Spur mused.

Sunlight slanted harshly across the barren landscape as the stagecoach bounced nearer the pocket of civilization that was to be their stop for the night. Little River, Arizona Territory, was one of hundreds of similar small towns scattered throughout the west.

Not far from Mexico, the whole town consisted of two streets that intersected near a large, wooden building that housed the sheriff's office, the hotel and barber. Eight or nine other businesses—including the standard livery stable, saloon, bank and general store, lined the streets every five hundred feet or so. About a dozen ill-constructed houses and a central, tiled well completed the town's highlights, along with several dusty mesquite trees and a few straggly desert junipers.

Little River wasn't much more than a glorified stage stop, Spur mused as the driver reined in the sweating horses. The coach pulled to a stop before the hotel. He disembarked, retrieved his saddle and carpet bag from the top of the rickety stage, and surveyed his surroundings as the two old biddies gave him a wide berth on their way to the hotel.

Four horses solemnly drank at the water trough before the Cat's Eye Saloon. A young buck escorted his plain, humble wife along the dusty street. An aging cowboy enjoyed the porch shade on the ten feet of boardwalk that fronted the general store.

Spur thought of his supply of cash. He may be carrying priceless dies but he had to think of the immediate future. He was nearly out of small change and, since the town was graced with a bank, McCoy figured he might as well try breaking a twenty.

Hauling the saddle over his back with one hand and the well-worn carpet bag with the other, Spur walked the short distance to the squat, ugly building and strolled inside.

"What the hell you want?" a nervous-eyed, gaunt man asked as he looked up from his ledger.

"Change." Spur clipped the word. He set down the bag and yanked a well-crumpled twenty-dollar bill from his pocket, unfolded it and handed it to the man who sat behind the hardwood desk.

The man frowned and examined the bill as if he'd never seen one before.

"This is a bank, or did I read the sign wrong?"

"Hell yes this is a bank!" The black-suited, string-tied man grunted and walked to the safe at the back of the small, plain office, clutching the twenty. "Cain't be too careful," he said, spinning the tumblers swiftly in several directions before opening the large iron door.

Spur grimaced as the man stuck his head inside the well-guarded cavity. Friendly town, he mused.

'I kin give you ones.''

"Okay. Fine."

The man quickly returned with the change and threw it onto the desk. "Count it yerself," he said gruffly, plopping down into the chair. "I got work to do." The banker bent over his stained, scrawl-covered ledger and dipped his pen into the splattered ink well.

Spur retrieved the stack of bills and counted them carefully. "Thanks for your friendly consideration," he said.

"Git yer ass outa here!" the man thundered.

Spur chuckled as he folded and pocketed the bills. He left the bank and turned toward the hotel to get a flop for the night.

A lone rider quietly entered Little River well after dusk. The man had pulled his hat brim down low, over his eyes as he tied up his frothing, slick horse at the hotel's hitching post. He quickly rubbed her down, soothing her tired, aching muscles. The horse drank deeply and whinnied as he slapped her left flank. He was almost as tired as she was.

Maybe tonight, the figure mused, as he turned for the hotel. Maybe tonight he'd get them. If not he could wait. He done a lot of that so far—two week's worth.

After all, it was a sure thing.

The bullet hit the bottle, shattered it and sent whiskey and deadly splinters of glass showering down on the saloon table. Spur pushed back his chair and dove under the stained table. He squatted beside his saddle as another bullet zinged overhead through the saloon.

"I'm fuckin' mad!" a brusque voice needlessly announced.

Spur looked questioningly through the table legs at the man who'd squatted with him and suddenly realized he'd dropped his cards in the excitement.

"Don't worry about ol' Sam," the snaggle-toothed young man said.

"I'm not worried, just wonderin'." He'd been well into a good game of poker with the kid—the one he'd seen squiring around his plain wife when he'd arrived in Little River—when the firearm had sounded and broken up the game.

"Don't blow up the place again, Sam!" the barkeep barked. "You'll pay for every goddamned bottle you shoot! And you damn well better be able to afford it!"

An ear-splitting explosion and subsequent shatter told Spur that Sam had racked up another charge.

"What's gotten him so riled up?" Spur asked the card-clutching man across the table from him as the scent of gunpowder and blue smoke surrounded them.

"Hell, I dunno. It doesn't take much. Happens about once a week. He drifted into town a few months back." The kid grinned. "Why'n you duck back up and git yer cards?" the toothy youth suggested. "No sense in lettin' him ruin our game. I'm gonna empty your pockets, stranger!"

What the hell. Spur poked his head above the table and grabbed the cards, got a quick look at the big, red-faced man, who stood reloading beside the bat-wing doors, then returned to the relative safety of the floor.

"Heck, Buck—he's this saloon's apron—he ain't mad. Sam gives him more business'n the rest of us." The youth glanced at his cards. "Where wus we?" he asked, scratching his head. "Your raise or mine?"

Spur couldn't remember.

After the trigger-happy fool had gone, Spur returned to his drab room for some shut-eye. He

surveyed the surroundings and quickly realized he
was vulnerable there. The door had a lock but he
had been given no key. Additionally, the room was
on the ground floor and there wasn't a chair he
could push under the door knob.

At that hour the cheery Mexican hotel keeper
would be well into his *siesta*. Spur laid on the bed
and tried to relax, but figured he wouldn't get any
sleep until he was again on the stage.

Two hours later, however, he'd dropped off. Spur
tossed on the lumpy mattress, sweating, his brain
crammed full of disgusting images of those two old
hags from the stagecoach forcing him to sexually
service them.

The nightmarish scenes quickly dissolved and he
woke to full consciousness as he felt a cold, round
steel object pressing into his mouth.

3

Spur automatically started to struggle in his darkened hotel room, then lay still as he focused his eyes. He was staring down the eight-inch barrel of an old Army revolver. The muzzle inched closer to his throat.

"Think twice about giving me any trouble," its owner said, and laughed. "Nothing'd please me more than pulling this trigger and watching your head split open. You just lie still. Okay?" he asked.

Spur nodded toward the man. In the darkened room he couldn't see the face but the voice was vaguely familiar. Spur cursed himself at being caught in this situation but he relaxed. It wasn't over yet.

The gunman eased the barrel out. Spur flinched as the fixed sight scraped along the roof of his mouth before flopping past his upper lip.

"Talk," the man said, keeping the revolver trained between Spur's eyes. "What'd you put in the bank this afternoon?"

Spur shook his head. "Nothing. I just changed a twenty-dollar bill."

"Bullshit!" the man said, exploding with fury.

"It's true," Spur said. "Go ask the guy for yourself. You got any more questions? I need my sleep."

The man laughed hollowly. "I'll give you some sleep—eternal sleep if you don't tell me the truth!" He jabbed the 8-inch barrel between McCoy's eyes.

Spur thought quickly. His holster wasn't where he'd hung it over the bedpost. The man must have stashed it somewhere. A glint of steel near the door told him that it was well out of reach. Think, he told himself. Think to save your ass!

"You must have me mistook for someone else, mister. I didn't put anything in the bank. Hell, I'm leaving on the stage in the morning. I've been wandering around looking around for a place to settle down and happened to end up in this dusty excuse of a town. I don't know what you want, but you've got the wrong fuckin' man!" Spur spread innocent indignation over his hard, planed face.

"Good story—but not good enough." He poked the barrel against Spur's forehead, pressing it against the skin. "Talk, asshole!"

"You want my money? I—I put it in my saddle. Everything you want's in there." He motioned to the saddle that the man had placed against the wall under the solitary window.

"Everything I want?" He grunted. "Maybe you are telling me the truth," he said. "But I ain't gonna go over there and get it. *We're* gonna go. Move, fuck-head!" he growled. "Sit up nice and easy like."

With the cold steel digging into his forehead, Spur rose to a sitting position.

"Slowly, asshole, slowly swing yer skinny legs to the edge of the bed. Try anything and I'll blow your brains out!"

He stared into the man's beady, shining eyes and nodded. Pressing his hands on either side of him on the soft mattress, Spur lifted his booted legs, violently swung them up and smashed them into the man's mid-section.

A howl of surprise shot up from the man. He
lifted the revolver. Spur knocked it from his hand
with a solid, hard punch, drove his right fist into
the shadowed man's stomach and another to his
chin.

The big man doubled over as Spur sprung to his
feet and drove his knee against the prominent chin,
sending the man reeling backward.

Spur dove for the Army revolver, slid along the
warped floorboards and felt the satisfying slap of
the gun's walnut stock in his hand. He spun
around on his hips just in time to see the dark,
groaning figure crash through the window.

Spur rose and stared out. Nothing. The man
wasn't in sight. McCoy checked the deserted
streets once again and then looked down at the
handsome .44. He turned it over in his hands. Nice
piece, he thought; not as fine as a genuine Remington '58 but not bad.

He looked out the broken window again. The
town was small, there couldn't be more than two
hundred or so people there, but they weren't the
friendliest folks he'd met.

He was sure no one had seen or heard anything
that would lead to his finding the would-be bandit.
Spur weighed his natural urge to stalk the man
with his main job—moving the dies safely to San
Francisco.

McCoy sighed. He'd let the bandit go. Besides,
the man hadn't mentioned the dies. He'd just
wanted his money. For all he knew it was old Sam,
the one who'd shot up the saloon, looking for funds
to pay off the barkeep.

Yeah, the voice had sounded vaguely familiar,
but Spur had spent the better part of three hours in
the saloon that night. He'd probably heard every

male Little River resident talking, boasting or swearing in that time.

So he'd gotten a revolver out of the night's entertainment and a sore mouth. He coughed and shook his head. He wouldn't miss Little River when the coach pulled out of there in the morning.

The ride to Juniper was uneventful. The two sexless, sex-crazed hags had, fortunately, decided to stay an extra day in Little River, presumably deciding to risk another twenty-four hours in the rough town than a second close-quarters ride with McCoy.

When the coach stopped in Juniper just after dark to change horses, Spur got off. Sneezing and spitting eight hours of dust from his lungs and nose, he hauled his 28-pound saddle and carpet bag to the nearest saloon, The Fancy Garter. Juniper was a larger town than Little River, Spur thought, though he didn't see much of it in the dark. He slid through the batwing doors, sidled up to the crowded bar and ordered a whiskey from the scar-faced bartender.

He downed half of the cracked glass's contents in one gulp. As the bitter, woodsy liquid poured down his throat and warmed his insides Spur glanced around the room.

Three poker games were in session. Two cowboys, surrounded by empty whiskey bottles, snored loudly from a table's slick, alcohol-covered surface.

A fourth table was occupied by a brassy-haired, big-bosomed woman packed into a red and white, tight-waisted, puff-sleeved dress.

Interested, Spur studied her. She was no saloon girl, he decided. The redhead lacked the tired, list-

less look that most of the *Pistol Packing Peggys*
and *Squirrel Faced Shirleys* carried as they used
their thighs to squeeze as much cash out of as
many lonely men as they could.

Maybe she'd had too much to drink and her man,
disgusted, had left her there to fend for herself.
Maybe she didn't have a man and thought she had
to dress that way to attract one. Spur certainly
wasn't complaining as he looked her up and down,
but he wondered why none of the other men had
jumped her yet.

Maybe they had and she was just resting,
though she looked fresh enough.

The blue-eyed beauty saw him, smiled and
eagerly tapped her table. Maybe he was wrong.
Spur motioned for her to wait and, carrying his
saddle and carpet bag in one hand, walked to the
bar to get a fresh whiskey.

"Who's the filly?" he asked the scar-faced
barkeep.

"Hell if I know." The man refilled his glass.
"Lena something. Been coming around here for a
week, always drunker than a skunk. Never seen her
before that." He spit a long brown stream of
tobacco juice onto the floor.

Spur paid the man and walked to her. She smiled
broadly as he set down his glass and tipped his
Stetson. "Ma'am," he said.

"Sit down, go ahead, sit down!" the woman said
eagerly—too eagerly.

He obliged, dropped his saddle and bag to the
floor and grabbed his whiskey. He took a healthy
gulp.

"Lena Mac Dougal," she said, offering her hand.

"Frank Burch." He automatically used his cover
name as he pressed her hand.

"You're not from around here, are you?" she

asked. "I never forget a face."

"Nope. Just arrived a few minutes ago. What's a nice girl like you—"

The brassy-haired beauty laughed. "Brother, whaddya think I'm doing here?" Her blue eyes sparkled, her painted lips were a bit loose and her cheekbones were rosy.

She was drunk.

"You don't work here, do you?" Spur bluntly asked. Something about this otherwise delectable woman made him vaguely uneasy.

"I work where I want to." Her voice was defensive as she pouted and adjusted her breasts with a delicate, white hand. "Buy a girl a drink?" she asked lasciviously.

Spur laughed. She'd fooled him. "Sure." He started for the bar but stopped when she gripped his hand.

"Not here. My place."

Lena stood, offering him her left arm. They walked out of the saloon as Spur dragged his saddle and carpet bag with his left hand.

They moved down the boardwalk. Juniper, Arizona Territory, was preparing for the night. Lamps had been lit throughout the town, creating a fantasy of white, yellow and golden shimmering lights.

"Seriously, what are you doing in this place?" Spur asked, enjoying the cool night air and the feel of the young woman's hand on his arm.

"Just passing through on my way to Frisco. I've taken stage coaches and trains since St. Louis. I never intended to even stop here but one of the horses had thrown a boot and, well, after they got it back on his foot I somehow seemed to get stuck here."

"Shoe."

"I beg your pardon?"

"Horses have shoes, not boots."

"Oh." She giggled. "I'm really a city girl," she explained. "I don't know a lot about horses."

"Keeping busy out here?"

She turned to him and smiled. "You might say that. Lots of lonely men here in Juniper. Why, I wouldn't dream of leaving just yet."

He smirked. "Must give you a warm feeling inside, knowing you're helping out all those poor men."

"Oh yes; I come from a long line of charity workers." The laugh rippled from her painted lips as they entered her hotel.

Once in her room, the red-haired woman sat on her bed and began undressing. "You still haven't told me anything about yourself, Frank Burch." Her voice was faintly accusing.

"Neither have you."

Spur leaned against the door, arms crossed over his broad chest. He'd enjoy watching her remove every article of clothing almost as much as he would seeing her without them on.

Lena smiled, struggling with her dress buttons. "You know all about me—I'm a working girl spreading love and affection throughout this great land. Now tell me what you do. You're no drummer, are you?"

Spur laughed. "No. Guess again."

She sized him up. "You don't look like a bank robber."

He shook his head.

"I give up—on you and these darn buttons."

"Let me help you."

He moved to her then, sat beside the woman and undid her dress. Their thighs pressed together.

"Oh no!" she said as her dress fell forward into

her hands. She pushed it against her body.

"What? Having second thoughts? Think I can't pay you or something?"

Lena shook her head and searched his eyes. "You —you aren't some kind of *lawman* or something, are you?"

Spur smiled. "No," he lied. "What makes you ask that? Do I look like a lawman?"

"I don't know."

"You have something against lawmen?"

Lena smiled and stood, dropping the dress to the floor. She was completely nude. No chemise, bloomers or petticoats obscured her body. The soft kerosene light illuminated her curves, fuzzy groin and pink nipples.

"No. It's just that—well, daddy was a lawman. In St. Louis. And—and ever since I—"

"I see."

He didn't know what she was talking about, but he certainly did see her—all of her. When she stood before him, however, Spur again sensed something was wrong. He realized what it was when she pushed her hand between his legs.

Lena frowned at what she felt. "Hell, boy, what's the matter with you? Aren't I pretty enough?" she said, massaging his limp bulge.

"No. I mean yes, hell yes you're pretty. Prettiest thing I've seen in a long time." He looked down at her busy hand. "I don't know. Maybe I'm just tired. I've been traveling for a long time."

"Yeah? Where are you headed, Frank?"

She redoubled her efforts, stroking, massaging, running her tongue in and out of his ear, but it didn't work. He was as limp as a dry sheet in the breeze.

"Nowhere in particular. Just wandering around, looking for a place to settle down."

The woman continued her efforts for a few minutes, furiously trying to stir lust into his groin. When it was clear that it wasn't going to work she finally sat beside him.

"Look, boy, I don't know what your problem is," she said angrily. "Maybe you've been spending too much time with your horse."

Damn! Spur thought. Why the hell couldn't he give her what he'd given so many other women? Maybe it was something about the girl, something he just didn't like. "I don't have a horse—not here, anyway."

"I guess you're not gonna have me neither." Lena unpinned her hair, shook it back and ran a hand over her forehead. She frowned. "It coulda been good, Frank. It coulda been real good. I'm the best there is."

"I can believe it." He stood and shrugged. "Maybe some other time."

"When you leaving Juniper?" she asked, a curious urgency in her words.

"In the morning."

"Well, okay, be that way." She pouted again. "I hope you fall off your danged horse!"

"I don't—" Spur sighed, picked up his belongings and walked out of the room, leaving the frustrated girl sitting stark naked on her bed.

Spur didn't really mind, though he couldn't remember such a thing happening to him more than a few times in his long, sweat-packed, body-bucking history. That woman was more than she appeared to be, he thought, and somehow it had bothered him—even that part which was rarely bothered by anything.

He put it out of his mind. Time he checked into a hotel, ate and played some poker. He might as well enjoy himself on this job.

Besides, he realized, as the hard leather saddle
straps cut into his shoulder, there were millions of
women out there waiting for him. He didn't mind
disappointing one of them.
Much.

4

"Lawson, honey, I'm sorry!" the tear-streaked woman said. "I tried my best but he wouldn't tell me a damn thing! Hell, he wouldn't even screw me!"

The burly, six foot-one, black-haired man raised his hand again, sending the fully-dressed woman cringing against the far end of his hotel room bed. She stared up at him from lowered lashes, panting. A bright pink spot on her left cheek showed the result of his last slap.

"You tried!" he thundered. "That's not good enough, not with all this at stake!" He stared down at her, fuming, threatening her again and again with another hard slap. Finally he lowered his hand. "Damn! I shoulda known he wouldn't tell you anything. He's too smart for that."

His hard brown eyes softened as he gazed at the beautiful, buxom woman who cowered against the iron headboard. "Did I hurt you much?" Lawson Amory's voice was suddenly tender.

The red-haired woman pouted and rubbed her shining cheek with slender, white fingers. "No. Not much. I've had worse. Lots of men have slapped me around." She sniffed.

"Look, Lena, I'm sorry. I figured you—of all the women in this damned town—could get anything you wanted out of him. Guess I was wrong."

Lena MacDougal wiped her cheeks, visibly relaxing now that the danger of another solid blow had passed. "He wouldn't tell me nothing, not a word about what he's doing here."

Lawson nodded. "Did you feel his pockets like I told you to?"

"Yeah, I felt his pockets—I felt all over between his legs." Lena half-smiled. "He didn't have anything in his pockets except for what felt like a wad of money." Her blue eyes focused on his. "What do you want from him, anyway, Lawson? It can't be that. You've got tons of money."

"Yeah, what I haven't given you." Amory laughed shortly. "Hell, don't worry your pretty little head about it. I knew it'd be hard."

Her eyes lit up. "I hope it's hard. Hell, that guy couldn't get it up if a dozen girls lifted their skirts and stuck their behinds into his face!" Lena smiled. "You're more of a man than him. I think he's partial to horses!"

Amory smiled at the insult. The girl's passion was infectuous; he felt a tightening in his crotch. "Come on over here, gal! I won't hurt you again."

Lena squealed delightedly and rolled across the bed until she bumped against his muscled thigh.

"Get to work," he said harshly as she gazed up at him. "I'm paying you so I might as well enjoy it."

"Yes sir!"

Lena MacDougal fumbled with his fly, ripped it open, pushed her hands past his shorts and hauled out his rising organ. She slipped it's hard, mushroom-shaped head into her mouth and moaned.

A rush of warmth flooded through Lawson Amory as he forced himself deeper into the woman.

Enjoy yourself, he thought, as Lena started to work him over. He'd have to bide his time. Didn't want to risk a confrontation with the man here.

Lawson Amory allowed himself to relax as he

enjoyed the woman's mouth. Hell, he could wait. He relished the satisfaction of knowing that long before Spur McCoy could board that ship for San Francisco the dies would be his and the Secret Service agent would be lying in a puddle of blood.

He'd enjoy watching the man die.

The sun hung directly overhead, burning the desert into an arid wasteland. The Butterfield Express stagecoach rattled down a dusty, rude trail through the desolation as it moved toward Clover, the next town along the line. The vast, barren landscape stretched out to infinity around it.

Bizarre rock formations lay strewn over the ground up ahead. They rose hundreds of feet into the air—twisted, broken pinnacles of long-dead mountains worn down by centuries of sand and wind.

Inside, the heat was oppressive. It radiated from the ceiling overhead and in through the windows. Dust-laden air hung around the four men seated there.

"Indians," the black-suited man said. He sat beside Spur in the bouncing stage. "I know they're out there."

"You worried?" McCoy lazily asked the man. They'd been talking about the dangers of the untamed countryside to pass the time.

"Hell no! No sense in worrying about what might be." Bart Clemons mopped his slick, dust-coated forehead with a stained handkerchief and stuffed it back into his pocket. "I'm just curious. Never seen real live Indians before."

"Injuns, hell!" The unshaven cowboy seated across from Spur lit up a cheroot with a sulphur match and inhaled the bitter smoke. "Let me at 'em. I'll blast those soulless devils to hell! They're lower 'n animals!''

"They're not soulless devils, asshole, they're human beings," Ted Malbrough said. The thin, bearded salesman stared out the window. "As much as ah hate to admit it, they have ev'ry right to attack us."

"How you figure that, Malbrough?" Clemons asked.

His thin lips bent into a harsh smile. "We took their land, slaughtered their people, stripped their huntin' grounds, burned their fields and took away their religion. Those that still got breath in 'em are just trying to stay alive, and ah don't blame 'em a bit!" The New Orleans salesman's accent was as thick as the silt-laden Mississippi River.

"Mighty high-faluting talk, drummer! But I still say they're soulless devils." The cowboy snorted and inhaled again, then blew out the smoke in perfect circles.

"Might as well keep a watch, just in case," Spur said, and looked out at the lonely countryside through the small black window.

The stage drew nearer to the mass of sharp, sheer rocks that jutted dramatically from the desert floor. The trail that wound through them looked vulnerable.

That'd be the best place to stage an attack, Spur thought. Plenty of prime hiding places in the broken cliffs above them, lots of spots to set up crack archers.

The six horses whinneyed as the driver urged them forward up the slanting road. Their hooves broke sharp rocks into dust as they strained against the increased weight.

"See anything?" Spur asked.

"Nope," Clemons answered, as he strained his neck out the opposite window.

"Hell, you worry too much!" the cowboy said. "I ain't afraid of no yellow-bellied Injuns!"

A sharp cry issued from above them.

"What in hell was that?" the banker asked.

Spur stuck his head out the window in time to see the driver's arrow-riddled body fall past him on its way to the ground.

"The driver. He's dead!" Spur said.

"Indians!"

The horses, suddenly freed from pressure on their reins, panicked. They surged forward, snarling and snorting, up the sloping trail. Clemons and Spur searched the overhead rocks from the bouncing windows.

"I don't see a plum thing!" Bart yelled.

"They have to be out there somewhere!" Spur strained his eyes but saw no movement, no Indians.

An arrow whizzed past. The slender wooden shaft dug two inches into the right rear horse's flank.

The mare screamed. Her pain-racked leg faltered, stumbled. The six teamed horses veered to the right, sending their pounding hooves into a deep gulley created by centuries of intermittent rainfall.

"Holy shit!" Malbrough said, clutching to the jerking seat.

The coach lurched sickeningly and jolted sideways as the horse's hooves caught in the deep slot, tangling their legs. It stopped suddenly. The wounded, whinneying horse fell to the ground, pulling the rest of the kicking, screaming team with it.

The Butterfield Express coach's left wheels shot into the air as the horses pulled vertically against it. The seat slanted sharply, slamming the cowboy and the drummer against Spur and Clemons.

"We're going over!" the banker yelled.

The coach teetered on its right, iron-wrapped wheels for five endless seconds before crashing onto its side with a bone-rattling crunch.

The four groaning men, piled on top of each other on the wall below them, tried to untangle their limbs as the horses snorted and groaned in agony from snapped ankles. The impact had knocked the breath out of Spur. He gasped, picked himself up and shook his head.

"Everyone all right?" he asked.

The three men yelled affirmitively.

"Git yer smelly boot outa my face, banker!" the cowboy said.

"I will if you get yours outa my back, cowboy!" came the retort.

Spur gripped his long-barreled Colt .45 and poked his head out the now overhead window.

A lone Indian rider crashed down the cliff toward them, whooping triumphantly, swinging his bow above his head as his horse slid along the incline.

Spur lined up his shot and waited until the brave was within thirty feet. Just as the man drew back his arrow McCoy fired, slamming a load of hot lead through his chest.

The surprised Indian slid backward off his mount as his heart exploded. He dropped to the gorund and lay motionless as his frightened mount charged forward down the hill and veered onto the trail.

Lucky shot, Spur thought, as he ducked down into the carriage. The three men were settling themselves on the coach's side which now served as the floor.

"How many of 'em?" Bart Clemons asked.

"Used to be one but you can bet yer ass there's more out there." His face was grim.

"What're we gonna do?" Malbrough asked, shaking, his lips tight.

"Get ahold of yourself, drummer! You and Clemons see if you can kick some firing holes through the floorboards. Do it now!"

The two men nodded as they squatted before it.

They pounded their boots against the warped surface.

"Hurry, goddamn it!" Clemons said.

Spur turned to the cowboy, who sat slumped against the floor rubbing his jaw. "Where's your big words now, cowboy? I thought you were going to take care of the Indians singlehanded."

The sullen man fixed his eyes on the bright window opposite him.

The men pounded the dilapidated floor with their thick-soled boots. The old, felt-covered wood took the force at first, then buckled, splintered and cracked. Seconds later sunlight shone through four holes.

"Good enough. I sure hope you boys can use those things," Spur said, as the two men drew their weapons.

"Now's as good a time as any to find out!" Clemons checked his revolver.

Dozens of hooves pounded the hard-packed desert floor outside, growing nearer and louder, as the whole Indian raiding party approached them.

"Land sakes!" Clemons said. "Here they come!"

"Then stick your weapons through those holes and get ready to fire. This thing ain't over yet!"

5

The overturned Butterfield stagecoach seemed to grow even hotter as the four men huddled in it. Clemons and Malbrough, squatting and pressing their noses against the floor, peered through the firing holes they'd kicked through it.

Spur slid a sixth round into his .45. "What's the count?" he barked as the sounds of the approaching Indians grew louder. "How many of them?"

"Jesuz!" the salesman said. "Must be hundreds of 'em comin' down the cliff!"

"You're plumb crazy, Malbrough!" Bart Clemons said. "I see five—six of them."

"Anyway, there's more of them than us. Ah don't like them odds, not one bit."

"Quit yer bellyaching and use those guns!" Spur thundered.

The cowboy, who'd sat slumped in the corner since the coach had rolled over, jumped to his feet.

"I gotta get outa here!"

"Sit your butt down!" Spur said.

"No. I can do it. I can make it." The cowboy gripped the window above him and stuck his head fully through the hole.

"Shit-for-brains!" Clemons yelled.

Malbrough peeled off a shot at the approaching Indians, using a higher hole for sighting.

The cowboy screamed and dropped from the

overhead window onto the floor. A feathered arrow had turned his left eye into a mass of blood and tissue.

"Hell!" Spur snarled as he looked at the bleeding, mortally wounded man. The arrow had slammed into his brain, lodging deep inside the vital organ. "Had to go and get yourself killed!"

The cowboy's lanky body shook. His boots rattled on the wall beneath him as he gurgled out a scream. Moments later he lay silent.

Outside, loud whoops surrounded the coach. The Indians were closing in for the kill.

Malbrough blasted a bullet through the cracked floorboards. "Got one!" he shouted in joy.

Arrows rained down around them and slammed into the coach with dull thuds. One flew in through the window but fell harmlessly beside Spur's feet.

"Five to go," Clemons said, squatting.

Spur straddled the dead cowboy's body and lifted his fully-loaded .45. Pressing it against his chest he pushed his head and the Colt out through the window.

Spur lined up a shot. His .45 spoke and tore a hole through an approaching Indian's chest. The man howled, dropped his bow and bent forward on his mount. Just as McCoy ducked down into the coach again he saw the Indian flop to the ground.

"Good work!" the banker yelled at Spur. "That's four to go!"

Clemons and Malbrough fired repeatedly, furiously, filling the cramped coach with blue smoke and resounding explosions. Sweat squeezed from their foreheads as they alternately reloaded and struggled to sight the Indians as they circled on their prancing, saddleless mounts.

Repeated whacks told of dozens more arrows piercing the stage coach.

"Hold still, damnit!" Malbrough yelled.

"Yeah, make it easy for us!" the banker said sarcastically. "You think they're gonna line up?"

As Spur looked up at the window, ready to rise through it, the whole door above him suddenly swung open. Spur fired at the leering Indian as the man sent an arrow flying into the stagecoach. The strangled cry told him he'd hit his mark. The Indian slid off the coach.

Spur ducked back up through the opened door and quickly killed a fourth Indian.

"Damn. Sweet Jesus! I'm dying, man I'm dying! That bastard got me!"

Spur shot a look behind him. Bart Clemons lay against the wall, his face a mask of agony and terror. The hastily fired arrow had torn open his gut. Half its length stuck out from the banker's stomach.

"Damn! It hurts!" he howled, grasping the arrow with trembling hands.

"What—what do we do?" Malbrough asked. He gazed at the wounded man.

Gut wound, Spur thought. Nothing much they could do about it here. If they were in town maybe a doctor could patch him up. Here, miles from civilization, the Dodge City banker was doomed to a slow, painful death.

"What do we do?" Malbrough asked again, twisting his head from the groaning man to Spur.

He slowly shook his head. "Pray, drummer. Pray that you're not next."

"Can't we take that arrow outta him?" the man asked, his face white. "We gotta do something. We gotta!"

"No. The damage's been done." He shook his head again and hardened his voice. No time to waste. "Just get to work with that hogleg of yours."

He blocked out Clemon's screams. Two more to go. Just two Indians between life and death.

The banker's agonized groans increased in

volume. Marbrough hadn't moved. "I said forget about it," Spur said. "Spit some lead at those damned Indians!"

"Okay, you heartless bastard!" Marlbrough moved to the holes again.

Sudden fury poured through Spur's veins. He stood upright through the opened door and blasted two rounds at the arrow-wielding Indians. At ten yards the shots were easy. Seconds later both fell to the ground, moaning, dying as the hot desert sun shone on their blood-spurting wounds.

Glancing quickly around the area, Spur counted seven dead, including the first he'd killed. Adrenaline ran through him as McCoy sat down and sighed.

Bart Clemons spluttered near his feet. His wounded belly rose and fell like a roaring sea around the murderous arrow. The banker's vital organs, ripped and torn, poured poison throughout his system.

The dying man looked at Spur. "Hell, guess it's time I cashed in anyway." He managed a short, wrinkled smile before wincing again as pain shot through his body.

"You're gonna be fine," Spur lied, smelling fresh blood. "We'll get you to a sawbones and—"

"Don't bullshit me!" Clemons said, and groaned. He nodded with his chin. "They all dead?"

McCoy nodded.

The man closed his eyes. "Then git yer butts outta here and let me die in peace. I don't need a goddamned audience."

A new wave of intense pain flooded through the banker. He doubled up and rolled onto his side as he rode it out.

Ted Malbrough squatted before Clemons, breathing heavily, his eyes wide and round.

"C'mon, Ted. Least we can do is give this man his last wish."

The man looked up wildly, his lips parted, then nodded.

After checking to ensure that all seven Indians were dead and not just unconscious or lying in wait, Spur put the wounded coach horses out of their misery. All six soon lay dead on the sand.

The dead Indian's mounts had scattered across the desert and were nowhere in sight. Spur realized that he and the salesman had a long walk ahead of them.

He retrieved his carpet bag and saddle from where they'd been lying on the ground since the accident and hauled them a hundred yards away. Ted Malbrough was sitting there, silently, since they'd left the stage.

As they waited outside, ignoring the banker's agonized screams, the drummer got his bag of fixings and tried to roll a cigarette. His thin hands shook so much that he'd emptied half his tobacco onto the ground before successfully finishing the simple task. He struck a sulphur match and was soon puffing away on the stick.

Watching a light breeze scattering countless, tiny grains of sand against each other, Spur pushed all thoughts of the dying man and the attack out of his mind. San Francisco, he told himself, mulling over his assignment.

Two hours later the stagecoach was finally silent. Clemon's death screams had ended as he drifted into unconsciousness and eternal oblivion.

The two men outside sat quietly, paying their last respects.

"He—he dead?" Malbrough's voice was barely a whisper as he blew out a thin stream of acrid smoke.

"Yeah."

Ted's eyebrows crunched together as he glanced at the man sitting across from him. "Ah ain't used to this. Never seen nobody die before. First the cowboy and now Clemons.''

"Maybe you'll be lucky and won't see it again.'' He sighed. "Come on, we have work to do.''

"Work?'' the young man asked, taking a last puff before tossing the smoke behind him.

Spur's voice was grim. "We're not leaving until we've given those men a proper burial. Even the cowboy deserves that much.''

Malbrough nodded.

Using a small shovel they found in the wreckage of the coach, the two men took turns digging through the soft sand. Harsh sunlight made them sweat until their clothes hung on them.

The heat radiated up from the ground, baking them. Spur's throat ached. He needed a drink of something—anything.

He called a rest. They found two canteens on the coach. The men slaked their thirst and returned to the work.

Soon they'd managed to dig two shallow graves. They hauled out Clemons first and quickly covered him over with sand, then the cowboy.

They hadn't spoken to each during the entire time. As they stood staring down at the sandy mounds, Spur wiped his forehead and sighed.

"Ain't ya gonna say something?'' Malbrough asked. "Shouldn't we read a Bible verse?''

"Know any?'' he asked.

The man shook his head.

"Neither do I. Then we're done. The next stage stop shouldn't be more'n six miles or so. Passed one not long before the attack.''

The drummer stood and stuffed his canteen into his black leather luggage. "Ah ain't goin' with you.''

"Why in hell not, Malbrough?''

He frowned, wrinkling his slick, salty face. "Hell, ah shouldn't be out here. Realized it when those Indians attacked us. This ain't my place, so ah'm going back to Juniper, get the first stage ah can, and head home. Ain't gonna stop for nothing 'till ah see the Mississippi again.''

Spur grunted. "Don't blame you. Best of luck, Malbrough.''

The drummer nodded and turned toward the trail.

McCoy packed his canteen, slung the heavy saddle over his shoulder, gripped his carpetbag and started out down the trail as the sun slanted further before him.

The stage stop couldn't be too far away. He should get there long before dark.

Spur was well aware of his vulnerability. He was alone, on foot, with little water and no food, travelling through Indian territory. But he was alive and the dies were still safe. Things could be worse.

He walked relentlessly, following the crude trail, his boots kicking up clouds of dust. The harsh sunlight worked on him as it had on the desert for untold thousands of years.

The ground pounded below him. The trail beckoned for Spur to follow it toward the distant stage stop. The heat made his head light.

Hours later he stopped to rest under a cliff that provided welcome shade. He dribbled a bit of water onto his tongue and relished the liquid before gulping it down.

He leaned back against the cool rock wall and slowed his breathing. A pair of scorpions slithered across the sand. They halted, startled at the smell of human sweat. Raising their poisonous, curled tails, the pair threatened him for a moment, then thought better of it and scurried beneath a mass of dead cactus. Moments later he continued his journey.

For two hours Spur saw no living thing save for

a coyote cub who'd lost his mother and a few hawks riding the updrafts, training their keen eyes on the landscape in their endless search for prey.

The secret service agent flexed his mind as he strained his muscles, planning out each day that lay before him until he reached San Francisco and delivered the priceless package to the mint.

For the thousandth time Spur wondered how the news of the dies—especially the fact that he was moving them—had leaked out. The drunkard who'd yelled at him from the dark alley in Hastings damn well knew what he was transporting. But how had he known?

He shook his head, sending salty droplets onto the hot sand where they sizzled and evaporated. The man wouldn't cause him any futher trouble but he knew that others certainly would. He sighed, then McCoy fixed an image of San Francisco in his mind—the glittering lamps along the bay, the dark blue water lapping against tall ships, the bracing scent of sea water and the fancy ladies with smouldering eyes and tight satin dresses who invited with a flick of their eyelashes.

The picture soon faded as he hiked up a steep, rock-strewn incline. For the next hour he passed dozens of these rises. McCoy knew that they'd been carved out of the desert floor by infrequent, heavy rainstorms that had dumped their fury on the usually arid landscape. The rain had gathered and roared through the area, flooding masses of runoffs seeking the lowest point. As they surged across the sand they'd gouged deep gulleys as testimony to their primeval presence.

He struggled up another one. The next ridge, he kept telling himself, as his legs ached and his shoulder throbbed. Over the next one he'd see the stage stop.

Then, finally, as he gained its top, he saw the building far ahead. The tiny corner of human habitation shimmered in the intense heat. It was an oasis of civilization where food, water and rest waited.

McCoy redoubled his efforts, crashing down the sloping ground, nearly tripping over his feet. At the bottom he lugged the saddle onto his right shoulder, gripped his carpetbag with his left hand and pumped his legs hard.

His sweat-soaked clothes hung from his lean body. His head pounded from the intolerable heat. His chest painfully heaved, but he was almost there.

The stage stop dropped out of sight behind a small range of cracked mountains. As he continued his journey, snorting super-heated air through his nostrils and exhaling explosively through his mouth to nourish his aching lungs, Spur detected a bitter scent in the air. Woodsy. Spicy. The unmistakeable odor of smoke.

The aroma sent McCoy's stomach churning. Food. Someone was cooking in the now-invisible stage stop. Beans and steak and coffee and apple pie. He could almost taste them.

Slow down boy, he told himself. Think about getting hungry when you're there. Besides, the smoke didn't smell right. It seemed stale, old.

Twenty minutes later Spur stopped in his tracks, gazing at the stage stop that lay two hundred yards ahead. Even at this distance he realized that all was not right.

His worst fears had been realized. Though still standing, the small barn, squat wooden building, even the outhouse were laced with thick dark stripes of charcoal. Dead horses lay still on the ground. No humans moved there.

The stage stop had been burned.

6

Desolation surrounded him.

Spur dropped his saddle and carpetbag, slicked his forehead beneath his Stetson and stood in shock among the cold, charred remains of the stage stop. As he took in the scene of destruction and carnage, as the finality of it penetrated his brain, his nostrils flared. The acrid stench of burned human flesh rose up from the ground and hung in the air.

Near his feet lay the pitiful remains of four men, burned beyond recognition. A stagecoach lay in pieces beside the single-story structure. Arrows riddled the buildings. The troughs had been overturned, dooming the precious water to evaporate on the sand. Twelve horses lay heaped on each other, peppered with arrows, their huge eyes staring sightlessly out at the desert, their limbs twisted and broken.

Indians, he thought, and grimaced.

The fire they'd set—probably by overturning the cookstove—had barely scorched the surrounding land. Horses had apparently chewed nearby bushes and scrub to the ground, so the fire hadn't spread. Not far away lay a thicket of cottonwoods and maybe, just maybe, water.

He surveyed the area. No survivors, no dead Indians even. They must have stormed in and attacked before the people had a chance to defend themselves.

McCoy shook his head and moved laterally away from the buildings, away from the gut-churning stench of overcooked human meat. He dropped to a squat, panting. He was almost too tired to comprehend the sight, too hot and thirsty to take it in. Had he walked so far only to come to this?

He closed his eyes and breathed deeply until his heart had returned to its normal pace and he'd rested. First things first. He checked his canteen. Almost half full. If he didn't find water he couldn't start out on the desert, not alone, not in this heat. He didn't know the local waterholes and couldn't risk the trip.

He'd have to wait until the next stage plodded up and hope he could get a ride.

Spur sighed as he rose and glanced again at the dusty cottonwoods. Worth a try, he thought, and started for them. He ignored the aching in his boots as he covered the hundred yards to the area.

The trees grew thickly, their slender trunks caked with years of desert grime. Not the slightest breeze stirred the leaves or snaked the trunks back and forth, but the branches arching overhead cooled the air. McCoy walked into the welcome, soothing shade.

Cottonwoods were always a good sign of water, he remembered. In this place they could be his salvation.

As he moved into the grove, small patches of bright green appeared on the sand below him, not cactus but some sort of small leafy plant. Encouraged, Spur eagerly walked on the soft sand. His boots crushed dozens of fragile plants that had eeked out survival in the grove.

Then he heard it just ahead—the refreshing trickle of water splashing on rocks, the sound of constant dripping, of liquid spilling into liquid: the miracle of the desert.

A spring, he thought, grunting and smiling to himself. Good place for a stage stop—at least, it had been.

A distinct, sharp intake of breath ten feet from him, a miniscule rattle of bushes, set Spur's mind in motion. He froze and turned his head toward the sound's apparent place of origin.

An innocent, three-foot patch of horehound stood in the dappled sunlight. It was still, dense, intensely green. He approached it.

Another gasp, another rattle. Someone was in there. Had he surprised an Indian?

"Don't—don't—!" the bush said.

Spur smiled. It was a woman. By god, a woman!

"I'm not going to hurt you, ma'am," Spur said, halting seven feet away. He put his hands on his hips and stared at the bush. "You believe me?"

"Yes, I—I do." The voice was high, strained.

"Fine. Now why don't you come out of there? I'm not an Indian."

Silence, rustling, then the bush gave birth. A tall, striking blonde woman rose from it, her chin high, eyes wild with fright. The checkered tatters hanging from her body showed the remains of a calico travelling dress. Her face was smudged with smoke and dirt, her hair matted with leaves.

Her aquamarine eyes glowed. "Thank god you're not an Indian!" she said, relieved.

"Frank Burch, ma'am," Spur tipped his hat.

"I—I'm Beverly Thomas." The woman stared at him as if she'd never seen a white man.

"You all right, Miss Thomas?" Spur approached

her, cautiously, slowly.

She nodded and smiled. The simple act seemed to transform her, and Spur was struck by the incomparable beauty that lay beneath the traces of dirt, smoke and leaves.

"I'm fine, Mr. Burch." She coughed. "Tired, scratched, hungry—but fine."

"You gonna come outa that bush?"

She looked down and blushed, then stepped toward him, freeing her feet from the tangle of soft green branches. "I'm not myself. Please excuse the way I look—" She halted her sentence and eyed him sardonically. "Listen to me! You'd think I was back in Boston!"

"No need to apologize," he said gently. "I understand. What happened?"

, Her smile faded. "The Butterfield Stage had stopped here to change horses. We—me and Parson Thomas—had just finished eating. The parson was reading his bible, something in Revelations, I think. I—" she blushed deeply, coloring her soiled cheeks, then looked away. "I'd left him to go off to the bushes to, well, *you know.*"

Spur nodded.

Beverly looked at him timidly. "Anyway, I'd just ducked into some bushes on the edge of the cottonwoods when I heard these unworldly voices coming out of nowhere. Then, horses running. Lots of them. I didn't know what was going on so I just stayed where I was, crouching inside the bushes, and—and watched." She folded her hands before her and closed her eyes, brushing her high checkbones with long, blonde lashes.

"Look, Miss Thomas, if this is too painful for you, you don't have to tell me."

She looked up sharply at him. "I have to tell someone!" She bent down and plucked a handful of some nameless, tiny white flower. Clutching it, she took a deep breath. "The trees were in the way, but I saw Indians riding up. I'd never seen any before. The driver was yelling his head off and Parson Thomas dropped his bible as he tore out from the kitchen."

She took a deep breath and continued. "Before I knew it they were all dead—the preacher, the driver and the two old men who ran that place. I looked away in fright and disgust but I heard something fall over. As they rode off I saw the fire they'd started and—and—." She squeezed her eyes shut again. "And they'd set fire to the men! All of them! There were four men I'd eaten with, one of them a man of God, and they were burning like birch twigs." She shivered and looked at him again. "So I just stayed here, walking farther into the trees. I'm not going back out there. Ever!"

Spur nodded. "Well, Miss Thomas, I think you could call yourself powerfully fortunate." He thought of what they would have done to her.

"I know." She nodded, her eyes cold. "I count my blessings every time I remember what it looked like back there. I fondly recall the day I decided to leave Boston and look up Trevor in San Diego!" Color burnished her cheeks, the product of frustration and anger.

"I'm sorry, Miss Thomas."

Her light blue eyes softened. "Don't be. I knew it was dangerous travelling alone across the Territory of Arizona. And call me Bev, not Miss Thomas. Okay?"

He nodded. Even though she'd been through hell, Spur couldn't help but notice that her dress had nearly slipped off her firm, rounded body. His eyes darted down quickly. "You have anything else you can wear?"

She paled and laughed, vainly trying to cover up the large patches of bloomers and chemise that showed plainly through torn checkerboard dress. "My heavens! I'd forgotten that I was nearly naked!" Bev laughed joyously. "Leave it to a man to take a girl's mind off her troubles. Yes, I have two bags, but they're out there." She pointed toward the burned stage stop. This slight motion ripped apart the few threads that held up the right shoulder of her dress. It dropped down, revealing a portion of her smooth, white upper shoulder and the top of her chemise.

She giggled. "Oh hell!" Beverly slapped a delicate, lightly scratched hand over her lips. "Whoops! You probably think I'd be mortified to be seen in this condition—and by a man at that. But with all I've been through, it just doesn't matter anymore. Not at all!"

He liked her. Spur was entranced by this dirty but beautiful blonde. He admired her courage and her openness. "I'd better go get your bags before that dress falls off." He flashed her a wink and turned toward the burned buildings.

"Would you? I'd appreciate it. They're the lilac leather cases!" she called.

Spur hurried out to the burned buildings, found the two small suitcases and ran back into the trees.

She smiled as he placed the bags at her feet. "Thanks. Aren't you the gentleman!"

He smiled and solemnly turned around, folding his arms over his chest. "It's okay, Miss Thomas. You can change now. I assure you I won't look."

She laughed. "Heck, call me Bev! And why should I mind if you looked? You practically saved my life!"

He stood stoically. The woman's proximity reminded him of his own condition—he must stink to high heaven. "How much water's up ahead, Bev?" Cloth rustled behind him.

"Lots. There's a spring and a big pool. The water's cold but it sure is refreshing."

He nodded. "Think I'll have a bath."

"Okay." She sighed. "I guess I won't have an audience after all."

He grunted and moved ahead to find the spring.

A dozen shades of green surrounded the six-foot pool of glistening water. The endless flow from deep within the parched earth had carved a large, deep bowl. Spur bent over it, cupped up some water and sucked it into his mouth. It was cold all right, he thought, and savored it as it travelled down to his stomach.

He ripped off his salt-caked clothing and threw it onto the ground. Sitting on the leaf-covered bank Spur tussled out of his boots and socks, stood and poked a toe into the water. Maybe too cold, he thought. Its temperature numbed his foot.

What the hell. Spur whooped, jumped up and splashed down into the spring. The water slipped around him like ice, jarring his body with intense pain and knocking away his breath. He gasped and hopped from one foot to the other as the water lapped at his waist. His whole body screamed in agony as he waited until it had adjusted to the sudden, glorious temperature change.

The sound of feet rustling through dead leaves behind him made McCoy spin around.

"I do declare!"

He glanced up, surprised.

Beverly Thomas, dressed only in her bloomers and silky chemise, locked her gaze on the long slab of flesh that swung between Spur's legs.

She sucked in her breath and smiled. "Aren't you a sight for a girl's sore eyes!"

7

Spur McCoy grinned up at Beverly Thomas as she stood gazing at him. He felt the heat of her eyes as she drank in his naked body.

"I thought you were changing," he said, somewhat uncomfortable. He shivered as a tiny wave of ice-cold water hit the small of his back.

Bev smoothed her hands over her chemise. "And miss all this—all of you—all of *that*? Not as long as I'm alive. I never miss an opportunity to see a buck-naked man." She pouted. "You probably think I'm a fallen woman, watching you like a dog in heat."

"Well," Spur said, noticing the swelling of her breasts beneath the flimsy chemise, "you've been through a lot. You're still in shock."

"The hell I am!" Bev smiled smugly at him. "Boy, you're just what I needed to make me forget my troubles." Her eyes sparkled at him for a moment before she dropped her gaze again.

Spur felt like a cow at auction as the beautiful woman studied his crotch.

"Mr. Burch, you've got more between your legs than the last three men I've been with put together!"

"I appreciate that, Beverly."

She jumped into the pool beside him. The result-

63

ing splash sent him into another shivering fit. Bev yelled in delight, rubbed her face clean, then arched her back before him, holding her arms high above her blonde-tressed head.

The woman's clinging, wet chemise revealed every detail of the pert mounds that lay beneath them. Spur forgot the cold water as he drank in her breasts—perfect globes that proudly jutted out from her body. They were topped with hard, red nipples that plainly showed beneath the wet silk.

Beverly finished her stretch and fixed her aquamarine eyes on his. "Look, Burch, I never was a woman who waited to be asked. I want you. Right now! To hell with the stage stop, to hell with Trevor, to hell with all that's right in this world! Frank Burch, love me!"

"I never say no to a lady." Spur felt the flush of warmth at his groin.

"Haven't I made it clear by now that I'm not a lady?" She curled her upper lip, batted her eyelashes and parted her lips. With a blissful sigh Beverly threw her head back and melted against him.

Spur gripped the woman's slender waist and, crushing her slick body to his, peppered her face with kisses. He murmured against her throat. then lifted his lips to hers. They met in a long, lingering, tongue-thrashing kiss. Spur felt his erection pounding against her stomach in spite of the cold water that splashed between them.

He broke the kiss. Beverly stared up at him with her honest, enflamed eyes. "Undress me. Now!"

Excited by her lust, McCoy gripped the chemise and slid it up off her body as she held her arms above her head. He pushed his mouth onto her left breast, touched his tongue to the hard, red nipple, then pushed it into his mouth.

"Mmmmmm. I like that." Her voice was husky with sexual passion.

Spur sucked the nipple, flicking his tongue over the hard nub. She moaned as he gently ran his teeth back and forth.

"Why, what is this thing?"

He lifted his head. "Hmmmmm?" he asked.

"This thing here!" She was teasing him.

His erection floated on the water between them. "You know damn well what that thing is!" he said, his desire growing stronger and stronger. The woman radiated sex. Her half-nude body seemed to heat the water by its mere presence.

"I just hope you know how to use it."

Beverly gripped his penis and stroked it tenderly. "My goodness, Frank honey, I've never seen anything like this. I mean, one this big!"

He squirmed as her delicate fingers pulled and prodded. The erotic pressure sent bolts of fire through his veins. She increased the pressure and speed of her strokes, groaning and marveling at the massiveness in her hand.

Spur quickly brushed it away. "You keep that up and I won't have a chance to use it."

Beverly smirked. "Okay. Let's get out of this danged water and get down to business!"

They lay on the mossy bank, entertwined like jungle vines. Spur ripped off her bloomers, cursing as they entangled on her feet. Beverly giggled.

"Don't you want me?" she asked as he rolled her onto her back.

Spur grunted. The blonde fuzz between her legs beckoned to him with a siren's song. He moved above her and, lifting himself on his hands and the balls of his feet, hung in mid-air. His penis nudged her pubic hair.

"I want you and I'm gonna have you!" Everything about the woman stimulated him, made him harder and ready to go.

Beverly stopped giggling and opened her eyes wide. "What kind of a lady do you think I am?" she asked, with mock indignation.

"You're not a lady. You're a woman. A woman in heat. A woman that's got me in heat." He positioned himself between her legs. Beverly lifted her hips in anticipation as he rubbed his erection against her opening.

He pushed. Hard. Beverly's mouth opened. Her eyes went glassy and she arched her back as he slipped into her, filling her with his desire.

Spur slowly pushed into a world of warm, moist velvet, opening her, pleasuring her. When he was in all the way he sighed and released the breath he'd been holding.

Their bodies joined at their crotches, Spur looked down into the aquamarine eyes of the woman who'd seduced him. The artifice, the teasing, the coquettry was gone, washed clean by the fire of pure erotic passion.

"Oh . . . oh . . . you're such a big man!" Beverly grasped his shoulders and pulled his body down onto hers.

"Am I too heavy for you?" Spur asked, nuzzling her right ear.

"You're not too anything for me," the breathy woman said. "But hold it there for a bit," she said, as his hairy chest crushed her breasts. "It's been . . . a . . . while."

He did so, unwillingly, but after enjoying their motionless connection for a few moments Spur felt the old urge building within him. He reared back and thrust.

"Yes!"

Again.

"Oh yes!" Beverly chewed on his stubble-covered chin and groaned.

Spur McCoy began stroking her, slowly at first, enjoying the ripples of emotion that shot across the woman's face as she took his penis. Bev clutched him, digging her fingernails into his back as he increased the tempo.

"Oh Frank, fuck me. Fuck me! Make me your woman!"

Spur's passion rose at the woman's use of the word. Snarling down at her trembling face, at her sex-misted eyes, he pounded between her legs, driving into her with sensual fury, luxuriating in the sensations their bodies were producing.

"Fuck me!"

Beverly lifted her thighs and locked them around Spur's. She came alive, bucking her hips upward, meeting his thrusts with her own, trying to drive him even deeper into her body. She reached around him and flicked her fingers across his bouncing, slapping testicles.

"Beverly, you feel good!" Spur said, his voice hoarse. He pumped into her faster and faster. "You feel so damn good!"

"So . . . so . . . do . . ." Her short, hard breaths blasted against his face.

He slammed his mouth down on hers, driving his tongue into her mouth, matching his thrusts into her vagina. She moaned and sucked it as their lips molded together.

He broke the kiss. Beverly's head flopped back as she frantically bucked her groin against his.

Spur lifted himself on his hands and stared down at the woman in wonder, in lust, watching her creamy white breasts bounce and shake as he opened her wider than she'd ever been before.

"Oh Frank, I'm gonna . . ." she began, panting.

"I think I'm gonna . . ."

Spur drove deeper, harder into her yielding opening until his hips became a blur. His vision blurred as wave after wave of pleasure shot through him. He groaned, driving them both toward that final moment.

"I'm gonna!" Beverly said, gasping.

He slammed into her with the violence of passion, celebrating her womanhood, reveling in his maleness. Spur's sweat rained down, splashing against her naked body like a summer thunderstorm.

Lightning struck her. Beverly moaned, gasped, closed her eyes and flipped them open. A high-pitched scream issued from her throat, followed by another and yet another. The woman's face flushed and grew slick as she shuddered through orgasm after orgasm, rubbing her clitoris against his erection, gripping his pumping thighs with hers as if to beg him to continue, to ride her forever.

Beverly's contractions, her cries of pleasure, her shuddering body drove him on and on. His mind went blank. His hips jerked spastically as he rammed into her, smashing their pelvic bones together.

Beverly gripped his hips and urged them faster. Spur felt his balls tightening in their sack as they banged against her buttocks. He felt his chest heaving, the pressure in his groin growing beyond denial. His vision blacked out. McCoy looked at the sky, screamed his primitive male cry of release and spurted deep within her.

Withdraw. Thrust. Spurt. He roared and shook and blindly slammed into her, ejaculating like a wild animal with no thought but for their mutual pleasure.

As she took his seed, Beverly shook through yet

another orgasm, clamping her legs around his spasming body, screaming and tearing at her hair as she shuddered through another mind-bending moment of pure sexual bliss.

After an endless time, it was over. Spur dropped down onto the woman. Their heated, slick bodies trembled as they maintained their union.

Slowly, slowly, Spur returned to normal consciousness. He felt Beverly's thighs relax and slip down from where she'd held them around his. With a great effort he lifted his head to look at the woman.

Beverly stared at him, astonished, her lips a dry, red bow. Her oval-shaped face glowed with satisfaction and her eyes narrowed as his penis jerked inside her. She squeezed her legs together around him.

"Anything wrong?" he asked, amused.

"No. I'm just surprised. I—I've never had it happen more than one time!" she stammered. "Never! Not even with the best! Jesus, Frank! You're amazing!" Beverly Thomas' voice was filled with wonder.

Spur smiled. "You're one hell of a lady—I mean woman, Bev." He tenderly kissed her lips.

"And you're a man and a half." Beverly pushed her hand down between them, past his hard stomach, and ran her fingers through his pubic hair. Spur groaned as she gripped the base of his erection. "You're still hard!"

He shrugged comically at her. "I guess it's the company." He started to withdraw.

"Don't take it out." Her voice was a whisper. "Don't ever take it out!"

He did, finally, a half hour later, after he brought them both to another shivering release. Spur rolled off the blonde woman and lay on the sandy bank of the spring-fed pool. They stared at the interlacing cottonwood trees overhead and, beyond them, at the deep blue afternoon sky. Beverly grabbed his hand and held it tightly.

"Jesus, Frank, after that I feel like I can face anything." She sighed deliciously and nestled her head against his shoulder. "I guess it's time to leave."

"Maybe you're right," Spur said. "Though I kinda hate to think about it."

She smiled. "Come on; we have to leave sometime. Besides, there's lots of time for more loving—later on. We'd better get dressed, get on your horse and ride out of here."

Horse. Spur frowned. How could he break it to the woman? "We can't."

Beverly looked at him, curiously. "What do you mean?"

He stalled. "We can't leave now. It's too late in the day to go very far before dark."

"Well, I don't mind riding after dark!" Beverly pushed herself up on her elbows and looked at him. "Besides, it'll be sexy with you pushing your thigh against my rump." Her eyes sparkled. "I may not know much about riding, but I'm a fast learner."

"We won't be riding." Spur sighed as the full brunt of their dangerous situation flooded back through him. They were in the middle of a harsh desert, miles from other humans. "I—I don't know how to tell you this, Beverly, but I don't have a horse." He looked squarely at her.

She smiled. "What are you talking about? Come on, don't tease me about a thing like that, Frank! Of course you have a horse!"

"No, I don't," Spur said sullenly.

She shook her head slowly, her eyes narrowing. The aquamarine circles seemed to pale. "You didn't ride up here then?''

"No. I walked."

Beverly laughed nervously. "Come on, Frank! You expect me to believe that you walked all the way across the desert? Well, I don't believe you!"

"It's the truth. Look. I took the Butterfield out from Clover. About halfway here we got attacked. The stage coach was wrecked, the driver killed, the horses put out of commission. So I walked about six or eight miles to reach this place. I don't have a horse, Beverly. That's the truth."

Beverly caught her breath. Her high cheekbones colored. "Attacked? You—you mean?"

He nodded. "Indians. Came out of nowhere. Killed two other men besides the driver."

She shivered. Anguish slipped over her face. "Well . . . what're we going to do?" she asked, squeezing his hand so hard that it hurt. "I mean, how are we gonna get out of here?"

"I wish I knew, Beverly. I wish I knew."

8

Spur pulled on his shorts and pants, stuffed his feet into his dirty socks and boots, slapped his Stetson onto his head and went back to the ruined stage stop. The bloated, dead horses reeked after baking in the sun as he passed them and walked into the charred building.

Sunlight glanced into it here and there where flame had licked holes in the timbers. Beside the overturned stove McCoy found a cache of canned goods. Most had burst from the intense heat, spewing their multi-colored contents onto each other, but he found a can of tomatoes and one of peaches that were still sound.

Poking around further revealed an untouched can of Arbuckle coffee, as well as a pot in which to brew it and two cracked metal cups. He also found a mass of sun-dried jerky and a barely singed loaf of bread no more than a few days old.

He went outside with the supplies. Two faded red blankets had been lain over bushes in back of the building to dry. Spur placed the goods onto them and wrapped them up, retrieved his saddle and carpetbag and headed back into the cotton-woods.

He and Beverly had spoken about their plans. They'd spend the night in the woods as Spur kept watch, then start for the next town a few hours before dawn to take advantage of the cooler night air.

As he arrived at the spring-fed pool Beverly Thomas was dressed in a bright yellow, high-waisted dress that she'd taken out of her travelling bags. She pulled and tugged the cotton material into place around her luscious body.

"Food?" she asked as he approached her. Bev was once again her vivacious self. She seemed to have shoved all thoughts of their dangerous predicament into the depths of her pretty little head.

"Food," Spur said, smiling. "Not much, but at least we can eat."

The blonde smiled. "Great! It seems like years since I've eaten anything."

Spur built a fire of the plentiful dead wood around them. The two ate in silence, alternately locking their gazes together and then letting the visual contact end. Spur pushed a fragment of the hard bread into the bright red tomato juice and ate the refreshing liquid.

Afterward, Spur poured the last of the coffee into the two metal cups he'd found in the burned building and they finished off the jerky and peaches.

"How long until dark?" Beverly asked as she delicately wiped the corners of her mouth.

"Not long. About an hour or so."

"And then tomorrow we'll walk to the next town. I don't know about that part. I never was the most active girl."

"You're active all right." He squeezed her left breast. "Active enough."

She giggled. "Frank Burch! That's not what I meant and you know it."

Spur released her orb. "We don't have a choice. We'll make it. You'll see."

"I guess we'll have to."

"Still think coming out here was a bad idea?"

She paused and then firmly shook her head, tossing her yellow hair around her like a halo. "How could I think that? I couldn't stay in Boston. Everyone there was so *stuffy*. That's no place for a girl like me to live. So in spite of everything that's happened, I'm glad I came. Besides, if I hadn't, I never would have met you."

"Thanks," he said.

"It's not every day a girl meets a man who can pleasure her the way you can." She smiled fondly at the memory, set down her coffee cup and lazily yawned. "All this loving and all this food's made me tired. I think I'll take a nap." She pulled a faded red blanket around her as she settled down on the soft sandy bank.

They rested until dusk. Spur woke and kept watch as the moon crawled overhead across the sky. The fire had burned down to glowing embers. He studied the moving pictures which the lines of red and orange created within them to keep awake. The steady, soothing trickle from the spring kept him company.

As Beverly slept all he could think about was the San Francisco mint and his saddle.

A lone rider walked his exhausted horse up to a ruined building. The thin moonlight was sufficient for him to survey the area.

"Hell!"

The tall man spat on the ground as he saw the overturned trough and the charred bodies eerily lit by moonlight that lay scattered around the place.

No water here, he mused. He'd just have to push

his horse farther. He surveyed the surroundings. Might be a stream nearby, he thought, looking at the dark shapes that jutted from the stark landscape not far from where he stood.

The man slid from his saddle and walked the protesting, lathered horse to the trees. He tied its lead to a sapling and walked a few feet into the grove. The darkness surrounded him, closing in on both sides where the branches choked out the glow of the moon. His boots crunched sand and dried twigs.

He paused in his tracks. A thin eddy of breeze trickled through the cottonwoods, sending their thin leaves whispering to each other.

It was nearly pitch-black. He shook his head. Maybe there was water ahead, somewhere in the woods, but he wasn't going to waste more time. His horse could make it. He'd give her the rest of the water in his canteen and go thirsty.

He returned to his mount and rode the bay toward the west, toward the next town and—he hoped—the start of his new life of wealth and leisure.

Spur poured sand over the dead fire and sighed. The last thing he needed on his mission was a beautiful woman to protect. But he figured he could take her to the next nearest big town— Yuma, he assumed—and then get on toward San Francisco.

Not that he minded. Meeting her had been the high point of his trip so far.

A distinct crackling sound broke the stillness surrounding him. Spur froze, listening. Six more crunches echoed through the woods, halted, then trailed away.

Someone—or something—was there in the

woods. He glanced down at Beverly. The beautiful woman was sound asleep, lying on her side, her arms pressed close to her breasts. Shallow puffs of air slipped through her lips. She'd be fine until he got back.

McCoy rose and moved like an Indian among the trees, soundlessly, without wasted motion. He walked among the cottonwoods for two yards, following the retreating footsteps, before he heard the unmistakable whinney of a horse and, seconds later, its hooves hitting the hard desert floor.

A horse! He ran out from the grove, no longer caring if he could be heard, and burst out from the trees just in time to see the diminishing figure of a rider rounding a nearby ridge west of the stage stop.

Friend or foe, help or threat, the man was long gone. Spur sighed and quietly returned to the spring, unsure whether he'd just spared himself further trouble or missed easy passage out of the desert.

Beverly was sitting up, stretching, as he walked up. "Something wrong?" she asked dramatically.

"No, nothing. I was just looking around." There'd be time to tell her tomorrow what had happened. She needed her sleep.

"Okay." She laid back on the blanket and dropped off again.

Spur frowned as he watched her sleep. In spite of his fortune in meeting Beverly Thomas, this hadn't been the luckiest day of his life.

Long before dawn tinted the eastern sky, McCoy and Beverly packed up their belongings and started on the long trip to Clover. They moved slowly across the silent desert, their passage unnoticed save for a pair of curious owls who hooted back and forth to each other.

Despite her earlier protests, Beverly proved herself a good walker. She'd changed her high heels for sturdy flat soled shoes. Spur was pleased that he hadn't needed to stop for rest nearly as often as he thought might be necessary.

They'd brought as much water as they could, plus an additional can of peaches that Spur had found moments before their departure. The sweet syrup and fleshy fruits would taste especially refreshing once the sun had reached the peak of its intensity.

They walked on and on, ignoring their personal edges of exhaustion, pushing harder, blocking out the misery that their bodies telegraphed to their brains. Beverly panted. Spur swore. Together they made their way toward the town.

It was sundown before they reached the outskirts of Clover, Arizona Territory. Once a Mexican ranching settlement, it was ringed with ranchos. Beverly had been tempted to stop at one of them on the way in but Spur had convinced her to wait for more satisfying luxuries—like private beds and real food—in the town itself.

The tall, muscled man and blonde woman attracted little attention from the citizens, a mixture of Mexicans and Anglos, as they dragged themselves down the manure-laden main street. Spur saw a sign on a false front with just one word—hotel.

They quickly checked into rooms, both on the second floor on opposite sides of the hallway. After they'd washed their faces and changed their clothing they went down the steep stairs to the front desk. Spur quickly ordered food, telling the Welsh proprietor that they were hungry.

He shook his head, saying that supper wouldn't be served for an hour yet and there was no way he was going to open the dining room early. Frustrated, Spur handed him a ten dollar bill. On seeing the money the greasy man hustled his eldest son into the kitchen.

Soon Spur and Bev were devouring mountains of potatoes, barbecued ribs, tortillas and beans. They washed down the hearty if simple feast with gallons of strong black coffee, then returned to their rooms, satisfied, weary from their long trek.

He saw Beverly safely to her room, kissed her forehead and unlocked his door. As he walked in and turned on the kerosene lamp, Spur realized he'd been too tired to worry about his saddle. He was relieved to see that it was still there where he'd lain it, over the pillow on the narrow wooden bed. He threw his hat into the corner and stretched out on the mattress. Sleep, he thought. He needed sleep.

Even the thought of Beverly's sexual favors—she'd made a half-hearted offer after their meal—wasn't enough to keep him awake. He drifted off into a faraway land where a broad, wide bay glistened in sunlight; where fog surrounded gleaming white houses; and where a white marble building waited the double-eagle dies that he'd been guarding.

A piercing feminine scream rocked him out of his sleep. Shocked by sudden consciousness, dazed by the scream, he twisted over and crashed to the floor.

"Beverly!"

9

Spur stumbled out of his hotel room and into the hallway, wiping sleep-grit from his eyes. A woman had screamed. Was Beverly in trouble?

He nearly bumped into a large object directly in front of his door. McCoy lurched back, focused his eyes and saw a short, fat, black-bonneted old woman poking her head into the room across from his. The elderly woman yelled and repeatedly slapped her beaded purse against some unseen object within the room itself.

"Thief!" she hissed. "Robber! Tryin' to take advantage of an old lady! How dare you break into my room and steal my things, you criminal!"

A red faced, huffing thin man—dressed only in his underdrawers—warded off the blows. "Now look, ma'am, this here's my room! I ain't trying to steal nothing from you. You're just all mixed up like."

"Rapist! Criminal! Gun-slinger!" the woman rattled on. "Think you're above the law! I'll show you what you get when you try to hoodwink Amelia Barrett!"

"But ma'am!" the protesting man said.

Spur shook his head in a vain attempt to strip it of the liqueur of sleep. This was the woman he'd heard screaming, he thought dully. Beverly must be fine.

Still unsteady on his aching legs, McCoy stared at the floor and turned on his heel. He bumped into the hotel manager as he rushed up to the scene. The unexpected impact sent Spur reeling back and banging against the far wall.

"Mrs. Barrett, please!" the sweaty, nervous little Welshman said.

She turned on him. "Mr. Jones, thank the Lord you've come!" the elderly woman said, smiling as her heavy purse connected with the 'robber's' left shoulder.

"Mrs. Barrett, you're waking up half the town!" The manager wore a striped shirt that hung below his knees.

"I don't care." She halted her blows. "I came back from havin' a drink and this man was in my room! Probably trying to steal my jewels or waiting to—to *rape* me!" She spat the hated word.

"I wasn't—hell, this is my room, Jones! I don't know what's gotten into her!"

Jones shook his head. "He's quite right, Mrs. Barrett. You're on the other side of the hall."

Amelia Barrett opened her mouth in surprise, glanced at the number on the door, at the blushing male hotel guest, then at Mr. Jones. " I—" She heavily sighed. "I'm sorry." Her sweet smile deepened the wrinkles that covered her face. "I guess I made a mistake. I'm an old woman; I don't see very well."

"Yeah, I guess so," the battered man conceded. "But that don't give you the right to—"

"Now Mrs. Barrett," Jones said, cutting him off. "Why don't you go to your room and get a good night's sleep." Jones put his arm around her and steered her to the opposite door. "Let's just forget about this."

"I guess I should. I'm so sorry to cause you so much commotion." Amelia glanced down at the innkeeper's bare legs. "And to get you out of bed too."

"That's fine. Get a good night's rest." Jones glanced at Spur, curtly nodded and walked down the hallway, peppering his movement with soft curses.

McCoy watched it all in a daze, leaning against the wall in rumpled clothing, his reddish-brown hair tangled around his hatless head.

Amelia Barrett turned to Spur as the male hotel guest slammed his door shut. "My my, young man. You must think I'm an old fool. I don't know what got into me. Except maybe age." Her clear gray eyes fixed on Spur's. "I do declare. I *do* declare, young man. You're the 'xact image of my son Dale!"

Spur nodded groggily. "I'm . . . I'm happy for you." He started for his room.

"No, no, I mean it!" she said, catching his arm.

He wearily turned toward her. "Ma'am, I appreciate it, but I'm bone tired. If you'll excuse me." He groggily tipped an imaginary hat to her.

"Why, it's *remarkable* how much you look like him. If you were a little older there wouldn't be any difference a'tall! Not a'tall!" Her beady eyes shimmered in the dim light thrown by the kerosene wall sconces that lined the hotel hall.

Sleep, Spur thought. After forty-eight hours without it the last thing he needed was an old woman grabbing his arm. He thought of the bed that lay waiting for him—and his saddle.

"Tell me something about yourself!" Amelia said, as a smile rewrinkled her dry skin. "You remind me of him ever so and it's comforting to see you, to be reminded of him."

"I'm sorry. I gotta get my sleep."

"No!" She thought for a moment, then looked openly at him. "I need a drink, after that I definitely need a drink."

"Drink it in good health."

She gripped both his shoulders. "Young man, you don't mean to tell me that you'd let this old woman go to the saloon all alone, do you?"

Spur shook his head at her. "No," he said. "I mean yes. Hell, I don't know."

"I should think not! A fine upstanding man like you don't have any reason to let an old woman like me expose herself to all sorts of who-knows-what!"

"Frankly, ma'am, I don't have the time or the inclination. I need to get some sleep!" Spur felt anger rumble through his veins and, at the same time, felt foolish directing it toward a sweet-faced, gray-haired, old woman.

"Well then, do you—" She hesitated. "Do you think you could go to the saloon and get me a bottle of something?" She opened her beaded purse and retrieved a few dollars. "Anything that's got a kick to it?"

Spur sighed. If it meant he could get back into bed any sooner he'd agree. "Sure. Just let me get my hat." He went into his room, stuffed it onto his head, visually checked the saddle, went out and locked the door.

Amelia Barrett handed him the money. "I'll be in my room," she said sweetly. "Thank you ever so much, Dale!"

He smiled at the mistaken identity. "Okay."

McCoy walked to the saloon, cursing the woman with every step. If he hadn't checked on the scream he'd be asleep by then, but if it had been Beverly— no, he'd done the right thing.

Two blocks down he bought a small bottle of red wine at the saloon. It was still early in the evening and he passed several men and a few women on his way back to the hotel. As he watched one young, delicate thing sashaying by, his right foot pressed into something soft and gooey. Spur looked down —he'd stepped in a pile of horse droppings.

Scowling, he scraped off his boot and hurriedly returned to the hotel. He walked down the hallway —and saw the door to his room lying one-third open.

He had closed and locked it. The last traces of mist left his mind as he approached the opened door. Soft kerosene light made a golden arc on the well-rubbed wooden floor below it. McCoy slipped his hand down to his holster and lifted the long-barrelled Colt .45.

He kicked the door open.

"Oh!"

Spur dropped his aim as he saw the intruder—a gray-haired woman wearing a bonnet. She straightened up over his carpetbag. What the hell was she doing in his room? And how did she get in?

"Young man, what do you think you're doing, barging into an old woman's room like that?" Amelia demanded, her face red with rage.

Spur didn't buy it. Something was up. "Get lost again, Mrs. Barrett?" he asked sardonically.

The old woman faltered, looking like a naughty boy who'd tipped over an outhouse, then opened her mouth and let out a piercing scream.

"Shut up!" Spur said. He threw the wine onto his bed, stormed over to her and shook her shoulders. "That's not gonna work this time, Mrs. Barrett!"

The scream trailed off.

"What're you doing here? You can't convince me

that you've accidentally stumbled into two locked rooms twice within an hour—no matter how bad the locks or your eyes are."

"But I—"

"No. Don't say anything, grannie! We're going to talk to Mr. Jones."

Amelia Barrett retrieved her beaded bag from the bed. "All right! Maybe he can keep all these wicked men like you out of my room!"

Spur closed and locked his door, then escorted her to the front desk and banged on the bell. Soon afterward, as he firmly held the woman, the beleaguered innkeeper appeared.

"What in tarnation is it this time?" the Welshman thundered, then stopped. "Mrs. Barrett!"

"I think this sweet-faced old lady's a slick thief. Far as I can figure she cases guests and then breaks into their rooms when she thinks they won't be inside."

Jones turned to Amelia. "That right, Mrs. Barrett?"

"No! Why that's the most absurd thing I've ever heard! He's just trying to—to—"

"To explain why you've been caught breaking into other guests' rooms twice tonight?" He turned to Jones. "I just found her in my room after she sent me out on a little chore." Spur frowned.

"That's a little hard to believe."

"Sure; that's why it has to be true. Who'd expect her of something like that?" Spur pointed out.

"Hmm. Come to think of it, a young couple on their way to Yuma did find some things missing in their room yesterday. They left this morning." He scratched his stubbly chin.

"How long has she been staying here?" McCoy eyed the woman, who stubbornly kept her mouth shut.

"A week now. Says she's resting up before heading on out west."

"Appears she's doing more than resting. You better go get the law, Jones."

The innkeeper looked up quickly at Spur, then nodded. "Be right back. Don't let her go anywheres." He ran off.

"Well, Mrs. Barrett—"

"I have no apologies!" she said, her chin firm. "An old woman has to make her own way in this man's world as best she can. So just shut yer trap, you young buck!"

Spur smiled at the old woman.

An hour later Jones, McCoy and the sheriff checked the woman's room. They found three travelling bags full of paper money, gold coins, jewelry, pocket watches and various other items that the woman had pilfered. It amounted to a small fortune.

"Lock her up, sheriff!" Jones said.

Spur dragged himself into his room, locked the door and soon was fast asleep.

In the morning, Spur met Beverly in the hallway. She looked radiant in the bright sunshine that filtered in through the windows at each end of the passageway.

"How you feeling this morning?" he asked, grunting in appreciation of the way her bright red dress hugged her curved bust and hips.

"Wonderful!" Bev's eyes glistened. She dropped her dirty lilac bags, raised up on her heels, threw her arms around him and kissed his lips.

"Good morning to you too," Spur said, as she ended the kiss and licked her lips.

"When do we leave?"

"We?" Spur asked.

"Yes! When do we leave this miserable desert

behind and get on toward the coast, to San Diego and my cousin Trevor?"

Spur looked at her in silence. "Beverly, there's something I have to tell you."

Her smile faded. "What?" Bev seemed perplexed.

"Not here. Come to my room."

"Gladly!" She hefted the bags and followed him in.

Once there, Spur glanced at the saddle before turning to her. "Sit down—on the bed."

She did so happily and started unbuttoning her dress. "I was hoping you were in the mood!" The blonde giggled.

"No, that's not what I had in mind—" Spur said. He struggled to keep his thoughts clear. "Please, Beverly, just listen to me."

She stopped fumbling and sat quietly, folding her hands on her lap. "Okay, I'm listening."

"Beverly, I just want to warn you that I don't think it's a good idea for you to go with me to San Diego."

Her jaw fell open. "But why?"

"I can't tell you. It'd be dangerous for you to go with me. That's about all I can say."

She laughed. "Hell, what do you think it's been like without you?"

"No, Beverly, you don't understand."

She studied him. "What aren't you telling me? You aren't some kind of bank robber or something, are you?"

"No. Worse."

She thought for a moment, a finger to her lips, then shrugged. "Well, if you can't tell me then you can't tell anyone. And you can't give me a good reason for not going with you!" Beverly studied him. "Frank Burch, after what I've been through I don't relish the thought of travelling alone—not through these lands."

"I realize that, and sympathize with you, but there's quite a bit about me that you don't know. First of all, my name's not Frank Burch."

She nodded. "I didn't think so. The way you said it—" She shook her head.

"My name's Spur McCoy." He paused. How much should he tell her to let her know of the danger she was exposing herself to? "I'm a sort of lawman. I work for the government."

She smiled slyly. "A lawman! First one I ever had—or who's had me. So why all this secrecy?"

"I'm working on an important mission. I can't tell you what it is, but it's so dangerous that I—" He lowered his eyes. "I don't think it's a good idea for you to go with me."

"Why don't you let me be the judge of that, Spur McCoy!" she tilted her chin. "I kinda like the sound of that. You sure spurred me the other day." Beverly sighed. "Okay, all right! When's the next stage for Flagstaff tear outa here?"

"Noon today."

"Fine. Then I'll be on it. If you happen to be on it too, well, I'll just pretend I don't know you." She molded her lips into a pout. "I'd *hate* to get in the way of your precious mission."

Before Spur could respond to her taunt the woman dissolved into giggles, sending her breasts rolling and bouncing beneath the crimson dress.

"Beverly Thomas, you stop that!" Spur said. "I'm warning you, girl!" Spur's defenses weakened as she continued to explode before him. She collapsed on the bed and laughed.

"Allright, Miss Thomas. I can't stop you from riding the same stagecoach. But just remember—I warned you."

Her laughter trailed off as she sat upright and stared at him. "I'll remember. Now why don't you live up to your name and spur me again? Who needs breakfast?"

He obliged.

Five hours later they'd boarded the stage. Its grizzled driver, Mack Reynolds, grumpily took their money and hauled their luggage onto the rack. "Might as well leave now," he said, as Spur let Beverly onto the stage first. "No other customers today. Ever'one got off here."

Spur sat beside Beverly. Their thighs pressed together and she slipped his hand in hers as the carriage bolted into life and shot out of town.

The blonde woman laid her hand on Spur's shoulder. "I want it to be like this forever," she said, and licked his neck. "I don't want you to leave me."

Spur shivered as he felt the liquidy sensation. "Just remember, girl, we're not travelling together!"

Six hours later they'd started into mountainous terrain. The trail to Flagstaff rose dramatically from the desert floor. As they bounced higher and higher along the shoulder of a sweeping mountain Beverly clung to Spur. Her left hand slipped between his legs and gripped his crotch.

"Mmmmm," she moaned.

"Ah, Beverly, the driver," Spur said, enjoying the feeling.

"Let him get his own woman!"

As he responded to her intimate touch Mack Reynolds yelled and reined in the horses, sending them to a shuddering, hesitating stop.

"Damn!" Spur said, as Beverly retrieved her hand. They'd ridden into a small, isolated, high-altitude town. Poking his head out the small window as he adjusted his groin Spur saw a sign—they were in Flagstaff.

They hurried off the stage. "We stop here for the night," Mack Reynolds said. "Be on the stage first thing in the morning, right after sunrise." The driver leaned forward and threw Spur's saddle on the ground.

"Hey!" McCoy said, bending to grab it. "That's valuable merchandise! Don't go throwing it around, Reynolds!"

"I've waited a long time for this day, Spur McCoy!" someone said behind him. The voice was thick with Latin nuances.

Spur spun around. A short, stocky, long-haired Mexican man stood five yards from him, legs spread, feet planted on the ground, both hands hovering over his twin holsters.

"I've waited a long time to watch you die, gringo!"

10

"Have we met?" Spur asked the puny Mexican gunslinger as they faced each other off in the streets of Flagstaff.

"You know we have! You killed my men. Tucson, a few years ago. I watch them die when you shot them. Remember, gringo? Remember how you killed?"

Spur shook his head and dropped his saddle. "Never been to Tucson. You must have me mistaken for someone else."

He did recognize the man—Roberto Costa, a notorious, small-time crook who robbed banks and held up stage coaches. His face was plastered on walls throughout the west.

"Why, his name's not McCoy!" Beverly said, walking up beside him. "It's Burch. Frank Burch."

"Beverly, go away," Spur warned.

"*Si*, pretty lady. Wait for me in hotel room." Costa sneered at her.

"But—"

"Go!" Spur shouted.

Frowning, Beverly moved to the other side of the stagecoach and glanced up at Mack Reynolds, who rubbed his hands together in apparent delight at the excitement.

"I don't know who you are or what you want, but

93

I'd suggest you get the hell outa here before you go and get yourself hurt." He held his own hand over the holster strapped to his thigh.

The small Mexican laughed throatily. "You scare me," he said. "I shake in my boots."

Spur stared the man down. "I guess you do. Look, Costa—"

"Ah! You remember?" he asked.

"Yeah, I remember. I couldn't forget your ugly face if I tried. You're wanted for bank robbery, extortion, murder, rape, and horse-stealing!"

The Mexican crook frowned. "I never steal horse! You lie! I buy horse."

"There's a $5,000 reward on your puny little head, Costa. Every lawman in the area knows that. You're damn stupid to show your face to me again."

Costa grinned. "I have friends here. I get protection. I was not planning, just saw you. So watch your back, McCoy. You not leave Flagstaff alive!"

"And you won't leave Flagstaff at all." Spur took a step forward. "Just come with me to the sheriff's office, Costa. Your riding days are over."

Costa laughed. "No, lawman! No fuckeen way!"

"Shoot him!" someone nearby said. "Shoot the old snake!"

"Yeah, Costa, blow his brains out!"

"Yeah, prove how good a shot you are!"

Saddened by the show of humanity around him, Spur scowled. If he drew, he'd force the man's hand. Too many innocent bystanders around to shoot it out right there and then. Besides, he knew Costa was a lousy shot. Quick on his feet, but couldn't hit the side of a barn. That's why he had been so dependent on his men.

"Costa, you couldn't kill me if you tried. You'd miss if you pushed your six-guns to my gut and fired."

The man's face reddened. "What you say to me, gringo? You make insult?"

"You're the worst shot for a hundred miles, Costa! That's why you've been laying low here; you can't find any good men to ride with you. You're nothing without your backups; a coward, a knee-shaking, yellow-bellied coward!"

A dollop of spit oozed over the man's lips. "You —you are asking for it!"

"Go ahead and draw. I'm sure all your 'friends' here would love to see the ground soaking up your smelly blood!" Spur's hand danced over his holster, his fingers twitching.

"You talk big, McCoy. Too big. Now you no more talk." The short bank robber flipped up both shimmering silver-plated weapons and trained them on Spur's mid-section.

"Go ahead, asshole! Shoot! Do it in front of all these people you've been lying to! Let 'em see what a lousy shot you are! Waste your bullets in the street! Go ahead!" He folded his arms on his chest.

"No!" Beverly cried.

"Damn you, McCoy!"

"Yeah, shoot the big-mouthed bastard!" a wizened old cowboy said nearby.

"Go ahead, Costa; you've been talkin' big, do it!"

The man shook. His hands trembled as his gaze burned into Spur's.

"Coward!" McCoy barked. "Shoot me!"

"Please, Spur, I mean Frank, I mean—oh hell, don't do this!" Bev shouted.

Costa shook with rage. "You bastard!" His twin guns spoke.

Beverly screamed. Spur stood his ground. The slugs slammed into the dirt at his feet.

As the explosions died out the citizens of Flagstaff murmured to each other.

Roberto Costa stood panting, gasping, his eyes blank, as his streams of blue smoke drifted from the barrels.

Spur strode over to him and slammed his fist into the man's jaw. Costa jerked backward. The weapons flew from his hand as his chin split open, pouring out blood. The groaning Mexican hit the dust.

"You won't be robbing any more banks," Spur said. He glanced up, saw a man with a star pinned to his striped blue and white shirt. "You the law here?"

"Yeah!"

"He's all yours. That's Roberto Costa, wanted for three or four robberies. Big reward." He shot the man a glance. "But I guess you knew that, didn't you?"

The man arched his left eyebrow. "What can I say? Thanks! I—I shoulda done somethin' about him before, but I—I—"

McCoy felt a warm body pressing up against his. Beverly looked up at him, relieved, her face flushed.

"You sure know how to show a girl a good time!" Bev said.

"Come on."

Four blocks down the street in Flagstaff, a tall, wiry man busily pumped away on a stained mattress. He stared down at the plump woman beneath him, at her bored eyes, her slack jaw, her half-hearted attempts to show passion and involvement in their activity.

"More," Joanna said. "Oh yes. I cannot stand it. More. You're killing me with that thing. Do it harder." The whore's voice was flat, hollow.

He grinned. "I'm not paying you to talk."

"Okay, so I won't talk." She stared at the ceiling, avoiding her customer's empassioned, almost frightening leer. "Hurry up, wouldja? I'm hungry."

"Okay, missy. It won't be long now."

Lawson Amory closed his eyes as he worked the woman over. The thought of his future wealth heightened his excitement. His hips moved faster, his strokes grew more powerful, until each thrust sent the woman's head banging against the wall behind the bed.

"Hey, watch it!" she said.

"Fuck you!" Lawson said.

"You are, big boy, you are!"

"You little cunt! Hell, if you were any good I'd buy you and take you home."

"Oh sure," Joanna said. "Talk big to me."

"You don't know a damn thing about me. You don't know who I am or what I'm doing."

"I know what you're doin'." The whore smiled, showing a broken front tooth.

He snorted. "Tomorrow I'll be the richest man in the whole territory. Maybe richer."

"Right, and I'm Betsy Ross." She flared her nostrils with a sigh.

"No, damnit!" Lawson slowed down, frustrated. Her talk had taken him away from the edge of release. He sighed as he moved within her. Okay. He'd do it again, just one more time. It was worth it—who'd listen to a fat Flagstaff whore? Besides, it was the only way he'd been able to shoot for the past three weeks.

So he told her everything. As he talked the fire

burned between his legs. Sweat slicked his body,
his blood boiled as he related every move he'd
made, the defeats, the triumphs, all the planning
that had gone into his mission.

She took it in, bored, uncomprehending. He
smiled as he told her of how he'd sell them to the
hightest bidder, set himself up for life and kiss the
U.S. Government goodbye forever.

The image of the woman below him blurred. He
squeezed his eyes shut as he saw himself weighed
down with gold, every pocket overflowing, gold in
his hands, between his teeth, wallowing in it,
nearly suffocating in it.

He slammed into the squealing woman and
sealed his vision with the pure energy of raw sex.

Moments later, she pushed him off her. Lawson
luxuriated in the feeling of release. Warning bells
went off in his head—he'd showed his hand again,
threatening his whole mission.

But one look at the dead-eyed whore satisfied the
doubt. She was so stupid she probably didn't
understand a word he's said.

He was safe for another day or so until the next
whore.

Beverly Thomas and Spur McCoy sat down to
dinner in the hotel dining room. Four others were
there as well, nudging each other as they
recognized the man who'd brought down the
Mexican bandit in the street earlier that afternoon.

"I can't believe it!" Beverly said.

"I told you it was dangerous, hanging around
with me." Spur sipped a cup of bitter coffee.

"Dangerous?" She laughed. "It's about as
dangerous as collecting buttercups in a field in
Boston on a summer's day! You know how to take
care of yourself, Spur McCoy." She clasped his

and over the table. "Honestly, I can't think of when I've felt safer."

He smiled and shook his hand free to dig into his dinner.

"That man had two guns!" Beverly said, breathlessly. "Two! And you just stood there, begging him to shoot you!" Her light blue eyes were wide with admiration.

"That wasn't bravery," Spur said. "He really is a lousy shot. Let's just forget about it, okay?"

"Okay." Beverly made a visible effort to temper her enthusiasm.

They ate in silence, aware of the stares that the other diners darted at them—and of their whispers concerning the man who'd brought Roberto Costa down before their eyes.

Mack Reynolds, dusty from the stage coach, hurriedly undressed as the naked, dim-eyed saloon girl lay on her bed. Joanna watched him as he revealed his pitiful, white, fat body.

Another screw, another dollar, she thought idly.

"I want something extra," the stage coach driver said as he rustled out of his black pants.

"Like what?"

He shrugged. "I don't know. Surprise me."

The woman sat up. "How about some information?" Her mind raced as she formulated her words.

"Don't you talk fancy, girl!" Reynolds said, grinning. "Information? What kind of information?" He dropped his drawers.

She flinched at the sight of his ugly genitals. "Good information. Mister, you like to make money? I mean, real good money?"

"Yeah, I guess so, but I like to spend it too." He flipped her a silver dollar.

It landed on the bed beside her. Revulsion rose in

her throat as the smelly, smiling man sat beside her. She flinched from the touch of his body. She had to get out of this town, out of this business, and into a good marriage. She just couldn't take it any longer. Making some extra money that she wouldn't report to her boss would be a good start.

"Mister, I got some news that you might be interested in."

"What kind of news?" he asked, impatience hurrying his words.

"Just the kind that could make you rich."

He guffawed. "C'mon, Joanna; how'd a girl like you know something like that?" Reynolds cupped her left breast.

She squirmed away from him and pressed her back against the bed. She slid her legs firmly together. "I hear things. Lots of things from my men. And I heard something today." She shook her head. "You wanna know what it was?"

Reynolds slid a calloused hand between her thighs. "Sure, girlie. Tell me everything. Just spread 'em wide-like."

"Five dollars and I tell you everything." She caught his hand and, with forced playfulness, threw it back at him.

"Hey, what is this?" Reynolds asked.

"It'll be worth it, believe me." Joanna inhaled through her mouth to keep from sickening herself smelling the man's acrid sweat.

"And then you'll let me have fun with you? If I pay this extra money, I mean?"

She nodded. "Sure. You can fuck me every which way."

He quickly got the money and held it out to her. "This'd better be good, dolly, or I'll take it back from you."

She tucked the six silver dollars beneath the

mattress and stretched out on the bed. The slobbering man eased himself down on top of her, crushing Joanna with his weight.

"Tell me!" he said, growing aroused. "Tell me my five dollar's worth!"

Joanna took a deep breath, closed her eyes and repeated every word the tall man had told her about the dies for the gold double-eagle coin that were in town.

11

As Spur and Bev ate breakfast in the hotel's dining room, McCoy saw the stagecoach driver arguing with a young couple outside the window. They seemed to want to get on the stage but, apparently, he wouldn't let them on.

"It's time," Beverly said, wiping her lips with a lace handkerchief.

They'd already checked out, so the pair hauled their luggage—including Spur's saddle—out to where the stage was parked at the hotel's board-walk. The two teams of horses looked fresh and eager to be off.

"Some kind of problem?" Spur asked as he handed his saddle and carpetbag to the driver.

"Who? You mean that young couple?" Mack Reynolds snorted. "Wanted to ride for free. I told them what they could do with their free ride!"

"Can't you hurry?" Beverly asked. "The faster we get to Yuma the closer I'll be to the coast."

Reynolds jumped onto the driver's seat and feigned a bow. "If you'll step in, ma'am, we'll be on our way."

Spur helped her inside and sat across from her on the seats. "Guess we're alone again," he said pensively.

"So? Isn't it wonderful? Us here alone and him

103

up there where he won't bother us."

Mack Reynolds yelled and snapped his whip. The horses burst into action as the coach sped out of town.

"Yes . . . I guess it's wonderful." He shook his head.

She smirked. "What's wrong now, Spur? I mean, Frank?"

He'd told her to use that name when they were in public. Although she didn't know why, she had agreed to the plan.

"We'll be going through Indian country again pretty soon. A couple more able-bodied men who can shoot wouldn't be too bad."

"You can take care of us. And me."

Spur shook off the doubt. "You? Beverly, I don't know a thing about you. I feel like we've known each other for years but we only met a few days ago. Where you from?"

The blonde unpinned her bonnet and sat it on the seat beside her. Her hair fell to her shoulders. "There! That's better!" She affected a British accent. "I was born in Dover, in merry old England." Switching to her normal voice, Beverly explained, "But I really don't remember it. My father had gone to England on business—he was a ship-builder—and my mother happened to have me there just before they came back to the States.

"Anyway, I grew up in Boston in a big, old, ugly brick house by the bay. I can't complain about my childhood, I had everything I wanted, including this little gold-colored rope. All I had to do was pull it and a maid would show up and do whatever I asked." She shut her eyes. "I grew up wearing French dresses, eating caviar and *pate fois gras* for breakfast, had more money than I knew how to spend—but I was unhappy."

Spur smiled. It was a familiar story, but he asked her why.

"I didn't have any friends." Her high prominent cheekbones colored. "We lived four miles from the nearest road, out on a point of land. On one side the waves crashed below us and, on the other, trees stretched out to the road." Her face turned bitter. "My mother and father never talked to me, never kissed me goodnight or tucked me in. My family consisted of maids, butlers, groundsmen and stable boys."

Spur was silent.

Beverly brightened. "But that was okay. I didn't like them—either of them, so I pretended they didn't exist. It worked out fine, since they did the same thing to me."

"Why'd you leave home?" Spur asked. "Did you get married?"

Her eyes danced. "Not exactly. Oh, they tried. They tried to force me into marrying for six years, but I hated every man they introduced me to. They were all stiff-necked millionaire's sons whose wallets were probably bigger than their . . . well, *you know.*"

Spur nodded.

"Anyway, not long ago father went out looking for me. He found me out back near the trees with the stableboy. My bloomers were around my knees and, for some reason, the young man wasn't wearing his pants." She smiled at the memory. "That was too much for my parents. They handed me a thousand dollars, made me pack my bags and sent me off."

She paused. "So I thought I'd look up my cousin Trevor in San Diego. And that's why I'm here."

"I see."

Spur tried to picture Bev in those expensive

trappings but couldn't. She'd been raised to be a lady but—as she herself had said—she was much more than that. She was a woman.

"Enough about me," Beverly said. "Tell me about you. Why all this secrecy? Why this phony name and all that?"

Spur glanced behind him. The coach's noise probably drowned out most of their words so that the driver couldn't hear. But no sense in risking matters any further. He took her hands and leaned to her.

"No!" she said. "Don't say it! Let me guess. You can't tell me now." She studied him for a few seconds, lips pursed. "Is it something about that Robert Caustic or something?"

Spur smiled. "Roberto Costa and, in a way, it is something to do with that."

Beverly frowned at him.

"Believe me, Bev, it's better that you don't know."

She threw her hands up in the air. "Okay! Okay! Don't tell me. I'll just sit here and twiddle my thumbs until we get to Yuma."

"It's also safer if you don't know."

"All right! I won't ask you again." Beverly tossed her head, ran a hand through her mane, then drummed ten polished fingernails on the hard seat on either side of her. "So you're a lawman."

Spur laughed.

"And you're on some kind of secret mission."

He stared at her, darting his pupils back and forth.

"And it's dangerous, and somehow it involves Mexican—what's the word?—*banditos* and San Diego. How close am I?" Her eyes shone in the slanting sunlight.

He remained silent.

"Well, it looks to me like you're just lazing around, travelling from town to town, not doing much of anything, except helping out poor women in distress and inviting people to shoot you—and walking across the desert."

Spur grinned, crossed his wrists, laid them on the back of the seat and leaned his head against them. Beverly was amusing; he was enjoying this.

"I don't think you are a lawman, Sp—I mean, Frank Burch! I think you're just a—a—damn; I don't know what the hell you are!" She looked at him, perplexed.

He laughed out loud, jumped to the seat beside her and kissed her cheek.

"What's that for?" she asked as he pulled his lips from her face.

"For not asking me again!"

Two hours later Spur's butt was aching from constantly pounding on the hard seat. The stage coach rattled over the rocky, mountainous countryside, passing tall peaks. Some, thousands of feet high, were frosted with unreal-looking snow that glistened in the altitude-weakened sun.

They passed through tall, stout pine trees as they slowly made their way from Flagstaff. The driver let the horses pick their way down, not forcing them.

The time seemed to crawl by, Spur thought. Beverly, clasping his hand, had fallen asleep on his shoulder. He watched her as she napped.

Spur had begun snoozing himself when the stage came to a complete stop a few minutes later. He woke with Beverly at the snap of the reins and the driver's harsh voice. Spur stuck his head out the window.

"Why're we stopping?" he asked.

Mack Reynolds looked down at him, grim faced.

"You better come on out here, mister, and look at this."

"What the hell is it?" he asked.

"Just get out here!"

Cursing under his breath Spur opened the door. As his torso jutted out from inside the stagecoach McCoy felt a powerful blow strike his head. He groaned in surprise and pain and staggered forward for two steps. The agony increased, filling his brain and smothering his consciousness. His vision went black. His knees buckled. He was out before he hit the ground.

"Come on, shitface! Wake up!"

Spur groaned. The dull ache in his head, the hard ground pressing against him and the taste of dust in his mouth all told him where he was.

He opened his eyes. The brightness intensified the pain. As he closed them, Spur was aware of more pain coming from his ankles and wrists.

A low growl forced him to open his eyes again. Three feet away a scrawny, open-mouthed mountain lion snarled at him, saliva dripping from his razor-sharp fangs.

Spur groaned and shook his head. He ignored the pain as he looked at the big cat. It had been tethered to a dead, thin sapling. It tensed the rope and looked hungrily at McCoy, licking its lips, its eyes unblinking.

Beverly gasped. "Spur, I thought you were—"

"Shut your mouth, woman!" Reynolds yelled.

Ignoring the mountain lion, Spur tried to ease the strain in his shoulders and thighs but soon realized he couldn't. Ropes bit into his wrists and booted feet. They'd been tied together near the small of his back, completely immobilizing him.

He was hog-tied! Spur fought the bonds, struggled against them, flopping around on his belly like a gasping fish, as the cat continued to growl.

He heard a laugh. McCoy looked up and saw Mack Reynolds, the stagecoach driver, standing over him. "Save yer strength," he said. "You're gonna need it for talking."

"Spur, don't tell him—"

Reynolds spun on one boot and slammed his opened palm against Beverly's cheek. She screamed and wilted against the stagecoach.

"You bastard!" she said, rubbing the bright red hand-imprint.

"You'll get worse if you don't keep your fuckin' mouth shut, bitch! Maybe I'll feed you to the cat first! Hell, I ain't the kinda man who'll hurt a pretty woman, but you just might change my mind!"

Beverly fumed at him, but was silent.

Spur looked up at Reynolds as he turned back toward him.

"Well, Mr. McCoy, all comfortable?"

"Yeah." He blocked out the pain that rolled around in his skull and boiled up in his gut. "Reminds me of a saloon girl in Dodge City. This was her specialty."

Reynolds roared with laughter. "Cats and ropes? Hell, I ain't no saloon girl," he needlessly said.

"No. You're lower'n that. What the hell are you doing, Reynolds? Having a little fun?"

He tussled against the bonds, sending them scraping against his wrists and the tops of his boots. Spur McCoy was helpless. How the hell was he going to get out of this one, especially with that starved mountain lion staring at him?

"Sure, I'm having fun." He glanced at Beverly and groped his crotch. "I'll have some more fun later."

"If you lay one hand on me I'll kill you!"

"Hoowhee! I like a girl with spunk! But right now I'm all business."

"You look all bullshit from where I am," Spur said.

"You mean on your belly, hog-tied, seconds away from getting eaten by that big cat?" the driver snorted. "If I was in your position I'd shut my yap and listen. That's all you can do, far as I figure."

"What do you want, Reynolds?"

The man squatted before Spur, his back to the lion, and gazed down at him. "I want the two double-eagle dies you're transporting to San Francisco," he said evenly. "The ones you've had since you left Denver. And I want them now!"

Spur sighed. Again? Not again! "Reynolds, you must have shit fer brains. Where in hell'd you get such a stupid idea like that?"

He smiled. "None of your damn business! Are you gonna tell me where you're keeping 'em or do I have to use this?" He yanked a Bowie knife from his boot, waved it menacingly around McCoy's face, then pressed it against his neck.

"Maybe I could cut off your arms and legs, one at a time, until you told me. Or maybe I could start with your ears or fingers. Just chop you up into little pieces. Make it easy for that cat to gobble you up."

Beverly screamed again.

"Shut your mouth or I'll start on you, girl!" Reynolds yelled without turning from Spur. "What'll it be, lawman?"

Spur smiled. He had a plan. "Okay. So what happens if I do tell you? I suppose you'll just let me and the girl go. Right? Just leave us here . . . alive . . . with that mountain lion."

The driver spread out his hands. "But of course.

I'm not a violent man." The sunlight glinted on the razor-sharp blade as he waved it in the air.

The cat growled.

"I don't believe you."

"You got no choice, mister. No choice!"

The stagecoach driver's words stabbed the air, sending a fine spray of spittle onto his face.

McCoy flinched, then nodded. "Okay. I'll tell you."

12

With his hands and feet lashed together behind his back, Spur glanced over at Beverly. She shook her head at him, urging him not to, her eyes wild. He smiled at the blonde.

"Okay, I'll tell you where I hid them," Spur repeated.

"About time, McCoy!" Reynolds thundered. "I already know they aren't in your carpetbag or in your pockets. Hell, I looked under your hat and took off your boots to look there, but didn't find them. And hell, I had to put 'em back on. Your feet stink. So where are they?"

Spur thought fast. "My boots."

"I just tole you I looked in your boots!" Reynolds screamed. "What're you trying to pull?"

"Did you look inside them?"

Reynolds scowled. "You want me to let that big cat chew on you for a while, McCoy? Don't talk shit. What the hell do you think I just said?"

"Did you look *inside* them?"

"Hell, boy, talk straight? I'm getting damned tired of this bullshit!" He knelt and pushed the big Bowie knife against Spur's neck again.

Beverly gasped as the steel blade drove into the soft tissue a fraction of an inch. A bright red droplet rolled down from the wound. The mountain lion sniffed the air and roared at the smell of fresh blood.

"Did you look inside the heels?" Spur asked.

Reynolds withdrew the knife and sat back. "What're you talking about?"

"The heels. My boot heels. Did you look inside them, or just inside my boots?"

Reynolds laughed. "Matter of fact, I didn't. Mighty fancy place to hide 'em, McCoy! I never would've found them there. Now you just hold still while I take a look." The driver moved over to Spur's feet. His big, calloused hands gripped the squares of black leather and tugged on them.

Spur gazed at the mountain lion as the man worked over his boots. "Nice kitty," he whispered.

"You better not be shittin' me, McCoy!"

"I ain't."

Spur glanced up at Beverly. She stood still, hugging herself, shaking her head.

After struggling with them for a few seconds Reynolds tore his hands from the boots. "How the hell do I get into those damned things? I don't see no cuts anywhere, no place where you plugged up a hole!"

"You gotta take them off," Spur said. "I pulled up the lining, dug holes in the soles and stuffed the dies in. Then I glued the lining back down so it wouldn't attract attention, just in case."

"You could have told me that in the first place!" Reynolds huffed. "I guess we'll just have to get these things off."

He tugged at Spur's boots, pulled on them, yanked as hard as he could, but they wouldn't budge. The rope he'd tied around them kept them firmly planted on his feet.

"Take it easy!" Spur said. "Christ, you wanna

ip my feet off?"

"Better me than that cat. Damn! They're not comin' off!"

Spur was silent as the man thought it out. Go ahead, he said in his mind. Go ahead and do it.

"Guess I have to untie 'em after all. Don't go and do anything stupid, asshole! That cat smells its dinner. Now that I know where you hid 'em, your life ain't worth shit to me."

"I won't do anything stupid," Spur said, pretending weariness.

Mack Reynolds worked quickly. First he cut the head between Spur's bound wrists and feet. McCoy obediently let his feet and hands flop down. He felt the man's knife slice through the knotted rope around his boots, tearing away at the coarse fibers a few at a time, working the blade into the mass until the last strand popped open.

His feet were free.

"Hold still," Reynolds said.

Spur waited until the big hands pressed around his ankles. He sharply yanked his legs apart and sent both feet rocketing up to smash into Reynold's face.

"Shit!" the man said, as the hard leather soles broke his nose and split both lips.

His hands still bound behind his back, Spur scrambled up into a sitting position and drove his boots into the groaning driver's stomach. The Bowie dug into the ground as the big man toppled over, yelling, covering his torn face with his hands.

Jumping to his feet, Spur struggled against the ropes. They wouldn't break. Reynolds hadn't left him enough slack to wriggle out of them.

The driver stumbled up into a standing position directly in front of the now pacing mountain lion. Blood poured from his nose. Spur gritted his teeth, bent at the waist and charged at him. His head slammed into Reynold's stomach. The driver grabbed McCoy's shoulders just as he tipped over.

Spur wrenched himself free. The big hands slipped off. Mack Reynolds crashed down onto the dead tree that held the mountain lion and broke it in two, releasing the animal.

The enraged cat, surprised at its freedom, roared and jumped onto the stagecoach driver. Reynolds screamed as vicious teeth tore into his arm, slicing through veins and arteries, ripping apart the skin. The mountain lion's mouth turned red with blood. The big man tried to fight off the cat but its teeth held him close.

Spur stood watching for a second, then turned and searched for the knife. There it was.

"Beverly!" he yelled above the agonized screams of the lion's living human meal. "Beverly!" He shouted louder.

She turned to him, tears streaking her cheeks.

"Get the knife and cut me loose! Hurry!"

"But—" She pointed at the wrestling man and mountain lion.

"Do it!"

Blubbering, she retrieved the Bowie from the dirt.

"Come on, cut the rope!" Spur turned his back on her.

Bev worked quickly, her sobbing increasing as Mack Reynold's screams intensified.

Cat and human thrashed on the dirt as Spur finally felt the pressure vanish from around his wrists. He shrugged out of the rope fragments and grabbed Beverly's hands. "Let's get the hell out of here!"

"But that man—he's—"

Spur picked up his saddle where it had been

hrown on the ground and yanked the blonde
oward the stagecoach. He threw it inside.

Mack Reynolds passed out as the mountain lion
ipped off his left arm at the shoulder and gnawed
ontentedly on it. Pints of fresh blood oozed from
is maw. Torn muscle tissue and arteries stuck
etween his reddened teeth.

"Come on!"

Spur pushed Beverly Thomas into the stage,
lammed the door shut and hopped onto the
lriver's seat. The horses were skitterish, whinney-
ng at the violence and blood. He slapped the reins
nd yelled. The two teams jolted forward into
ction, happy to tear away from the scene of
arnage.

As they reached the rocky trail Spur stood and
hanced a look behind him. He watched as five
ingers slipped down the big cat's throat.

Hours later in a dusty Yuma hotel room they
istened to mariachi music filtering up to them
rom the street below. Fresh from their baths, Spur
at slumped on the bed while Beverly nestled her
ead in his crotch and closed her eyes.

"I can still see it—all of it."

He kissed her head. "I know. I can too."

"It was so—so horrible, Spur. I mean, that lion
te him alive!"

"Just be thankful it wasn't us."

She shivered. He smelled roses in her hair.

They'd made it to the next stop and had
xplained to its proprietors most of what had
appened. Not all of it, just that the driver had
een killed by a mountain lion during a piss-stop.
After digging into his funds, Spur had rented two
orses and a saddle from the stage stop's
roprietors.

They'd eaten, loaded up on provisions and water and then rode through the rest of the afternoon and night, finally reaching Yuma just before dawn.

Now, as they listened to the loud, cacophonous music of the roving Mexican band, Spur rubbed his lips against Beverly's.

"We've made it," he said.

She looked up him hopefully.

"This far."

Beverly was silent for a moment. "And what about tomorrow?"

"We'll have to wait that out."

During their long trip Beverly hadn't pressed him for details. She hadn't asked him about the double-eagle dies or anything else that the man had said. However, he did notice her glancing at his boots at odd moments.

Once, while they were riding side by side on the trail to Yuma before dark, she gazed at his right boot for several seconds, her eyes moving as it bobbed in the stirrup. When he'd caught her looking she shifted her gaze to the ground below his mount.

Spur figured that she either didn't want to know or didn't want to bring back the horror of the driver's death by asking him about it.

"I didn't put them in my boots," he said softly, still looking into her eyes, as they lay on the bed.

"You didn't put what—oh." She moistened her lips. "Where did you put them?"

He shrugged. "Guess. You're the lady detective."

Beverly frowned, then looked around the room. "That man said they weren't in your bags. If they aren't in your boots or in anything you have on—" She looked up at him triumphantly. "Your saddle. You put them in your saddle!"

McCoy smiled. "Very good, young woman, very good. You are an astute observer."

"Oh, thank you kindly, sir. And just what is my reward for being such an astute observer?"

Spur smiled. He recognized the fire in her eyes and realized there was only one way for Beverly Thomas to exorcise the terror she'd been through.

Though he was bone-tired, though his wrists were slashed with red rope-burns, the tiny hole on his neck stung and his back still ached from the uncomfortable position, he felt his excitement growing.

What the hell, he told himself. "You know what your reward's gonna be," he said, and smiled at her.

She slid to the floor and began tussling with her dress. "Close the curtains, will you, Spur? I think they can see in here from the building across the street."

Spur nodded and went to them. As he reached for the dust-caked, flimsy curtains his gaze zeroed in on the figure of a tall man walking down the street in the early morning light.

For some reason the face captured his interest. McCoy strained his eyes as the man approached the hotel.

Lawson Amory, Spur thought, when the face came into focus. Lawson Amory in Yuma!

"Spur, you coming back to me?" Beverly asked.

He shut the curtains and turned to the blonde woman. "Sure, honey."

"Anything wrong?"

"No. Just thought I saw someone I knew."

What was a Secret Service agent doing in this town? Why hadn't he been informed that Amory would be here? And why did Spur have this nagging feeling.

13

Lawson Amory walked down the dusty street, spitting trails of saliva. Spur McCoy should be in town by now, he mused, watching the men who passed him, searching for the now familiar mutton-chop sideburns and the brown hat ringed with Mexican coins.

Yuma was the last town in Arizona Territory before the border of California. Even in the early morning sun it baked with a dry heat. But it was alive.

Chickens scurried before a large Mexican woman who flailed her arms in a vain attempt to catch them. Drifters slept off their whiskeyed nights in the shadows that hugged adobe walls along the broad avenue. A boy of fifteen tagged behind a colorfully dressed—but far from talented—mariachi band as it blasted its way down the street, alternating music with vociferous announcements that somebody-or-other's cantina had just opened for business.

Amory saw no sign of the Secret Service agent but knew he would find the man. He always did. And this time—this time he'd get the dies from him.

Amory had known that it wouldn't be an easy task. He'd prepared as well as he could, for Spur

McCoy's ability to handle himself with his body
and mind were legendary throughout the service.
McCoy was held up as the supreme example of
what a good agent should be like.

As he wandered down the dusty street, sweat
popping out on his neck, Lawson Amory felt
energized. He was going up against the best. He
was going for the biggest prize. He'd risked everything, given up everything for it.

And soon, after he'd tired of playing with the
man, it would be his.

After his latest sexual romp, Spur trailed the
chilling water over Beverly's left breast. Beverly
squirmed as the white cloth pressed against her
mound and droplets slid down her naked body to
soak onto the towel below her.

"Too cold?" Spur asked as he dipped the cloth
back into the flower-festooned ewer.

"No. It's delicious."

They bathed each other until the last traces of
sweat and sex lay seething in the clouded water
and the pitcher sat empty.

As he towelled Beverly, Spur thought back to
what he knew about Lawson Amory. The man was
an agent, that much was for sure, for they'd been
introduced at some party during one of his
infrequent trips back to Washington, D.C.

Amory was tall and wiry and an excellent shot.
Spur seemed to remember hearing that he was
skilled in Indian ways, knew how to move through
heavy brush, could live off the land if he had to.

They'd been introduced—how long ago was it
now? A year? Two? Spur couldn't remember. But
the name, the man's craggy face and height had
stuck in his mind.

Spur dug the towel between Beverly's round, full

white buttocks. She giggled as he moved it lower
and touched it to her lips.

The image of a shadowy face flashed through his
mind. McCoy yanked away the towel.

"Hey! Just when I was enjoying it!" Beverly
said, protesting.

When he didn't respond the bare blonde bent
over and looked at him between her shapely legs.
"You still there, Spur!"

"Yes. Just thinking."

She sighed and grabbed the towel. "If you're
gonna think let me do you now."

Spur was barely aware of her attention as he
remembered the face he'd seen—briefly—in the
darkened Little River hotel room. Amory? It could
be. Lawson Amory might have been the man who'd
broken into his room, stuck a revolver into
McCoy's mouth and threatened to pull the trigger.

It didn't make sense. Agents didn't go around
threatening each other. Unless . . . unless he had
been mistaken. Unless the man had gone crazy.

Or unless Lawson Amory no longer worked for
the U.S. Government.

"Mmmmmm." Beverly roughly stroked Spur's
hairy, muscled thighs and dabbed at the droplets
of water that clung to his pubic hairs.

He shook the confusion from his mind. No sense
in wasting energy just wondering. He'd better
send a telegram to the home office and find out
what the hell was going on.

The soft cloth moved lower. Spur smiled. " Dry
me some more there."

The towel flicked back and forth, up and down.

Perhaps Amory had heard about the movement
of the dies. He was certainly in a position to do so.
Maybe over drinks with one of the other pseudo
couriers he'd heard the news and had seen his

opportunity.

Maybe.

Spur smiled down at Beverly. "Let's get dressed. I have some things to do."

A half hour later Spur had sent a telegram to General Halleck in Washington. In it, in plain, simple language, he asked what Lawson Amory's current job was. Might as well end that avenue of thought quickly if the man was still in the service or if he was somewhere else in the country.

After all, he could be wrong about seeing Lawson there in Yuma and about identifying the man in his Little River hotel room as Amory.

Bevery had donned a bright yellow sun dress, with a matching bonnet and a small parasol. As they strolled down the boardwalk, dodging Mexicans as well as Anglos, Spur searched for the tall Secret Service man.

The smell of Yuma rose up around them. Onions, peppers, frying tortillas and beans, spicy pork and stale lard filled the air. The pungent aroma of horse droppings littering the street mixed with the more appetizing odors, causing Beverly to push a handkerchief over her face.

"I don't like this place," she said summarily behind the silk cloth. She surveyed the flat, barren land. "There's no trees, no flowers, only dust and dirt and sand and that horrible music."

Spur smiled. "Come on; it's not so bad when you compare it to where we were this morning. At least there's no mountain lion here."

She shivered. "Thanks for reminding me."

They approached a long, solid-looking building. "What's that?" Beverly asked.

"It's a great place to visit," Spur said with feigned excitement. "That's the Yuma Territorial Prison."

She pressed closer to him. "I knew I didn't like this place!"

He laughed as they passed it.

Soon they saw a crowd gathering on a corner up ahead and joined it. The object of their attention was a round-cheeked, sweating, bald-headed man holding up a mysterious blue-glassed bottle.

"Yes, ladies and gentlemen; the miracle cure of the 1800's! Professor Johnson's Liquid Elixir! Cures whatever ails you! Chills, infirmities, colds, weak hearts? Just take a spoonful of this magic philtre and be cured!"

"Does it grow hair on your head?" a cowboy asked.

The bald-pated snake oil man smirked. "That's the only thing it won't do, sir! Barrenness? Deformities of the limbs? Curvature of the spine? This'll do the trick! Professor Johnson's Liquid Elixir! Patented in the year of our Lord 1860! Good for whatever ails you! One thin dollar per bottle to cure your fatigue and fainting spells!"

"I'll take a bottle," a grizzled old-timer said. He proffered a dollar bill.

"Bless you, father," the salesman said, quickly exchanging bottle for money. "Potions and lotions and nostrums! Good for whatever ails you! Who'll be next?"

"What—what's he doing?" Beverly asked. She was fascinated by the man's tirade.

"Trying to make some drinking money," Spur said.

"I've never seen anything like this," Beverly said, her aquamarine eyes shining below her bonnet. "I think I'll get a bottle."

"No, Beverly, don't. You're just wasting your money. Trust me."

"Well, if nothing else it'll be a keepsake. And the

bottle's pretty too." She dug into her purse and handed a dollar bill to the drummer.

"Thank you, young lady," he said. "Good for women's sickness too."

Beverly grasped the thin bottle in her hands and removed the cork. She smelled it and wrinkled up her nose.

Spur smiled and surveyed the crowd. Across the street, near See's Livery Stables, Spur saw Lawson Amory glance at the crowd and dawdle aimlessly down the street.

Spur was certain the man hadn't seen him. He fought off the urge to follow Amory, unwilling to drag Beverly into the problem or to leave her alone on the street. Itching to confront the man, he glanced back at her.

Beverly held the opened bottle in her hands. "Might as well try it." Before Spur could stop her she put it to her lips and tilted it, swallowing half of its pinkish contents.

Beverly immediately pulled the bottle from her mouth, dropped it and retched. She pressed one hand against her chest and coughed, gagged, as the 'medicine' tortured her throat.

"You all right?"

The beautiful blonde woman paled and coughed, bending at the waist as her body tried to expel the liquid. She shook her head.

The crowd—and the drummer—turned to watch the choking woman.

"Hey, salesman, that's what your miracle cure does?" Spur escorted the gasping woman back to her hotel room.

Beverly stretched out on the bed in her sun-splashed room, fanning herself and sipping a glass of water.

"You all right?" Spur asked, turning over the

lue bottle in his hand.

"I'm fine now. I feel so foolish, being taken in by
hat—that—"

"Snake oil man." He frowned. "This curing elixir
eems to be nothing but castor oil, grain alcohol, a
ash of perfume and some kind of coloring." Spur
lanced at her. "It could have been worse."

Beverly nodded. "I know. Thanks."

Two hours later, Spur felt all the coffee he'd
runk that morning threatening to split him in
wo. He excused himself and headed for the two-
ole outhouse behind the hotel. He pushed the
ickety door open and stepped inside, turned and
hut it.

Spur grabbed his buckle. The door suddenly shot
pen. Surprised, McCoy looked up. Lawson Amory
tood pointing a shotgun at his gut.

"We meet again, McCoy." Amory smiled.

"Yes, I guess we do, Amory. What the hell are
ou doing in Yuma? You on government
usiness?"

Amory stepped into the doorway. "Not really.
ust setting myself up for the future."

The barrel prodded Spur's stomach.

No time for talk. McCoy kicked the door. It
umped forward, groaned on its hinges and banged
gainst the shotgun. Spur jumped as the big
veapon exploded, peppering the door with lead.

"Bastard!" Amory yelled outside.

Standing on the seat, Spur yanked the door open
nd drove a foot into Amory's face. The tall man
roaned and reeled backward, firing another load
f buckshot into the air.

McCoy pounced on the man, knocked him to the
ock-strewn ground and straddled his legs. He
vrestled the weapon from the agent's hands and

bashed the stock twice into Amory's forehead before the man gurgled and lay still.

Panting, Spur rose and stared down at the unconscious man. He hadn't been wrong. Lawson Amory wasn't on any assignment. He was in Yuma to steal the dies! Hell, he must've been following him from the day he left Denver.

McCoy didn't attract any attention as he hauled the man to the local sheriff's office.

"What's this?" Sheriff Oscar Tate said as Spur entered the small, squat building with Amory in tow.

"This man attacked me while I was tryin' to piss." Spur dumped Amory on the floor and wiped his gritty neck.

"And who the hell are you?" The thick-waisted man looked at Spur with narrow eyes. He ran a finger through his thick, prematurely-grey beard.

"Spur McCoy."

The man laughed. "Sure, and I'm President Grant."

"You've heard of me?"

"Of course I've heard of Spur McCoy—not you. Every lawman this side of the Mississippi's heard of McCoy. You got some kinda proof?"

Spur sighed and dug out the telegram he'd received from General Halleck detailing his latest job. He handed it to the doubting sheriff and looked down at the prone man.

Tate grunted. "Well, okay, suppose'n you are Spur McCoy—and I ain't saying you are. What the hell you want me to do with this man?"

"Keep him locked up. I don't know exactly what's going on here but I intend to find out. I sent a telegram to the home office in Washington; should get a reply soon. Maybe that'll clear up this whole matter."

Tate looked down. "You know who he is?" The sheriff planted his folded hands on his protruding belly.

"Lawson Amory. Do me a favor, sheriff; just keep him under lock and key until I get back."

Tate nodded. "Tell me more about this mission you're on."

Spur frowned. "I can't talk about it, Tate. And I'd rather you didn't tell folks around here who I was. Got that?"

"Sure, sure, sure. Okay, I'll corral him for now. What's the charge? Assault?"

"Attempted murder would do as well. He pulled a shotgun on me."

"Okay, okay, McCoy." Oscar Tate smiled amicably. "Good to have you in this hell-hole, if you really are who you say you are."

"Right." Spur grimaced and returned to his hotel room.

Three hours later, after playing ten hands of cards with a completely-recovered Beverly, he checked at the telegraph office.

"Just came in," the squinting clerk said. Leaning on a cane, he walked to a box stuffed with envelopes and rifled through them. "Here we go, sonny."

"Thanks." Spur walked out into the sunlight and read the message that the clerk had recorded in his barely legible scrawl.

LAWSON AMORY NO LONGER EM-PLOYEE OF U.S. GOVERNMENT . . . STOP . . . TERMINATED HIS EMPLOY-MENT THREE WEEKS AGO . . . STOP . . . NO WORD ON CURRENT WHERE-ABOUTS . . . STOP . . . GOOD LUCK . . . STOP.

It was signed General Wilton D. Halleck
(retired).

Spur crumpled the yellow paper and stuffed it
into his pocket. Amory wasn't a Secret Service
Agent? It was time he talked to the man.

He dug his heels into the dirt and sped toward
the sheriff's office.

Oscar Tate was stuffing a huge forkful of deep
dish apple pie into his mouth. He waved at Spur
and motioned to his busy mouth.

Nodding, Spur glanced at the two cells behind
the man. Both were empty.

Blood pounding in his brain, McCoy slammed a
fist onto Tate's desk.

"Where the hell's Lawson Amory? Where's the
man I brought you just a few hours ago?" he demanded.

Tate swallowed and licked crumbs from his lips.
"I let him go."

"You what?"

"I let him go! Hey, McCoy, anyone can make a
mistake." He tongued apple goo from his teeth and
gulped it down. "Seems the man you had me lock
up was some kind of lawman too—the Secret
Service, I think he called it." Tate shook his head.
"Anyway, he showed me some kind of document
that looked pretty damned convincing to me. He
told me you're Spur McCoy all right and said you'd
made a mistake. So I let him go."

"Damnit, Tate! You don't know what you've
done!"

"The hell I don't!" The sheriff's face grew red.

Spur retrieved the crumpled telegram he'd just
received and threw it at the sheriff. It landed on
the pie.

"Get a mouthful of that!"

Grumbling, the corpulent man removed it from

his dessert, smoothed out the paper, read it and frowned. "So what's this mean?" The fat sheriff burped.

"Can't you read? Lawson Amory is no longer an agent. You let a renegade Secret Service man out of jail—a man who just tried to kill me. Jesus, Tate, you don't deserve to wear that star on your chest!"

"Like I said; anyone can make a mistake." He curled his upper lip. "But I don't care who you are, get the fuck outa my office!" Tate filled his mouth with more apple pie.

Spur grabbed the telegram and stormed from the place, his face reddened with rage. He cooled off as he neared the hotel. Served him right for trusting that slick-tongued man to a small-town sheriff.

So Amory was free again. The ex-Secret Service agent was somewhere in town, waiting for his next chance.

And Spur had better be ready for him.

14

In a dry wash five miles outside of Yuma, Lawson Amory rubbed his aching head and took another swallow of whiskey, then another. The alcohol soothed the dull throbbing in his forehead, tranquilized his bursting hatred, lulled him into a hazy, peaceful state.

Moments later he smiled in spite of himself, as he remembered how he'd woken in the cell, quickly collected his thoughts and outsmarted that stupid sheriff into setting him free.

As the wood-flavored liquid burned down into his stomach Amory tipped some water from his canteen into a small coffee pot and hung it from the crude tripod he'd constructed. As it brewed he settled back against the hard-packed sand wall and thought of how he'd come to be there.

He'd been born to a common whore in Philadelphia and left on the steps of an adoption agency at the age of two. Three years later a wealthy Philadelphia family, unable to have children of their own, adopted him and brought him into their world.

Lawson had grown up knowing he was an outsider, and his adopted father and mother had continually reminded him of how lucky he was to have been spared the torture of living in an adoption agency until his eighteenth birthday.

With his increasing years—including stints at private schools—Amory became less and less enchanted with his parents. When he was nineteen years old he'd balked at his father's offer to join the business—cash register and scale manufacture —and accepted a lucrative offer from one of the old man's major competitors.

Summarily disinherited by his family and bored at his new job, Amory joined up during the great war. He excelled in combat and enjoyed promotion after promotion. His father, intrigued by his son's advancement and the extra prestige it would give him in the yankee business world, pulled strings to get Lawson a lieutenant's commission.

Once the North had won and he'd entered civilian life, his father had again approached him to enter the family business. But again he'd snubbed the man.

Looking for a new career, Lawson Amory had joined the Secret Service shortly after it had been created to ferret out counterfeiters and to protect U.S. currency. During his army career he'd acquired a taste for danger and felt a rush of intense, undefineable excitement every time he faced another human being and blasted him into the next world.

However, Secret Service life wasn't what he'd thought it would be. Sure, there were times when he saw action, when he never knew if the next breath he took would be the last, but for twelve months he'd been doing nothing but sitting in Washington D.C. squiring around gold shipments and romancing senators' daughters.

He'd wasted his days and spent his nights locked between the thighs of plump women yearning for a real life, the kind that could only be won or lost by his skills at firearms.

During his years in the Secret Service he'd heard of the exploits of one Spur McCoy. The man was damn near famous for his ability to complete his assignments no matter how tough, impossible or dangerous they were.

A few weeks ago Harris, a new agent who'd been with the service for only a year, took him out for a drink to celebrate. Harris's new assignment, the greenhorn had told him, was to act as a decoy courier.

Amory hadn't been too interested until he heard who—and what—he was the decoy for. Dissatisfied with his life, thirsting for excitement, Amory saw his chance to live the moneyed life he'd once enjoyed, as well as the opportunity to pit himself against the foremost Secret Service agent.

He'd spent a week gently grilling Harris for details, then quit the service once he'd learned of Spur McCoy's plans and had mapped out his journey.

Somewhere between Denver and San Francisco he'd get the dies and settle down where the women were pretty, the whiskey was full-strength, and life was a mosaic of shootouts, spent shells and blood-soaked dirt.

A low hissing noise brought Amory back to the present. The water was boiling over the fire. Amory lifted the pot from the tripod and quickly set it on the sand. Soon, he told himself. Soon he'd be ready.

The dark-skinned man looked down and ripped the home-made knife from the uniformed guard's bleeding back. He pressed a shaking hand against the man's neck. No pulse.

Good. He was dead.

Glancing both ways, the prisoner bent and quickly stripped the guard. He had no more than two minutes. Once the dead man lay in his underwear, the Mexican tore off his drab clothing and dressed. The pants were too long, so he rolled them up. The shirt was far too big but he tucked in the tails and tried to smooth its billowing back against his body.

Working methodically, breathing evenly, the prisoner stuffed his feet into the black shoes and stood upright. He mentally checked himself, running his fingers over the buttons, making sure everything was in place.

It seemed right. He gripped the dead man's hat and put it on his head, then padded softly down the blank corridor. The door at the far end grew closer and, with it, his chances for freedom.

Ten more yards, the prisoner thought, as he moved in the uncomfortable, two sizes too big uniform.

"Hey! You there!" an American called as he passed an intersecting hallway.

The prisoner grunted and continued on.

"Hell, I'll tell you later."

The prisoner released his breath. Five more yards. Two. One.

He pushed the key into the lock. It hesitated, locked and turned the tumblers. He yanked it out and burst outside.

Free from the prison, the Mexican bolted down the darkened street. Few people were on the street; the stores were closed. The smell of tobacco and whiskey urged him into the first saloon he passed but the prisoner fought his desires. There were more important things to do.

He breathed heavily with excitement and fear.

He'd gotten out. He'd escaped! The bumbling Americans had left him the perfect opportunity and he'd taken it. All he had to do was get out of town. Somehow.

A familiar uniform approached him a block up the street. The prisoner panicked and bolted down a dark alley. Think, his mind screamed. A narrow stairway led to the second floor of the back of some building.

The Mexican went up it, three steps at a time, and tried the knob at the top. The door opened. He slipped inside and pressed his back against the wall.

A hotel. He was in a hotel corridor. The Mexican smiled. He'd need regular clothes anyway. He stuffed his hands into his pockets and once again retrieved the small ring of skeleton keys. It was worth a try.

Footsteps resounded from below. Someone was coming up the stairs. He ran three steps to the door opposite him and stuffed a key into the lock. It wouldn't budge. Frantic, he fumbled with the ring, found another key and pushed it into the hole.

It turned. The knob opened under his sweating hands. Inside, he slammed the door shut. The kerosene lamp was low but he saw the carpetbag on the bed and the saddle on the pillow.

Hurry, he urged himself. Change and get the hell out of there. Before they put you back into the living hell that is the Yuma Territorial Prison!

"Honestly, I can't wait to see the blue waters of the Pacific Ocean." Beverly sipped a glass of milk as they ate in the hotel dining room.

"It's not much different from the Atlantic," Spur observed. "Just another ocean."

"Oh Frank, you're such a romantic," the woman

deadpanned. "I don't care. It's so—far away, so mysterious." She smiled and wiped her lip with a napkin. "California!" Her voice was breathless. "Flower-draped *ranchos*. White missions shimmering in sunlight. The smell of golden poppies."

"That's not why you're going there."

She pursed her lips. "No. You're right. But I can dream about it anyway, can't I?"

Spur shrugged. "Sure. Until you realize it's an untamed, harsh, barely civilized frontier."

"It can't be any worse than this place."

"I won't argue with you there. San Francisco's a big town but San Diego's just a fishing village with a mission."

"My cousin Trevor said he's doing quite nicely in that 'fishing village,' buying and selling land."

"We'll see once you get there." He pushed away his plate and stifled a burp. "Boy, that was one good dinner."

Beverly's eyes sparkled. She leaned closer to him. "Would you like dessert—in your room upstairs?"

He squirmed as the whisper tickled his ear. The woman was insatiable. "Sure."

She gripped his hand as they climbed the stairs. "How long until we get to San Diego?"

"Two, three days at most."

"And then you'll be going to San Francisco?" Beverly asked as they reached the landing.

"That's right."

"Hmmmmmm."

Spur stopped them in front of his door. He pushed the key into the lock but the door opened.

"Stay back, Bev." Spur banged the door open.

The room was empty, the lamp still low. He turned up the flame.

"Everything okay?" Beverly asked as he walked in.

Spur hesitated. His carpetbag had been over-turned. His belongings were scattered across the polished wooden floor. Spur's gaze darted to the bed. The pillow was creased with deep impressions —and his saddle was gone.

"No, it isn't."

15

"Can I come in?" Beverly Thomas asked, peering into Spur's hotel room.

"It's gone!" Spur thundered.

"What's gone?"

"I left it here an hour ago—less than an hour!" Spur yelled. "Of all the stupid things . . . ."

Beverly glanced around the room. "My god! You've been robbed!" She pressed her hand to her mouth.

"Yeah, and the saddle's missing." Had Amory stolen it? Not likely. He didn't know where the dies had been hidden. Noticing something that had been pushed under the bed, Spur pulled out a dirty, torn prison uniform.

"You mean the saddle that you—"

Spur nodded, rose and flipped her his key. "Lock the place up. I'll be back—sometime." He strode to the door.

"What's that supposed to mean?" Beverly asked, fumbling with the slender iron key.

"I'll be back when I find that saddle and not before!"

The air outside was still warm from the heat of the day. Two carriages rushed by, kicking up clouds of dust. Spur pumped his arms as he headed

141

for Sheriff Tate's office. As he arrived there he saw
four men tying their mounts to the rail before it.
Dim light spilling out from the windows of the
sheriff's office lit the men up.

"Where's Tate?" Spur asked the first man he
saw, a tall, gangly youth with bright red hair
sticking out beneath his hat.

"He'll be here any minute. We wuz just out
catching a runaway prisoner. Seems he broke into
the hotel and stole someone's clothes."

"And saddle," Spur said darkly. "It was my
room he broke into. I was just there and found
out."

"I'll be? This's your lucky day. Here he comes,"
the carrot-topped youth said.

Sheriff Oscar Tate rode slowly up to his office
holding a rope. Beside him the prisoner—wearing
Spur's clothing—trotted along, gasping for breath.
Tate yanked on the rope, forcing the prisoner's
bound hands painfully upward.

"Was he on a horse, Tate?" Spur asked as the
man handed the leach to the redhead.

"Why the hell do you want to know, McCoy?"
Tate asked as he recognized the man, dismounted
and brushed off his pants.

"My room was broken into, my saddle and some
of my clothes are missing. He's wearing my pants
and shirt. See a saddle too?" Spur calmly asked.

Tate laughed harshly. "Hell, if I'd a known that
was your saddle I would've thrown it into the
bushes. But yeah, he was riding; his mount'll be
coming soon."

A man rode up leading a riderless horse. As it
neared the office Spur saw the saddle on its back.
He sighed in relief—it was his.

"Look, Tate, let's forget about what happened
earlier. I don't like it any more than you do.

Lawson Amory could charm the dress off a preacher's wife. It wasn't your fault.''

"Damn straight it wasn't my fault!" the hefty man said, huffing. "But I'm glad you got yer damn saddle back. Go ahead and take it and get the hell outa my sight!''

"Well, what about his clothes?" the red-haired youth asked. "Shouldn't we give 'em back to him too?''

"Hell, boy, you want me to strip that prisoner right here and parade him through the streets of Yuma butt-nekkid?''

"That's okay. I don't want them back," Spur said, as he unstrapped the saddle. "Let him keep them.''

"I can't blame you," Tate said. "That man smells pretty powerful.''

McCoy uncinched and untied and finally pulled the saddle off. The horse seemed to relax as the weight left his broad back. Spur slung the saddle over his right shoulder.

"Go ahead and get your ass outa here!" Tate said. "I got work to do.''

"Right." Spur hurried to the hotel, up the steps and banged on his door.

Beverly unlocked and opened it, saw the saddle and smiled. "That was fast," she said. "Thought I'd have to wait up all night.''

"I had some help." He tossed his hat onto the floor and the saddle on the bed. It bounced twice before laying still.

"Don't put that thing there, Spur McCoy!" Beverly said.

He looked at her. "Why not?''

Beverly's eyes sparkled. "Not unless you intend to ride me in that saddle!''

* * *

Lawson Amory started his ride west hours
before dawn. His horse managed to pick out the
trail by thin moonlight and dim starshine.

Okay, Amory thought, as he bounced in the
saddle over the uneven ground. So he hadn't had
the best luck so far. He was enough of a
professional to wait for the best opportunity.

That time at the outhouse behind McCoy's hotel
was just a preliminary move, something to get
Spur's guard up, to inject the mission with some
excitement. Though his ultimate goal was to
obtain the dies, he figured he might as well have a
little fun with it.

Sure, he could have shot the bastard that night
in Little River and, eventually, found the dies, but
that would take half the challenge out of the
mission.

San Diego looked to be the end of this game—
and of Spur McCoy. He kicked his horse's flank,
impatient for the next round to begin.

The stage passed through narrow ravines, box
canyons and rock-strewn washes. It climbed up a
long, treacherous route, rising 5,000 feet from the
desert floor. The scenery changed—pine trees and
ancient oaks replaced cactus and scrub. Mountains
occasionally gave way to emerald-lapped valleys.
Streams and lakes glistened far in the distance,
reflecting the blue of the overhead skies.

Spur and Beverly rode the stage for three more
days before finally entering a deep valley several
miles long. Far in the distance, at the mouth of the
river beside which they traveled, lay the Pacific
Ocean.

Beverly drummed her fingers on Spur's thigh as
they sat next to each other in the stage. She'd
grown increasingly anxious as they neared their

latest destination. The slightest ease in their progress, the quick, regular stops for a change of horses or to eat seemed to rile her. She wanted the trip behind her.

A gleaming white structure topped with several bells sat on the cliffs to the right of them, on the far side of the river. "That's a mission!" Beverly said.

"You're quite right. Almost there now," Spur said, looking at the Christian building.

She squeezed his leg, eliciting a look of abhorrence from the middleaged woman sitting across from Spur and one of delight from her eighteen year-old son.

An hour later the stage halted in San Diego. The town consisted of a wide variety of buildings and houses, from brick monstrosities to ramshackle dwellings. Many were of adobe, constructed in a quaint Latin style, reminders of the area's colorful Spanish Colonial history.

As they crossed the street to a plain-appearing hotel—the Lomita—Beverly gasped. The sun sank low onto the western horizon, charging the water with oranges and reds, spilling multihued light through the clouds above it.

"Honestly, that doesn't look like the ocean we have on the other side of the country," she said, setting down her luggage and taking in the view as a light breeze slapped their faces.

"True. That's a bay."

Beverly looked at the rock arm that jutted out into the color-shot water. "But beyond that point of land out there, that's the ocean."

Spur smiled. "I never argue with a lady—I mean, a woman."

They went into the hotel.

After registering, Spur walked down to the docks and booked passage to San Francisco on a freighter, the only ship that was scheduled to leave in the morning. It wouldn't be luxury accommodations but he figured he could suffer for a while.

Once back at the hotel Beverly laced her fingers with his.

"Feels good, Bev. Well, you going to look up that cousin of yours tomorrow? Trevor?"

She hesitated. "I don't know."

Spur was incredulous. "You've come all this way and you're backing out now? Why?"

Beverly looked away. "I'm not backing out; I'm just putting it off for a while." She paused. "I think I want to see San Francisco."

Spur blew out his breath. "I see."

"So—so I'm going on the boat with you." Beverly set her chin and looked at him quizzically.

He smiled. "Sorry. I only booked one passage—not two."

"I'm sure we'll manage."

"I guess so. As long as you don't mind sailing with tons of hides."

Beverly swallowed. "Hides?"

"Yeah, new leather on its way up to San Francisco. It was the only ship leaving tomorrow."

She thought about it and nodded. "Well, why not? I do want to see the city, after everything you've told me about it these past few days. Why not? It's no skin off my back."

Spur squeezed her hand.

The next morning, Lawson Amory leaned against a Chinese laundry near the docks. He watched as Spur and some woman boarded the FLYING BUCKSKIN.

After the two were well out of sight, he walked up the gangplank and asked if they needed another hand.

The whiskered skipper looked him up and down, nodded his assent and wordlessly directed him on board. Amory hurried onto the ship.

He'd spent a sleepless night in San Diego. The trip had taken longer than he'd planned. Amory hadn't arrived until well after midnight and, at that hour, hadn't been able to find McCoy. So he decided to follow him all the way to San Francisco.

Things weren't working out right, Amory thought, as a deckhand described his duties. Hell, it'd be too risky to try anything on the ship, so he'd keep out of sight until they'd docked.

Then the prize would be his!

16

Beverly leaned against the railing as the heavy
freighter steamed into San Francisco Bay. The
deck rolled gently on the calm water as they passed
several other small boats and various other forms
of watercraft.

"Oh, it's glorious!" she said, clasping Spur's
waist as a salty breeze pummelled them. "Just
look at all the buildings! How many people live
here?"

"A lot," Spur answered.

"I just know I'll love San Francisco, Spur! More
than I ever could have imagined!"

"I'll like it a helluva lot better once I've made my
delivery."

She turned to him and frowned. "Spur McCoy,
always thinking about work."

"That's what they pay me for."

He regretted bringing her along but he knew it
was far too late for that now. He'd just hope for the
best.

The sun was setting behind them, casting a deep
orange light onto the glistening water and painting
the buildings that studded the twisting, steep hills
with the same hue.

Faint glows showed behind hundreds of distant
windows as kerosene lamps were turned up. The

ship neared the docks, bringing into sharper view
dozens of vessels of all sizes and descriptions tied
up along the wooden arms that jutted out from the
land. Squat, round-sailed Chinese junks competed
with fishing boats; a row of U.S. Navy warships
sat beside freighters. The bay was a confusion of
movement and color as smaller craft tooled around
on the water.

A breeze suddenly swept down, kicking up
whitecaps on the water and nearly blowing
Beverly's bonnet off her head.

She tightened the bow beneath her chin. "It's
more beautiful than I'd imagined," Beverly said.
"What a big city!"

"Then you're not disappointed you came with
me?" Spur asked.

"How could I be? At least I'm still with you. Are
you sorry about that?"

Spur paused. "No. Not really. You're taking a
big risk but I guess you're used to that. Anyway,
my assignment will be over soon."

Beverly turned to him. "I know. And then?"

He looked at her blankly.

"I mean, what will you do after that?"

"Well—"

"I know, you'll be off to who-knows-where." A
smile played on her lips. "I know I'll never see you
again. But at least I've spent these days with
you." She kissed his cheek. "I wouldn't have
missed them for the world!"

As Spur gripped her firm, round bottom a tall
figure watched them from the prow.

"When are they expecting you?" Beverly asked
as they climbed the steep hill that led up from the
docks into the heart of the city.

"Either today or tomorrow. I didn't give them

an exact time."

"Well, in that case, do you think we could slow down and rest for a minute?" Beverly panted. "I'm not used to these darned mountains."

"They're hills, and I'd rather I got the dies safely delivered as soon as I can."

Beverly sighed. "Okay. But it just figures—no carriages for rent at the docks."

"And if we didn't have all this luggage we could have rented some horses. No problem. It's isn't far now, not more than two miles or so."

The blonde sighed and turned to him. "How do you know they're still in there? In the saddle? I mean, you haven't looked or anything, have you?"

Spur shook his head. "No. It'd be obvious if someone had torn it apart. Besides, no one's thought to look in there—certainly not that prisoner who stole it."

Beverly shivered in the cool evening air. The sun had sunk into the western sea, enveloping the city in darkness. They moved from one streetlamp to another pausing in the pale pools of light that they cast on the street.

"I'm just glad I wasn't in your room when he broke in. That prisoner, I mean."

They passed a small shop covered with bright red Chinese characters. Inside, a confusion of silk lanterns, tea cups, religious images, kites, robes, strange, small books and lacquerware vied for floorspace. The pungent aroma of incense filtered out from it.

"Let's stop here and look inside," Beverly asked eagerly. "Just for a minute!"

"We've got to go on," Spur said firmly. "As soon as I make this delivery we can stop wherever you want. We'll have dinner in a good restaurant, too. Beverly, you weren't this tired while we were walking in the desert."

She shrugged. "I didn't *let* myself feel this tired there. Here, with all this civilization around us, it doesn't make sense to wear ourselves out."

A carriage slipped past them.

"You wanted to come along."

A man darted from an alley directly in front of them and stood, hands on his hips. His face was dark.

"Hey, doll, you're looking mighty fine tonight!" the man said. His teeth glowed in a smile.

"Can't say the same for you," she retorted.

"Get out of her way," Spur said in a warning voice.

"No."

Beverly walked past him.

"Hey, dump that joker and come on up to my room," he called as they slowly walked away. "I got a bottle of whiskey and a warm bed." The man ran out into the street and stopped in front of them again.

"Leave her alone, pal," Spur said.

"Ignore him, doll. Let's go." His knees wavered as he looked at her, licking his lips.

"I said, leave her alone!" Spur darted forward to the leering man and dropped his carpetbag.

"Get your butt outa here, cowboy! She don't want you; she wants a real man!"

McCoy balled his fist and smashed it into the drunk's stomach. He doubled over, howling in pain, then came up holding a long-bladed knife.

The man waved it in the air. "You want this, huh? You want this to slice open your guts? Huh, cowboy? Show off for the fine looking lady!"

Spur swung the saddle over his shoulder and down onto the man's head. It connected, cracked into the skull and sent the drunkard to the ground.

Beverly gasped as they hurried on. Spur non-chalantly stepped over the downed man. "Beverly, you sure do attract attention," he said, as he picked up his carpetbag and the two hurried down the street.

"Thanks, Spur," Beverly said. Her face was hidden in the darkness; the streetlamps seemed to be farther apart the higher they climbed up the hill.

They finally reached its crest and turned around, breathing heavily. They looked out on the barely visible string of lights that surrounded the bay and at the vast void that lay beyond them.

"Come on," Spur said. "Not far now."

The streets were nearly black. Clouds shot across the sky, cutting off the thin moonlight, blanketing the city in darkness. The saddle cut into Spur's shoulder as they hurried from corner to corner. He roughly knew their destination. The mint shouldn't be more than a few more streets down and two to the left.

The encounter with the drunkard sent McCoy's mind working. Where was Amory? Spur hadn't seen him since he'd deposited the ex-Secret Service agent in Sheriff Tate's jail. He lamely hoped the man had given up but Spur had a feeling that that wasn't the case.

They moved down the inky street, passing warehouses and packing plants that had closed up hours earlier.

Beverly yelped. "Hell!" she said. "I tripped." She poked her boot at a piece of splintered wood.

"You okay?" Spur asked, reaching for the dim form before him.

"I'm fine. Let's just hurry. This dark city gives me the creeps. Where's all the big houses? Where's the fancy restaurants that serve lobster and pate and caviar? Where's the bright lights and fancy carriages and flower boxes?"

"Far from this part of town," Spur said wryly.

He steered Beverly across a rutted, bricked street. They moved laterally from their original direction. Suddenly, in the darkness up ahead, McCoy heard a rustle. The sound of a can scraping along the broken sidewalk.

"What was that?" Beverly asked, freezing.

"I don't know."

Spur cautiously advanced. The darkness was so intense that he could scarcely make out the sidewalk.

He glanced ahead—twin yellow pools of shimmering light swung up toward him, blinked, and then raced off to the left accompanied by the sound of claws.

Spur relaxed. "Just a cat."

A distant meow seemed to echo his comment.

"Spur, I'm exhausted!"

"We're almost there, Beverly. You can make it."

Spur heard a similar sound behind him as they moved through another intersection.

"Another cat?" Beverly asked.

The sound halted, then continued, growing louder, advancing on them.

"I don't think so, Bev."

"Then what is it?" she loudly asked. Her voice was infused with fear.

"Shhhh." They stopped. The sound halted. "Grab my arm and stay close, okay?"

"I can't," Beverly complained. "My hands are full of my luggage."

"Then stay close." Spur's voice was barely a whisper. "There's no telling who's back there. This is a big city, it's dark and we're not walking through the best part of town."

"Okay."

They walked quickly, Spur's boots clicking on the sidewalk. The shuffling behind them continued unabated as they moved.

Damn, Spur thought. Were they being followed? The image of Lawson Amory flashed through his mind. Might as well find out; no sense in taking chances.

He leaned his head toward Beverly. "We're going across the street again."

The man and woman raced across it and continued on down an alley between two three-story buildings. Their boots clattered on the worn cobblestones.

"Quiet!" Spur said.

"Why?"

"Shhh!"

The shuffling approached them again from behind.

"We're being followed," Spur whispered.

"No! How far's the mint?"

The footsteps grew louder.

"Not more than two blocks. It's one street back the way we came."

"We'll make it!" Beverly said.

They ran, shooting down the alley into the comparatively light street beyond it. Spur figured it was better to deliver the dies than to get involved in any more trouble. As they raced along the street Beverly dropped both small suitcases. They banged open as they landed.

"Hell!" she cursed.

"Leave them!" Spur yelled.

"But—"

"Beverly, come on!"

"But all my money and—and—"

Spur gripped his carpetbag with the hand that secured his saddle, grabbed the woman's slender arm and ran.

She stumbled forward but stopped complaining. "I'll pay you back."

One more block, Spur thought, as they crossed another intersection. He dragged the remarkably fit woman down the cross-street, back to their original route, and saw the huge, marble building in the distance. Soft light shone through a few windows, and the steps that led up to the building seemed to glow with an eerie light.

"That's it!" Spur said. "That's the U.S. Mint!"

"Thank God! You're about to pull my arm off!"

A deep, impenetrable fog suddenly fell onto them, effectively drowning the area in silent, wet darkness. McCoy looked down. He could see the lower half of Beverly's arm but that was it. The rest of her was invisible.

Two riders stormed down the street as Spur pushed himself and the girl harder, urging her faster and faster toward the lights that faintly glowed in the distance.

Beverly's arm wrenched from his grip. "Damn!" she said.

"What's wrong?" he asked.

"I—I tripped again." Her voice seemed to be coming from the street. He reached down with one hand, shifting the saddle so that it wouldn't fall off. The sound of the footsteps suddenly echoed through the eerie fog.

"Where are you?" Spur whispered.

"I'm—" Beverly's words were cut off.

A low, ominous rumble shook through the area.

"Beverly, where are you?" he repeated.

Silence. The fog deposited thick droplets of water on his face and hat as he stood desperately searching for the blonde woman.

"Looking for something?" a voice called out

from behind him.

Lawson! Spur thought. He spun around but the fog completely concealed the speaker.

"Beverly!"

"I'm afraid she can't answer you now, Mr. McCoy. Why don't you give me what I want? You can have the girl back."

Spur walked toward the voice. The fog was confusing; he couldn't see three feet in front of him.

Then it cleared—as quickly as it had descended the fog swirled up into the sky, accompanied by a strong, salt-laden breeze.

Lawson Amory stood ten feet away. He clutched Beverly Thomas to his chest, a gun pointed at her throat.

"No more time for talk, McCoy!" Lawson said bitterly. "Give me the dies or I'll kill her!"

17

The thick, wet fog swirled down around Spur, Beverly and the man who held the gun to her neck, temporarily cutting them off from each other's view.

"Do it now, McCoy!" Lawson Amory said. "Throw your gun into the street, lay the saddle down beside it, then turn around and walk away. You'll get the girl—unharmed."

Spur laughed. "What makes you so interested in my saddle?" he asked, peering through the shifting, dense cloud that enveloped them.

"Don't give me that, asshole! That's the only place you could've hidden the dies. I've got to hand it to you; that was pretty smart."

Beverly squealed in the darkness. Spur stepped forward three feet. The fog suddenly lifted, revealing the pair again. Beverly cringed at the man's touch but was completely immobilized.

"You're crazy, Amory. You think you're so smart. What makes you think I've got the dies? Hear some story from another agent? Hell, use your brain. I'm one of the fake couriers that General Halleck sent out to put bastards like you off the trail of the real one. Sorry, I don't have them. The courier with the real dies won't leave

159

Denver for two weeks. You've failed your last mission, Amory.''

Lawson pulled Beverly's head back, gripped her mouth and jabbed the barrel under her chin. She gave out a muffled yelp. "Good try. Now do what I say or I'll kill you both!"

Spur snorted. "Hell, Amory, I always heard you were one of the brightest agents. I can't believe you fell for that stupid story. Who'd you hear it from? Did you get one of the other couriers drunk?"

"I've followed you from Denver," he said, his voice rising. "I've tracked you every step of the way. You've got them and you're gonna give them to me!" He ran the barrel back and forth on Beverly's throat. "Or do you wanna see this pretty little lady die?"

"She ain't no lady," Spur said. "But if you're so interested in my saddle—here, take it." Spur swung it off his shoulder and threw it as hard as he could. It skidded to the cobblestones ten feet from Lawson.

"Your weapon too, damnit!" the man yelled.

"Sorry. I don't give that up too easy. You have to take it from me."

"I'll kill—"

"Cut the crap, Amory!" Spur said, snarling. "You know you won't hurt her. You're not the kind. Where's the excitement, the danger? Killing an unarmed, defenseless woman's about as tough as shooting fish!"

A low rumble shot through the area. The ground shook. Buildings swayed in the night air. Somewhere in the distance a window fell, breaking the silence as it shattered on the street far below.

"Let her go, Amory. If you want the dies let's do this man to man. You really need to threaten a woman to get them from me?" Spur put his hands on his hips, daring the man. "You really need to hide behind a girl? That's not your reputation. That's not your style. I thought you had some guts, Lawson. Am I wrong? Hell, I don't think you quit the service. I think they kicked you out cause you're scared."

"Bastard!" Amory said.

The earth moved and shook. Lawson looked around him wildly. "What—what the hell's happening?"

"It's just an earthquake. Christ; even that scares you!" Spur laughed raucously and cracked his knuckles. "You don't need her. Let her go, Amory!"

"Say goodbye to your piece of ass, McCoy! I'm tired of all your jabbering!"

He cocked the .45 Beverly closed her eyes. Amory started to pull the trigger.

The ground split open a dozen yards from them, swallowing an entire one-story building. The earthquake nearly knocked Spur's feet out from under him. He staggered, his eyes riveted on the ex-Secret Service agent, waiting for his chance.

Tons of shaking earth produced a cacaphony of destruction. Windows shattered. Thousands of bricks splattered onto the street around them.

"Let her go!" Spur said, regaining his balance.

"What the hell, take her!"

Lawson Amory thrust the woman toward him and darted for the saddle that lay in the middle of the street. Spur drew his long-barrelled .45. The wall ten feet in front of him buckled and started to collapse. Spur darted forward, grabbed Beverly and yanked her to safety. They slammed onto the ground as dust and debris rained down on the sidewalk, just missing them.

Beverly sobbed, hiding her eyes as the tremor continued to shake through the city.

The dust diffused the scene. Spur coughed and choked on the vile wall-particles as he stood on the shaky ground. He wiped stinging grit from his eyes as he struggled to fix his aim on the man who bent down to retrieve his saddle.

He had the Colt lined up, ready to fire. The quake increased in force, roaring directly underneath them. The street seemed to liquify, rippling and shifting as the earth shook and tossed both men onto its surface.

"Goddamnit!" Spur shouted, picking himself up from the ground as Amory rose to his feet again. His left leg ached.

"Don't do it, Amory!"

The man hoisted the saddle.

"Is it worth it?"

The man's answer was lost in an ear-splitting crush. Four windows fell, splashing the ground between the two men with thousands of razor-sharp fragments.

Amory turned to run, still gripping the saddle. Spur fired as the street boiled beneath him again. The shot went wild, slamming into a large pane of glass.

"Damn!"

Lawson Amory laughed as he ran through the darkened street. "Can't shoot better than that, Spur?"

Furious, McCoy darted toward the departing figure. His boots crushed the glass to dust as he moved over the slippery, hazardous terrain. His ears ached with the earth's roar.

Amory rounded a corner up ahead.

Spur reached it and halted. He breathed heavily

as the tremor rattled through the city and slowly died off.

The silence was eerie. McCoy pressed his back against the warehouse's wall, waiting. No sounds of footsteps. Amory must be standing just around the corner, waiting for him to step out.

"McCoy! You want the dies? Come and get them!"

The voice was near—too near. Spur glanced down at the street, bent and hoisted a two-foot-long piece of wood that had been wrenched from the building by the quake. He threw it past the corner.

Two shots pierced the night.

"Nice try, McCoy!" Lawson said.

Spur heard Beverly's sobs far away. He silenced his breath, poured all his concentration into his right hand, into the finger that gently gripped the cold metal trigger.

He had to move fast. He wouldn't have a second chance, no time to correct his aim.

Spur spun around the corner and fired.

Amory screamed as the slug slammed into his left arm. The agent's .45 spoke, spitting hot lead as Spur darted back around the corner.

He heard the heavy sound of leather slapping the street as Lawson dropped the saddle.

"Give it up, Amory!"

"No fuckin' way! I've worked too long to let some bastard like you—"

Another spin, another shot. The bullet slammed into Amory's right arm, ripping the muscles apart, severing veins and arteries.

He ducked back around the corner as Lawson screamed and fired four slugs at Spur.

"I won't kill you," McCoy shouted. "Unless you

force me to. You know the rules." He emerged from the corner and faced the man.

"Shit!" the agent said, pulling on empty chambers. He threw the harmless weapon at Spur.

McCoy ducked and it rattled beside him. Amory crumpled to the street, beside the saddle, and pressed his head to his knees.

"Come on, Amory. Get up. Time we got those wounds looked at." Spur approached the man cautiously.

"Damnit. Damnit! *Damnit!*" The big man howled like a wounded deer. Blood soaked his shirt from the open holes through his arms.

"Amory, let's go." He walked to within five feet of the downed man.

"Never!" The man bent upward, screamed and hurled a ten-inch piece of glass straight at McCoy's stomach.

Spur fired automatically. The bullet shattered the glass and continued on its path, slamming deep inside the man's chest. Lawson choked, coughed, his eyes wild with pain and surprise.

He fell onto his back, panting, wincing as white-hot pain shook through him. "Damn!" The word was harsh.

Spur watched him die. Lawson Amory, ex-Secret Service agent, squeezed his eyes shut. A shudder travelled through him. His breath grew faint; the pounding in his chest ceased.

The man's body fell limp. His face relaxed, the muscles easing into limpness, never to contract again.

The death-rattle shook the big man. A long, lingering stream of air hissed out between Amory's lips like a hot summer breeze.

Lawson Amory was dead.

Spur checked his neck to confirm it, shook his

head and picked up the saddle.

Beverly Thomas ran up, wiping tears from her face. She stopped as she saw the man lying on the street.

"Spur, I—I—"

"I know."

Bev went to him. She stared into his eyes and held out her arms. "Hold me!"

"I will, as soon as I deliver this damn thing to the mint. You understand?"

She nodded, wrapped her arm around him and walked away from the scene.

In an office on the top floor of the San Francisco Mint, a black-suited man sliced through the leather, snipping away the seams that the Denver saddlemaker had so expertly resewn.

Beverly stood next to Spur in the darkened office. The man worked in a pool of light cast by twin kerosene lamps in his walnut-panelled office.

"It should be right there," Spur said as the official peeled back a layer of leather.

"There it is." Mason Galde pointed to the small cloth-wrapped box that had been inserted into a hole dug into the layers of leather. He removed it from its hiding place and set it on the desk. Coughing, he relit his cigar, removed the cloth and opened the metal box.

Inside, gleaming in the soft light, were two small metallic objects, each a perfect negative impression of one face of the American double-eagle, the $20 gold coin.

Spur looked down at it and shook his head. How many men had died trying to steal the harmless pieces of metal? How many lives had been destroyed in the vain quest for these small pieces of magic?

Mason Galde puffed on the big stogie and turned over the dies in trembling hands. "They're in perfect condition." He set them down. "I can't tell you how happy I am to see them. You did a fine job, McCoy." He proffered a hand.

Spur shook it.

"I'll be sure to telegraph General Halleck and let him know how much I appreciate this. Any trouble along the way?" Galde asked.

Spur shrugged, glanced at Beverly and turned back to the man. "A bit. Nothing I couldn't handle."

"Glad to have made your acquaintance. You too, Miss Thomas." He took the dies to a safe in his office, worked out the combination and stashed them inside. "We'll put this in the main vault in the morning. Even I don't have the full combination to that. It takes three of us to open it." Galde smiled. "Well, what can I do for you folks? Need a ride to your hotel?"

Spur smiled. "That would be great."

18

A light breeze sent the lacy curtains into motion. Outside the window the San Francisco Bay was a glorious deep blue extravaganza. The city that hugged its waters shimmered in the late morning sunlight.

Spur sat in an embroidered chair, stretching his back. The dies had been safely delivered and everything had been cleared up with the local law regarding Lawson Amory's death. It was time to relax for a couple of days, to regroup, to catch up on his sleep.

A murmur behind him touched off Spur's smile. He turned and looked at the blonde woman who yawned in bed.

"Good morning," he said, scratching his stubbly chin.

Beverly gazed at the naked man sitting in the chair, widened her eyes, then smiled. As she sat up the sheet fell off her body, exposing her perfect, china-white breasts. Beverly Thomas lifted her shoulders and yawned again, heightening her cheekbones. She covered her mouth.

"Sleep well?" Spur asked, rising and walking to her.

She nodded. "Hmmm. For a moment—for just a

167

moment—I didn't know where I was. I thought I was at home in Boston." Bev's smile broadened. "Then I saw you and everything came back." She looked at the rumpled bedclothes beside her, at the place where he'd slept. Beverly's face darkened. "It really did happen, didn't it? It wasn't all a bad dream?"

"No, but you can remember it that way." He sat beside her and kissed Bev's forehead. "You hungry? We never did have dinner last night."

She shook her head. "I don't think I'll be able to eat for a while. Why don't you come back to bed." Her voice was dreamy but full of promise.

"I'm not sleepy."

"Neither am I."

Spur laughed and rolled on top of her, their bodies trapping the soft sheet between them. He held her head, ran his fingers through her golden hair and drank in her essence as he buried his nose against Beverly's neck.

"When I think of what I would have missed staying in Boston," Beverly said.

Spur responded by pressing his crotch against hers. He ground it—tenderly, gently—against the naked woman.

"Oh, Spur. You know just what to do." She lifted his head and, smiling, pressed her teeth around his lower lip, nibbled and sucked.

McCoy moaned as she chewed and then lashed her tongue along his lip. He pushed his groin harder against her as Beverly raised her mouth. Their tongues met in fiery, liquid passion, darting together and slashing inside their joined mouths.

Spur slid his tongue along hers, deeper and deeper, toward the back of her throat. Beverly moaned and sucked it in. She grasped the man's shoulders and pulled him closer as they locked together in oral bliss.

His erection pushed against her, rubbing the sheet, heating it up with his passion.

Beverly twisted her mouth from his and gasped. "I can't wait any longer."

Spur nodded, lifted up and ripped the sheet down. He kicked it off her legs.

"Just a minute," Bev said, as she slid out from under him. "I want to give you pleasure too."

Gentle hands on his chest urged him to lie down. Spur relinquished control and settled down on the firm mattress. Beverly gripped him with delicate, warm hands.

"I've told you I'm not a lady; now I'm gonna prove it to you."

Hot breath shot against his penis. Spur trembled as it grew more forceful. He looked up and saw Beverly's opened lips settled over its tip. She exhaled again.

"Beverly!" he said, and groaned.

She snaked out her tongue and touched it to his shaft. The contact sent McCoy out of his mind. He bucked on the bed as she licked and explored, spreading a thin film of saliva all over his rock-hard erection.

"Where the hell'd you learn to do something like —like—oh god!"

Spur shut his eyes as her lips closed around the mushroom-shaped head. Beverly groaned and pushed lower. It slid into her mouth and, after a slight hestitation, pushed down her throat.

McCoy felt his passion rise to new heights. Hot sensations of pleasure shot through his body as she raised and lowered her head, working his erection slowly, accepting him, nourishing herself from his body.

He opened his eyes and gazed at her in wonder as she slurped and sucked. Beverly's lips made a tight seal around his penis as she bobbed up and down, forcing it deeper into her throat with each stroke.

Something within him threatened to explode. Spur gently gripped her head and pulled her off him. He gasped as Beverly looked up at him, passion igniting her aquamarine eyes, her lips slick and glowing.

"Beverly, you may not be a lady but you're one helluva woman!"

She giggled as Spur moved to kneel between her legs. He gripped her ivory thighs, spread them and stuffed his face into her mystery.

"Oh, Spur, I've never—never—"

He chuckled as he sniffed her scent. It exploded in his brain and sped directly to his crotch. Spur lapped at her pink lips, swirled the soft yellow hair aside and plunged his tongue into the tight opening.

Beverly groaned as he worked it in and out, lapping, licking. He lifted his tongue higher and teased the hard button that lay above.

"Spur McCoy, you stop that now!" Beverly warned him.

He sucked and gently teethed, his passion rising tenfold with each salty, unforgettable taste. He buried his face in her crotch and ate.

The woman trembled. Beverly locked her thighs around his head and lifted her lips. He concentrated on her clitoris, pounded it with his tongue, sending her into ecstasy.

"Stop!" she pleaded. "Don't stop!"

He attacked her, slurping savagely. Beverly strangled out a short cry as her body shook and rocked and rolled through an orgasm.

Spur thought he might suffocate between her legs but didn't care. Her passion enflamed him, forced him to give her more pleasure than she'd ever had with any man.

Beverly finally eased off her pleasure and relaxed. She lowered her legs and freed Spur's head.

He looked up at her, grinned and licked again.

"Spur McCoy, the way you treat a woman!" Beverly said, her face slick, eyes dancing.

He pushed up and laid on top of her. His erection slid between her legs and rubbed against the furry patch.

Their gazes locked—Spur's eyes were strained, excited, almost violent, while Beverly's were misty and full of the pleasures of her recent release.

Spur gripped his penis and rubbed it up and down Beverly's opening.

She groaned as the hot flesh parted her lips. "Now, Spur. No more teasing. Just give it to me!" She urged him with her eyes and parted her legs.

McCoy stared at the aroused woman. "What do you want?" he asked.

"I want you to fuck me." Beverly said, as if she was asking him to take her to dinner. "Now. Fuck me, Spur! Make me feel like a woman again!"

He pushed. His penis slid into her, spread her wide, filled her up.

Beverly gasped. "Oh lordy; you're so big!"

"Should I stop?"

She groaned. "Hell no. Deeper, Spur; deeper!"

Another inch. Two more. Spur kissed her again as he slid full-length into her velvety vagina.

The woman below him shook as their bodies fitted together. Spur revelled in the sensuous feeling, in the woman's arousal, in her tightness.

He pulled out to the head. Beverly squealed in

frustration at the emptiness his withdrawal had caused, then sighed as he slammed back into her.

"Fuck me, Spur!"

The brass bed banged against the wall as he pounded into her. Beverly gripped his waist and lifted her hips to meet his.

"Oh yes. Oh god! This is what life's all about! This is it, two people giving each other pleasure. Harder, Spur, do it harder!"

He obliged until he was hammering into her. He raised up and altered the position of his entry just enough to slide against her clitoris. Beverly gasped at the new sensation. Her cheeks shook and her breath was harsh.

She shivered through another orgasm, tightening herself around him. The added pressure was more than Spur could handle. He felt his balls rise in their sack as they slapped against her thighs.

Spur arched his back and screamed as he shot, spurting liquid white fire deep inside her. Again and again he squirted, again and again he thrust, sending himself over the edge and past all rational thought.

The room whirled around them. The bed spun on a cloud of misty sexual bliss as they clutched together, their slick bodies locked in the eternal embrace of woman and man, washed with the warm sweet breeze of the ultimate release.

Spur lay heavily on top of her as reality returned. Beverly groaned. As he opened his eyes she looked up at him, smiling in wonder and appreciation.

"Don't worry," he said. "I won't take it out yet."

Beverly smiled as he gripped her shoulders and rolled onto his side, maintaining their union.

She nuzzled against his chest, licking the salty fluid that clung in crystalline droplets to the hair that grew there. Spur groaned as her tongue flicked and licked and drank.

Finally, after an immeasurable time, he felt himself softening, his passion fading in favor of a deep satisfaction mingled with genuine affection for the blonde woman.

"That was just what I needed," she said, as he pulled out of her. "Just what I needed to forget about last night, forget about all the—"

He nodded. "Me too."

"You're incredible, you know that?" she asked, looking up at him.

He smiled. "Hell, Beverly, I'm just a man and you're just a woman."

She shook her head. "No, it's more than that. Something—something I can't explain."

"Maybe it's what you've been through—what we've been through—this past week."

"Maybe." Her aquamarine eyes sparkled. "Hey, Spur, aren't you tired of your line of work yet? I was just thinking—dreaming, really. We could settle down together somewhere. Maybe here, right here in San Francisco."

He smiled. "It's tempting, Beverly, but I can't. I have to do my duty."

She sighed. "I know. I was just dreaming." She reached down and gripped his penis, nursing it back to life with insistent fingers.

"Again?" Spur asked, enjoying the feeling. "You want to go again?"

"Sure." Beverly kissed his right nipple. "If we can't settle down and get married, let's play husband and wife for just one more afternoon. Okay?"

Spur looked at her. He'd have time to send wires to General Halleck in Washington and his office in St. Louis tomorrow. Might as well enjoy himself while he could; he'd have another job soon enough.

Life returned to his shaft. "Okay," he said, grabbing the girl with the aquamarine eyes.

GIANT
SPECIAL EDITION

SPUR

DIRK FLETCHER

In these Special Giant Editions, Secret Service Agent Spur McCoy comes up against more bullets and beauties than even he can handle.

Klondike Cutie. A boomtown full of the most ornery vermin ever to pan a river, Dawson is the perfect place for a killer to hide—until Spur McCoy arrives. Fresh from a steamboat and the steamiest woman he's ever staked a claim on, McCoy knows the chances of mining gold are very good in the Klondike. And to his delight, the prospects for golden gals are even better.
__3420-4 $4.99 US/$5.99 CAN

High Plains Princess. Riding herd over a princess touring the Wild West isn't the easiest assignment Spur has ever had, especially since assassins are determined to end young Alexandria's reign. But before the last blow is dealt, Spur will shoot his pistol aplently and earn himself a knighthood for seeing to the monarch's special needs.
__3260-0 $4.50 US/$5.50 CAN

LEISURE BOOKS
ATTN: Order Department
276 5th Avenue, New York, NY 10001

Please add $1.50 for shipping and handling for the first book and $.35 for each book thereafter. PA., N.Y.S. and N.Y.C. residents, please add appropriate sales tax. No cash, stamps, or C.O.D.s. All orders shipped within 6 weeks via postal service book rate. Canadian orders require $2.00 extra postage and must be paid in U.S. dollars through a U.S. banking facility.

Name _____
Address _____
City _____ State _____ Zip _____
I have enclosed $_____ in payment for the checked book(s).
Payment <u>must</u> accompany all orders. ☐ Please send a free catalog.

GIANT SPECIAL EDITION

BUCKSKIN

SIX-GUN SHOOTOUT

— KIT DALTON —

More girls...more guns...
more rip-roarin' adventure!

Only a man with a taste for hot lead and a hankering
for fancy ladies can survive in the Old West—a man
like Buckskin Lee Morgan. And when an old girlfriend
calls on Morgan to find the gutless murderer who
ambushed her husband, he is more than ready to act
as judge, jury, and executioner. For Morgan lives by
one law: anyone who messes with his women is a dead
man!

_3383-6 $4.50 US/$5.50 CAN

DIRK FLETCHER

The pistol-hot Western series filled with more brawls and beauties than a frontier saloon on a Saturday night!

Spur #37: Missouri Mama. When a master forgert starts spreading enough funny money to dam up the mighty Mississippi, Spur discovers the counterfeiter has a taste for the town's trollops. And the only way McCoy can catch the bastard is by making pleasure his business.

_3341-0 $3.50 US/$4.50 CAN

Spur #38: Free Press Filly. Sent to investigate the murder of a small-town newspaper editor, McCoy is surprised to discover his contact is the man's busty daughter, who believes in a free press and free love.

_3394-1 $3.99 US/$4.99 CAN

Spur #39: Minetown Mistress. While tracking down a missing colonel in Idaho Territory, Spur runs into a luscious blonde and a randy redhead who appoint themselves his personal greeters. Now he'll waste no time finding the lost man—because only then can he take a long, hard ride with the fillies who drive his private welcome wagon.

_3448-4 $3.99 US/$4.99 CAN

ROBERT E. MILLS

It takes a man with quick wits and an even quicker trigger finger to survive in a vicious world of fast guns and faster women—it takes a man like the Kansan. Get a double blast of beauties and bullets for only $4.99!

The Cheyenne's Woman. When Davy Watson's lovely lady is carried off by the vicious Cheyenne warrior Grey Thunder, the Kansan refuses to rest until he's rescued his beautiful lover. He heads for a showdown with the Indian that'll be a fight to the finish for one man—or both.
And in the same action-packed volume....
The Kansan's Lady. When his beloved Deanna is held captive by the ruthless Scotsman, Duncan Stearns, it's Davy Watson's last chance to even the score with Stearns and rescue his sweetheart. Either he saves Deanna—or he'll go down in one final blaze of glory.
_3450-6 $4.99